THOSE WHO SURVIVE

THOSE WHO SURVIVE

Kir Bulychev

Translated by

John H. Costello

Fossicker Press - Peabody, MA

Copyright © 2000 by Kir Bulychev.

Library of Congress Number: 00-190120
ISBN #: Hardcover 0-7388-1560-8
Softcover 0-7388-1561-6

All rights reserved. No part of this book may be reproduced or transmitted in any form or by any means, electronic or mechanical, including photocopying, recording, or by any information storage and retrieval system, without permission in writing from the copyright owner.

This is a work of fiction. Names, characters, places and incidents either are the product of the author's imagination or are used fictitiously, and any resemblance to any actual persons, living or dead, events, or locales is entirely coincidental.

This book was printed in the United States of America.

To order additional copies of this book, contact:
Xlibris Corporation
1-888-7-XLIBRIS
www.Xlibris.com
Orders@Xlibris.com

CONTENTS

CHAPTER ONE	7
CHAPTER TWO	38
CHAPTER THREE	75
CHAPTER FOUR	96
CHAPTER FIVE	117
CHAPTER SIX	146
CHAPTER SEVEN	176
CHAPTER EIGHT	202
CHAPTER NINE	243
CHAPTER TEN	275
CHAPTER ELEVEN	304
CHAPTER TWELVE	343
ABOUT THE AUTHOR	385

CHAPTER ONE

In all the world the only place Oleg knew he would ever be dry and warm was in this house.

A fly was buzzing the candle that sat lit on the wooden table. The candle should have been extinguished hours ago, when the sky turned gray. Mother had forgotten, of course. Out on the street gloom reigned in the constant, misty fog.

Oleg lay sprawled on his cot where he had awakened only moments before. He had been spending his nights guarding the settlement, chasing off the zhakals. On his last night a whole hunting pack had crawled up to the barn and almost carried him off instead.

The night had left him drained, a feeling of emptiness and boredom had overcome him, as though he had no reason at all to feel any excitement about what had happened, and about what was to come, and no right to feel terror. It was either or, fifty-fifty, you returned or you didn't. And what were the odds of survival at fifty percent to the fourth power? *One half times a half times a half times a half times....* There should have been some regularity, there should have been tables, or else you're always re-inventing the bicycle. Of course they would have to ask the Mayor what a bicycle was. There was a paradox here. There were no bicycles, but the Mayor kept reproaching them for not hunting for the meaning hidden by the words.

From the kitchen Oleg heard his mother start to cough. So she was home.

"You didn't go?" Oleg called out.

"You're awake? Want some soup? I've cooked some." His mother asked.

"Then who went after the muzhrumes?"

"Marianna and Dick."

"That's all?"

"Some of the children may have tagged along."

They should have awakened him! Called him! Marianna hadn't promised, but it would have been natural for them to have called him.

"I'm really not hungry."

"If the rains don't stop the kewkumbers won't ripen before the frost sets in." His mother said. "Mold's growing on everything."

Oleg's mother came into the room, chased the fly away with the palm of her hand, and extinguished the candle. Oleg looked up at the ceiling. The spot of yellow mold had grown, changing its shape. The night before it had resembled Vaitkus's profile with a potato nose. But today the nose had puffed up as though stung by a wasp, and the forehead had been distended with a new bump.

Dick's going into the forest was alarming. Why would *he* want to pick muzhrumes? Dick was a hunter, a plainsman, or so he kept telling everyone.

"There are lots of flies." His mother said. "They find it too cold in the forest."

"So you've found someone to feel sorry for."

The house was divided down the middle; on the other side of the partition lived the Mayor, and the Durov twins the Mayor had taken in after their parents had died in the last epidemic. The twins were always sick with something: as soon as one recovered the other immediately fell ill.

If it hadn't been for their constant howling and whimpering at night Oleg would never have agreed to be town watchman. He could hear them now begin to snivel in chorus — they were hungry. Starved. The Mayor's monologue — unintelligible, distant, ever present like the wind — cut off and a bench squeaked on the wooden floor. That meant the Mayor had gone into the kitchen. Immediately his students started to make a racket.

"And why do you have to go?" Oleg's mother said. "Don't go!

You'll be lucky if you return in one piece!"

Now his mother began to cry. She was often crying now-a-days. She would mumble something, turn toward him and then turn abruptly away, and begin to cry silently — you could tell because she wiped her nose. And she begin to whisper, like some invocation or chant: "I can't take it. I can't take it any more. It would be better if I were dead . . ." Oleg, if he heard, froze lest he show he wasn't sleeping, as though he were looking at something he had no right to see. Oleg was ashamed to realize there was no way he could comfort his mother. She cried about things that meant nothing to him. She cried about countries he would never see, about people who were not here and never had been.

Oleg did not remember his mother ever being any different, only the same as she was today. She was a thin, stringy woman with straight, mottled hair gathered behind her in a bun; heavy strands of hair were always getting loose and hung down her cheeks and she had to blow them away from her face. Her face was red with willowwasp pockmarks, there were dark bags under her eyes, and her eyes were too bright as though they were on fire..

His mother sat down at the table and rubbed the coarse palms of her callused hands. *Well, start crying, why don't you?* Will she reach for the photograph now? He was right. She pulled the box towards her, opened it, and pulled out the photograph.

On the other side of the wall the Mayor was cooking the twins something to eat. The twins were sniveling. The students were shouting and horsing around, helping the Mayor feed the infants. As though this was going to be a typical day. As though nothing out of the ordinary were about to happen. But what were Dick and Marianna doing in the forest? *It will be noon soon. They'll come back for lunch. It's time they got back.* They knew what can happen to people in the forest.

His mother kept looking at the photograph. She was in it, with his father. Oleg had seen it a thousand times and a thousand times he had tried to find a resemblance between himself and that man. He could not. His father's head was covered with curly blond hair, the lips were full, the cleft chin jutted forward. In the picture his father was laughing. Mother said he was always laughing. Oleg resembled his mother more — not the way she was now, but back when the photograph with his father had been taken. Straight black hair and thin lips. Wide, steep eyebrows like arches over bright blue eyes. Skin so pale the red blood vessels showed through. Oleg burned easily. He had thin lips and black hair, like his mother in the photo. His father and mother had been young and very happy. And striking. His father had been in a uniform, and his mother in a dress without shoulders. Something called a sun dress.

That was twenty years ago and Oleg hadn't been born. He was now a little more than fifteen.

"Mother." Oleg said. "Don't, please."

"I won't let you go." His mother said. "I won't let them send you. Over my dead body."

"Mother, enough already." Oleg said and sat up on the cot. "I'd better have some soup."

"You can have it in the kitchen." His mother said. "It hasn't gotten cold yet."

Her eyes were moist. She'd been crying just the same, as though she had buried him already. Or maybe she was crying for his father. For her the photograph was the man. But as much as he had tried, Oleg could remember absolutely nothing about his father.

The boy got to his feet and went into the kitchen. The Mayor was at the hardened clay stove, trying to set fire to some dried wood.

"I'll do it." Oleg said. "You want the water boiling?"

"Yes." The Mayor said. "Thanks. But I have to finish the lesson now. Come get me when it's ready."

***

Marianna had filled the basket with muzhrumes. She'd been lucky. True, she had to go some distance, all the way to the gorge. With Oleg along she would have had too much sense to go so far from the settlement, but with Dick she felt more confident, because Dick felt confident with himself, everywhere, even in the forest, even if he preferred the plains. Dick insisted he was a born hunter, but in fact he had been born earlier, before they had built the settlement.

"But you know the forest as well as you know your own home." Dick said.

He spoke too loudly. He was walking in front and a little to one side. A leather jacket with its fur out sat on him like his own skin. He had sewn the jacket himself. Few of the women in the settlement could have sewn it as well.

The forest was sparse and uneven, the trees here rose to hardly more than man height before bending their tops to the side as though they feared to stick out from the mass of their neighbors. The trees were being sensible. The fierce winter winds would have torn away anything that stuck out too far above the rest. The needles dripped chill rain. Marianna's hand gripping the basket had frozen; she stretched her fingers and moved the container to her other hand. The muzhrumes in the basket had begun to shake and chitter. The girl's palm hurt; one of the muzhrumes had stung her with its barb while she was digging them up. Dick had extracted the stinger so there would be no infection and Marianna sipped the bitter antidote from the bottle that always hung from her neck.

Marianna spied a violet blossom nestled between the fat, slippery white roots of a payn.

"Hold on, Dick." She said, "There's a flower there I haven't seen before."

"Don't you think we can do without flowers?" Dick asked. "It's time we got home. I just don't like this place." Dick had a nose for danger.

"Just a second." Marianna said and knelt down by the trunk.

The spongy soft blue bark that covered the payn pulsed slightly, its veins were pumping themselves full of water, and the roots had shot out tendrils so as not to miss a single droplet. What she had noticed was a flower. An ordinary flower, a violet, only somewhat brighter in color and larger than those growing around the settlement, and with longer thorns. Marianna yanked it from the ground and held it too high for the flailing roots to grasp hold of the payn, and a moment later dropped the violet into the basket with the muzhrumes that were chirping and twittering so much, Marianna even began to laugh and paid no attention to Dick's cry.

"Duck!"

The word and the danger sank in; Marianna jumped forward, fell, dove into the warm mass of pulsing roots. But too late. Her face burned as though she'd been struck by a whip.

"Your eyes!" Dick shouted. "Are your eyes all right?"

Dick grabbed the girl by the shoulders, pulled her clenched fingers out of the mass of roots and made her sit still despite the intense pain.

"Keep your eyes tight!" He told her and quickly started to extract the thin needles from her face; he continued angrily:

"Idiot, we can't let you loose in the forest. You have to listen. It hurts, doesn't it."

Unexpectedly he threw himself on Marianna and pressed her into the roots.

"That hurts!"

"Another one just flew past." Dick said, half rising. "We'll take a look later. It managed to dust my back."

Two willowwasps had flown past three meters above the ground; spheres taut and fat with needle-like spores, but lighter than air with their hydrogen fill. They would fly until the wind carried them against a tree or drove them against the cliffs. Billions of spheres died without issue, but should one find a baer it would riddle the warm pelt with needles carrying its young. In the sporing season you had to be careful in the forest or you would be scarred for life.

"Well, that's all." Dick said. "No needles left. And most important, none got in your eyes."

"Is it bad?" Marianna asked quietly.

"You're beauty hasn't been damaged." Dick said. "Now let's

get home fast. Let Egli smear you with grease."

"Right." Marianna ran her palm along her cheek.

Dick noticed and grabbed at her hand.

"There are more than enough muzhrumes, you got a flower. Are you off your head? Do you want to get it infected."

In the meantime the muzhrumes had escaped from the basket, crawled in among the roots; a few even managed to bury themselves halfway into the ground. Dick helped Marianna gather them, but they never found the violet. Dick gave Marianna the basket back; it was light but he wanted to keep his hands free. In the forest you only had seconds to react, and the hands of a hunter had to be kept free.

"Look." Marianna said, taking the basket. She caught at Dick with her thin, frozen hand. "Is my face spoiled?"

"Don't be silly," Dick said. "We all have marks on our faces. Me too. Is my face spoiled? They're our tribal tattoo marks."

"Tattoo?"

"You forgot? One of the Mayor's history lessons, how wild tribes decorated themselves with special marks. As a badge of honor."

"But those were savages." Marianna said. "And this hurts."

"We're savages too."

Dick was already walking ahead. He didn't turn as he spoke, but Marianna knew he was listening to everything. He had a hunter's hearing. Marianna jumped over the gray stem of a hunting vyne.

"Later on you'll itch, it'll be impossible to sleep. The most important thing to remember is, don't scratch yourself. Then you'll be scarred permanently. Only everyone scratches."

"I won't." Marianna said.

"You'll forget while you're sleeping, and scratch. . . ."

The rain drove down harder, but they moved along slowly. Anyone who ran without looking where they were going ended up dinner for a vyne or oke. The muzhrumes beat against the sides of the basket, but Marianna didn't want to throw them away. Soon they would see the clearing and then the settlement. Someone would certainly be on guard by the stockade. She saw Dick pull his knife out of his belt and shifted his cross-bow into a more comfortable position. She unsheathed her own knife as well, but the blade was too narrow, too thin, and good only for cutting vines or digging out muzhrumes. If a pack of zhakals found you the knife would be of little use. No better than a stick.

***

Oleg finished the soup and placed the pot with the leftovers on a shelf higher up. The students' feet pounded on the hard clay floor of the next room; through the arrow slot in the wall Oleg saw them rush out the door and jump into an enormous puddle that had swollen over the past few days, splattering mud everywhere. Then one of them shouted: "Wyrm!" and they swirled around in a mass, grabbing for the wyrm.

The critter's scarlet tail rose out of the water and struck at the students' legs. Ruth, Thomas's red haired little girl, began to wail: apparently the wyrm had swatted her bare hand with its burning sucker. The little girl's mother stuck her head from her house opposite, shouting:

"Have you gone crazy! Don't go poking in the water! You could lose your hands. It's home for you all. Now!"

But the students had decided to carry the wyrm over their heads, and Oleg knew why. As the wyrm dried it changed color, first to red, then blue, then it became very interesting, but only to those who did not panic at the sight of wyrms, harmless and cowardly critters that they were. Unlike mothers.

Linda, Thomas's wife, stood at the edge of the puddle and called her daughter, and Oleg, guessing what his mother was about to ask him, said:

"I'll go now."

He went out into the street and looked down to the end, toward the gates in the fence where Thomas stood tense with a cross-bow in his hands. *Something's wrong.* Oleg thought. *Wrong, just like I thought.* Dick must've really led Marianna somewhere far off, and something happened. Dick doesn't realize she's different and he didn't watch over her.

The children continued their dance with the wyrm over their heads; the animal had aleady become quite black, it couldn't adapt to captivity any more. Linda Hind pulled her red haired daughter from the parade and dragged her home, captive. Oleg ran off toward the fence and only halfway there did he realize he hadn't taken a cross-bow and would be completely useless if anything happened.

"What's up?" Oleg asked Thomas.

"Zhakals lurking about. A pack." The man didn't bother to turn around.

"The same ones as last night?"

"Don't know. Didn't used to hunt at night. Waiting for Marianna?"

"She went off hunting muzhrumes with Dick."

"I know. Let them through myself. No need to worry. With Dick, nothing will happen. Born hunter."

Oleg nodded. It was embarrassing, but Thomas had no desire to insult the boy. Dick was simply more useful. Dick was a hunter. Oleg wasn't much of one. As though skill at hunting was the greatest thing you could have in the world.

"Of course I understand." Thomas suddenly laughed. He lowered the cross-bow and leaned his back against one of the great boles that formed the fence. "It's a question of priorities. In any small scale society, ours being the example at hand, abilities in, say, mathematics, are in less demand than the ability to kill a baer. It just ain't fair, but it is understandable."

Thomas's smile was polite, the long lips bent at the corners of his mouth as though they had trouble fitting a face that was a mass of deep scars, and eyes darker still. And the whites of Thomas's eyes had turned yellow. Thomas's liver was diseased. Perhaps that was why he had gone completely bald and coughed all the time.

But Thomas was a survivor and knew the road to the mountain pass better than anyone else.

Thomas pointed his cross-bow and, without sighting, fired a bolt. Oleg's eyes followed after the bolt, there was a yowl, and the wood stuck from the hide of a zhakal that hadn't dodged in time. The creature fell out of the branches, as though the tree had been holding on to it but now let it drop. The zhakal's black maw gaped open, the individual hairs of its white coat stuck out like needles. The critter crashed onto the meadow, twitched, and grew quiet.

"Great shot."

"Thank you. We'll have to drag it away before the croes come."

"I'll do it." Oleg said.

"No. He's not alone." Thomas stopped him. "Get your cross-bow first. If the kids do return, they'll have to walk through a pack of them. How many zhakals were there last night?"

"I counted six." Oleg said.

Oleg had just turned to run after his weapon when Thomas's whistle brought him up short. The whistle was loud enough to be heard anywhere in the settlement.

Stop now? No, better get the cross-bow first! It would only take a minute.

"What's happening?" His mother stood in the doorway.

He darted around her, grabbed the cross-bow from the wall, and almost cried out in alarm. Where were his bolts? Under the table? Had the twins carried them off?

"Behind the stove." His mother said. She had hid the quiver from the twins. "What's happening? Is Marianna all right?"

The Mayor had run out with a spear; he could hardly fire a cross-bow with only one hand. Oleg ran around the Mayor, pulling a bolt from the quiver as he ran, although he'd always been taught never to do that. All the settlement's children were hurrying to the fence.

"Get back from there!" Oleg shouted in his loudest voice. No one listened to him.

Sergeyev was already standing next to Thomas with a long

bow in his hands. The men were listening tensely. Sergeyev lifted a three fingered hand and ordered those running toward them to stop.

And then a cry reached them from the straight gray wall of the forest. A human cry, from far off, and brief, cut off; endless silence followed from the settlement. And Oleg imagined — no, he could *see* – Marianna and Dick out in the forest, behind the wall of rain and thick white trees, in the living, breathing, crawling forest. Marianna stood with her back against the warm and smarting bark of a payn and Dick, half fallen to his knees, blood dripping from a hand torn by the teeth of a zhakal, trying to pick up the spear.

"Mr Mayor!" Thomas shouted. "Boris, stay at the gate. Oleg, with us."

Aunt Luiza caught up with them at the forest edge; in one hand she carried the enormous ax she'd used to chase off a baer last year, in the other hand she carried a burning torch. Aunt Luiza was a large, fat and terrifying woman — short gray locks of matted hair rolled down the sides of her head, her loose coveralls blown by the wind to bell shape. Even the trees dragged back their branches in fear and the leaves twisted out of her way; Aunt Luiza was like the wolfwind that ripped down the gorge in winter. And when she stumbled over hunting vynes they slithered behind the nearest tree in fright.

Thomas came to a halt so abruptly Sergeyev almost ran into him. He put two fingers into his mouth and whistled. No one else in the settlement could manage such a deafening whistle.

When the sound died away Oleg realized the others had grown completely still. The forest feared human trampling, human fears and human rage. All they could be heard was Aunt Luiza's heavy breathing.

"Here!" Marianna's voice sounded quite close by. She had hardly shouted enough to be heard from one end of the settlement to the other. They ran on and Oleg heard Dick's voice — rather his roar — and the furious barking of a zhakal.

Oleg dashed to one side to be able to shoot around Aunt Luiza, but he was blocked by Sergeyev's naked back; Marianna's father hadn't had time to dress, he had come running at Thomas's call, pulling up his leather trousers.

Marianna stood with her back pressed into the soft white bole of a fat old payn just as in Oleg's premonition; it had begun to cave inward as though it were trying to embrace the girl. But Dick still stood; he had driven back an enormous gray zhakal with his knife. The critter dodged the blow, hissing and twisting. Still another zhakal was writhing on its side on the ground, an arrow sticking out of the fur. And five of the critters sat in a row to one side like an audience. The humans had never been able to explain zhakal behavior. The animals did not fall on their prey in a pack but took turns. If the first failed to take down the prey the second took his place, and so on, until they won, without pity or concern for their own fallen. Sergeyev, when he had dissected one of the animals, had difficulty finding the brain.

The audience of zhakals, as on command, turned their muzzles to the people who had rushed onto the field. Oleg thought for a moment the red points of the zhakals' eyes were sizing him up. Could it be they were all going to attack together? That wasn't in the rules.

The zhakal trying to grab Dick's knife with its teeth suddenly jerked to one side; an arrow poked out from the base of the long neck. Thomas had managed to fire while Oleg was still trying to decide what to do. Dick, as though he had been waiting for this, immediately turned on the remaining zhakals and ran at them with his spear. Alongside him were Sergeyev and Aunt Luiza with the ax and firebrand. Before the zhakals could understand what was happening, two lay sprawled dead in the meadow and the rest turned on their claws, the tips of their scaly flat tails arched to the bare backs of their heads, and vanished into the depths of the forest. No one went after them. Oleg went over to Marianna.

"You okay?"

Marianna was crying. She was clutching the chittering basket to her breast and crying bitterly.

"I was stung by a willowwasp." Marianna cried. "Now I'll be marked."

"It's a shame you came so fast." Dick said, wiping blood from his cheek. "I was just beginning to have fun."

"Don't talk like a fool." Aunt Luiza said.

"The third or fourth would have had you for dinner." Sergeyev added.

***

On the way back to the settlement Dick began to shake from the toxins of the zhakal bite. They hurried to Vaitkus's house. Vaitkus himself was sick in bed, but his wife Egli pulled lotions and antidotes for zhakal poison from the medicine box in the corner for him, then washed Marianna's wounds thoroughly and made her lay down and get some sleep. Dick left; the fever had come on him, he felt sick and looked bad, and he did not want other people to see him.

Egli put a bowl of the sugar they obtained from the roots of one of the swamp grasses on the table. Only she and Marianna were able to distinguish the sweet sedge from the usually poisonous variety, and a few of the younger kids who knew by smell which grass was sweet and which bit back. Then Egli poured hot water into the cups, and everyone ladled out himself a spoonful of thick gray sugary gelatin. No formalities. Everyone liked visiting the Vaitkuses.

"Nothing too serious?" Thomas asked Egli. "Dick can still go?"

"He's like a cat. He'll heal fast."

"Any doubts?" Sergeyev asked the other man.

"No doubts . . ." Thomas answered. "No other choice, really. Are you prepared to wait three more years? We'll die out from poverty."

"We won't die out." Vaitkus said from his bed. His beard and a mop of hair on his head covered all his face. All anyone could see was the red nose and the bright points of his eyes. "We're going terminally wild."

"All the same." Thomas said. "If I could get my hands on Daniel Defoe I'd wring his neck! Miserable liar!"

Vaitkus laughed; it sounded more like a cough.

Oleg had heard this conversation before. Now it was all small talk and banter. He'd have preferred to drop by the barn where the Mayor and his students were preparing the dead zhakals' hides, to have a word with the Mayor. Simply speak with him for a while. But then he looked at the bowl with sugar and decided to stay and have some more. He and his mother had finished their sugar ration at home the week before. He started to draw the spoon through the bowl but took only half a spoonful. Well, he hadn't come here to have dinner.

"Drink this, Marianna." Egli said. "You're tired."

"Thank you." Marianna said. "I'll go let the muzhrumes soak first, then I'll get some sleep."

Oleg looked Marianna over, as though he was seeing her for the first time, the spoon hung idly over the bowl. Marianna's lips were drawn precisely, a little darker at the edges, very remarkable lips, unlike anyone else's in the settlement. Although she did look a little like Sergeyev. Quite a lot. Of course she also resembled her mother, but Oleg didn't remember the woman. And maybe she looked like her grandfather as well? A remarkable thing, genetics. The Mayor had conducted an experiment for the students with peas in the hothouse pit behind the barn, Marianna's domain. Well, not with real peas, but with a local plant that could pass for a lentil. Everything had agreed with theory, but with some differences; different rules for assortment of the chromosomes, evidently.

Marianna had a triangular face, wide cheekbones and forehead, and a sharp chin, so there were a lot of spaces for eyes to rest on her face, and Oleg's eyes occupied all the free spaces. And a very long neck, with a long red scar she'd had since childhood on one side.

Marianna was used to it, and she'd survive the willowwasps.

And it hardly mattered if someone had marks on their face or not, did it? Everyone had them. And instead of a necklace of pearls around her neck Marianna had a string with a wooden flask of antidote, like everyone else in the settlement.

"You should reconsider; this little jaunt might end tragically." Sergeyev said.

"If I thought that I wouldn't have anything to do with it." Thomas said.

Vaitkus began to laugh again, a gurgle that started from somewhere in the middle of his beard.

"Fellows, Dick and Oleg are the hope of our colony, its future. Thomas, you are one of our four last men."

"Amen to that." Luiza said in her basso voice and began to blow loudly into her cup to cool the boiled water.

"You haven't convinced me." Thomas said. "But if you're so much afraid, let Marianna stay here."

"I'm afraid for my daughter, yes. But we're talking about more important things."

"I'll go soak the muzhrumes." Marianna said and got easily to her feet.

"Skin and bones." Aunt Luiza looked after her.

Walking past her father, Marianna ran the ends of her fingers along his shoulders. He lifted a three fingered hand to touch the back of his daughter's palm but she had already taken her hand away and quickly headed for the door. The door opened, letting in the rain's gentle droning, and closed loudly behind the girl. Oleg had almost darted after Marianna, but stopped himself. Somehow he felt uncomfortable.

One of Vaitkus's sons toddled out of the second room. How old was he now? The first boy had been born in the spring, and the other not long ago, when the snow fell. That meant half a year. In all Vaitkus had six children. The world record.

"Sug-gaa.." The child said angrily.

"I'll show you sugar!" Egli said in exasperation. "You want

your teeth to ache. Like mine? And who said you could walk barefoot? Did I?"

She picked up the boy and carried him out of the room.

Oleg saw he had forgotten himself and begun to spoon sugar from the bowl again. In anger he poured the spoon full back. Then he wiped the empty spoon with his tongue.

"Let me pour you some more hot water." Aunt Luiza said. "I keep worrying about our children. They're always so underfed."

"There's nothing more we can do." Egli said, coming back into the room. After her came the deep-throated wailing of a Vaitkus-*fils*. "We can go muzhrume hunting now. They have vitamins. Worse with proteins. . . ."

"We'll be going now." Aunt Luiza said. "You look quite worn out."

"You know why." Egli tried for a smile, but the smile became a grimace; the thought was painful.

A month ago Egli had given birth to another child, a stillborn daughter. The Mayor said she was too old to give birth now. And her body was exhausted. But she thought it her duty. "The species has to continue. Don't you understand?" Oleg understood, although talk about such things was unpleasant, because for some reason it was as though they weren't supposed to talk about such things.

"Thanks for the hospitality." Aunt Luiza said.

"How you manage to put on weight I can't understand." Thomas said, watching Aunt Luiza's enormous bulk moving toward the door.

"Not from living the good life, I can tell you." Luiza said without turning. At the door way she stopped and said to Oleg: "With all the commotion you forgot to stop in at Kristina's. They're waiting for you. Naughty."

Of course. Damn! He should have dropped by more than an hour ago.

Oleg got to his feet.

"I'll go now."

"Well, it has to be done. I can do it, for discipline." Aunt Luiza said. "I'll drop by to see her myself. I'll go after I feed my own pack."

"You don't have to."

Oleg jumped off the house platform into the street after Aunt Luiza and immediately remembered he had forgotten to thank Egli for the hot water and sugar; everything had become awkward.

The two walked together; it wasn't very far. The whole settlement could be circumnavigated in about five minutes along the fence perimeter.

Two lines of houses sitting on stilts, under slanting lean-to roofs, huddled together, clutched at each other on either side of a straight swath of mud that cut the settlement in half from the gates in the palisade fence to the common barn and warehouse. Roofs covered with the long, flat, reddish leaves of water tulips glistened in the rain; puddles everywhere reflected the ever cloudy sky. Four houses on one side, six on the other. Of course after last year's epidemic, three stood empty.

Kristina's house was the next to last, with only Dick's beyond. Aunt Luiza lived opposite.

"Aren't you afraid to be going?" Aunt Luiza asked.

"It has to be done." Oleg answered.

"A true answer, worthy sir." For some reason Aunt Luiza started to laugh.

"Will Sergeyev let Marianna go?" Oleg asked.

"Your Marianna will be going." Luiza said. "She'll be going."

"Nothing's going to happen to us." Oleg said. "Four people. All armed. It's not our first time in the forest."

"In the forest, no." Luiza agreed. "But when you get to the mountains it will be totally different."

They stopped in the road between her house and Kristina's. Luiza's door had already been opened and they could see the boy Louisa had adopted, Kazik, waiting.

"The mountains are horrible." Luiza said. "I'll remember how we trudged through them the rest of my life. People died as you watched and you could do nothing. . . . When we got up in the morning . . . some people were frozen to the ground."

"It's summer now." Oleg said. "No snow."

"Don't delude yourself. There's always snow in the mountains."

"If we can't make it there, we'll come back." Oleg said.

"Just make sure you do."

Luiza headed for her own door. Kazik ran out to meet her. Oleg turned to Kristina's door.

Kristina's house was stuffy, there was a bitter smell in the air. The mold had covered the insides like wallpaper; although the mold was yellow and orange it did nothing to brighten the room; — there was never any light.

"Hello." Oleg said, holding the door open to see who was where in the dark. "You're not sleeping?"

"Oh, someone's come." Kristina said. "I thought you wouldn't, guessed you'd forgotten. What with preparing to go into the mountains why should you remember me?"

"Don't listen to her, Oleg." A small voice said almost in a whisper. That was Liz. "She's always grumbling. She grumbles at me. You get sick of it."

Oleg found a stool, groped for it with his hands and sought the candle; he pulled iron and flint from his belt pouch.

"Why are you sitting in the darkness?" He asked.

"The lamp's out of oil." Liz said.

"But where's the can?"

"We have no oil." Kristina said. "Who needs two helpless women like us? Who'd bring us oil?"

"There's oil on the shelf to your right." Liz said. "When are you leaving?"

"After lunch." Oleg said. "How are you feeling?"

"Okay. Just weak."

"Egli said you'll be able to get up in two or three days. If you want we can take you over to Luiza's."

"I won't leave mama." Liz said.

"Fine." Kristina said. "Get her away from here. Why should

she die with me?"

Kristina was not Liz's mother, but they had always lived together. When they had arrived at the settlement Liz was less than a year old, the youngest of the children. Her mother had frozen to death in the mountain pass and her father hadn't even made it that far. Kristina had carried Liz through those days. That was when she had been strong and brave. When she had eyes.

And the two of them had stayed together. Then Kristina went blind. It had been the willowwasps — at the time they hadn't known what to do. So now she sat. She rarely left her house. Only in summer. If it wasn't raining. Everyone else was used to the constant rain and didn't even notice it, but not her. If it rained she wouldn't leave the house for anything; if it was dry she would sit on the porch, guess who the passers-by were from the way they walked, and complain.

The Mayor said Kristina wasn't entirely normal any more. Once upon a time she had been a famous astrophysicist. Liz had once staid to Oleg: "Try to imagine being in her position; her life was looking at the stars, and then found herself in a forest where there weren't any stars, and then she went completely blind as well. You can't understand her."

Oleg looked around and found the jar of grease on the shelf. It wasn't empty yet. He poured some in the lamp, and lit it. Immediately the room became bright. He could see the wide bed on which Kristina and Liz huddled together under skins. Oleg was always surprised at how similar the two were; it was hard to believe they weren't related at all. Both had pale white skin and yellow hair, with wide squarish faces and small lips. Liz had green eyes. Kristina's eyes were closed, but the Mayor and his mother both said they had once been green as well.

"There's enough oil to last the week," Oleg said. "Then the Mayor will bring more. You don't have to ration it. Why sit in the dark?"

"I'm sorry I got sick." Liz said. "I wanted to go with you."

"You'll go next year."

"You mean in three years?"

"In a year."

"After this year means after three of our years. I have weak lungs."

"It's a long time 'til winter. You'll get better."

Oleg understood this girl with the wide face was not talking about what awaited him. When she spoke of going with him she didn't mean into the mountains. She wanted Oleg to remain with her always. She was afraid. She was completely alone. Oleg tried to be polite but he didn't always succeed. Liz was a pest — her eyes were always asking for something.

Kristina got up off the bed, picked up her stick and walked over to the hearth. She was able to do everything for herself but preferred her neighbors help her.

". . . go out of my minds." The woman mumbled. "I was someone. I used to do real work. And men would turn their heads when I walked by. Now I have to live in this sty and everyone's abandoned me . . . damned by fate. . . ."

"Oleg," Liz said. She rose half way on her elbows revealing a breast that had grown large and white since the end of winter. Oleg turned away. "Oleg, don't go. You won't return. I know you won't return. I have a premonition . . ."

"Can I bring you some water?" Oleg asked quickly.

"We have some." Liz said. "You just don't want to hear me out. Just for once in your life!"

"I'd better get going."

"Yes." She said bitterly.

Her words reached him at the door:

"Oleg, would you look for cold medicines there? For Kristina. You won't forget?"

"I won't forget."

"You will." Kristina said. "There'll be nothing surprising at all about that."

"Oleg!"

"What is it?"

"You haven't said good-bye to me."
"Au revoir."

***

The Mayor was washing himself over the basin in the kitchen.

"The critters you killed weren't fully grown." He said. "The coats are poor quality, summer coats."

"That was Dick and Sergeyev."

"Are you angry? Were you with Kristina?"

"They're all right. Just bring them some grease. And they're out of bowtatoes too."

"Don't get upset. Come into my room. We can finally have our talk."

"Just don't take too long." Oleg's mother called from behind the partition.

The Mayor grinned sourly. Oleg held the rag so the old man could wipe his left hand more easily. The Mayor had lost the right hand fifteen years ago when they had made the first attempt to go back across the mountain pass.

Oleg went into the Mayor's room, sat down at the table polished by the students' elbows and pushed the home-made abacus to one side, rattling the counters made from dried nuts in their grooves. How many times had he sat at this table? Several thousand, certainly. Nearly everything he knew, he had learned at this table.

"For me the worst thing is sending you." The old man said, sitting down opposite him in his teacher's seat. "I thought in a few years you will take my place teaching the children."

"I'll be back." Oleg said. He thought: *What's Marianna doing now? She must have finished soaking the muzhrumes already, then she has to go through the herbarium and select what she'll be taking along. Is she getting ready? Is she talking to her father?*

"Are you listening to me."

"Yes, certainly, teacher."

"But at the same time it was I who insisted they take you with them up to the mountain pass. In fact you're more necessary than Dick or Marianna. You can be my eyes and my hands."

The old man raised the one hand and looked it over with interest, as though no one was looking. And was lost in thought. Oleg said nothing; his eyes roamed the rest of the room. The old man sometimes fell silent like that, unexpectedly, for a minute or two. Everyone had some weakness of his own. The fire from the lamp illuminated the polished little pocket microscope on the wall. It had once been part of a much larger portable medical lab, but everything else had been lost; it didn't even have a real lens any more. A thousand times Sergeyev had told the Mayor the empty tube was just a great luxury. "Let me bring it to the workshop, Borya. I can get you two knives from it." But the Mayor never surrendered it.

"Sorry." The old man said. He blinked his gray eyes twice, stroked the carefully trimmed white beard that caused Aunt Luiza to call him 'Mister Fashionplate.'

"I've been doing some thinking. You know about what? Back in the history of Earth there were a number of cases — groups of people cut off from the general current of civilization by accident or disaster. And here we are in a position to carry out a qualitative analysis . . ."

The old man fell silent again and pursed his lips, lost in his own thoughts again. Oleg was used to this. He liked sitting next to the old man, simply saying nothing, and it seemed to him that the knowledge of the old man was so great the air of the room was simply filled with it.

"Well, naturally one should study temporal diapason. Diapason — it's a concord of notes, and by extension of that meaning a range of possibilities effected over time. remember?"

The old man always explained the words which his students hadn't encountered before.

"To regress a single individual to barbarism all you need is a few years. That's because man is born tabula rasa. a blank sheet of paper. It's known children who fell among wolves or tigers at an early age — they used to tell such tales in India and Africa — after a number of years were hopelessly behind their contemporaries in linguistic skills. They remained feral. A feral person is . . ."

"I remember."

"Yes. Hmmm. . . . They were never able live among other people afterwards. They even walked on all fours."

"What if they were adults."

"The wolves didn't take in adults."

"And on desert islands? Like Tasmania and. . . ."

"That depended on the circumstances, but people inevitably experienced regression. The degree of regression . . ."

The old man glanced at Oleg. The later nodded his head — he knew the word.

"The degree of regression depends on the level which the person had reached at the moment of isolation and on his character. But we cannot pose an historical experiment on a single developed personality. We are talking about the social experience of the group. Is it possible for a group of people under conditions of isolation to maintain the level of culture which held at the moment of separation?"

"Maybe." Oleg said. "There's us."

"You can't." The old man said. "For a child five years is enough to turn him into a savage. For an isolated band, if it doesn't die out, it will take two or three generations. For a large group or a tribe — several generations. For a nation — a century maybe. But the process is irreversible. It's been proven by history. For example, the Tasmanian and Australian aborigines . . ."

Oleg's mother entered the room. Her hair was combed and she had put on her best and only real dress.

"I'll come and sit with you." She said.

"Take a chair, Irina." The old man said. "We were speaking about social progress. Or, more precisely, regress."

"I've already heard." Oleg's mother said. "Have you decided how much longer it will take before we walk on all fours? I've already told you — we'll all be dead before then. Thank God. I've had enough."

"But Oleg hasn't." The old man said. "And my twins haven't."

"It's because of him I'm still living." Oleg's mother said. "So why do you want to send him to certain death?"

"In your point of view death threatens us here every day just because we get up, Ira." The Mayor spoke as the tribal Elder. "The forest out there — that is death. Winter is death. The spring floods are death. The hurricanes are death. A bea sting is death and a flee-bite is worse than death. There's no way of telling where death will come from or what form it will take."

"It will come whenever it wants and choose whomever it wants." Mother said. "One after the other until no one is left."

"There are more of us now than there were five years ago. Our main problem isn't physical survival, but moral."

"We are fewer! You and I are fewer! You understand. There aren't enough of us left! How will these puppies survive without us?"

"We might." Oleg said. "Would you go off into the forest alone?"

"It would be better to hang ourselves. I fear going out into the street at times."

"But I am going on the climb now. And I'll return. With the hoard."

"We almost didn't save Dick and Marianna today."

"That was an accident. You certainly know that zhakals don't hunt in packs."

"I don't know any such thing! Did they all run off as a pack or not? Did they?"

"Yes."

"Then they hunt in packs."

Oleg couldn't think of a reply. His mother grew silent as well. The Mayor sighed, waited for a pause in the argument and continued his monologue.

"For some reason or other I remembered another bit of history today. It seems like I haven't thought of it for a thousand years, but today I remembered it. Perhaps it was your going and this place . . .

"It happened in 1530 AD, shortly after the discovery of America. A German ship was hunting whales to the south of Iceland. It was caught by a storm and driven to the north west, into uncharted waters. For some days the ship sailed the waves among icebergs. Icebergs are . . ."

"It's a mountain of ice in the water. I know." Oleg said.

"Correct. After several days the snow capped, mountainous shores of an unknown land appeared. Now they call it Greenland. The ship let down anchor and the sailors went ashore. And you can imagine their surprise when they soon saw a half ruined church and then the remains of stone cabins. In one of the cabins they found the corpse of a red haired man in clothing sewn from sealskins, along with a worn down, rusty knife. And all around them emptiness, cold, snow . . ."

"Borya, there's no need to frighten the boy." Oleg's mother said. Her fingers nervously rapped on the table. "Pseudohistoric fairy tales. . . ."

"Just a moment. This is no fairy tale. It's been very carefully researched and documented. The dead man was the last of the Vikings. You remember what Vikings were, Oleg?"

"You told us all about Vikings."

"The Vikings were sea rovers. They conquered whole countries like France and England. They settled Iceland, came ashore in America, which they called Vinland, even founded a kingdom of their own in Sicily."

"And they had an important colony in Greenland. There were several settlements with stone houses and churches. Then the Vikings stopped sending their ships out to sea. Their colonies fell to other people or were abandoned. Contact with Greenland came to an end. And at the same time the climate grew worse. The herds of cattle died out, and Greenland's population started to drop. The reason for this was the loss of contact with the rest of the world. The Greenlanders, once heroic seamen, forgot the art of constructing sea-going ships, because they had no trees. Their numbers dwindled. It's known the last marriage in Greenland was celebrated in the middle of the fifteenth century. The descendants of the Vikings became primitives. They were too few to withstand the elements, make progress or even preserve what they had. You can imagine the tragedy — the last wedding in an entire country?" The Mayor glanced at Oleg's mother.

"Your analogies are less than convincing." Oleg's mother said. "However many the Vikings were, however few, nothing would have saved them."

"But there were alternatives. Had the German ship come thirty years earlier everything might have turned out differently. The Vikings could have sailed to the continent and returned to the human family. Or else once they had re-established contact with other countries, traders might have come, new settlers, perhaps even new tools, knowledge. . . . Everything would have been different."

"Well, no one is going to sail the seas to us." Oleg's mother said.

"Our salvation will not to be found in adapting to nature." The old man said with certainty. This time he had turned to Oleg. "We need help. Help from the rest of the human race. And that's why I insist that your son go to the mountain pass. We still remember, and our duty is not to break that thread of memory."

"Empty words." Oleg's mother said tiredly. "Shall I pour you more hot water?"

"Pour away." The Mayor said. "Let us indulge ourselves with hot water. We're threatened by loss of our past. The people who remember what we need all the fewer. Some are dying, some others are simply too busy staying alive from day to day. And now we have a new generation. You and Marianna are just the transition stage. You're like a knot uniting us with our future. Have you any idea, any image of what it's going to be like?"

"We're not afraid of the forest." Oleg said. "We know the muzhrumes and the trees, we can hunt on the plains . . ."

"What I am afraid of is a future ruled by a new type of man, a Dick-the-Hunter; for me he's a symbol of our failure, a symbol of the surrender of mankind in the struggle with nature. . . ."

"Richard is a fine boy." Oleg's mother said from the kitchen. "He hasn't had it easy growing up alone."

"It's not his character I worry about." Boris said. "It's everyone else becoming like him I fear. When are you going to learn to ignore trifles, Irina?"

"I may ignore trifles or not, but if Dick hadn't killed that baer this winter we'd all have starved to death."

"Dick already thinks of himself as a native here. He stopped coming to class five years ago. I'm not even certain if he remembers the alphabet."

"And why should he?" Oleg's mother asked. "There aren't any books at all and nowhere to write letters to. And no one else."

"Dick knows a lot of songs." Oleg said. "And he composes some himself."

Oleg had become somewhat ashamed that he was so pleased at hearing the old man's displeasure toward Dick he felt he had to defend the other boy.

"We're not talking about the songs. Songs are the dawn of civilization. But for the younger kids Dick has become their idol.

"Dick is the hunter!" The Mayor turned to Oleg's mother. "And for you he is an example. 'Look at Dick. What a good kid.' To the girls he's a knight in shining armor. Haven't you ever seen what sort of eyes he casts at Marianna."

"Let him look. They'll get married. That's good for the settlement."

"Mother!" Oleg couldn't stand it any longer.

"But what?"

As usual his mother had noticed nothing of what was going on around her. She lived in some sort of other world of her own, reliving the past.

"And does a world of Dicks suit you?" The Mayor was ashen.

He even slammed his fist on the table. "A world of successful, quick footed savages."

"And what do you offer in its place?"

"This." The old man placed his heavy palm on Oleg's head. "An Oleg-world. Your world and my world, the world you are so willing to toss away, even though there's nothing else to put in its place."

"You're not right, Borya." Oleg's mother said. She went into the kitchen took the pot with the boiling water from the fire and brought it into the other room. "The sugar's all gone."

"Mine too." The old man said. "The roots are almost dried out now, losing their sweetness. Egli says we'll have to wait another month for more. Have some bread. Can't you see our chances of rebuilding civilization are doomed if a world of Dick the Hunters replaces us."

"I can't, Borya." Mother said. "We should survive. I'm not talking about myself personally but about the settlement. The children. When I look at Dick or Marianna I have hope. You call them wild, and I think they might be able to adapt. And if they die now, we all die. The risk is too great."

"And you mean to say I haven't adapted." Oleg asked.

"You have adapted less than the others, yes."

"You're simply afraid for me." Oleg said. "You don't want me to go to the mountains. But I can shoot a cross-bow better than Dick."

"Of course I'm afraid for you. You're my only son. You're all I have left. And with every day you're drifting further and further away from me, going off somewhere, becoming strange."

The old man paced slowly about the room as he usually did when he was displeased with his students. Stooping down he lifted a globe from the stool. He had made it from a giant muzhrume which had grown that winter beside the barn. The Mayor had drawn all the continents and seas of the Earth from memory. The globe had turned pale with time, and in two years it had withered like a round apple.

Oleg saw a small point of reddish fungus on the table. Unlike the yellow fungus this was poisonous. He carefully wiped away the spot with his sleeve. It's dumb when your own mother prefers someone else to you. In fact it's a betrayal. A very real betrayal.

"We're going to die, you know." The old man said.

"I know it very well. We've lived long enough." Oleg's mother said.

"All the same we're not forcing the issue, we're clutching onto life as best we can."

"We're cowards." Mother said.

"You've always had Oleg."

"He's the only reason I chose to live."

"You and I are going to die." The old man continued. "But the settlement should live. Otherwise our lives would have no meaning."

"A settlement of hunters will have a better chance of survival."

"The settlement of Olegs will have a better chance of survival in the long run." The old man said. "If Dick and others like him rule our tribe, in a hundred years time no one will know who we were or where we came from. The rule of the strong will triumph, the laws of primitive tribes."

"And they'll be fruitful and multiply." Oleg's mother said. "They'll become many. They'll invent the wheel and, in a few thousand years, the steam engine." Oleg's mother began to laugh. To laugh and cry at the same time.

"You're joking, aren't you?" Oleg asked.

"Irina is right." The old man said. "A struggle for simple survival will lead to hopeless regression. To survive at the price of adapting to nature rather than adapting nature to us means surrender."

"And living." Mother insisted.

"She doesn't think so." Oleg said to the old man.

"No. She doesn't." The old man agreed. "I've known Irina for twenty years now. I know she doesn't think like me."

"In general, I prefer not to think at all anymore." Mother said.

"You're lying." The Mayor said. "We're all thinking about the future, fearing and hoping. Otherwise we stop being people. It is precisely the weight of the knowledge which Dick has chosen not to burden himself with, which will save us, not the simple laws of the forest. For so long as that alternative remains we can still hope."

"And for the sake of this alternative you are send my son to the mountain."

"For the sake of the preservation of knowledge, for your sake and mine. For the sake of the struggle with savagery, isn't that clear?"

"You always were an egoist." Irina said.

"But your blind maternal egoism isn't to be taken into account?"

"Why do you need Oleg? He won't survive the trip. He's too weak."

She should never have said that. She herself understood this and looked at her son, pleading with her eyes.

"I'm not ashamed. Mom." Oleg said. "But I want to go. I want to go more than the others do, maybe. Dick would rather not go at all. The dyr are starting to herd together. The real hunting's on the plains."

"He's needed for the climb." The old man said. "As much as I may disapprove of his power over us in the long term, today his experience, his strength might save us."

"Save us!" Mother tore her eyes from Oleg. "You harp on salvation. How can you deceive yourself? Our people have gone back up to the mountain pass three times. How many returned? With what?"

"That was before we even knew what we were doing. We didn't know the local rules. We went when there was still snow in the pass. Now we know it only melts at the end of summer. You have to pay for any knowledge."

"If they hadn't died how much better-off would we be? There would even be more hands providing food for the children."

"We'd still be regressing and powerless to stop it. Either we are a part of the human race and guard its knowledge or we're savages."

"You're an idealist, Borya. A bit of bread today is more important than an abstract pineapple."

"You really remember the taste of pineapple?" The old man turned to Oleg and added: "Pineapple is a tropical fruit with a very specific taste."

"I understand." Oleg said. "She's trying to be funny."

CHAPTER TWO

"Paper." The Mayor repeated. "Even a dozen pages."

"You'll have it." Thomas said.

Those who were to depart had gathered by the gate in the fence. The others had come to see them off. They were all pretending the climb was just an ordinary jaunt. As though they were going for roots in the swamp. But everyone knew their farewells could be forever.

Those going on the climb were warmly dressed — the clothing had been gathered from all over the settlement. Aunt Luiza herself had gone about collecting, taking this piece of clothing in or letting that out to the necessary sizes. Oleg had never before been so warmly dressed. Only Dick carried nothing not his own. He had done all his own sewing. The rain had almost stopped, and water-tygers were splashing and squeaking in the puddles around the bases of the trees that formed their palisade. That meant good weather.

Thomas looked over the water-tygers and said:

"The rain's stopping. You'll have to strengthen the fence."

"Don't think about it." Aunt Luiza said. "We'll handle it."

"What are you going to bring back for me, Pa?" Thomas's daughter Ruth asked.

"Don't." His wife Linda said. "Don't even think about that. All that matters is your father comes home. Bundle up or you'll catch a cold again."

"Coming back from the pass you head to the right." Vaitkus told Thomas again. "Remember?"

"I'll remember." Thomas laughed. "It's like I can see it now.

You should be in bed."

Oleg's mother held him by the hand and he was unable to tear the hand away. He felt Dick's eyes on him, smirking. Irina wanted to go with them as far as the cemetery, but Sergeyev wouldn't let her pass through the gate. He let no one else through but the Mayor and Luiza.

A number of times as they walked up the hill Oleg turned to look back. His mother stood there, her hand raised, as though she wanted to wave to them and had forgotten what to say. She was trying not to cry.

Over the gate he could make out the heads of the adults: Mother, Egli, Sergeyev, Vaitkus, and lower down, through the bramble laced chinks in the fence, the dark forms of the children. A tiny column of people, and after them, the sloping reddish roofs of a small cluster of huts glistening in the rain.

Oleg looked back for the last time from the hill. They all still stood by the fence, only some of the smaller children had run off to one side and made for the puddle. From the height of the hill he could see the street — a rut between the huts. And the door of Kristina's house. A woman was standing in the doorway, but from the hill he could not make out if it was Kristina or Liz. And then he walked further and the top of the hill cut the settlement off from view.

The graveyard was fenced in like the settlement of the living. Dick looked inside to see if some animal were lurking there before pulling the gate wide. *If it was me I'd have forgotten to do that.* Oleg thought.

Inside, it was eerie. The graves were weighted down with slates of a soft shale quarried from the nearby cliff. They numbered more than the people in the settlement, although the settlement was all of sixteen years old. Oleg's father wasn't here; he hadn't even made it as far as the mountain pass.

Dick stopped before two individual slabs better kept than the others. His father and mother.

The Mayor pulled his clothing tighter against the cold and damp of the rising wind and slowly walked from grave to grave.

He had known them all. Sixteen years ago they had numbered some thirty-six adults and four children. Nine adults and three of those children remained. Three. Dick, Liz, and Oleg. Twelve of the children had been born in the settlement, including Marianna. That meant, seventeen years ago there had been forty people, now there were a little more than twenty. The math was simple. No, not so simple. The graves were more numerous than all the children who had died or perished. The ones who were here.

Into his ear, as though she had listened in on his thoughts, Aunt Luiza said:

"The majority died in the first five years."

"Naturally." The Mayor agreed. "We paid for every bit of knowledge in blood."

Oleg stopped in front of the slabs in the center of the graveyard. The slabs were unkempt, dirty, crooked, the tenacious rusty paws of the moss had started to wind around them and turn them into little round hills.

Oleg wanted to go back, to take one more look at the settlement; he knew his mother was still standing by the gate hoping to see him again. Oleg even walked a little toward the gates in the fence but then Thomas said:

"It's time to go. It will be getting dark soon, and we have to make it to the cliff."

"Oh!" Marianna said. She was running her fingers nervously along the bag over her shoulder.

"Forget something?" Dick asked.

"No. Maybe. I wanted to take one last look at dad. . . ."

"Let's be going, Marianna." Thomas said. "The sooner we get going the sooner we return."

Oleg saw that Marianna's eyes were full of tears. Anything else and they'd pour down her cheeks.

Marianna trailed after the others. Oleg walked over to her and said:

"I wanted to go back too. Or just take another look from the top of the hill."

They walked side by side and said nothing.

Thirty paces from the fence the wall of underbrush, sticky and crafty, began.

Luiza kissed them all. The Mayor shook their hands. Oleg was the last.

"I'm putting my hopes on you." He said. "More than Thomas. Thomas will look after the interests of the settlement, for today. You have to think about the future. Do you understand me?"

"Pretty well." Oleg said. "Look after mother, make certain she doesn't sit around doing nothing but worry. I'll get you that lab kit."

"Thank you. Return as fast as you can."

Dick used the end of his spear to jerk back the sticky tentacles and entered the underbrush first.

"Stay close behind me." He said. "Before they can react."

Oleg didn't look back. There was no time to look back. If you turned back the branches would stick themselves to your boots, and whether you pulled them off or not you'd stink for three weeks. The underbrush worked at being unpleasant.

***

They made it to the cliffs by evening, just as Thomas had calculated.

The forest stopped some ways off from the cliff wall; the scarlet fangs of rock jutted up from naked valleys covered by circles of lichen. Rags of clouds flew by so low the sharp crags disemboweled them and they scattered to fine mist, lost in the gray overcast. Thomas had told them the cave where he had spent the night the last time was dry and could be reached easily. Everyone, other than Dick, was tired, but if Dick had been tired he wouldn't have admitted it to any of the others anyway. The only sign was that his teeth chattered.

"It was colder the last time." Thomas said. "We figured it would be easier to cross the swamp in the cold. But the mountain pass was closed. I remember we were right about this spot and we could hear the frosty ground cracking beneath our feet."

An off-white circular area about twelve meters in diameter lay between the travelers and the cliffs ahead.

"You were right about this spot when you heard the ground cracking beneath you, you say?" Dick asked. He was walking ahead of the others. Abruptly he stopped at the edge of the spot; the surface almost glistened like the bark of a payn.

"In fact, yes." Thomas stopped beside Dick.

Oleg held back. An hour ago he had taken Marianna's bag so she wouldn't be worn out. Marianna hadn't wanted to surrender it, but Thomas had said:

"He's right. Tomorrow I'll help you, after that, Dick."

"Why are we doing this now?" Dick had said. "We're carrying a lot of stuff we don't need in the bags and no one noticed Marianna can't carry as much as the rest of us. It should have been thought of earlier. Two months we've been getting ready for this and no one thought of it."

Interesting, and who was thinking of it? So you're a thinker as well as everything else. Oleg thought, but said, nothing.

Even though it was Dick who said it, they did have to carry a lot if they weren't going to worry about food, and he was going to eat. They had taken both preserved meat, roots, and dried muzhrumes, but most of the weight was in the form of dried wood, without which they could neither boil water nor chase away animals.

"You know what this looks like?" Marianna said when she caught up with the men at the border of the white spot. "The top of a muzhrume. The biggest I've ever seen."

"Could be." Dick said. "Best we walk around it."

"Why?" asked Oleg. "We'll have to clamber along the rocks at the base of the cliff."

"Why don't I test it, then?" Marianna got down on her knees and pulled out her knife.

"What do you plan to do?" Thomas asked.

"Cut off a small piece. And smell it. If it's one of the edible varieties think how great that would be! It could feed the whole settlement."

"It's not worth cutting." Dick said. "I don't like your muzhrume very much, if it really is one."

But Marianna had already thrust her knife into the edge of the spot. Before she could cut anything off the white spot suddenly distended, convulsed and twitched and then billowed in Marianna's direction, knocking the knife out of her hand. Dick grabbed the girl and pulled her back with him, and the two of them clattered across the stones. Thomas jumped back after them, his cross-bow raised.

From where he sat on the stones Dick began to laugh.

"To kill it you'd have to fire the arrow from the woods or beyond."

"Well I told you it was a muzhrume." Marianna said. "There was no reason to be afraid, Dick. It smells just like one."

The white spot continued to shudder; ripples, born in the center, moved to the edges like the circles raised in water by a stone. But the center of the muzhrume kept rising and rising, as though it were about to burst. Then dark cracks appeared in the center; the cracks ran to the sides, widened, and from the center emerged the spikes of enormous petals. The petals started to twist back and forth, although no flower appeared.

"That's beautiful." Marianna said. "It's simply beautiful, isn't it?"

"And you wanted to walk on it." Oleg said to Dick in the voice of an older person, although they were the same age.

Thomas threw his cross-bow over his back and bent down to pick up Marianna's knife.

"Researchers in the field find it useful to think first, then conduct their experiments."

"That may have nothing to do with us." Marianna said. "It's simply showing how beautiful it is!"

"So long as nothing is hiding in it." Dick said. "Shall we be going? It's getting dark and we still haven't found the caves. We came especially at this time so we could spend the night safe in a place we knew."

They walked around the white spot across a vast sloping field of scree at the base of the cliffs. From where he stood above it Oleg tried to look down into the core of the flower, but it was too dark. The petals gradually retracted again as the giant muzhrume slowly quieted down.

"What will we call it?" Marianna asked.

"Todestule." Thomas answered.

"Is that some kind of muzhrume?"

"Yes." Thomas wheezed out. "Large and poisonous. A red cap . . . white spots on red cap."

"Not very similar." Dick said.

"But it sounds pretty." Marianna added.

For a long time now it was Thomas who had the task of bestowing names on the beasts of the fields. The names he chose were familiar, and not always appropriate. Why think of new ones? Just so long as they had similar characteristics. Everyone knew muzhrumes grew in the earth and you could dry them out and preserve them. That meant the orange or blue balls that dug themselves into the ground, but which you could dry, fry and roast and eat if you first de-veined them henceforth bore the name muzhrume. The zhakals roamed in packs, devoured carrion, were cowardly and greedy. It was unimportant that the zhakals here were reptilian. And baers had coats of long, bushy hair and were large . . . Although here their fur were the sprouts of willowasps, which looked like long strands of greenish hair.

Oleg started to pant while they picked their way across the scree, the stones slipping from beneath his feet. Marianna's backpack dragged at his hand, his own weighed down his shoulders. Oleg was counting his steps. Where was that damned cave?

The air began to turn blue; the day had been overcast from the beginning and already he was having trouble making out objects ahead. A grey cloud lifted from the earth. It was time to go to ground. Even Dick wouldn't risk the forest at night. They left the darkness to the night prowlers. If you went outside the stockade at night you didn't come back. But here, so far from the settlement . . . Oleg glanced back; it seemed something was following him. Now, only a cloud. He didn't notice he had quickened his pace until Thomas almost raised his voice.

"Don't run into me. You'll knock me down. Keep a distance."

But despite everything Oleg could not get away from the feeling that something was following him.

Thomas's back vanished — he had cut in front of Marianna. Now Marianna was walking in front of Oleg. She had a narrow back, narrow even in a warm jacket. Marianna stumbled. She had trouble seeing in the twilight. Egli had called it night blindness. "Night blindness, but not the ordinary kind, rather it's endemic. Endemic means it's a property of the environment, the locality." Oleg found the Mayor's voice repeating the words in his ears, as though the old man were at his side.

"Do you want to take my hand?" Oleg asked.

They were walking side by side through the swamp in the mist, wallowing in it up to their knees.

"No." Marianna said. "Thanks anyway."

"Stop!" Dick's hollow voice reached them from far ahead. "The caves."

***

They were lucky to find the cave empty; a baer could have been using it or, worse, one of the night wraiths that roamed outside the stockade and sometimes shook at the palisade walls trying to get in. They were drawn to the human settlement and feared it.

Once Marianna had come home dragging a young gote out of the forest on a leash. The gote had a loud and piercing voice, worse than the twins'. A green mop of hair hung to the ground, it stamped armor-covered feet and howled.

"It bleats." Vaitkus had said with some pleasure. "I could get used to the voices of domestic animals."

"So we'll call it a gote." Thomas had said.

The gote had lived in the settlement until winter, when night stretched from hesitant dawn to abrupt sundown almost without interruption. It got used to people, ate almost nothing and stuck around the workshop where Sergeyev fashioned furniture and carved plates and bowls all the time, where it was warm and Oleg enjoyed helping Sergeyev. Then one night the wraiths came and carried the gote away. Marianna found a few scraps of green fur beyond the graveyard, but by then it was already spring. She could have been mistaken.

Vaitkus had looked at the remains and said:

"So we'll have to put aside the development of animal husbandry for the future, I guess."

"You mean gotes' milk, more to the point." Egli had added.

The cave had one drawback — a large entrance. They stretched a tent of sewn fish skins across the space and lit a fire — the night walkers hated fire. The cave grew warm and Oleg lay flat with pleasure on the smooth stone floor. Marianna lay down beside him.

"I feel exhausted!" Marianna said. "It was terrible."

"Me too." Oleg said quietly. "I kept thinking something was coming up behind us."

"I'm glad I didn't know that." Marianna said.

Dick untied the bundles of dried sticks. They had brought along the very best, slow burning wood. Thomas opened the bag of dried muzhrumes and reached for the tripod and crosspiece to hold the kettle over the fire.

"Oleg." He said. "Bring me some water."

Oleg had the water in a gourd container. All Thomas had to do was take two steps and grab the water himself. Oleg understood Thomas was speaking as his teacher. The older man didn't want to have to order Oleg to carry out this or that job. It wasn't as if he hadn't been working — they had hung the tent and lit the fire together. *Next time I won't be too tired to do housekeeping; I did drag Marianna's bag along today.*

Naturally Oleg said nothing aloud. He didn't even have a chance to get to his feet. Dick stretched out a long arm and deposited Oleg's bag by Thomas's side.

"Let him rest." Dick said without any feeling beyond indifference. "He's dead tired. He carried two packs today."

"Go lay down." Thomas agreed.

Oleg sat up.

"Is there anything that has to be done?" He asked. "If there's anything you want I can do it."

"Wait a moment, Thomas." Marianna said. "I'll boil the water myself. You don't know how many muzhrumes to put in."

"I had the feeling something was coming up behind us." Dick said.

"You too?" Oleg asked.

Then they heard heavy steps on the other side of the screened cave entrance. Dick ran for his cross-bow. Thomas leaned toward the fire to grab a log. The clattering animal steps died away and it grew very quiet. They could hear the occasional patter of rain dripping from the cave overhang.

"We got here just in time." Marianna said.

"Quiet."

The shiny curtain of fish hides reflected the dancing fire. It was dead silent.

Dick held the spear over his head and went to the curtain. He carefully edged the corner to one side and looked out.

Oleg looked at Dick's broad tense back and waited. He should have taken a spear as well . . . No, now the screen and what lay beyond it was Dick's business. The unfairness of the situation was evident to Oleg, but he could console himself that he was there for other reasons. He was here to spot things the others weren't interested in. The Mayor was counting on him. . . .

Marianna kept busy by the fire, going through the muzhrumes and the dried berries. She always cooked them separately and then mixed them together. She was on her knees, the sleeves of her jacket rolled up, her fine hands a mass of cuts and scars. Oleg thought Marianna's hands were beautiful. The scars were nothing: everyone had scars.

Thomas was looking a Marianna's quick hands. He was watching the girl bury herself in religious rites that held no meaning for him, who would always be a stranger here. He noted each scar on her hands — the price the forest extracted for each quantum of knowledge — and thought about the gulf which the settlement had dug between him and these teenagers. He watched them, delighted now to fall asleep on a stone floor, covered with nothing and not feeling the damp, penetrating cold. Nor did they find the smell of these short legged plants they called muzhrumes without his objections revolting. They knew all the different local smells. Even the children here smelled different. Even his own children. Should his own daughter Ruth ever find herself lost in the in the forest she might die or she might not die, but she certainly would not starve. The forest might be dangerous, insidious, and crafty, but it was theirs. If he, Thomas Hind, was a man in this forest, these kids were fawns, baby rabbits or even better, wolf cubs. They were not the strongest of the local fauna certainly, but they were more cunning than most, and they would survive . . .

Marianna examined a doubtful muzhrume, gave it a pinch, and threw it away. On the surface it looked just like any other muzhrume. . . .

Again something heavy was moving around outside in the darkness past the cave entrance; it almost touched the half transparent curtain. *Damned night stalkers. They make as much of a racket as elephants, and I wouldn't be surprised if they were poisonous . . . The kids are tired, but Dick looks like he's ready to go chasing zhakals in the underbrush. Oleg is weaker. Of course, the kid isn't stupid . . .*

Something touched the curtain, sending the sewn hides to shivering. Their night visitor had evidently decided to pull it down. Thomas lifted a burning stick and got to the curtain even before Dick. He looked out into the twilight and mist. A dark shadow floated off into the distance, merging with the gray fog as though some jester were trailing behind him a child's balloon. . . .

"I don't know what it is." Thomas said before the kids could ask him. "I've never seen anything like it before."

"We'll have to keep watch all night by the fire." Dick said.

"I'd rather not sleep at all." Oleg said.

"I could use a good pistol now." Thomas said.

"You'll have soup in five minutes." Marianna said. "Tasty soup. Aunt Luiza picked out all the white muzhrumes for us, or she tried."

Far in the distance some things banged and came crashing through the undergrowth. Then they heard the light hammering of numerous feet and bleating. A number of voices.

Marianna jumped to her feet.

"Gotes!"

"Yours got eaten long ago." Dick said. "What's doing the chasing."

"Alleyfants with fangs, and venom." Thomas blurted out unexpectedly.

"What?" Marianna asked in surprise.

Dick began to laugh. "We might as well call them that."

The bleating turned into a shrill cry, like the cry of a child. It cut off abruptly. All was silent but for the hammering of feet.

"I think they have something to do with the giant white muzhrume. I think it releases them." Oleg said.

"What?"

"The poisonous alleyfants."

"Those are evil spirits. Kristina told us all about them." Marianna said.

"There are no such things." Oleg replied.

"Go further into the forest and say that," Dick challenged.

"Quiet, all of you." Thomas told them.

The fleeing gotes were quite close by. After them came their pursuer, moving in soft and infrequent steps.

The people stepped back behind their camp fire, leaving the

flames between themselves and the curtain, and the strange and terrifying animals on the other side.

The curtain was jerked to one side. It was torn slantwise, and a green furred animal about the height of a man rushed into the cave; it had a rounded body on four legs, with a bony spine down the back jutting up out of the mat of hair like a chain of sharp hills from a forest.

The animal was shivering rapidly and softly. Small red eyes looked uncomprehending at their doom.

Dick took careful aim with the cross-bow.

"Stop that!" Marianna shouted at him. "It's just a gote."

"You're right." Dick whispered, not moving from where he stood, not even moving his lips. "It's meat."

But Marianna had already run around the fire and was approaching the gote.

"Wait . . ." Thomas tried to stop her. Marianna shook his hand away.

"It's my gote." She said.

"Your gote was something's supper long ago." Dick said, but he dropped his hand from the cross-bow's trigger; they already had enough meat. There would be no pleasure in just killing. A hunter should kill only as much as he can carry back.

The gote was terrified. And froze in its tracks. It was obvious that whatever crept around outside was more fearsome than Marianna. Marianna bent down and quickly picked up a tasty white muzhrume from the basket and offered it to the gote. The animal snorted, sniffed, opened its hippopotamus mouth wide, and obediently crunched down the gift.

***

Oleg kept the first watch. The gote didn't leave. It huddled in place by the cave wall as though trying to merge with it, kept one eye on Oleg and sniffed noisily from time to time. Then it began to rub its body against the wall.

"You're starting to get fleas." Oleg said. "Stop making a racket or I'll chuck you out."

The gote looked up at Oleg, eyes not blinking. The animal gave the impression it was listening to him and understood all he said. In fact the animal was listening to what was going on outside.

Staring at the dying fire Oleg found himself dozing off without realizing what was happening. It seemed he was not sleeping but watching the blue sparks and flames twist together in their final dance upward over the burning wood. Then the gote snorted and began to bleat, drumming hooves in terror. Oleg jumped to his feet, not realizing right away where he was, and it was only after a second or two he understood that the gote had left its old spot and had retreated in panic into the depths of the cave and a gray and pimpled mass, like extruded dough, was slowly insinuating itself into the cave through the hole in the curtain.

The mass seemed determined, eager, and the gote bleated in desperation, begging to be saved — the animal had evidently decided the dough had come especially for him.

Oleg reached his hand over the stones but could not find his crossbow nor could he drag his eyes away from the approaching mass. He was able to think that, even for a night crawler, this mass of dough was exceptionally ugly. It exuded a stiflingly bitter smell. Then he saw a cross-bow's bolt suddenly appear — impaled half way into the side of the creature, and the mass easily and quickly gathered itself up, pulled back, and vanished; the awning fluttered gently as it pulled the last of its body out through the hole.

Oleg was finally able to move his eyes; his cross-bow lay two centimeters from his outspread fingers. Dick was sitting on his side, alert, awake as though he hadn't laid down to sleep. He put down his cross-bow and said:

"Maybe it wasn't worth shooting. I should have waited."

"Shot what?" Marianna asked, not getting up, but reaching out her hand and stroking the armored hooves of the gote, which had turned to Marianna in terror for comfort, sobbing like a child.

"Oleg froze, and the critter almost got him." Dick said without the desire to upbraid Oleg or shame him, just saying what he was thinking. He always said what he thought. "There was no time to start the fire going again."

"You fell asleep?" Thomas asked Oleg.

Thomas was laying with the bag of dried meat under his head, wrapped in his blanket, shivering. *He's never gotten really used to the cold. None of the adults have. He'll have the worst trouble of any of us when it becomes really cold.* Oleg thought.

"I fell asleep. I didn't even notice it. The gote woke me up."

"Smart of the gote." Marianna said.

"Good for the gote." Dick said, turning onto his side. His palm rested on the cross-bow's gunstock; the wood was intricately carved and polished. He had made it himself. "They'd have eaten us all . . ." He fell asleep without finishing.

Thomas couldn't sleep. He got up and took Oleg's place on watch. The boy only argued a little before agreeing; his eyes closed almost at once and he slumped exhausted on the cave floor. Thomas clutched the blanket tighter around his shoulders. It would have been better to throw more wood on the fire's embers, but they had to guard and ration out their supply. They didn't have very much, and it would be cold . . . Thomas remembered the first time they had come across the mountain pass. Fatally, hopelessly cold. Even worse when they went the second time. Of course, only two of them had returned from that second climb — he and Vaitkus.

Thomas glanced at the kids. Why didn't they feel how bitter and cold it was sleeping on the stone? What sort of changes had occurred in their metabolisms over the years? They were true savages, looking on him — the old man — with the native's polite condescension. That's why they frightened Boris so; with each passing year they became better adapted to this world of damp forest and gray clouds. And Boris was both right and wrong. He was right that the transition to savagery was unavoidable. Thomas could see that in his own daughter and the other kids. But what other solution, what other chance of survival did they have? There was the mountain pass, but that was a symbol no one believed in any longer, even if it was impossible to deny it.

The gote paced back and forth, clattering on the stones with armored hooves. Dick opened his eyes without moving, listened for a moment, and fell back to sleep. In her sleep Marianna had edged closer to Oleg and placed her head on his shoulder, to be much more comfortable. Far off in the forest something howled; a slowly dying roar transfixed him. Thomas pulled out one of the thicker logs and fed the fire.

* * *

It grew light at first dawning and a blue mist poured through the hole in the curtain; in the distance, in the forest, the early wakers were greeting the new day. Dick, who had kept the watch on the dying fire and busied himself by shaving down pieces of wood for bolts, carefully placed the sticks in his bag and quietly dropped off to sleep, so no one had seen when the gote left the cave. When Marianna awoke she was furious; she ran outside and checked around the base of the cliff wall outside, but she could find no trace of the gote anywhere.

"I hate him." Marianna said when she returned.

"Why, because he didn't thank you?" Oleg asked.

"He'd have been better off with us. Less danger."

"Too bad I didn't shoot him at dawn." Dick said. "I thought about it, but decided it would be better to do it during the day."

"That's rotten." Marianna said. "He did save us during the night."

"That's really irrelevant." Dick said. "Don't you understand? And anyway the gote was just thinking of his own hide."

Oleg picked up the skin bag and set off to search for water.

"Don't forget your spear." Marianna said.

"And don't walk off too far." Thomas added.

"I'm not a baby." Oleg shot back. But he took his spear.

The morning mist had yet to completely dissipate; it still hid out in hollows. The clouds had sunk almost to the level of the ground and in some places columns rose from the pillows of mist to connect the clouds and the land, as though the clouds were stretching out arms to the mist calling it after as they flew past. But the mist wanted to sleep and didn't like flying about the sky. Oleg had thought he would have agreed to fly off to the south with the clouds in the mist's place, to the great forests, in the direction of the sea, where Sergeyev had gone with Vaitkus and Dick last year. Poznansky had been with them at the time, but hadn't returned. They hadn't been able to get very far and hadn't seen the sea; the forests were too vast, filled with predatory vynes, animals and poisonous reptiles, and the warmer it got the more animals there were, all of them dangerous to human beings. But if you could fly with the clouds, then you could sail over the tops of the trees and over the sea like the floaters, which sometimes darted like shadows about the clouds in good weather, but which never come to ground. People could fly, evidently they could fly somewhat faster than the clouds themselves. But in the settlement everyone was forced to begin all over again at the beginning. And that was difficult because there were no tools and no time to make them.

Oleg had dreamed of building an aerial balloon, but for a balloon you needed far too much in the way of fish hides and thread, and no one other than the very youngest and the oldest had wanted to help him.

"In theory, it's not a bad idea." Sergeyev had said then. "In about a hundred years we'll certainly get around to it."

The Mayor had answered:

"In a hundred years we'll all have succeeded in forgetting the very idea. We'll have filled the clouds with invented gods who won't be thrilled at us mortals getting too close to them."

And nothing at all had come of the idea of the balloon.

As Oleg walked downslope he heard the sound of flowing water. There would be springs coming out of the cliffs. Then he went onto the stone scree and could see the top of the enormous muzhrume that had opened itself yesterday evening. The white spot had risen during the night and was sticking out of the earth. The cover of mist had flowed off the white circle, and Oleg saw the petals were once again slowly opening themselves from within the muzhrume, and from the mist on the far side of the little valley a series of spongy, soft looking gray spheres a little darker than the muzhrume rolled triumphantly out of the trees. They came in a line, one after the other, well spaced out. First one, then a second, a third, a fourth ... What had their night visitor been? The poisonous alleyfant, a piece of dough?

"The hunters return home." Oleg said in a low voice and suddenly realized the spheres were heading in his direction and moving faster than the uniformity of their movement hinted.

Oleg stumbled backwards on the scree and one after the other the spheres stepped onto the muzhrume's resilient top and headed for the center, to the yawning petals. Then the first sphere, gently pushing the leaves apart, passed inside. A moment later the second followed, then the third. A moment later, as if it was checking that everything was in order in the daytime world, the last. And vanished. And slowly, satisfied, the petals retreated to their position within the center, and the giant muzhrume sank gently into the ground, resuming the appearance of a frozen island.

Oleg started to shiver. An icy wind had sprung out of the west, stinging his face and hands. It was west they were headed. He remembered what was waiting for them. But this wasn't what frightened Oleg; he feared they would fail, they would not best the mountain pass any more now than they had in the past. Dick would be delighted — he could return to his beloved plains. Marianna would console herself in finding new grasses and muzhrumes. Thomas was used to failure and didn't believe they'd succeed anyway. The would only really disappoint Oleg. And the Mayor.

***

All day they walked through the open moorland, only infrequently encountering thickets of underbrush and no really tall bushes. These places were empty and devoid of life, but walking was easy, and they weren't tired yet. Thomas said they had guessed the time correctly. Summer this year was warm; last year at this time the barrenlands had still carried an impassable mantle of snow. Dick was bored, from impatience he vanished off to the side, reappearing after half an hour without any game, disappointed.

The gote was lucky. The animal reappeared during one of Dick's absences. Otherwise, Oleg decided, Dick would have certainly shot it. It was the same gote as the night before. It came blundering out of the underbrush with a crash, causing them meet it with raised cross-bows. But they recognized it from some distance away. A hairy giant, it's spinal comb taller than Oleg, noisily overjoyed it had met up with its friends from the night before again. The gote ran past them, throwing up heavy hind quarters, crashing spinal plates together and bleating deafeningly.

The gote was with them for the journey. He was even delighted when he spotted Dick's return from a kilometer off, and then crawled into the center of their file, not wanting to be either off to one side or the last, and getting underfoot. Oleg thought the gote would trample him with its sharp hooves but the animal proved far more agile than they first thought.

The animal's sense of smell and hearing were remarkable. It could sense the presence of living beings for several kilometers, and toward evening Marianna had already convinced herself there were real thoughts behind the sounds and the gote was telling them a field with tasty muzhrumes lay up ahead, but when they got to it and looked down they saw the ground was crawling with hunting vynes.

The party stopped for the night some time before dark. The real climb upward would begin just ahead of them, and Thomas said they would have to hunt for a particular valley in the morning. The mouth of a stream flowed out of it. Then they would head up the valley, which would then narrow into a gorge. They would be in the valley for no less than two days.

There was no cave or any other cover hereabouts and they slept in the tent, which the gote did not like, and although the there was no danger that night, the gote demanded they let him inside where it was warm all the same, and in the end he huddled on top of the tent, bleating his disappointment at all of them, but they endured it because the animal would be standing guard for them; it was already clear that if any undesired guest came the gote would raise such a cry he would wake them all.

***

Toward morning Oleg became terribly cold. He hadn't been able to sleep; he felt like he had been plunged into an icy swamp and was unable to extricate himself. Oleg began to shake. Then suddenly he grew warmer and slept more easily. He awoke when the gote decided to find itself a spot higher up on the tent. Oleg pulled up his feet, opened his eyes and saw Thomas had exchanged places with him in the night and now lay on the outside. The older man was white from the cold; he lay with teeth clenched, his eyes closed and pretending to sleep. Oleg felt ashamed. Even back in the village they had decided Thomas would have to be looked after when it became really cold. The old man's lungs were weak and he had difficulty standing the frosts. The children would have an easier time of it. They were healthy and adapted to the climate.

"Thomas." Oleg spoke in a low voice. "I've warmed up. Let's change places."

"No, don't." Thomas whispered, but his lips hardly moved.

Oleg crawled over him. The fish hide tent passed the cold through to its occupants and that night all of them had slept under blankets, even Dick who boasted he could sleep in the snow.

"Thanks." Thomas said. The man's body shuddered.

The gote had realized the humans within the tent had awakened and got to its feet. It stamped around in a circle, calling them out with its bleating, evidently having gotten enough sleep. Dick threw his own blanket over Thomas and crawled quickly outside.

"Hey!" Dick shouted from outside. "Get a move on. Come on, look; it's great!"

Oleg forced himself to crawl out after Dick.

Snow had fallen during the night, covering the valley ahead of them. It sparkled white and clean, brighter than the clouds which, in contrast, appeared quite violet. The gote stood a short distance off shaking icicles from its fur. The white curve of the valley rested against the sharp incline of the tableland. The bushes growing along the slope were slowly shaking their branches, filling the air around them with clouds of snow.

Their firewood was going faster than they had expected back in the settlement. That disturbed Dick, but he only told this to Oleg in a low voice when they had walked a short distance from the dirty little hill that was their tent.

"We shouldn't have taken Thomas along." He said. "He's getting sick."

"It would be harder to make it through the pass without him." Oleg said.

"It'll be even harder with him." Dick said, and fired a crossbow bolt at a dark niche on the cliff face. Oleg had seen nothing there, but snow exploded from the niche and a ribbit flew out in enormous leaps, its proboscis tossed over its back, speeding away. Dark drops of blood marked its trail.

"I'm going to pick it up." Dick said. His opinion remained unchanged.

It was difficult to argue with Dick; when he was convinced of something he didn't argue. He just left. And Oleg only found reasonable words afterwards, and left Dick unanswered even if he was wrong.

And how are we supposed to get there without Thomas? Oleg found himself continuing the argument with Dick in his mind. *It isn't just we don't have a road, it's what we're going to find when we get* there. We've never even seen a bicycle, so how are we to know one from a steam engine? Dick thinks he knows everything of use to any man in the settlement or in the forest. Maybe he's afraid of finding himself in another world, where he's not the strongest, where he's not the fastest?

Marianna had lit the fire. The gote, having already seen flame before, decided he had nothing to fear from it, and had edged up to the campfire. Marianna shouted to Oleg to drag the damned animal away. Dragging an adult gote anywhere was nearly impossible, but Oleg tried. He struck at the gote with the handle of his knife until he grew tired, but the animal evidently decided Oleg was caressing it and squealed with pleasure.

Thomas was running around in the snow to warm himself; he was wrapped in the blanket and stooped, and looked to Oleg like a wizened old man, although the boy knew Thomas was only forty. Egli had once mentioned the processes of aging were faster in the settlement. Aunt Luiza had retorted that, on their diet, all of them should have kicked off long ago. Everyone had diarrhea and indigestion most of the time, as well as allergies; the older generation's kidneys simply couldn't cope. It was true the children were comparatively healthy. The settlement was just plain lucky the majority of local microfauna hadn't adapted to the human metabolism. "At least not yet." She had added.

"It's too bad we're not in the swamp." Marianna said. "I could have found the grasses he needs, I know which ones."

"Why didn't you pick them earlier?" Oleg asked. Marianna could tell the different grasses apart better than anyone else in the village.

"Don't be silly." Marianna was surprised. "You have to eat them right away, while they're fresh. How could you preserve them?" She always thought it strange other people didn't know what she knew.

"Oleg." Thomas called. "Come over here."

Thomas had lowered himself down on the tent; there was more pain than usual in his face.

"My back's hurting again." He said. "Lumbago."

"Then I'll massage you." Marianna said.

"Thanks, but it doesn't help." Thomas laughed. He looked like the crow they'd seen drawn in the Mayor's biology lessons. A dark bird with an enormous sharp beak. "Listen, you remember where I've put the map? If anything happens to me."

"Nothing is going to happen." Oleg said. "We're all going there together."

"And we're not going to take any risks. Are you certain you've familiarized yourself with the map?"

The map was drawn on a piece of paper — the settlement's greatest treasure. Oleg had always felt a special awe toward it. Paper, even blank sheets, was a magical force connected with knowledge. It had been created to express knowledge. Paper was, as it were, an aspect of divinity.

Thomas spent some time coughing, then made Oleg point out the road to the mountain pass on the map. The route was familiar, they had already taken it in thought with Vaitkus and the Mayor. The reality was different. It was impossible to feel the essence of the journey, the cold and the desperation, at home in the settlement where it was warm, comfortable, where the lamps were burning and rain drummed against the other side of the wall. . . .

Dick brought back the ribbit. For some reason the lifeless meat frightened the gote and it bounded off up the slope and stood there, sadly shaking its head.

"It can sense what's in store for it." Dick said. He threw the ribbit down. "Let's eat now, it's better to go on full stomachs. And it will be better for Thomas. It would be even more useful if he'd drink the warm blood; I always do when I'm out hunting. Go on, try some, Thomas!"

Thomas shook his head. *No.*

"What are you doing? Going over the map again?" Dick asked.

"Thomas asked us to practice in the event for some reason he doesn't continue . . ."

"Idiots." Dick squatted down and began to skin the carcass. "You can still walk. And if it gets bad we'll go back."

Oleg realized Dick didn't want to embarrass Thomas. Dick had thought Thomas wouldn't make it from the beginning.

"It's nothing." Thomas said; not showing his displeasure at Dick's casual tone. "It's better if we have some insurance."

While they were drinking tea made from a local root the gote padded closer to the fire on the side away from where Dick had tossed the ribbit's skin, as though it were shielded from the pelt by the fire and the tent. He hooted loudly and Marianna threw him some dried muzhrumes.

"Now that's too much." Dick said. "We need the muzhrumes ourselves. It might turn out we won't be able to find anything. How will we get back?"

"There is food there, on the other side of the pass." Thomas said.

"We don't know it is still there." Dick answered. "It's stupid to starve to death. And we have to eat a lot to keep going in this cold."

"If it comes to that we can eat the gote." Oleg said.

"What do you mean 'If?'" Dick asked. "Of course we'll eat him. And soon. Before he runs off."

"Don't even think of it." Marianna said. "Don't."

"Why?" Dick was surprised.

"Because he'll return with us to the settlement and live there. It's time we had our own animals."

"I can bring you a thousand gotes like him." Dick said.

"Wrong. You're just bragging. You couldn't. At least not alive. There aren't that many of them in the forest, and if it wasn't willing you couldn't lead it anywhere."

"I'll take you along and you can talk to the animals." Dick said and began to cut the ribbit into equal portions for each of them.

"I'm not going to let you kill it." Marianna said. "He's going to have little ones."

"Who?" Oleg asked.

"The gote." Marianna said. "The she-gote."

"You mean it's a 'nanny'?" Thomas asked.

"Yes. She-gote. Nanny. I know."

"If Marianna is right, then let the she-gote live." Thomas said. "It's a very useful thing to think there's going to be a tomorrow."

"And even better to know you're not going to die today." Dick said.

"We can feed the gote enough to keep it going with us." Marianna said.

"I don't think so." Dick said.

"I'll give it my own." Marianna looked straight at Dick, her chin pointed forward. Dick tilted his head, examining Marianna as if she were some animal he'd never encountered before.

Thomas got to his feet first and started to fold the tent. He was shaking.

"Don't you think you should go back?" Dick asked him.

"It's too late." Thomas said. "I'm going on."

"Think what you're saying!" Marianna flared up at Dick. "Thomas can't go back to the settlement alone.

"Oleg could return with him." Dick said to have the last word.

"It's time to move on." Thomas said. "If it all goes well we should make it up to the tablelands today. The last time we got bogged down in this gorge. The snow was up to our belts and we had a blizzard."

Thomas walked ahead along the wide stream bed. Only a trickle was flowing down now, just enough to break off the flat pieces of ice that had grown along the shore during the night.

At first the gote rushed forward as though it were showing them the road, but then thought better of it and stopped. Dick threatened it with his hand, but then the gote honked and plodded after the people, although at times it stopped and howled disconsolately, cautioning them to head back.

The air grew a little warmer; the snow under their feet turned to water and the ground to slippery mud. Over the course of the day they had to cross the stream flowing down the valley, jumping from bank to bank a dozen times, and everyone's feet became battered and sore.

***

All the next day the tiny valley through which the stream flowed closed in on them, the dark stone walls angled upwards and drew close, covering the stream in constant shadow. The noise intensified the gloom, it reverberated from wall to wall, growing louder. Other than Thomas none of them had ever been in the mountains; even Dick lost his eternal self-assuredness; he stopped leaving the party to forge ahead. Dick looked upwards constantly, as though he feared falling stones, and he kept asking Thomas:
"Soon now? Will we be out soon?"
"By evening." Thomas answered.
Thomas, like the others, had grown warmer; he was even sweating from the exertion. The coughing had stopped and he was walking faster than yesterday. He only clutched his side in pain occasionally.
"Do you recognize where we are?" Marianna asked.
She had been walking behind them, urging the gote on. The animal had long since grown tired of the journey and was often stopping and looking backwards, as though begging Marianna to let her go back to the open spaces of the forest.
"Like I told you, the last time we didn't make it this far in." Thomas answered. "But when we were coming from the mountain pass fifteen years ago there was snow here, the days were short, and we hardly had time to look around. At the time we had hopes. That was the first time we'd even begun to hope . . . But we were exhausted. The trip from here to where the settlement is now took more than a week at the time, what with the state we were in."
Dick, waking ahead, suddenly froze. He lifted his hand.
Everyone stopped. Even the gote, as though it understood his order.
With his crossbow at the ready Dick slowly walked ahead. He bent down.

"Look at this!" Dick shouted. "They really were through here."

Behind a large boulder, shining dully and reflecting in the coppery river, lay something wonderful. It was made of white metal and resembled a flattened sphere with a white excrescence on top. Attached to it was a cord so that it could be carried over the shoulder.

Dick lifted the object and said: "A rock fell on you here, right?"

"No. No stone. Nothing like that." Thomas said and went over to Dick, taking the thing from his hands. "We called a halt here and someone... Vaitkus! This is Vaitkus's flask. He'll be delighted when we bring it back to him!"

"It's called a 'flask'?" Marianna asked.

Thomas shook the thing in the air and they all heard water swishing around inside it.

"Useful item." Dick commented.

"They're made flat deliberately." Thomas explained, carefully unscrewing the stopper. "To make it easier to carry on your side."

"Wonderful." Marianna said.

"I could use it hunting." Dick said. "Vaitkus doesn't need it; he's sick all the time."

Thomas brought the flask to his nose and sniffed,

"Damnation!" He said. "I must be mad!"

"What's happening?" Oleg asked. He wanted to hold the flask.

"Kids, this stuff's cognac! Have you any idea what cognac is?"

The gote had walked a short distance away and began to bleat in surprise, calling them.

Oleg walked over to her. In the hollow behind a pile of water washed stones lay another pile — of metal cans and small pans; he had never seen such a treasure hoard before in his life.

"Thomas!" He called. "Look. Here's something else you forgot!"

"Not forgot." Thomas said. "You must understand, at the time we knew we were going into the forest and ate here for the last time. These are cans, containers for prepared and preserved foods, do you understand? These are cans we didn't need any more."

"Didn't need?"

"So it seemed to us at the time." Thomas brought the flask to his nose and sniffed again. "I'm out of my mind. I must be. I'm dreaming."

"That means it's true." Dick said. "You did come through here. I always thought that you didn't — I thought the settlement just always was here."

"You know, sometimes I think the same thing myself." Thomas laughed.

He drank out of the flask, a single mouthful, and closed his eyes tightly.

"I'll live." He said. He began coughing, but he didn't stop laughing.

Marianna had gathered the empty cans and was packing them in a bag. The gote was honking and groaning. She didn't like the cans. They were strange.

"You don't want to carry them." Thomas began to smile. "Really you don't. If you really need them you can get thousands of them. Understand?"

"I don't know." Marianna said soberly. "But if we don't find anything else, we can always put these to good use. We won't be returning empty handed. Father can do a lot with these cans."

"Then pick them up on our return." Oleg said. He was beginning to want to try the cognac which had so enlivened Thomas.

"What if someone takes them?" Marianna asked.

"Who?" Thomas shot back. "No one's taken them in the last sixteen years. The gotes don't need cans."

But Marianna gathered up all the cans, even the ones with holes.

Dick said:

"Let me try it, Thomas. What's in the flask?"

"You wouldn't like it." Thomas said. "Children and wild men don't like cognac."

But he handed Dick the flask.

I *always have to ask.* Oleg thought. *I always just think about doing something, and Dick's already gone ahead and taken it.*

"Just be careful." Thomas said. "Just one small sip."

"Don't worry." Dick said. "If you can do it, I can do more. I am stronger than you are."

Thomas said nothing. Oleg thought the older man was laughing.

Dick upended the flask and swallowed a mouthful. Evidently, this cognac was very bitter; he threw the flask away and began to cough terribly, clutching at his throat. Thomas just managed to catch the flask without spilling any of the contents.

"I did tell you." Thomas said, wasting no sympathy.

Marianna ran over to the red faced Dick.

"Everything's burning. . . ." Dick sputtered.

"Why did you do that?" Marianna was angry at Thomas. She began to dig around in her bag. Oleg knew she was hunting an ointment for burns.

"It will pass in a minute." Thomas said, "You really are a wild man, Dick. You should approach an unknown liquid as if it might be a poison, first with the tongue. . . ."

Dick waved him off angrily.

"I did." He said. "You drank it first!"

Dick had been utterly humiliated. He couldn't stand it.

"Here." Marianna said. "Chew on this herb. It'll help."

"I don't need it." Dick said.

"It will all pass." Thomas said. "He should be feeling warmer already."

"No." Dick said. "You lied."

"Do you still have the desire to warm yourselves?" Thomas asked. "No, my brave tribespeople? By the way, the Indians — the North American ones — did call this 'fire water.'"

"And then they ruined themselves and sold their land to the white colonists for trinkets." Oleg remembered the history lessons.

"Precisely. Only those potables were of, ah, somewhat greater strength."

Thomas hung the flask over his shoulder. Dick looked at it with envy. He wanted to pour the damned cognac out and fill it with water.

They stretched out over the stones to take a rest. Marianna gave them a handful of the dried muzhrumes and a slice of dried meat each. She gave muzhrumes to the gote as well. Dick scowled but said nothing. The gote crunched the muzhrumes almost delicately, then looked at Marianna hoping for more. The gote was having trouble finding food so high above the living forest. She was hungry.

"Was all your food in these cans?" Oleg asked.

"No just cans." Thomas sighed. "Our food was in plastic bags and boxes. Containers, bottles, tubes, bulbs and lots of other things. Let me tell you friends, there was a lot of food. And there were even cigarettes, something I also dream about a lot."

And suddenly Oleg understood finding the flask, the preserved food cans, the remains of the camp had produced an effect not only on him or Dick. Even more, it had changed Thomas. It was as though the older man hadn't really believed they had eaten out of shining cans and drunk cognac out of flasks on the other side of the mountain pass himself before now. And this strange world, a world Oleg desired and Dick found unnecessary, had cast Thomas out.

"Let's get going." Thomas said and got to his feet. "Now I nearly believe we'll get there, although the most difficult part of the journey lies ahead."

They went on. Marianna stayed closer to Dick, she was worried he felt bad. Marianna felt sorry for him. *She'll feel sorry for anything.* Oleg felt jealous. It was perfectly evident Dick was healthy, although his eyes were watery and he talked louder than usual.

"It's a door." Thomas said. He was walking close to Oleg. "It's a door I've stepped through and my memories begin here. Do you understand?"

"Yes." Oleg said

"Before this it was something I could only dream about." Thomas continued. "And I completely forgot about this halt. Your mother was carrying you in her arms. She was totally exhausted but she wouldn't give you up to anyone else. And you were silent. Dick was bawling. That was normal; he was tired and hungry. But you were silent. Egli kept hovering around your mother; the two of them were really both still girls, about twenty-five years old, and they'd been friends before . . . Egli wanted to see if you were alive or not, but your mother wouldn't hand you over. She had nothing left to live for, only you."

Thomas suddenly began to cough, he doubled over, leaning his arm against the stone cliff face and Oleg noticed how yellow and thin his fingers were. Dick and Marianna had already run forward and vanished around the bend.

"Let me carry your pack." Oleg said.

"No. It'll pass. I can make it." Thomas laughed guiltily. "After all, I should be leading, setting an example for you kids, but I can hardly carry myself. You know, it seems if I drink enough cognac everything will be all right. It's nonsense, but that's the way it feels."

"You can still drink the rest . . ." Oleg said.

"I mustn't. I have a temperature. Just let me make it to the mountain pass. I should be in a hospital getting a good rest and competent treatment, not climbing a mountain."

Two hours later the gorge came to an end. The stream they had been following to its source began as a small waterfall flowing over a short precipice. It was only about two meters high but getting up it proved complicated. Thomas had become so weak they were forced to drag him. They pulled the gote on its rope, and it was a miracle the frightened animal didn't trample someone to death with its armored hooves.

Covered by snow, with occasional patches of bare stone, the tablelands stretched on for many kilometers until they came to nestle against the wall of mountains. It was a strange sensation: for two days they had been ascending through the narrow, twilit gorge, hearing only the water rushing over stones and then, suddenly, around them scowled a vast and merciless plain, the like of which Oleg had never seen before.

Looking back the way they had come the plateau dropped down the endless sharp slope, flowing into a wide, at first stony, valley. Beyond the valley grew the individual points which were bushes and trees, and ever so distant, to the horizon, these points flowed together, thickened into the endless forest. There, four days march distant, was the settlement. From here it was lost in the wilderness.

"It was right here we realized we weren't going to die. Or, at least, not yet." Thomas said. He was still trying to catch his breath. "We had come out of the mountains, those of us who'd been able to walk, crawling some times, dragging the sick and injured. We were freezing. We didn't really believe there was any point in going on. And then, without warning, we came to the edge of the plateau. As you can see the land toward the mountains is flat until it reaches the edge so it wasn't until we got to this point we knew we had any hope at all. It was snowing of course, a blizzard.... Who was the first? Boris, it seems. Yes, it was Boris. He was walking out ahead of the rest and suddenly stopped. I remember how he just froze, but I was so tired I didn't understand why. When I reached him he was crying, and his face had gone white. The visibility that day was terrible, but from time to time the curtain of snow parted and we knew that down there, in the valley, were trees. That meant there was life . . ."

The wind was blowing, fortunately it wasn't very strong. The gote began to jump and frisk about, glad to be done with the narrow valley, throwing up furry hindquarters and leaving deep triangular tracks in the sheet of snow. It stopped beside a barren patch and it began to dig into the frozen earth with the horny ridge on its nose, hooting, groaning and bleating — evidently, it had smelled something edible.

"There's no game here." Dick said, his voice telling them who he blamed. He turned to look at Thomas.

"In about three days if everything goes okay, we'll be there."

Thomas said. "Or after the fourth."

"But they said you had to walk for two weeks."

"We walked for thirteen days. It was winter, there were a lot of sick and injured, and now we're traveling light. Remarkable, it's as if it just happened this morning; we stood with Boris and looked down."

They made it to the mountains before dark.

***

At night the air froze. Dick and Oleg put Marianna and Thomas in the middle. Thomas was so exhausted he didn't even argue. He was burning, but there was no way he could get warm, and when he began to lapse into a dry cough Oleg closed his arms around him and Marianna made him drink the mixture she had prepared for the cough. Marianna couldn't sleep; to hurry the night she whispered with Oleg, but Dick, who wanted to sleep, turned over. Then he said:

"We won't be taking any rest stops tomorrow, is that clear?"

"What do you mean?" Oleg asked.

"I'll be making you walk no matter how much you want to sleep."

"Don't worry." Oleg said. "I won't be holding us back."

"It's not you I was thinking of."

Oleg didn't bother to argue. He understood Dick had Thomas in mind. He thought that Thomas, asleep, had heard nothing. But Thomas had heard, and said:

"I'm not competent to issue a diagnosis. Just my opinion, but I have pneumonia. I'm sorry things turned out this way, friends."

They had worked the tent into a large niche where it was sheltered from the wind and the gote paced alongside, wheezing, then began to paw the earth.

"What's she looking for?" Marianna whispered.

"Snayls." Oleg said. "I saw her find one."

"I thought it was too cold here."

"We can live here. I guess other things can too."

"There's nothing here." Dick said. "Get some sleep."

Thomas began to cough; Marianna made him drink more medicine. They could hear his teeth chatter at the edge of the cup.

"You should have gone back." Dick said.

"Too late." Thomas said. "I'd have never made it to the settlement."

"You're an idiot, Dick." Marianna said. "You've forgotten the law."

"I haven't forgotten anything." Dick spoke up louder. "I know we should look after the sick. I know what my duty is — better than you do. But they've been pounding into our heads that if we don't reach the mountain pass now, if we don't bring back metal and tools, the settlement will die out. But I don't think so. I don't believe we will. We can get along perfectly well without a lot of things. I can take down a baer with my crossbow from a hundred paces."

"That's because you have steel tips on your bolts." Oleg said. "If Sergeyev couldn't forge them how would you take the baer?"

"I can make my points out of stone. It's not a matter of the materials but of skill. Now they've made us come up here, to the mountains . . ."

"No one's made you come up here; you're here on your own . . ." Oleg said.

"Yeah. Sure. But you know it could start blowing snow real hard at any moment. And if we drag this out at all we might not make it back."

"So what do you propose to do?" Oleg asked.

Neither Thomas nor Marianna had said a word while the two of them spoke; the others just listened. Even the gote was quiet, listening.

"I propose we leave Marianna behind with Thomas. We give them the blankets and food. And just you and me travel light to the mountain pass."

Oleg didn't answer, but he realized he couldn't leave Thomas behind. It would take away the man's reason for living. That would kill him. But what if Dick thought he was afraid to go ahead, just the two of them together?

"Are you scared?" Dick asked.

"Not for myself." Oleg answered finally. "If Thomas becomes sick, he can't defend Marianna. Or Marianna him. What if there are animals? Predators? How will she cope?"

"Marianna, can you cope?" From Dick it wasn't a question, it was a command. Dick felt he had the right to give orders.

"I am going on." Thomas said. "I'll make it, don't worry about me. I have to get there. I've been going there for sixteen years now." Thomas's voice ran hot with his words, as though filled with tears.

"The get some sleep." Dick said after a pause. No one agreed with him, and he had convinced no one of anything either.

But in the morning the argument was moot.

Oleg got up first; his head hurt, his feet were blocks of wood, his back was ice. He pushed his way out of the niche and looked around; on the white snow was a chain of enormous indentations. Oleg couldn't guess what had made the tracks; it looked like someone had come along stamping the snow with gigantic barrels.

Oleg shook Dick awake and the two of them followed along the trail in the direction the tracks seemed to be headed, looking about warily. The trail ended at a sharp precipice — whatever the animal was, it could climb cliffs.

"What was it?" Oleg asked in a whisper, drawing back from the edge.

"If we followed it home we could pounce on it." Dick said. "We could catch it there."

"Forget it!" Oleg said. "Even with your cross-bow. You won't get a chance to try on its fur."

"I can try." Dick said.

"Where were you?" Marianna called out when she saw them. She was lighting the fire. "Thomas's temperature has fallen. Great, isn't it?"

"Fine." Oleg said.

They told her about the tracks; Marianna hadn't noticed them. She shrugged. There could be few such animals around in this barren wilderness. Not all could be dangerous. The animals were going about their own business.

"Sit down." Marianna said. "Have some breakfast."

Thomas crawled out of the tent. He was pale and weak. The man held the flask in his hand. He sat next to Oleg, opened the flask, and took a swig.

"I have to get warm." He said hoarsely. "Once upon a time doctors used to prescribe Cahors — a type of wine — for the weak and sick."

Marianna reached for her bag. A single muzhrume tumbled out of it.

The bag had been torn open. Chewed open. It was empty.

"Where are the muzhrumes?" Marianna asked Thomas, as though he should have known where they were.

Dick jumped to his feet.

"Where was the bag lying?"

"I was so tired I thought I put it in the tent." Marianna said. "But I must have left it outside."

"Where is that beast?" Dick asked quietly.

"Are you crazy?" Marianna began to shout. "It might not have been the gote."

"Who? Was it me? Or Thomas maybe? What will we eat now?"

"We still have some meat left." Marianna said.

"Show it to me. Or is that gone too?"

"Why would a gote eat meat?"

Dick was right. When Marianna counted the portions the gote had missed two dozen dried strips of meat remained for them.

"This time I'm not joking." Dick picked his cross-bow out of the snow. The gote sensed what threatened her, and jumped back down the slope.

"You won't get away!" Dick said.

"Wait a moment." Oleg said. "Wait, if you have to, you can do it. You can always do it. But Marianna does want to start herding them. You understand important it will be for the settlement. It would mean we'd always have meat."

"It's important for the settlement we don't die up here." Dick said. "The gote won't get to the settlement if we don't. She doesn't have anything to eat either. She'll run off."

"No, Dick, please." Marianna said. "The gote's going to have little ones, remember?"

"Then we go back." Dick said. "Our trip's over."

"Wait." Thomas said. "The decision's still up to me. If you want, I'll let you go back. I don't doubt you'll make it. I'm going on. And anyone else who wants to come with me."

"I'm going on." Oleg said. "We can't wait three more years until next summer."

"I'm going too." Marianna said. "And Dick will go on too." She told Oleg and Thomas. "He isn't evil, don't think that. He just wants to do what he thinks is the best for everyone."

"You don't have to explain." Dick said. "I'm going to kill the animal anyway."

"We have food for today." Marianna said. "It will be more useful to take the gote back with us."

"We could even load her, use her as a pack animal." Thomas said.

Thomas swallowed another sip of cognac and swished the flask around. From the sound it was clear very little remained of the fire water.

Marianna busied herself by the camp fire, wishing the water would boil. She still had some sweet roots left, about two handfuls.

"We still have one more day before it's too late to return." Dick turned to the older man. "And that concerns you more than the rest of us, Thomas."

CHAPTER THREE

After two hours' march Oleg was forced to draw the conclusion Dick had been right all along. They were walking along an empty, snow-covered country without marked paths. The route led upwards, but they would still have to go around a chain of cliffs, work their way along a line of crevices, and cut across glaciers. The cold cut through their furs, their breathing strained. Oleg was used to never being able to eat enough to fill himself, but before now he had never really starved — the settlement had always managed to have some sort of stores on hand.

But here hunger, having wandered into the neighborhood, quickly became Oleg's constant companion; as soon as it became clear they had days ahead of them without food Oleg caught himself looking at the gote with desire, wishing that she'd fall into a crevasse and break her neck and he would have more to eat than his own words — *Oh well, we'll find another*, he hammered the thought in silently. *We'll find another.*

And, as though he had been listening to Oleg's thoughts, Thomas said:

"It's our good fortune the meat is walking on its own. Otherwise we'd have to carry it."

"Stop."

That had come from Dick's. Dick walked over to the gote, carrying a strong rope woven out of water rushes, and slipped it over the animal's neck. The gote just stood there without making a sound while they tied her up. Then Dick extended the rope's free end to Marianna and said:

"You lead her. I don't want to risk it."

They did make a halt that day. They rested for longer than usual because they were all exhausted, but Thomas was still on his feet even if he was tottering so badly they wanted to support him. The man's face had gone scarlet and his eyes were half closed, but he held himself erect and put one foot in front of another as he trudged straight ahead, towards his mountain pass.

About two hours after they made their stop Thomas started to feel very uneasy.

"Wait a moment." He said. "Unless we've gotten lost there should be a camp around here. I remember those rocks."

Thomas was sitting on top of a boulder. He smoothed the map with his trembling hands and began to trace the outlines in the air with his fingers. Dick said nothing about this; he went ahead a little, hoping to shoot game.

The map had been drawn with ink back when they had still had ink; Oleg remembered the thick paste that had filled the pens. He's seen them, but he'd never written anything with them himself.

"We're here." Thomas pointed. "We're already more than half way there. I hadn't considered we could go so fast."

"We've had good weather." Oleg said.

"Judging from everything we'll spend the night here." Thomas said. "There should have been tracks, but there aren't."

"It's been so many years . . ." Oleg said.

"It has." Thomas mumbled. "a group of cliffs. . . . three cliffs . . . no . . . four. Oh yes, I almost forgot . . ." The adult turned to Oleg, handing him a small box. "Take this. Don't set foot in the ship without it. You remember?"

"That's . . . Oh, the radiation detector, isn't it?"

"The radiation counter. You know why we couldn't stop; there was too much radiation there. But the lack of heat made it just as bad . . . Hard radiation and no heat! Fry and freeze at the same time."

"Perhaps you should get some sleep." Oleg asked. "And then we'll go on. . . ."

"No. We can't stay here. That would be fatal. I'm responsible for you. . . . Wherever the camp was it will have to be dug in deeper. . . . We got them buried, but we weren't strong enough to dig very deep, you understand, it should have been deeper . . ."

Oleg reached to support Thomas, who had begun to slide down from the stone.

Dick had returned; he saw Oleg wrap Thomas in the blanket, while Marianna fanned and blew on the campfire to get enough heat to turn their frozen medicines liquid. Dick was silent, but he seemed to say: *Well I told you so!*

Oleg unstoppered the flask himself, sniffing the cognac; the smell was sharp, almost inviting, but he didn't want to drink any. It had other uses. He lifted it carefully to Thomas's cracked lips. The man whispered something almost inaudible, swallowed and for some reason said: "Skoal."

They were able to go on only toward twilight when Thomas came to his senses. Oleg carried his pack, Dick took the cross-bow. Coming out of this rest they walked, and scrambled, along a slope dusted with enormous stones that wobbled beneath their feet; an hour or two, no more, then it became too dark to see and they had to search out a place to stay the night.

It had grown cold; the sky held a different color. In the forest it was always gray, but toward evening the sky here acquired a reddish tint that frightened them — in the sky there was no reliability.

They were starving. Oleg was ready to chew stones. And as soon as they took their packs off and lay them on the ground that impertinent gote ran up to them, trying to open them with her beak, as though people had nothing better to do than hide food from her.

"Get away from me!" Oleg shouted at her. He threw a stone at her.

Exit gote, bleating.

"Don't." Marianna said. Her face had become darker, thinner.

The girl was vanishing. "She doesn't understand. She thinks we'll give her something to eat. She needs more food than people do."

That was the evening Dick struck Marianna.

It was their final meal. They were chewing their last scraps of meat, then washing the dry slices down with hot water. It was more self-deception than a meal; human beings need more to eat than three slices to feel satisfied. But Marianna slipped her own food to the unhappy gote, thinking no one would notice. Other than Thomas, who was only half conscious, they all did. Oleg said nothing. he decided then to tell Marianna later it was stupid to feed a gote whey you were soon going to starve to death yourself.

But Dick couldn't shut up. He stretched his hand across the fire and gave Marianna a sharp hard slap on the cheek. Marianna screamed.

"What was that for?"

Oleg threw himself on Dick. Dick brushed him aside easily.

"Idiots." He said "You're a pack of idiots. Do you really want to starve yourselves to death? You're never going to make it to the mountain pass!"

"That was my piece of meat." Marianna said, her eyes were dry and angry. "I don't want to eat."

"Of course you do." Dick said "And we only have two slices of meat left for each of us for tomorrow. It will have to last all the way to the mountains. Why was I crazy enough to ever come with you?"

Suddenly Dick grabbed his knife and threw it at the gote as hard as he could. It bounced off the mass of greenish fur and fell back against a stone, doing no harm to the gote. Dick jumped up, the gote roared back, pulling on the rope. Dick picked up his knife. The point had broken on the rocks.

"Idiots!" Dick shouted. "Why don't you get it through your heads we're not going to make it back!"

He wasn't looking at the weeping Marianna but at Oleg, who couldn't think of anything better than to give Marianna his last slice of meat, as though she were a little child. She pushed his hand away. Dick quickly unfolded his own blanket and stretched out to his full length on it and closed his eyes. He fell asleep. Or he pretended to sleep.

Thomas was coughing weakly; coughing took more energy than he could muster.

Oleg got to his feet and wrapped the man in the tent. Then he and Marianna lay on either side of Thomas to keep him warm. It started to snow. The snow wasn't cold. It covered them with a thick layer. The gote came over in the darkness and lay beside them; she understood they would all be warmer together.

Oleg hardly slept that night; it seemed to him he didn't. Something enormous went by not far away, cutting off the blue morning light. Then Oleg suddenly grew colder — the gote had gotten up and went off in search of forage.

And then the flee bit Oleg. Where it had come from wasn't clear. It might have been hiding in their clothing or in the gote's long fur.

Oleg sensed it first as a cold prick, as though a needle of ice had been injected beneath his skin. Most victims awaken immediately and freeze in terror and helplessness, and know they have an hour of sanity left.

There was nothing he could do. The snow flee's toxins were in his blood. He might shout, call for help, but the results were as unavoidable as death. There was nothing to be done. It would start in an hour.

The course of the illness would be the same for him as for everyone else. The wise, the stupid, the young, the old — for half an hour or an hour Oleg was going to be quite violently, uncontrollably mad. The Mayor had said if he had even one of the smaller portable medlabs he could have dealt with the illness; he would have understood how the pathogen acted on the nervous system. . . .

Oleg knew he would howl in rage, he would run wild. He would recognize no one. He would kill the people he loved most in the world and remember nothing of it later.

The first time it had occurred in the settlement no one had

even known what was going on. It was only after several terrible incidents they had realized the flee sickness couldn't be fought — you could only bind the victim tightly, lock him or her away and wait for the rage to subside and reason to return. That was all. Sometime, when they learned to treat the fever, it would be different. But now there was only one course of action . . .

When it happened in the settlement the victim would run to people himself and ask them: "Tie me up!" And then the terror really began. The victim was still seemingly healthy, but he knew his sanity was doomed; he still had some minutes left before his mind was gone and in its place was a raging, unreasoning animal. And everyone saw how it happened in others. And everyone knew it could happen to him.

"Dick?" Oleg called. "I'm sorry. Do you have your rope close by?"

"What?" Dick jumped up, beginning to grope his hands in the darkness. Dawn was a streak of light on the horizon. Thomas was wheezing in his sleep. He didn't awaken.

"Oh not that!" Marianna started to wail. "A flee bit you?"

"Yes."

Dick yawned.

"We don't have to hurry. You have an hour, at a minimum an hour."

"It happened a little while ago." Oleg said. "Everything's going wrong."

"Yes. We can't take any more of this." Dick agreed.

"I'll cover you with a blanket." Marianna said. "I'll sit next to you a while."

"Hell." Dick said, looking around for the rope, "We won't be able to start on time again."

"I'll get over it." Oleg said.

"After the onset you'll have to lie down for two hours at least; I had to." Dick said.

He wasn't angry with Oleg; he was angry at the total disaster this climb had become.

The sensation of cold where the flee had bit him in the thigh remained. Oleg felt the bite and imagined a tiny drop of poison flowing through his blood, pulsing, heading toward his brain to attack him and deprive him of his mind.

Dick took his time checking out the rope. Marianna began to re-light the fire.

The dawn was blue, different from the constant gray of the lowlands.

"Oh well." Dick said finally. "It'll have to do."

"Just so long as he doesn't hurt himself with anything." Marianna said. "Poor Oleg!"

"This won't be the first time I've tied someone up." Dick said. "These flees are a terrible business. Just relax as much as you can, Oleg. And try to think about something else."

First he tied Oleg's hands behind his back, then wound the rope around the other boy's chest and feet. The rope dug into his body, numbing his arms. Oleg gritted his teeth and said nothing; with the onset the victim became as strong as a baer. If they tried to make him comfortable now it would go so much the worse for them all later.

Thomas started to moan. He stuck his balding head out the tent and squinted, unable to understand where he was. Thomas's eyes were bleeding at the sides, his face was red, inflamed. Finally he looked at Dick who was still tying the ropes around Oleg, Oleg laughed in embarrassment. He was angry at himself for being such a bother to the others. It reminded him of what the Mayor had once said, how back in the Middle Ages epileptics and abnormal women had been called witches and even burned in bonfires.

"A flee." Thomas said. "There are flees everywhere . . . There are critters everywhere. . . ."

"Go back and get some more sleep." Oleg said. "I won't be coming to my senses very soon, you know. Get some rest."

"It's too cold." Thomas said. "I can't sleep. I have to go on watch soon; the computer's been acting up. It was bit by a flee . . ."

"Why the hell are we here?" Dick said. "They should never

have sent this circus to the mountains."

"There was no one else to go." Marianna said. "Something you very well know."

Gradually the cold spread throughout Oleg's body; it wasn't the usual cold, but an itching, tormenting irritation, as though an enormous number of tiny icicles were pricking at his chest, his feet . . . Thomas's head began to grow bigger . . .

"That's it." Dick said. "I've trussed you up as good as I can. It's not stretching, is it?"

"Everything's stretching." Oleg tried to laugh, but already there were cramps in his neck and jaw muscles.

"Look. . . ." Dick turned around to Marianna. "Where's the gote?"

"The gote? I heard her during the night."

"I asked you — where's the gote?" Dick's voice rose, high from anger like a little boy's. "Didn't you tie her down?"

"Of course I tied her down." Marianna said. "She must have gotten undone."

"I asked you where she was?"

The irritation and anger accumulating in Dick had to find an exit, and the gote had become the symbol of all their failure.

"Richard, don't get angry." Marianna said. She had started to cover Oleg with a blanket. "It's just gone off to find something to eat."

"There's nothing to find around here. Why didn't you tie it down?"

Dick had pulled his cross-bow from out of the tent and sheathed his knife in his belt.

"Where are you going?" Marianna asked. She knew perfectly well where.

Dick was carefully examining the snow around their camp, looking for tracks.

"She'll return." Marianna said.

"Yes she will." Dick agreed, "As dressed meat. She'll do. I don't want to die of starvation because of your stupidity."

Oleg saw Dick grow and grow; soon his head reached the sky, but he could knock the clouds to pieces, clouds of glass, solid clouds ... Oleg pressed his eyelids tightly shut and then opened them again to drive the hallucination away. Thomas was sitting on the blanket and rocking back and forth, as though he were silently singing.

"Marianna ... heat some water ..." Oleg's voice seemed to grow strong and loud, but he was only whispering barely enough to be heard. "For Thomas. He's getting worse."

Marianna understood.

"Right away, Oleg. Of course."

But she couldn't tear her eyes from Dick.

"Just like I thought." Dick said. "She's gone back. Down. She could have gone about twelve kilometers during the night."

"Dick, stay here." Thomas suddenly became loud and clear. "Marianna will find the gote herself. It's you the animal's run from."

"There's no doubt about it." Dick said. "We've had enough of this stupidity."

"I'll find her." Marianna forgot about the hot water. "Don't leave here, Dick. Thomas is ill and you have to look after Oleg."

"Nothing's going to happen to them."

Dick ran his fingers in his mat of thick hair, tugged it, shook his head and, not looking back, began to lope after the gote's tracks, down the hill from where they'd come in the morning.

"I'd rather you went." Thomas told the girl. "You'd have brought her back; he'll kill her."

The world around Oleg was shifting and changing dimensions constantly, becoming ever more unsteady and unreliable, but he still retained the capacity to think. He said:

"You can understand Dick ... He can't carry us all on his own."

"We only have a short ways left." Thomas said. "I know. I'm sure of it. We're going fast. We'll be there the day after tomorrow. We'll make it there without the gote's meat. Won't we? And there is food on the other side of the mountain pass, Dick, I promise!"

Dick lifted his hand to show he had heard them — the sounds carried that far over the snow covered slope — but he didn't slow his pace.

"We have to catch the gote." Thomas turned to Marianna. "We need her. But she mustn't be killed. There's no sense in that. . . . Something is burning me. How hot. . . . Why does my liver hurt so much? It's not right. We're almost there."

"He'll kill her. . . ." Marianna said. "He'll really kill her . . . Dii-ck!" Marianna turned to Oleg and Thomas: "What can I do? Tell me! You're so wise. You know everything! How can I stop him."

"I can't reach him. I haven't the slightest idea how." Thomas said. "He stopped seeing me an authority figure long ago."

"Now." Oleg said. "Just you untie me. I might be able to get him before the fit comes on. I might."

Marianna just waved her hands in annoyance. She made two steps after Dick, turned and looked at Thomas and at Oleg:

"I mustn't leave you."

"So run then." Thomas suddenly began to shout. "Run faster than he does."

Marianna rushed down the slope after the vanishing Dick as though her feet were hardly touching the snow.

"Poor girl." Thomas said. "She's gotten fond of that gote."

"Too bad." Oleg said. "It's very strange but you don't have just one shape. For a while you're fat, and then you become real thin like a match."

"Yes." Thomas agreed. "Just lay back and try to make yourself comfortable; that poison starts to work on your vision first. I remember the few times I was bitten. But don't be afraid; there are hardly any side effects. Don't worry."

"I understand. But I'm afraid of losing control of myself. Here I am now, but soon I won't even exist. . . ."

Oleg was sliding down into the blue water, and it was very difficult to stay on the surface of the water, because his feet were entangled in water plants and he had to free them, he had to free them or he'd drown. . . .

***

The blanket covering over Oleg flew off. The fit took the boy and he twisted out onto the snow. His eyes were closed and his lips shivered. Oleg's face had grown dark from the tension as he strained to break his bonds. Thomas wanted to help him, to cover him or maybe place the boy's head on his knees. That was desirable to do in such situations — support the head. Thomas tried to get up, but his legs wobbled and refused to support him. Oleg arched his back and literally flew into the air, hammered at the ground with his bound fists and slowly worked his way toward the precipice. He turned over a number of times, striking at the rocks and ice protruding out of the snow, and stopped. His jacket had torn open; snow did not melt on his naked chest.

It's no good. Thomas thought. *I'll have to get to him somehow. Damn that gote. Damn Dick with his Alpha male personality. Dick's so certain he's right. He's convinced himself what he's doing is for everyone's good. And with his savage's view point he is right since there really isn't any future any more than there is a past . . . How could civilized human beings go wild so quickly. We were wrong to let the kids grow up like wolf-cubs even if it did mean they could survive better in the forest. But Dick didn't have any choice. Only sixteen years since we adults were cut off from the mountain pass. And we wouldn't have had the slightest hope of reaching it if Dick and Oleg hadn't managed to grow up. How old am I now? More than forty, must be. Respiration labored and painful — I don't have to be a doctor to diagnose double pneumonia. If I don't reach the ship I'm done for. No gote-fat's gonna help me. And I have to get there on my own two feet — the kids can't carry me to the mountain pass . . . What about Oleg? The snow flee's the worst luck. Maybe fate doesn't want us to return to the human race? It's dragged us here to the mountains, and the forest wants to make us over in its own image, turn us into two-legged zhakals. It's agreed to permit our settlement, but only for its own ends.*

I can see a gap on the other side of the broken ice and snow I can see the a break. It's probably only a small cliff but the fall will kill Oleg. Where's the rope? There was another rope . . . I have to tie him to that stone . . .

Thomas crawled downslope, thankful it was down, it was easier for him to crawl downslope, even if the snow burned him. For some reason the powdery snow penetrated all the small openings of his clothing and burned his chest terribly. When he coughed, no matter how much he tied to hold back so as not to strain his lungs, the convulsions billowed and burst from his chest, and he doubled up in agony.

Thomas crawled downslope, dragging the rope after him. The rope which seemed unbelievably heavy, leaden; the rope uncoiled like a sneaq and dragged at him. Oleg beat his head up and down like a pecking bird trying to break his chains asunder, the back of his head dribbling on the stones. Thomas could feel the pain that held Oleg in madness, pain that held him in a nightmare, but which was no less the real for having been transformed into a hallucination. Oleg thought he was at home and the roof of the house had fallen on him. Only about ten meters separated the older man from Oleg, no more. Thomas knew the boy couldn't hear him, but he called anyway:

"Wait up, I'm coming." But he tried to lift his head to see if Marianna or Dick were returning.

The most important thing was to get there, get there before Oleg tumbled over the edge into the crevasse, when it would be too late. . . .

"Why is my head spinning now?"

When Thomas reached Oleg he lost consciousness for several seconds; all his strength had gone into the downhill crawl. His body refused to obey him any more — the desire to move wasn't enough to give strength to his arms and legs — as though it had done all it was capable of doing.

A gust of icy wind carrying a barrage of snow and perhaps the almost inaudible whisper of his and Oleg's hoarse breathing brought Thomas back to his senses. Thomas only wanted to close his eyes; to lay down, to do nothing, to think about nothing, to reside in a warm and comfortable fairy tale . . . . *a consumption devoutly to be wished* . . .

Oleg had managed to move a meter away, his body twisted and jerked about, trying to tear him free of the rope; he kicked at the clods of ice and snow with his bound feet. Thomas hauled the rope in, trying to figure out how to tie the rope to the rocks so the boy couldn't get away again, but he couldn't figure out how to do it, and then he found his hands empty. He had thrown the rope away, the end lay several meters from him and he didn't have the strength to return to it. Thomas reached out to grab onto Oleg's feet, but the boy twisted and kicked Thomas away. The boy's body had ceased to feel pain.

Thomas realized he couldn't hold on to Oleg: even bound hand and foot the boy's body was the stronger. Thomas resumed his slow advance on the crevasse. He would have to place himself between the crevasse and the boy, to act as a barrier, an unmoving block. Thomas felt he had been crawling for hours; he spoke as he moved, praying, begging Oleg to wait, to lay back peacefully, but by the time he managed to crawl onto the narrow shelf separating Oleg from the crevasse Oleg had moved so close Thomas had to elbow his way between the boy and the sharp stones that lined the edge.

Certainly Thomas would have been able to drag Oleg back upwards to safety if he himself had been able to remain on the shifting edge of consciousness.

***

Marianna returned to the camp at a run, her chest heaving from exertion and the thin air. It seemed like she'd been gone only a few minutes, although in fact she had been away for more than an hour. She ran straight to the tent, not immediately realizing what had happened. She saw only that the camp was empty, and at first even lifted up the edge of the tent thinking Thomas and Oleg were huddled there away from the snow, although the tent lay flat on the ground and no one could have hidden beneath it.

Marianna looked around in confusion and found the tracks in the snow leading downslope toward the cliff; it looked like someone had been dragging a heavy weight in the snow and all she could imagine was a terrible scene. The animal that made the circular, barrel sized tracks had dragged both men away and it was all her fault. She had run off to save the gote and had forgotten about her own people, she had abandoned sick people in a snow covered desert and it had all been for naught because she had never reached Dick and hadn't found the gote, had gotten lost among the rocks, terrified she'd never find the path back to the camp, terrified for Thomas and Oleg who were helpless. She had run back, and was too late.

Marianna picked her way down the slope, sobbing and repeating:

"Mama, mama . . ."

Why was the rope on the snow? Had Oleg gotten free?

She made her way around gray hillocks of snow and ice and saw Oleg laying tied up at the edge of the precipice; Of Thomas there was no sign.

"Oleg, oh Oleg!" She shouted. "Are you alive?"

Oleg didn't answer. He was sleeping solidly. The fit had passed. He was alone, but the track from his body continued down, toward the drop, and when Marianna glanced over the edge she saw Thomas on the ground about five meters below. He lay so quietly and comfortably Marianna did not immediately guess he was already dead.

After, when she had gotten down into the crevasse. hurrying and falling and cutting her hands and legs on the icy stones, she pulled at him for a long time trying to awaken him, and suddenly she understood Thomas had died. The back of his skull was caved in. Above her on the cliff Oleg had come to his senses, heard the noise and her wailing, and asked in a weak voice:

"Marianna, is that you? What's happened?"

Oleg remembered absolutely nothing of how he had pushed Thomas over the edge, and it was only by the tracks and the fragments of Oleg's nightmarish visions they could understand how and why it had all taken place, and guessed how Thomas had died.

***

Dick returned to the camp two hours later. He hadn't caught the gote and had lost her tracks on the great stone field. While returning he had encountered the tracks of an unknown animal and went after it, thinking he would return to camp with at least some game. Then he could say he left the gote alone on purpose because he was wanted to spare Marianna's feelings. And he had already convinced himself; the idea of failure terrified him.

When he learned what had happened in the camp during his absence he turned more sober and quieter than the others and said to Oleg:

"Don't spout nonsense. You didn't kill anyone and you're not guilty of anything. You of all people know what killed Thomas. You should be thankful he tried to save you. He might not have been able to do anything, most likely he was able to do nothing, but all the same he wanted to save you. Perhaps it was for the best; Thomas was very ill. He could have died at any minute. He wanted to go to the pass so much he would have made us drag him, and we would all have died."

"Are you actually trying to calm Oleg?" Marianna answered; she was rocking back and forth where she sat from pain; she had frozen her hands and gotten them covered with blood when she had tried to revive Thomas. The two of them, Oleg still staggering from weakness, had dragged the older man's corpse up to the tent.

"You want to calm Oleg? But it's the two of us who are guilty. If we hadn't run after the gote Thomas would still be alive."

"You're right." Dick said. "You didn't have to run after me. That was stupidity, female stupidity."

"But of course you don't have any responsibility at all, do you?" Marianna asked.

Thomas lay stretched out silent between them. His head was covered with the blanket, but he was a participant in their conversation none the less.

"I don't know." Dick said. "I went after the gote because we needed the meat. We all need it. Me less than the rest of you because I'm stronger."

"I don't want to talk with him any more." Marianna said to Oleg and the world in general. "He's as cold as the snow."

"I want to be fair." Dick said. "Why are we wasting our time moaning over it. It's not going to get any better. We're wasting time. The daylight's almost half done."

"Oleg's still too weak to walk." Marianna said.

"No. It's nothing." Oleg called out. "I can make it. Only we have to take Thomas's map and radiation detector. He told me if anything happened we had to take those things."

"Don't bother." Dick said.

"Why?"

"Because we're going back." Dick said quietly.

"And how did you come be the one to decide that?" Oleg asked.

"It's our only chance to save ourselves." Dick said. "In two days we can be back in the forest and I can find game there. I'll get you back to the settlement, I promise."

"No. We're going on." Oleg said.

"That's stupid." Dick said. "It's hopeless."

"We have the map. "

"And why do you believe that thing? The map's old; it all could have changed. And no one knows how long we still have to walk without food in this icy desert."

"Thomas said we were going so fast there was only a day left."

"Thomas was wrong. He wanted to get there so much he was deceiving us."

"Thomas never deceived us. He said there was food there and we would be safe."

"He wanted to believe that. He was sick. His judgment was gone. We're still alive, and we'll remain that way only if we go back."

"I'm going on to the mountain pass." Oleg said. He was looking at the blanket covered body; it was his farewell to Thomas.

"I'm going too." Marianna said. "Why don't you understand that?"

"Marianna, the Mayor's pulled the wool over Oleg's eyes." Dick hit his large fist against a stone, beating in time to his words as he spoke. "The Mayor always kept telling Oleg he was the smartest, better than you or me, that he was special. Oleg could never be better than us in the settlement or in the forest; he always fell behind. He couldn't even keep up with you in the forest. You've got to understand; Oleg needs this fairy tale about the mountain pass and about the savages you and I are becoming but he's not. But I'm not a savage. I'm not dumber than he is. Let Oleg go on if he's so sure of himself. But I'm not letting you go on; I'm taking you back down."

"Stupid, stupid, stupid!" Marianna shouted. "The settlement sent us; they're waiting for us and hoping we'll succeed!"

"We'll be more use to them alive." Dick said.

"I'm going." Oleg reached toward the blanket to get the map and radiation counter from Thomas's body. He said silently: *I'm sorry you won't be making it; I'm sorry I have to take your treasures.*

He pulled back the edge of the blanket; Thomas lay with his eyes closed, his face ashen. In death his lips had become even thinner. Oleg couldn't force himself to touch to Thomas's chilling body.

"Wait, I'll do it." Marianna said. "Wait."

Dick got to his feet, walked over to the cliff edge, lifted the flask from the snow and shook it. The cognac swished inside. Dick pulled out the stopper and poured the cognac out onto the snow. The bitter, unfamiliar odor hung in the air. Dick replaced the stopper and hung the flask over his shoulder. No one said anything. Marianna handed Oleg the folded map, the radiation counter, and Thomas's knife.

"We can't bury him." Dick said." We'll have to carry him over the drop and cover him with stones."

"No!" Oleg said.

Dick lifted his eyebrows in surprise.

And it was stupid to answer that Thomas should not be covered with stones. Thomas was dead after all; he wasn't going to object.

Dick did everything. Oleg and Marianna only helped him. They didn't say anything else. Oleg and Marianna silently packed their bundles, picked up the very light packs (only enough wood remained for one or two campfires), and divided the last slices of dried meat into three portions, Marianna handed Dick his share; he put it in his pocket and said nothing. Then Oleg and Marianna started off up the hill, without looking around, toward the mountain pass.

Dick caught up with them after a hundred meters. He caught up, then passed them and insisted on leading the way. Oleg was still staggering from the last effects of the fit. Marianna limped; her legs were bruised from when she had scrambled over the precipice. They managed to make about ten kilometers before they were forced to stop for the night.

Oleg collapsed in the snow and immediately fell asleep. He didn't even awaken to drink the hot water and their dwindling supply of sweet roots. And he didn't see what Dick and Marianna saw when it became dark enough. The clouds broke overhead, splitting to reveal a blackness they had never seen before filled with tiny points of light, the stars, which not one of them had ever seen before. Then the sky closed up again. Marianna soon fell asleep as well, but Dick sat longer by the warmth of the dying fire with his feet almost in it, looking up at the sky and waiting for the clouds to part again. He had heard about stars, but never before had he suspected they would inspire such awe, or guessed the magnitude the tiny colored points nestled in an infinity of dark would reveal. Dick understood why they could not return to the settlement.

***

The three got up early, melted snow into hot water to drink, and finished eating the sweet roots which only increased their hunger. That day dragged slower than usual; even Dick was dead on his feet.

They did not know if they were following the correct path or not. There were directions drawn on the map, but they did not correspond to anything they could see. The last time people had come this way had been in winter in the midst of a blinding snow storm, through bitter cold and fog, and now everything looked totally different.

So despair set in; the mountain pass was an abstraction you could not believe in, any more than you could imagine a sky filled with stars if you had never seen them before and knew them only from stories. Oleg mourned that he had fallen asleep and missed the sky; perhaps the phenomenon would recur the next night. The clouds filling the sky had become thinner — sometimes a patch of blue burst through and suddenly the land around them became far brighter than the forest lowlands.

During the day they were all dead on their feet. Dick gave the order to stop and began to wipe snow on Marianna's frozen cheeks; it was then that Oleg noticed a blue patch in the snow off to one side. But it was more than a hundred paces walk further off and Oleg didn't even have the strength to speak.

Finally, when Dick said it was time to move on again, Oleg pointed at the blue patch. They walked toward it, every step quicker now.

It was a short blue jacket made from some thin, unwoven

material; it was half frozen into the snow; one sleeve was filled with snow and stuck up in the air. Dick was cutting the snow around it away to get it free, but suddenly a painful impatience gripped Oleg.

"Don't bother." He barked. "Why? We'll get there soon; you understand; we're on the right track!"

"It's strong material." Dick said. "And Marianna's almost frozen."

"I don't need it." Marianna said. "Let's just go further."

"Go on; I'll catch up with you." Dick insisted. "Go on."

Dick caught up with them fifteen minutes later, carrying the jacket in one hand, but Marianna refused to put it on, saying it was damp and cold. But mostly it was because the jacket was someone else's. And if it had been brought along and then thrown away the owner was dead. They all knew seventy-six people had come out of the mountain pass, and little more than thirty reached the forest.

They didn't reach the mountain pass on that day, although to Oleg it seemed the pass must be just ahead — for now they had to skirt the tongue of a glacier. . . . and the mountain pass will be just ahead, now they passed a field of broken stones. . . . and the pass . . . And the rise of the land became all the more sharper and the air thinner and less substantial in their lungs.

They spent the night — more precisely, they survived until the darkness ended — piled together, wrapped in all the blankets and covered by the tent. Despite their exhaustion they could not sleep from the cold, they only dozed off from time to time and woke up to change places. For Marianna, who lay in the center, there was hardly any warmth; she had become almost incorporeal and sharp, her bones were showing through her skin. They got up at dawn with stars over their heads fading into a purple sky, but they didn't look at the sky.

Then, gradually, it turned light. The clouds were transparent like mist and through them shone a sun, small, cold, and blinding, which they had never seen before either, but they weren't looking at the sun. They trudged along, walking around the fissures and cracks in the ice and snow, the fields of talus rock and precarious ledges. Dick insisted on taking the lead, choosing their path and falling down more frequently than the others, but not once did he surrender his lead.

So he was the first of them to see the mountain pass, not suspecting they had reached their destination because the declivity along which they clambered had flattened out into a plateau so gradually they had not noticed it, and then they saw the jagged mountain peaks ahead of them. Peak after peak, a chain of snow-capped mountains glistening under the sun, and an hour later below them opened a saddleback in the middle of which, even from their kilometer's height, they could see the fat disk of glistening metal. It lay on its side half buried in snow and ice in the very center of the hollow. The captain had aimed the ship for the saddleback after the explosion in the engineering section had cut off the thrusters; he landed it in the middle of a storm, in the night and fog of the terrible local winter.

They stood in a line, three tattered, worn out savages, crossbows on their shoulders, bags of animal hides on their backs, bruised, frostbitten, black from hunger and exhaustion, three microscopic figures in an enormous, empty, silent world, and looked at the dead ship that had crashed on this planet sixteen years ago and would never rise into the sky again.

Then they began to descend the steep slope, clutching at the stones, trying not to run on the treacherous scree, yet running ever faster as though their feet refused to listen to their pleas of caution.

An hour later they stood in the bottom of the hollow.

CHAPTER FOUR

Sixteen years before, Oleg and Dick both had been a year old and Marianna yet to be born, and none of them remembered how the exploratory ship *PolarStar* had crashed here in the middle of the mountains. Their first recollections were connected with the settlement, with the forest; they had learned about the habits of cunning red muzhrumes and hunting vynes before the mayor had told them about the stars and of other worlds. And the forest was much easier to understand than tales of starships or buildings that might each hold a thousand people. The forest's laws, and the rules of the settlement which arose from the necessity to preserve a handful of people who had not evolved for this environment, worked to push the memory of Earth from their minds. In place of that memory arose the abstract hope that someday they would be found and it would all end. But how long could one hope to wait? Ten years? Ten years and more had passed. A hundred years? Then they would find not you but your grandchildren, assuming the settlement survived that long. Hopes still alive in the old, did not exist for the second generation — they only interfered with the everyday struggle to survive in the forest. But for the adults not to at least try to not transmit that hope on to their children was unthinkable. The adults knew they were going to die, but the species must continue. Death would only reign the moment they gave up hope for a future.

Therefore the Mayor and the teachers — everyone who could — tried to instill in the young the feeling they belonged to the Earth, the idea that sooner or later the separation would come to an end. And the greatest single hard fact connecting them with the old world remained the starship crashed beyond the mountain pass. It existed. It could be reached, if not in this local year of a thousand endless cold days, then next year when the children had grown and could go into the pass themselves.

Dick, Oleg and Marianna descended into the hollow, to the ship. It grew. It became as corporeal as it was enormous. But it did not stop being a legend, their Grail, and none of them would have been surprised if it had vanished into smoke the moment they touched it. They were returning to the house of their fathers, which frightened those who had been here only in their dreams or in legends told under dim lamplight in a few stolen moments when a blizzard raged beyond slit windows stretched tight with fishskins.

The fact the ship existed gave birth to dreams and legends, and the young generation had created a Ship of the Mind out of their imaginations that bore little resemblance to the reality of this giant. The Mayor and the other adults found this conflict difficult to understand; for them the story of catastrophic explosion, the failure of light and life support, the flight through the corridors as the lights died, the silence of the drives and the chattering of the radiation counters, the escape to the snowy wastelands, was no mere tale.

For their listeners — for Oleg and his generation — only the snow storm had really been understandable. They associated corridors with images of forest thickets or dark caves; their imaginations were fed by what they had seen and heard themselves.

Now they could understand how people had fled from here, dragging the children and the injured, grabbing the things which should have been immediately useful on the run, at a moment when no one really understood they would have to live here forever and die on this cold world — even here the gigantic scale and unbelievable power of interstellar civilization instilled a false sense of confidence that everything that happened, however tragic it might have been, was only a temporary break, an accident that would be fixed as accidents had always been fixed.

In front of them was the airlock.

We shut it when we left, so the Mayor said, *and we put the emergency stairway we came down to one side, under an overhang. The spot is marked on the map.* They did not have to search for the stairway — the snow had melted and it lay unmoving, its blue paint weathered over the years. When Dick picked the stairway up the impression left behind in the snow was blue.

Dick kicked at the metal rungs to test it.

"It's light." He said. "We've got to bring it back."

The others were silent. Marianna and Oleg stood a short distance away, heads thrown back, examining the ship's rounded belly. The ship seemed completely intact, ready to take off and fly further. And Oleg even imagined it blasting off from the hollow, falling ever faster into the blue sky and becoming a dark circle, a point in the heavens. . . .

The exhaustion was gone. Their bodies felt light and obeyed their minds, and the impatience to look inside this marvel as fast as possible became mixed with a terror of becoming lost forever inside the ship's closed sphere.

Oleg cast a glance at the round emergency lock; he could tell what it was because it was outlined in black. Numerous times the Mayor had repeated to Oleg:. "*The emergency lock wasn't sealed, you understand. We only drew it closed. You get up to it on the stairway and the first order of business is to check the level of radiation. There shouldn't be any now. Sixteen years have passed, but you must check it with the counter. Back then the radiation was just one of the reasons we had to leave so quickly. The cold and the radiation. Forty degrees below zero, the life support systems were all off line and the radiation counters were screaming. It was simply impossible to remain.*"

Dick scouted the ground around the ship, extricating bags and cans from the snow, many things people had dragged out of the ship and been forced to leave behind.

"Well?" Oleg asked. "Let's go in."

"Why not?" Dick raised the stairway and placed it against the base of the lock. Then he climbed up the stairs, put Thomas's knife in the thin crack and pushed as hard as he could. The knife broke.

"Could they have locked it?" Marianna asked below.

"There are no more knives like this one left in all the world." Dick said.

"The Mayor said the lock was open." Oleg noted.

"The Mayor's forgotten everything." Dick said. "You can't believe the old people."

"Nothing happened?" Marianna asked.

Clouds had started to cover the sun; it was quickly becoming darker, more familiar.

"Wait." Oleg said. "Why are we running around in circles. Why push like at home? What if doors into the ship open differently?"

"I'm coming down." Dick said. "I'll get a stone."

"A stone won't do any good." Oleg said.

The hatch was set back a little into the wall of the ship and seemed to extend below the edge of the metal. A thin crack in the hull seemed to run along one edge on the inside of the black circle. What if you tried to push it to one side? He'd never seen such a thing before, but if the ship flew, it would certainly be best if the door didn't flap open itself by accident. Oleg told Dick:

"Give me the knife."

Dick handed Oleg the broken knife, stuffed his hands underneath his armpits and started to stamp: he was frozen. Even he was frozen.

A fine light snow began to drift down. They were alone in the world. They were dying of hunger and the cold. But the ship refused them entry.

Oleg placed what was left of the knife into the thin crack and gently tried to push the metal circle to the side. It slid quickly and effortlessly as though it had been waiting for him, and simply vanished into the wall. *All in order.* Oleg didn't bother to turn around although the others had seen how smart he was. He had solved the problem. Even if it wasn't a very complicated one, but the others hadn't. Oleg sheathed the knife in his belt and pulled out the radiation counter.

"Hey!" He heard Marianna's voice. "Oleg's opened it."

"That's great." Dick said. "Go on, what are you waiting for?"

The counter indicated no danger. *All in order.*

"It's dark in there." Oleg said. "Hand up the lamp."

Even when it had been horribly cold the night before they hadn't lit the lamps; they gave off too little warmth but burned a long time.

"Is it warm in there?" Marianna asked.

"No." Oleg sniffed the air. A strange, dangerous smell remained in the ship. To step inside was frightening. But Oleg understood now he was leading them and not Dick. Dick was afraid. Dick struck his flint and lit the lamp. In the light of day the lamp's flame was nearly invisible. Dick went half way up the stair and passed it to Oleg, but he didn't go any further. Oleg took the lamp and extended his hand inside. Ahead was darkness and a level floor.

Oleg spoke loud enough to drown his terror:

"I'm going in. Get your lamps and come after me! I'll wait inside."

The floor under his feet was springy like the bark of a living tree, but Oleg knew the floor was inanimate and there were no such trees on Earth. He imagined something lurked in front of him, and he froze. But then he understood it was only the reflection, the echo, of his own breathing. Oleg took another step forward and the lamp flared, illuminating a wall that bent gently upward to become the ceiling as well. A bright and shining wall. He touched it. It was cold.

So I'm home. Oleg thought. *I have a home — the settlement. But there's another home called Space Exploratory Ship* **PolarStar**. *I've dreamed of it a thousand times, but the dreams are nothing at all like it turned out to be in reality. But I was here. I was even born here. Somewhere in the dark depths of the ship is the room where I was born.*

"Where are you?" Dick called out.

Oleg turned around. Dick's silhouette started to shadow the airlock aperture.

"Come on in." Oleg said. "There's no one here."

"If there were, they'd have frozen." Dick's voice reverberated down the corridor.

Oleg used his own lamp to light Dick's, then waited while Dick made room for Marianna and passed the flame on to her.

With the three lamps burning it immediately became much brighter, but the lamps could do nothing about the cold. It was far colder inside than outside.

The short corridor ahead ended in another door, but Oleg already knew how to open it. A small degree of certainty appeared in Oleg's actions, not very much, but he felt he belonged here on the ship far more than the others. The others still felt the ship was a terrible cave; if not for their hunger they would have remained outside. Had Thomas made it to the ship with them things would have been different. Oleg could not take on himself the role of conductor and interpreter of the mysteries; but Oleg himself knew he was better than nothing.

Beyond the door was a vast circular hall the like of which they had never seen before. The entire settlement could have been moved in there. Despite the light from the three lamps the ceiling vanished into darkness.

"This is the hangar." Oleg said, repeating the word's he had memorized from the Mayor. "This was where they stored the flitter and other tools. 'But the manual launching mechanism was rendered inoperative during the crash. This played a fatal role.'"

"'And compelled the crew and passengers to go through the mountains on foot.'" Marianna added.

At lessons the Mayor had insisted they memorize the history of the settlement by heart, beginning with this series of events to prevent them from forgetting. "If people lack paper, they memorize their histories." The Mayor had said. "Without a history, people stop being . . . people."

"'With enormous casualties. . . . '" Dick continued for a moment but could not complete it; he couldn't bring himself to speak aloud here.

In front of them, blocking their path, was a cylinder about ten meters long.

"This was the flitter they dragged out of the hanger by hand." Oleg said. "But they weren't able to take advantage of it and were forced to abandon it."

"It's really cold in here." Marianna shivered.

"The ship is retaining the winter's chill." Dick said. "Where to from here?"

Dick had accepted Oleg's leadership.

"There should be an open door over here." Oleg said. "It leads to the drive chambers. Only we can't go there. We have to find a stairway leading upwards."

"It's good you studied everything." Marianna almost laughed.

The three of them started walking along the wall again.

"There must be lots of things here." Dick said. "How will we bring carry them back?"

"The people who died here? Did they just walk away?" Marianna asked.

"You stop it!" Dick said.

"Obvious. . . ." Oleg stopped.

"What? What did you see?"

"I just figured out how we'll do it. If we take the flat metal steps of the ladder, then we can load what we'll take back on them and drag them behind us. Like the sledges Sergeyev made."

"Well I thought you saw a corpse." Marianna said.

"I thought so too." Dick said.

"That first door." Oleg said. "We can't go in there."

"I'll just take a look." Dick said.

"There's radiation for sure in there." Oleg said. "The Mayor was certain of it."

"It won't do anything to me." Dick said. I'm strong."

"You're hardly going to see it, you know. You studied it too." Oleg went further ahead, holding his lamp close to the wall. The wall was uneven: there were niches in it, open panels with buttons and cold reflecting surfaces he knew were called screens.

Thomas had been an engineer. Thomas had understood what these buttons had meant and what powers they commanded.

"Look at all they built." Dick said. He still hadn't made his peace with the ship. "And it's all broken."

"It was good enough to carry them through the sky." Marianna said.

"Here's the other door." Oleg said. "From here we can get to the living quarters and the astrogation department."

That's how it had always sounded: "Astrogation Department" and "Bridge." Like an invocation. But now he'd see the Astrogation Department for himself.

"Do you remember the number of your own room?" Marianna asked.

"Cabin." Oleg corrected her. "Certainly I remember it. Forty four."

"My father asked me to stop by and see how things were there. We were one hundred ten. You really were born on the ship?"

Oleg didn't answer; the question didn't really demand an answer. But it was odd Marianna was thinking the same way he was.

Oleg put his hand on the door and moved it to the side. The light came from nowhere and from everywhere.

Oleg jumped back. He had forgotten — of course this was to be expected. They had paints that gave off light for many years.

The Astrogation Department and some corridors were painted with them. It was bright. Bright enough to let them douse the lamps.

"Oh." Marianna kept her voice in a whisper. "Does this mean someone is still living here?"

"It's good there's light at least." Oleg said. "We can save the lamps."

"It's gotten warmer." Marianna said.

"It only seems that way." Oleg said. "But we'll certainly find warm things and we can sleep in the rooms."

"No." Dick said. He had stayed back from the others and still hadn't entered the lighted corridor. "There's no way I'm sleeping here."

"Why?"

"I'll be sleeping outside, in the snow; warmer there."

Oleg understood. Dick was afraid to sleep in the ship, but Oleg wanted to remain here. He didn't fear the ship. He had been frightened at first when it was dark, but not now. He was home.

"I won't sleep here either." Marianna said. "There are the shadows of the people who lived here. I'm afraid."

To the right the corridor wall sank away from them but was obstructed by something transparent, like a thin layer of water; a material Marianna remembered was called plast. And behind it were green plants. With tiny green leaves. There were no such leaves in the local forest.

"Won't they bite?" Oleg asked.

"No." Marianna said. "They're frozen. "And Earth plants don't hunt animals; surely you've forgotten how Aunt Luiza talked about them."

"That's not so important." Dick said. "Let's get going. We can't just walk around in here forever. But what if there's nothing to eat here?"

Odd Oleg thought. *I'm really not hungry at all. And I haven't eaten in so long I'm not hungry. Nerves.*

Ten steps later they saw yet one more niche; but the plast had been broken. Marianna reached in.

"Don't." Dick said.

"There's no problem. I can feel it. These are all dead."

She reached her hand out. At the touch of her fingers the leaves broke and fell to dust.

"Too bad." Marianna said. "If only there were seeds we could plant them around the settlement."

"There's a store room to the right." Oleg said. "Let's look for something to eat."

They turned to the right. A broken, half transparent bag lay in the middle of the corridor; a number of white cans had spilled out of it. The bag must have broken while the people were fleeing.

***

It was an odd, wondrous feast they had when they finally opened the cans. Dick tried to open them with his knife and failed; the blade didn't leave a mark, but Oleg found a way to remove the tops without a blade by pressing at the edge. The containers then heated their contents until they were soft enough to eat. They tried everything the cans and tubes contained, and nearly all of it was as tasty as it was unfamiliar. And of cans there was no lack, for there were entire rooms filled with cases and containers, endless numbers of cans and all kinds of other foods. They drank condensed milk, but there was no Thomas with them to tell them what it was. They gulped down sprats, another unnamed food. They squeezed preserves which seemed too sweet to them out of tubes, they chewed flour. Marianna became upset at the mess they were making on the floor.

Afterwards they dozed off — they had trouble keeping their eyes open, as though all the weariness of the last days weighed on their shoulders. Despite their exhaustion Oleg was unable to convince his companions to remain and sleep in the ship. The other two left, and Oleg, as soon as their footsteps had died away in the corridor, suddenly became afraid himself and scarcely was able to keep himself from running after them. He lay on the floor, pushed the cans away, and slept soundly for many hours. Time here in the ship was frozen as well; there was no way he could tell its passage.

Oleg slept without dreams, without thoughts, deeply and quietly, far more quietly than Marianna and Dick. Dick even in such weariness awakened and listened for danger several times during the night. He woke Marianna up as well; she had been resting her head on his chest. They were covered with all the blankets and the tent, and it wasn't cold because toward evening a thick snowfall had buried the tent, turning it into a snow drift.

Oleg awakened before the pair sleeping outside; he was freezing. He jumped up and down for a long time to warm himself, then he ate some more. It was a remarkable feeling: not to have to wonder if there was enough food — he didn't remember when the last time was he hadn't been hungry. His stomach even hurt — *Let it hurt more*, Oleg thought. It was almost shameful to look on the remains of their feast, and Oleg removed the empty and half empty cans over to a corner of the room. *I've got to go further.* he thought. *Should I go call the others? No, they must still be sleeping.* To Oleg it seemed his sleep had only lasted a few minutes.

He planned to look around a bit, then go outside to awaken Dick and Marianna. There was no one else in the ship, there hadn't been for a long time, there was nothing to fear. They would have to go back the way they'd come; the mountain pass would soon fill with snow. And they were sleeping here. How dare they waste time sleeping here!

Like a good denizen of the forest Oleg had no trouble finding his way around. Even in a starship. He wasn't afraid of getting lost and therefore quietly went up the metal stairway leading to the living quarters.

He found the cabin with a round metal plate marked "44" after an hour. Not because it was difficult to find, simply because he became distracted and spent too much time looking at what he found along the way. At first he found himself in a passenger lounge where he saw a long table, and there he took an immense fancy to a funny looking salt shaker and pepper grinder set and he even put the pieces in his pack, thinking his mother would be delighted if he brought such things back to her.

Then he examined a chess set for a long time; the box had fallen to the floor and scattered the pieces on the carpet when the ship had crashed. No one had ever told him about chess and he concluded these were sculptures of unknown terrestrial animals. And finally, the carpet itself was amazing. It was without seams or stitches, which meant it was skinned from the hide of a single animal. How could animals on Earth be so large, and what could cause them to have such strange designs on their hides? Obviously it had to be a pelagic animal. Egli had told the children the largest animals of Earth dwelt in the oceans and were called whales. Oleg saw so many more wondrous and incomprehensible things over the course of the hour it took him to reach cabin Forty-Four he was overflowing with impressions, and absolutely desperate with a sense of his own stupidity, from his inability to figure out what the things he found were.

Oleg stood for a long time in front of cabin Forty-Four's door, unable to decide to open it, although there was no reason why he should not look in there. But he did understand why.

Although his mother had said many times his father had died when the ship had crashed, that he had been in the drive compartment when the converter flared and fused, despite everything it seemed to him his father might be in there.

For some reason Oleg had never really believed in his father's death, and his father had remained among the living, on the ship, waiting, abandoned. Perhaps this had come from his mother's deep conviction that his father was still alive. It was her nightmare, her obsession which she carefully hid from everyone, even from her son. But her son knew all about it.

Finally, Oleg forced himself to push the door to one side. The cabin was dark; the walls were covered with normal paints. He was forced to wait outside, light his lamp, and his eyes did not quickly accustom themselves to the dimness. The cabin consisted of two rooms. In the first stood a table, a desk, and a divan where his father spent the night; his mother lived with the infant Oleg in the second, inner room.

The cabin was empty. His father had never returned. His mother was wrong.

But a different surprise awaited Oleg, a different shock, an expression of the other side of time, when the ship was alive, from the moment when the people had abandoned her to the day Oleg returned.

In the smaller room stood a child's crib. Oleg immediately

understood this soft device suspended in the air with undone straps hanging from the sides was intended for a small child. And that for some reason, a little while ago, the young child had been carried out of here in a hurry, even leaving behind one very small red bootie and multicolored rattle. Oleg, who had yet to finally realize he was coming face to face with himself, in this preserve of frozen time, lifted the rattle and shook it; the moment he heard the clattering sound, however strange it was, the memory came back. He finally came face to face with the reality of the ship, the reality of a world which was deeper and more real than the reality of the settlement and the forest. In everyday life you never come face to face with your past. Things get lost, all that remains is memory, like a souvenir. But here, in the loop attached to the side of the bed hung an unfinished bottle of milk, milk that had frozen, that he could warm and finish drinking.

And, having seen himself, having met with himself, having recognized and survived that meeting, Oleg started to search for the traces of the two other people who had lived on the other side of that frozen time, his father and mother.

Finding his mother was easy; she had fled from here carrying him, her son; so here in the depths of the ship he found a twisted, crumpled dress where she had thrown it on her bed. Soft slippers stuck out from under the bed. A book, his mother's place held by a sheet of paper, lay on the pillow. Oleg picked up the book carefully, fearing it would shatter like the plants in the corridor. But the book had weathered the frosts well. It was called "***Anna Karenina***" and someone named Leo Tolstoy had written it. It was a thick book, and mathematical symbols — formulae — were scribbled on the book mark — mother had been a theoretical physicist. Oleg had never seen his mother's handwriting before; in the village there had been nothing to write with. He had never seen a book; at the time no one had thought to bring any from the ship. Oleg had heard the writer's name at Aunt Luiza's lessons, but he had never thought a writer could write such a fat book. Oleg took the book with him. And he knew: however difficult it was to get back, he'd carry the book all the way back. And the sheet of paper with formulae. And then, thinking a little, he put his mother's slippers in the knapsack as well. They seemed very narrow for his mothers worn old feet, but let her have them anyway.

But traces of his father, although they were corporeal and obvious for some reason did not draw themselves so much to Oleg's attention as his encounter with his former self — at the moment the ship crashed his father was already dead. He had died earlier. He had gone on watch and had cleaned up after himself. Oleg's father had been a careful, precise man with no tolerance for disorder. His books stood in a file on their shelf behind plast, his things hung in the wall closet. . . . Oleg pulled his father's uniform from its place in the closet. Certainly, he hadn't worn it on board the ship — the uniform was quite new, blue, pressed, with two small stars over the breast over a jacket pocket, with thin gold stripes down the narrow trousers. Oleg pulled the uniform from the closet and held it close — the uniform was a little too big for him. Then Oleg pulled the jacket on top of his own and it proved to be just right for him. — all they would have to do was take in the sleeves. Then he pulled on the trousers. If his father lived in the village and walked around in this uniform, he would have let his son put try it on sometimes.

Now the ship finally belonged to Oleg. Even after he had returned to the forest he would always yearn for the ship and try to return here, like the Mayor had tried, like Thomas had tried. This was all to the good, it was a victory for the Mayor who had never wanted those who grew up in the village to be only a part of the forest. Now Oleg finally understood why the Mayor thought that way, and the man's words took on meanings that could be understood only by those who had been here.

Oleg turned to the covered desk and figured out how to open it; the inside turned out to be a mirror. Oleg only had occasion to see himself reflected before in puddles, he had never before seen himself in a large mirror. And, gazing at himself, he felt a split, but this split wasn't unnatural — after all, it was only him, little Oleg, who hadn't even finished drinking his milk, standing here behind the open door. But now he stood before the mirror in his father's uniform. Of course he didn't look much like his father now; his face was weather worn, wind-burned, the dark skin taut with early wrinkles from malnutrition and the terrible climate, but despite everything it was him. He, Oleg, had grown up, returned, donned his uniform and taken his place as a member of the *PolarStar's* crew.

In the desk he found his father's notebook; half the pages were empty, no fewer than a hundred clean white sheets, a treasure in itself for the Mayor who could now teach the children by drawing various things they had never seen before on the paper. And when they grew up they would return to the ship themselves. He also found there a number of volumes of colored pictures, photographs with views of various Earth cities. He packed them away to take also. A number of other things were totally incomprehensible, and Oleg didn't bother to touch them — he knew the return to the settlement would be difficult enough.

But he took something else with him. He guessed what it was immediately and knew how delighted Sergeyev would be, and Vaitkus, who had drawn this thing in wet clay and repeated again and again: "*I can never forgive myself that not one of us took a blaster with him.*"

"*You're blaming yourself for nothing.*" The Mayor had retorted, "*You'd have had to go back to the Bridge, and it was flooded with radiation.*" It turned out one blaster had been with Oleg's father, in his desk.

The handle fitted comfortably in his palm. To see if the blaster's charge remained Oleg pointed it at the wall and pressed the trigger — lighting flew from the blaster's mouth and danced over the wall. Oleg blinked and shut his eyes tight, but for a minute more the sparks jumped through his eyes.

Oleg went out the door with the blaster in his hand: now he wasn't just the master of the ship; now he could face the forest as more than just a supplicant. *You can't touch us!*

Out in the corridor Oleg hesitated; he wanted to head for the Astrogation Department or the Com Center, but it made more sense to return to the storeroom, because if Dick and Marianna had gone there they would be worried.

Oleg went back the way he had come quickly, but the store room was empty. No one had come by here. Well then, he would have to awaken them. And besides, although Oleg wasn't willing to admit it to himself, he wanted to appear before them in a spaceman's uniform and say: "You've been sleeping to long. Time to go back to the stars..."

This time he cut straight across the hangar; the way back appeared shorter than yesterday; he was already familiar with the ship's layout. A bright light appeared before him — the outside lock was still open. They had forgotten to close it. That wasn't really important here; the lock was too high for the animals, so why should they close it?

Oleg stood there for about a minute, squinted and let his eyes grow accustomed to the daylight again. The sun stood high in the heavens; the night had ended long ago. Oleg opened his eyes wide and grew frightened.

There was no trace of Dick or Marianna; during the night the snow had leveled off and smoothed out everything. Snow without a single dark spot on it.

"Hey!" Oleg said. Not too loudly. The silence was so thick it threatened violators.

And then Oleg noticed something was moving back and forth about twelve meters from the side of the ship by a low, rounded hill. It was an animal the like of which Oleg had never seen before; white, nearly blending in with the snow, similar to the lowlands reptiles but fur covered, about four meters from snout to tip of tail. Carefully, as though it feared frightening prey, it was pulling apart that hill. Oleg looked at the animal as though spellbound and waited to see what would happen next; he didn't associate the white snow bank with Dick and Marianna's night time camp. Even when the animal's paws had raked the snow aside and revealed the darker color of the tent below he just stood there unmoving.

But then Dick woke up; through his dreams he heard the animal pouncing upon them, and his nose caught the animal's dangerous alien scent. Dick had grabbed for his knife and burst out from underneath the tent, but was caught up in the blankets. When the column of snow shot upwards to Oleg it looked like the snow bank had unexpectedly come to life. The animal wasn't in the least frightened by the explosion; on the contrary, it was now convinced it had not erred in digging for prey; it grasped the fish hide tent with taloned paws and held its prey down in the snow, growling in triumph.

Oleg, the forest dweller, groped for the knife in his belt and aimed for a leap to the ground, his eyes already trying to guess where on that white body was the best spot to thrust in his knife. But, Oleg the inhabitant of a starship, and the son of the ship's engineer, grabbed the blaster in place of the knife. It was impossible to fire from where he stood, too high and far away. Oleg jumped down into the snow and rushed for the animal, clutching the weapon in his hands. The animal, seeing him, lifted its muzzle and started to growl to frighten Oleg away; it had taken him for a competitor and now fell on Dick without fear.

Oleg stopped and sent a blaster bolt into the mass of jagged teeth.

***

Dick and Marianna finished eating and started to drag what they would be taking back to the village to the exit. Oleg finally made it to the very top of the ship, to the Astrogation Department. He asked Dick to go with him but the other wouldn't go up — the booty was enough for him. Marianna refused to go as well; Oleg had shown her the hospital and she busied herself picking out the medicines and instruments Egli had described for her. But now they had to hurry. Snow was coming again and it was growing colder. It was still day, and they had to get out of the mountains — the snow would last many days and the temperature would reach fifty below. So Oleg found himself entering the navigation room alone.

He stood for a number of minutes in the joyous company of instruments in the center of a dead ship that was the inconceivable achievement of millions of minds and thousands of years of human civilization. But Oleg felt neither terror nor hopelessness now. He knew that now the settlement, at least for him, had been turned from the center of the universe into a temporary refuge until the ship could become their true home once again, until they understood it enough to find the means to tell Earth about themselves. For this he must — the old people had told him this at least a thousand times — repair and activate the emergency beacon.

Oleg went on into the com center; the Mayor had told him where to find the hard copy study guides and manuals he would have to understand before the Mayor died, or Sergeyev — the only ones who could help him with it. So he could help those who came after him.

The Com Center was dimly lit and it took Oleg a while to search for the hard copy instructions. He pulled out the manuals; there were so many of them, and no way of telling which he would need. But he knew he'd rather part with his mother's slippers than these books. He would have been happy to bring back with him any of the separate pieces of equipment or instruments which might come in handy, but he understood these would have to wait for the next time he came here, when he could make sense of the screens and displays.

And then Oleg's attention was drawn to a weak flickering in the corner of a display, half hidden by the operator's chair. Oleg walked over to it — carefully, as though it were a wild animal.

A green fire was flashing on the display. On. Off. On. Off.

Oleg looked the display over, trying to understand why this was happening, but he couldn't. He sat down in the operator's chair and began to touch the contact points in front of him. Nothing happened either. The fire kept flickering. What did it mean? What was it? Who had started it? What did it do? Oleg's hand drifted to one of the knobs which depressed slightly and moved to the right. And then from out of a small grating right next to the fire a thin human voice reached him.

"Earth calling . . . Earth calling . . ." After that was the hiss and buzz of a crackling fire, but now there was some thought he could not comprehend in the hiss. A minute later the voice repeated: "Earth calling . . . Earth calling. . . ."

Oleg lost his sense of time. He waited, again and again, until the voice had spoken, a voice he couldn't answer but which connected him with the future, when he would.

He was returned to reality by the beeping of a wristwatch — Dick had found it in his own cabin and given it to him. The watch beeped every fifteen minutes. Perhaps such things were necessary.

Oleg got to his feet and said to the voice from Earth:
"Good bye."

And then he set off toward the ship's exit, dragging the stack of still utterly incomprehensible hard copy manuals. Dick and Marianna were already waiting for him below.

"I was ready to go after you." Dick said. "What do you want to do, stay here forever?"

"I would stay." Oleg said. "I heard a voice from Earth."

"Where?" Marianna was surprised.

"In the Com Center."

"Did you tell them we're here?"

"They're not listening. It's some sort of robot. Com isn't working; have you forgotten?"

"Maybe it's started to work now?"

"No. No it hasn't." Oleg said. "But it will."

"What do you have there?"

"They're called books." Oleg said. "I'm going to learn them."

Dick snorted skeptically.

"Dick, please Dick." Marianna begged. "I'll just run up there and back to hear the voice. Fast. We can go together?"

"And how are you going to get them all back?" Dick asked peevishly. "Don't you know how much snow there is in the pass now?"

Dick already thought of himself as their chief again. The handle of the blaster stuck out from beneath his belt; but he hadn't thrown away his cross-bow.

"I'll get them back." Oleg threw the pack down into the snow. "Go on, Marianna; go hear the voice. And I've forgotten one of the most important things as well. Did you see anything that looked like the Mayor's small microscope in the hospital? Or a box marked 'JHG-4/H Medical Lab?'"

"Yes." Marianna said. "Several."

"Too bad." Dick said. "Then I'm going with you."

***

Harnessed to the sledges the three of them dragged their load first up the hollow's sharp slope, then along the plateau, then down to the lowlands. It snowed and they stumbled. But it wasn't cold, and there was more than enough to eat. They did not throw away cans as they emptied them.

On the fourth day the canyon through which they had first climbed upward to the plateau lay before them and they suddenly heard a familiar bleating.

The gote sat under the rocky overhang by the edge of the small waterfall.

"She waited for us!" Marianna shouted.

The gote had grown so thin it appeared she might be about to die. Three tiny kids were wedged against her side trying to reach her teats.

Marianna pushed the cover on the sledge aside and started to search in the bags for something to feed the gote.

"Just don't poison her." Dick said.

The gote looked beautiful to him. He was glad she'd gotten away, nearly as much as Marianna.

"You were lucky to get away." Dick told the gote. "I'd have certainly killed you. And now we can harness you."

In fact they were unable to harness the gote. Hooting through her trunk she howled so much she shook the cliffs, and her kids joined in the racket as well in support of their mother.

So they went onward: Dick and Oleg dragging the sled, Marianna supported them from behind, keeping it from toppling, and after them came the gote and her young pestering them for food — she was always hungry. Even when they made it down into the forest and there were muzhrumes and tubers she still demanded condensed milk, although she had no more idea what this sweet white substance was called than did Dick, or Marianna, or Oleg.

CHAPTER FIVE

So far this year the first hints of the spring thaw had stretched over two weeks.

From the calendar records they had so laboriously kept, spring was actually early this year, and everyone was hoping they had seen the last of the frosts.

The settlement maintained a double calendar. One was local, determined by the passing of the days, the onset of winter and summer as the planet swung in the long orbit around its star. The second was Terrestrial, which they retained as a formality. Like a law no one obeyed.

Once upon a time, nearly twenty years ago by the terrestrial count and six years by the local, when the survivors from the *PolarStar* had reached the forest, Sergeyev had made his first cut into one of the planks stuck into the edge of one of the huts. One cut was a Terran day. Thirty or thirty-one made up the month.

Gradually the calendar was turned into a forest of notched boards and sticks. They put an awning over them to ward off the rain and snows. The notches were of different sizes and depths. Some were larger, others shorter. Beside a few were commemorative marks. Marks for a birth and marks for a death. Marks for epidemics and marks for the Great Frosts.

When Oleg was little these sticks and their marks had appeared to be alive and all knowing, remembering everything. They remembered when he studied his geography poorly or when he disappointed his mother. Once Marianna had admitted to Oleg she feared these marks too. Then Dick just laughed and said he had wanted to cut out the record of a poor geography grade but the Mayor had caught him and boxed his ears.

Sergeyev's calendar was deceptive, and they all knew it. It lied twice over. First and foremost the days here on this world were two hours longer than those of Earth. Secondly because there were more than a thousand such days in a local year. A short summer, a long rainy fall, four hundred days of winter and cold, and an equally long spring. The torturous arithmetic had become a watershed between the older generation who remembered the ship and other worlds and their children. The Mayor and other adults pretended they believed the marks beneath the awning really did provide a count of the local years. The younger people accepted the local year for what it was. Otherwise, how else would you deal with a fall that lasted an entire year, and winter was a year as well . . .

So the thaw this year had stretched out over two weeks. The bands of snow along the ground grew narrower, vanished first in the clearings, then under the trees. The side of the graveyard hill that faced the village became wild, overrun and overgrown with the young tendrils of lichen in the belief spring had, at last, come. The settlement's only street melted into a single, long, mud puddle.

Beyond the rows of houses the band of mud split in two — the narrower end finished at the palisade gate, the wider ran to the workshop and barn. To the right of the workshop, before the new gote shed, an enormous green puddle had formed. In the morning the young gotes smashed the ice surface with their sharp claws and wallowed, hunting for wyrms. Then the kids started to play, howling, splashing gouts of slime everywhere, leaping into the mud, kicking and whirling with their feet — they too were welcoming the first breath of spring. Only the gote everyone just called Gote, the family matriarch, truly understood true spring still had yet to put in an appearance. She hung around outside the workshop, in the warmth that seeped through the slats in the walls, but from time to time she grew fed up with waiting and rose up on her hind legs, and then rubbed her shell against the walls of the building. Oleg would run outside and chase Gote away with a stick. On seeing Oleg come out, Gote rose, pranced about, coquettishly waved her forelegs over Oleg and bleated with joy. She was convinced she had delighted Oleg with her presence — why else would he strike her so delightfully with his stick?

Then Oleg would call Sergeyev to help him. The gote tumbled down and rolled over on her side on seeing him. "It is time, madam, for you to return to your maternal duties. You are neglecting your children." Sergeyev growled and threatened.

The gote was in no hurry to depart but slowly showed her enormous green rear. Her children remained neglected, however, for she made her way to the palisade walls and planted herself there, hoping her latest inamorata, a male three meters high at the shoulders, decorated with sharp bony plates, would show himself.

From time to time the male would appear at the edge of the woods and call Gote to come and accompany him on a stroll. Out of fear of the people he never came any closer to the walls. Gote would run to the gates and, if there was no one there, open the bolt herself and vanish for several days. From these amorous encounters she had thrice delivered litters and there were seven young gotes of various ages living in the corral.

So far the herd of gotes had been of little practical utility, but the gotes had become a part of the people's everyday life, proof of the vitality of the settlement, entertainment for the children who rode on their backs despite the evident displeasure of the animals and the propensity of the rides to end in inflicted bruises. In the final analysis the gotes could always be killed and eaten — the hunters certainly brought back wild gotes. In the middle of winter, when their food stocks had been at their lowest, Dick had offered to do the butchery himself. But Marianna had objected, and the Mayor supported her. Dick shrugged his shoulders, preferring not to have to argue, and went off into the forest in the middle of a snow storm. He returned late in the evening with the tips of his fingers of his left hand frost bitten, but with a medium sized baer over his shoulder.

Gote's continued existence and presence did offer one enormous benefit. She had turned out to be a valuable watchman. And she was teaching her young to guard the settlement as well. The moment anything strange approached the walls Gote's family raised such a ruckus that the entire settlement was awakened. True, then, if the gote determined the danger was serious she rushed to the first available house to hide herself. There she succeeded in overturning anything not nailed down and smashing all the clay pots and pans.

Gote, an even tempered and social creature, hated only Spytter. Most likely she had encountered his kind in the past. She would not permit herself to get close to the claws, but from a deferential distance she waited, stamping her six feet, threatening and shaking her enormous bony comb, bleating and demanding the settlement rid itself of such a disgusting inhabitant.

Kazik, one of Luiza's adopted children, had been first encounter Spytter.

In the spring, shortly after Oleg, Marianna, and Dick had returned from the mountains where the *PolarStar* had crashed, Kazik and Dick had gone on a long hunt, more than twenty kilometers to the south of the settlement, where the herds of muzdangs flocked in the fall.

Muzdang meat was inedible, even the zhakals would leave them alone, but muzdangs possessed a remarkable air bladder. The animals inflated them when they had to flee from predators. Then the muzdangs changed from a lean, sinewy, somewhat horse-like insect into a brilliant hydrogen-filled sphere and rose into the air. Their aerial bladders were elastic and strong and Sergeyev turned them into window panes, bags for water, and grain, and many other useful items. And the girls in the settlement played at fashion, inflating light cloaks and running about in them like butterflies.

Dick and Kazik had left the settlement at dawn. They encountered nothing interesting or remarkable in the forest. In those days the memory of the trip to the mountain pass cast shadows over everything, and therefore the normally taciturn Kazik was beside himself with curiosity and pestered Dick with questions.

That spring Kazik had turned thirteen, although to the adults he looked to be no more than ten. He was small and wiry, his dark skin covered in blue scars from willowwasps, his hands gnarled and horny, a long diagonal scar on his forehead. Kazik was at home in the forest, so much they had nicknamed him Mowgli.

Kazik kept up with the older boy easily, without making another sound, not even bothering to look twice where he was going, jumping over living roots, sometimes he bent down for cover and clasped with a quick motion of his hand a sweet muzhrume, and popped it into his mouth without stopping, sometimes he'd barge off to the side to sniff at a trail, but he immediately returned to the next question.

"It's all made out of metal."

"From composite compounds." That was easier to say than "The starship used to be as much energy as matter," which would have been more precise, but Dick didn't quite understand all of it himself.

"And it's bigger than the settlement?"

"Than the palisade. A lot bigger."

"And it's round?"

"Mowgli, you already asked that."

Dick disliked speaking in the forest; you could be heard too far off when you had to be listening for sounds indicating danger or food. This information never bothered Kazik; he could hear better than any of the animals.

If the other children were able to roam about the forest, and knew how to hide themselves from predators in the soft rootmass of the white payns if forced to spend the night away from the village, Mowgli could live in the forests for weeks. It was as though Kazik owned it. And the boy knew everything. The trees obediently withdrew their leaves from his path, the muzhrumes darted back underground, the hunting vynes lifted their tails and ran. Even the zhakals feared his scent. Mowgli never bothered with a cross-bow in the forest; he could he could pin a fly to a branch from the distance of fifteen meters with his knife.

"So I'll ask you again." Kazik answered right back. "It's fun asking questions. Will you take me with you to the *PolarStar* next summer?"

"Definitely. So long as you behave yourself."

Kazik snorted. He bobbed his head in mock obedience.

"I want to fly to the stars." Kazik said. "The stars are bigger than our forest, bigger than all the world. You know where I'm going when we return to Earth? I'm going to India."

"Why?" Dick was surprised.

"'Cause . . ." Kazik was suddenly taken aback. It wasn't something he had ever put into words inside his own head. "I just want to."

For a while both of them were silent.

"I'd rather stay here." Dick said suddenly. He had never spoken about it to anyone else before.

Kazik was silent. Suddenly he ran to one side, jumped on a low, horizontal branch of wood, grabbed for a cluster of squirming nuts and plunked them into his bag.

"We'll cook it in the evening." Kazik said, jumping back down to the ground.

Dick was annoyed. He was displeased with himself. He should have seen that cluster first. Dick had long ago come to view the forest as a field of battle; the forest hid dangers to be overcome, or avoided, as well as booty to be taken, predators and deadly monsters which had to be outwitted or killed or they would kill you. Kazik viewed the forest as a home, perhaps, just a bigger home than the settlement, because the existence of the settlement was alien to this world, and the forest grudgingly accepted them only because the people had proven themselves wilier and more dangerous. Kazik understood the forest and had no fear of it. He was not fighting an enemy. If he was stronger, he gave chase. And he avoided what might eat him. But in general he felt no special love for the forest, for the same reason he experienced no such feelings for the air or water. All his dreams, thoughts, hopes were connected with the world that lived on only in the adults' stories, in the memories of Luiza and the Mayor. That world — the realm of stars and starships, space stations and the Earth — he knew in detail better than any of the settlement's other children, although no one in the settlement had ever guessed it. Kazik had listened to everything the Mayor had ever said about the Earth and he remembered everything. It was waiting for him.

He knew the height of Everest and the principal dates in the life of Alexander the Great, the atomic weights of all the elements and the height of Brahmaputra. His small head was packed with figures and information that had not the slightest connection with the settlement and this permanently clouded, twilit world. History had captivated him; the numberless generations which had each lived, fought, built, one after the other, on the Earth. Billions of people and millions of events connected by a complex network of relationships, had turned the forest and the settlement into some sort of abstraction, much like a boring dream, which simply had to be endured. "I'd spend a year going to museums." He told himself. "The Hermitage. The British Museum. The Prado. The Pergamon. . . ." He'd never mentioned this to anyone. What reason for it?

When Marianna and Dick had gone off with Oleg and Thomas Hind to the mountain pass Kazik had dreamed of going with them and had followed them every step of the way with his thoughts. And long before they had returned he had stopped eating or sleeping — he had been listening for their return. He had even met the survivors some ten kilometers from the settlement while they were dragging their home made sledges loaded down with the treasures of the ship over muddy ground.

Kazik had exhausted each of them with detailed questions of what they had seen in the ship. He knew he would have to wait for next year before he could go to the *PolarStar* himself and the three years wait did not seem so long. Winter would pass as it always did, Oleg and Sergeyev would figure out how to fix the com system, they would build a radio, and then Earth would send a rescue ship.

When it became dark — and it became dark early, at the hour they called four o'clock for convenience sake — Dick and Kazik holed up for the night in a thicket of stinkweed. The forest animals avoided the stands, but if they had to find a bolt hole for the night they could get used to the stench.

The next morning Dick and Kazik found a herd of muzdangs, crept up to them from downwind, and selectively brought down a few of the older males. Dick shot with his crossbow; the blaster they had taken from the ship was in his belt but he didn't use it. The charge was to be saved. Kazik killed only one muzdang. His job was to send the animals toward Dick. He killed it, throwing the knife Sergeyev had forged for him. Sergeyev had made knives for each and every one of them out of the metal steps they had brought back from the *PolarStar*.

Dick stripped to skin the muzdangs, cutting off the bladders without damaging them. The work turned him into a bloody mess and he did it alone. Not wanting to waste time, Kazik headed down along the edge of the stream looking for snayls. They turned the shells into useful scrapers and saucers — the settlement's women would thank him for any he brought back.

Kazik got about three hundred meters. He was thinking of the marvels of India where Luiza had lived as a child; he had come up to the gates of a city with the fairy-tale name of Hyderabad, and suddenly he heard a splash, something flashed in front of his eyes, and the next moment Kazik realized he was standing in the middle of a small pond which, only a moment before, had not been there.

The pond was completely round, about three meters in diameter and about two or three centimeters deep, no more — grass and pebbles stuck out of its surface. It was completely flat and smooth and reflected a sky stretched with violet clouds. As though an enormous droplet had fallen directly on him.

Kazik froze. Like any denizen of the forest he did not like anything strange.

The forest was alerted to danger and grew silent. Kazik wanted to retreat and carefully began to lift his feet. But the liquid held onto the thick fish hide of his boots, as he watched the substance grew stronger and more glassy.

Kazik finally became alarmed and whistled, calling Dick for help. He didn't realize how far he had gone or that Dick could not hear him. Then the boy froze again, *Think!* What to do?

As he did the thick wall of leaves shook and parted and a creature similar to a carapace-less crab with a long, thin proboscis fixed in the front of the head crawled out of the woods. The creature was unfamiliar, and nameless, but it exuded menace. *Spydeure.* Kazik thought. *That's what Thomas Hind would have called it.*

On either side of the proboscis, lower than the unthinking olivine eyes, the spydeure had openings covered with membranes. The membranes scarcely fluttered, and Kazik intuitively understood where the danger he faced lay. So when the membranes opened and two streams of sticky yellow liquid shot from the holes, Kazik was ready; although his feet were immobilized in the hardened puddle he moved to one side and ducked. The liquid struck the puddle and splashed over it, like water over ice.

The critter was very annoyed at missing the boy. It was used to prey behaving in dependable, predictable ways. The critter turned its head, raised its proboscis to the sky, stamped its thin, fragile legs, and howled in rage.

Kazik even laughed, having seen how the critter closed membranes over the openings and started to puff, exerting itself, then it opened the membranes again, but all that shot out were two tiny spurts.

The critter sat back on its hind legs — evidently it was prepared to wait and think, if that was something it was capable of doing. It was clear that if Kazik were going to get out of this trap he would have to do it himself. As the glue dried it gripped his feet all the tighter. It was clear to Kazik he would have to abandon his boots.

Kazik started to ease his feet out of the leather. He would have to jump to the side, a distance of a meter and a half, without touching the glue with the bare soles of his feet. Watching Kazik, the creature started to become excited again. It touched the edge of the glue with the claws of its fore legs and realized its discharge still hadn't dried out and it could not take the prey with its bare legs, it began, slowly and unsteadily to touch the glue trap with its feet, searching for dry spots from which it could reach out to Kazik with its proboscis.

Kazik made a leap toward the side of the trap away from the critter, trying to land on his hands and pulling up his legs. He almost made it, but the bare heel of his right leg touched the edge of the glue puddle and stuck; there was a sharp pain. Pulling at his leg Kazik screamed so loud he thought he should have been heard in the settlement. The critter, realizing finally its fly had fled, hurried toward the boy.

Bending down, Kazik pulled his knife out of its sheath and waited a moment before throwing it. *Get myself free first!* he thought. And the knife might not do the critter any harm.

Kazik hurriedly tried to slash at the surface of the layer of glue, but his knife just slid uselessly over its surface. The proboscis was almost on him; the boy slashed about his feet, waved his arms and raised the knife to ward off the proboscis which was so close he could catch the cold, bitter, smell. . . .

Then Dick shot the critter with the blaster.

Dick hadn't heard Kazik's earlier whistle, but he heard the cry for help and came running, terrified something had happened to the boy. He shot until the predator's fragile body was a black, smoking pile of ash and the legs scattered like branches knocked from a log. The air stank of ozone.

Kazik looked at surprise at the calcined critter's remains and said:

"Why'd you do that. You'll drain the charge."

Kazik had never seen the pistol used before; it had always been too important to hold it in reserve.

"Idiot." Dick said. "It would have sucked you dry for supper.

Weren't you looking where you were going? Or were you already in India.... ?"

Kazik shut up. He had pulled his heel away from the glue, leaving skin behind. His foot was bleeding. He reached for the small bag with balm.

"I've lost my boots."

Dick covered the boy's foot with medicine and bandaged it with leaves and a piece of cloth, and carried Kazik back to the settlement on his shoulders. The boy was heavy, and Dick was bringing back the bag filled with the muzdang's flotation bladders as well. Kazik was silent, although his foot hurt, and for two weeks thereafter he had to hobble about on one foot.

But in the end, Kazik's adventure proved to be the impetus for the great undertaking. Kazik fired the first shot while he was sitting on a stool and watching his foster mother sew him another set of boots. Earlier in the morning Vaitkus had brought pieces he had cut from a fish hide, and the enormous Luiza was stitching the pieces together. The labor was in fact primitive. Although Marianna had brought real needles from the *PolarStar*, she had been unable to find actual thread, so as before they were using the dried stems of water plants thick enough to serve but rather too short for the work. As always Luiza grumbled; she hated sewing — it simply took too much time that could be spent on other necessary tasks. Kazik was looking at her, then he said.

"As soon as I get better I'm going to the forest to bring you back one of those spydeures."

The woman stopped and looked up at him. "Whatever for?"

"For sewing."

"What are you talking about?" She turned her eyes back to her work.

"You don't understand." Kazik said. "Not for sewing, for gluing."

Luiza paid no attention to what Kazik said, but the boy was insistent. As soon as he could get up from the bed he attached himself to the Mayor and acquired an extra net from him. The

Mayor went fishing with nets in the small lakes on the other side of the swamp. The nets were often torn and the Mayor, who considered mending nets the idea tranquilizer and therefore had accumulated a large number of them selected the largest and strongest and even agreed to participate in the expedition to go in search of the critter.

Later, Kazik, Kazik's foster sister Fumiko, and Vaitkus's oldest son Patrick, set off on their quest. At the last moment Dick insisted on coming to prevent them all from killing themselves.

They spent three days in the underbrush until they finally came across one of the glue spitting critters. Dick tormented it, running forward to get its attention and then darted out of the way of the stream of spit and the creature soon emptied itself of its store of glue. After that it was easy to net it and lug it back to the settlement. Their chief worry was not to damage any of the legs.

They installed the creature in a cage and fed it worms and snayls. Soon the critter's mood brightened, it covered the inside of its cage with a thick web of netting and felt at home. The critter was dull witted and sluggish, and no one gave a second thought to its repulsive appearance — the people in the settlement were used to monsters and worse.

They called the creature Spytter. It turned out the names spydeure and grabbe had already been awarded to other creatures.

The Mayor had noted the gradual changes in the terrans' language as they adapted themselves to their new environment long before. The font of words the children exhibited was but a small fraction of that utilized by the adults, so much of the remaining world was nameless. Therefore their language had inevitably become the poorer, despite the Mayor's insistence in school that his students memorize by heart poems he recited to them, or if he didn't remember the poem he summoned the other adults together and they cobbled the forgotten texts together.

"Kids on Earth have it easy." The Mayor said. "Their parents just enroll them in learning centers and what they don't learn there they pick up the street, from the 3V, or books. An earth child is logged onto the net and awash with information he doesn't even realize he's getting. And what do we have? Half a dozen adults who keep trying to remember just a few thousand words between them."

Oleg found himself disagreeing with the Mayor. In his view, the younger generation's language was hardly impoverished. The language had simply changed. The children had been forced to find words for new experiences and things unknown or just uninteresting to the adults. They had been forced not merely to think up new words themselves, but to impress meanings onto old words. Once, through the partition separating their room from the Mayor's, Oleg had heard six year old Nick Vaitkus explaining to the Mayor why he had been late for school.

"I took three burries on a stamp." He said. "About a nail deeper than Arnis did."

"Go sit down." The Mayor answered, pretending to have understood.

In fact he had not. But the meaning of the phrase was clear to Oleg. You could even use it to explain just how much the village's children knew about their world, about which the Mayor had only a vague understanding.

Sometime during the past summer certain bearies had fallen on the abballs that grew beside the palisade. These bearies were in fact sluggish red grubs which hung on the branches casually working their ways into the bark. Vaitkus had tried to get rid of them, drenching the trees with everything from acid to diluted zhakal venom, but nothing had altered their health or slowed their activity. And then one fine day the slugs vanished. The adults had noticed nothing, although Vaitkus had sighed in relief — the enormous, sweet fruits hanging from the trees were the source of much of their winter vitamins, but the bearies had changed into bluish sharp thorns, which dug into the earth just outside the palisade to wait out the winter. The children had called these thorns 'burries;' the adults could see no genetic relationship between the bearies and the burries. The buried thorns were if anything more active than in their tree dwelling stage; if a warm blooded animal passed by the area outside the fence the thorns worked their way out of the ground, and made for the animal's hide to plant their spores, which dissolved in human blood and were therefore considered harmless by the adults. But the prick of the thorn was painful, and carried the risk of infection.

The children devised a game. They took off their sandals, the soles stitched from the hard and pliable shells of forest cokernuts and which the children all called spoons, and teased the thorns. The thorns thrust themselves at the warm shoes and stuck in them. The winner was the child who gathered the most thorns and whose thorns had dug the deepest into the sole. The game was fun, but certainly not without dangers; the thorn might penetrate a hand. As a result, Nick's curious phrase indicated only he had been playing the game with Arnis and had won.

It was Oleg's mother Irina who came up with the name of Spytter and everyone soon accepted it. There was only one minor disparity — the adults called the creature's glue, glue; the children called it spit.

Spytter's appearance in fact improved everyday life, especially when Vaitkus noticed Spytter's glue would harden more slowly if it was mixed with a saliva which the animal also shot out from its proboscis. Sergeyev soon figured out he could repair broken ceramic dishes and pots on his carpenter's table using the dried glue, and if colored clays taken from the swamp were added to the glue and the glue to the pottery the colors stayed lacquered to the dishes.

During the winter Spytter hibernated and ate virtually nothing, and produced almost no glue. Before that, however, Vaitkus had stored a supply in sealed containers. With the arrival of the spring Spytter awakened from his slumbers and began to dance about his cage and to spit on everything whether they wanted him to or not.

***

The endless thaw brought with it runny noses, colds, bronchitis, and worsening rheumatism. Oleg's mother lay in bed with arthritis, and Oleg had to fix their meals himself.

Oleg had already convinced himself medicines operated selectively. Those who believed in their effectiveness grew well, those who disbelieved continued to be sick. In fact he based his conclusions without reference to the real medicines which he had helped bring back from the ship. But those medicines were for the real sicknesses, the ones that had killed so many in years past — infections, blood parasites, inflamed lungs. The medicines from the ship were few, and Egli Vaitkus guarded them, locking them away in a special chest.

Oleg's mother had a whole store of every kind of dried herb and preparation filling small boxes and containers. At that moment, although Oleg was very cold, the first order of the day was to warm water and pour it into a thick mixture to prepare a lotion. The hut was practically lightless, only the clay pot burned faint red on the small flame, and Oleg's mother lay under a pile of skins. She said.

"You're here finally. I was waiting. I was waiting all day. All I can do is just sit here in pain. I thought you could have come earlier."

"I'm here now, Mother." Oleg said. "It's ready now; I'll rub it on you."

"No, you go eat." His mother answered. "You're the one the settlement needs; everyone depends on you. And you're getting too pale and thin. I can wait; don't you bother. All that's wrong with me is arthritis. No one's ever died from arthritis."

On the other side of the hanging curtain the Mayor started coughing. The Mayor could have moved out of the hut long ago; they could have built a new one or the Mayor could have taken the empty house opposite the Vaitkuses, but they had gotten used to living together. The Mayor, Irina and Oleg were not one family, but they often ate together, and when the Mayor and Irina were alone they spoke for long times. The Mayor had become very voluble; he was chattering constantly now; it had become difficult for him to stay silent. Perhaps that was why he had begun the school, because he loved to talk so much. And Oleg's mother was sick and angry at life in general. All she had left was her fear for her son's safety, that he might be injured, fall sick, or vanish unheralded in the forest. Oleg would soon be twenty; he was a grown man. He spent whole days with Sergeyev in the workshop where they made things the settlement needed. The rest of the time he spent studying the hard copy manuals they had brought back from the *PolarStar*. The two of them had but one idea — fix the communications system so the *PolarStar* could signal Earth that people were still alive here. The settlement had lived two decades on the hope of returning someday to Earth, but before now hope had been timid and abstract. Now it had a chance of becoming reality. Oleg's mother kept saying over and over again:

"If the specialists and engineers who survived the crash could not fix the subspace radio then what can a boy and an old cripple accomplish?"

In fact she was terrified Oleg would have to go to the mountain pass where the starship had crashed for a second time. Her son had escaped from there once already; she knew he would not return a second time. But was it really better to live out his life in this stinking mass of hovels among crippled adults and stunted children while outside the monsters howled and rattled at the gates? No, she did not know what was worse, everything was worse.

Oleg brought the box of ointment; despite everything he was a good kid, really the best in the settlement. He had shot up over the course of the last winter and was now fully grown; his father would have been proud she had raised such a son.

Oleg applied the ointment and rubbed his mother's back. The touch of the burning liquid was pleasant, because the heat meant there was still life in her. Her body still lived and felt, and her son had hard warm palms and fingers and he was able to massage her back. He had done it as frequently as possible over the last year; it was a great joy there were such hands willing to grasp your old and very tired flesh and knead new life into it. Irina quietly cried from the unexpected pleasure.

From the other side of the partition the Mayor's voice reached them:

"Want some help, Oleg?"

"No, thanks." Oleg answered. "Come on over. I've warmed the soup; we can have supper."

"Thank you, I'm full." The Mayor answered, and Irina laughed through her tears because she had heard him — she had sensitive hearing and each sound spelt out every motion the Mayor took as he prepared to cross from his section of the hut into theirs; he washed his dishes, then started to get dressed. The Mayor treasured the idea of going into someone else's territory as an actual guest and approached the action with all due formality, even if it was only going from one room to another.

The three of them sat at the table; Irina became better because she had improved her mood. She believed in the value of a burning hot broth and therefore it helped her. The Mayor brought fried nuts for the soup; he had picked them himself and cooked them on the brazier. He had put on his new jacket; it had only one sleeve. Oleg was sometimes astonished someone could manage to do so well with only one hand.

"When you go to the ship the next time you'll have to bring back far more paper." The old man said, watching Oleg ladle the soup into their bowls. "It was a tragedy you brought back so little paper."

"I know." Oleg had heard about it many times before.

"When we had absolutely no paper at all we survived quite well without it." The Mayor continued to speak. "I'm afraid it went in a . . . a feeding frenzy, and it's all my fault. I even gave each of the children a sheet to write compositions; can you blame me?"

"Certainly not." Irina said. "It was perfectly understandable."

"And Linda Hind wrote that long poem about Thomas." Oleg said.

"People are used to confiding their thoughts to paper; that's why microtapes and videochips never entirely replaced it. Back on Earth I have a whole library of real books, something that would evoke surprise in no one. So you will simply have to bring back far more paper next time. The strength of a white sheet where someone can confide his thoughts or the images overcoming him is unbelievable. We'll have to find something else for teaching the children."

"We still have to make it through to the end of summer." Oleg's mother said. She was sitting up straight, tense, not moving; if she sat otherwise she knew she would feel the pain. "It astonishes me how all of you grown ups are now running to Oleg saying 'Don't forget to bring this back, or that . . . '"

"If I could get to the ship I'd recognize what had to be brought back far better than Oleg." The Mayor said. "I have the experience."

"And all I had to go on was intuition and guesswork." Oleg said lazily.

The hot soup made him drowse. Today they had finished hammering out the metallic parts for the mill so as to be ready to place it in the stream once the ice was finally gone. Then they put Oleg to studying electronics again, and just before dozing off he had managed to finish reading the paragraphs in the textbook, and in the morning before work Sergeyev would question him on them.

"The next time we'll bring back a whole treasure hoard." Oleg said. "I couldn't believe everything would vanish so fast."

"It didn't vanish. It was simply put to use." The Mayor said.

"And almost half of it went to Egli and Sergeyev." Oleg's mother said. Oleg couldn't tell if his mother was pleased or blaming Egli and Sergeyev.

"Of course." The boy answered. "Sergeyev needed most of it in the workshop and Egli has to keep track of the medicines."

"I even gave her the microscope." The Mayor sighed. He was quite proud of his sacrifice.

In the settlement, of necessity, everything was held in common, otherwise they would never have survived. But there were still private things; Marianna had her mirror, the Mayor his microscope, Oleg's mother the copy of *Anna Karenina*. Not to mention clothing or hand tools. This sometimes led to incidents.

Marianna had the only mirror.

Oleg had found a round pocket mirror on the ship and had given it to Marianna on the way back. The existence of the mirror had produced a profound effect on the life of the settlement. Before it arrived people hadn't had a chance to see themselves as others had seen them, other than in mud puddles and in window panes. But the mirror told people the often all too painful truth. Certainly the adults remembered themselves from the time when there had been many mirrors. And they were astonished at how much they had changed, grown old, and knew their youth had faded. The young people had never had a chance to see themselves before, and now, suddenly, they had been forced to, as it were, establish relations with themselves.

Marianna's opinion of herself had changed for the worse. When she saw her bony, weather-beaten face with hollow cheeks, her sharp chin and cracked lips in the mirror, all covered over with the tiny scars of willowwasps, she knew at once she was monstrously deformed and no one could ever do anything to restore her beauty. She didn't even notice her large grey eyes, her long black lashes, the ragged cut of her thick straight hair.

Liz, on the other hand, had seen her reflection and decided she was a beauty on a par with Anna Karenina. She started to put on airs and even blackened her eyelashes with ash to make herself more beautiful.

Then Liz stole Marianna's mirror. The other girl simply could not live without it. Marianna had given the mirror around — there were a lot of people who wanted to look at themselves — and Liz said the mirror was lost. Everyone was very annoyed, but several days later Kristina, although blind, figured out from the sounds that Liz was looking at herself in the mirror. She started to strike

Liz with her dry fist and cry in shame that Liz could be so deceitful, and she forced Liz to return the mirror to Marianna and own up to everything.

Liz returned the mirror and said she had found it in the crevice behind the bed. On the next day Kristina was sitting on her porch and recognized Marianna's footsteps passing by.

"Liz returned the mirror to you, didn't she?"

"Yes, thank you."

"She did tell you she didn't want to give it back?"

After a short pause Marianna said,

"Yes, she did."

Kristina understood Liz had said nothing. But no one spoke about the matter again.

Oleg distributed the brew to everyone, and he brought out sweet syrup; this year the syrup was especially tasty; Vaitkus had added abbals to the mix of preserves.

"I'm hoping we'll be able to make contact." Oleg said. "And then we won't have to lug more things back from the ship. I really don't want to have to drag another sled over the mountain pass if we don't have to."

"We'll have to be prepared for both alternatives." The Mayor said. "Obviously, they'll find us sooner or later. But we'll have to assume the worst and be prepared for it. "

"We've always been prepared for the worst." Irina said. "The worst never ends."

"Don't make promises you can't keep." The Mayor laughed dryly.

"Too bad the flitter was damaged." Oleg said. "But the landsled vehicle would never make it over the mountains even if we could have gotten it out of the ship. I was thinking if we can't fix the subspace radio Sergeyev and I might try to repair the flitter."

"That would be fine." The Mayor said. "But it would demand several trips to the ship."

"Maybe, maybe not." Oleg said. "Sergeyev and I have been

discussing it. Two or three people could remain on the ship through the winter."

"No way." Oleg's mother cut in. "I'll never allow it."

"Because there'll be light and heat. . . ."

"The temperature in the mountain pass drops to sixty degrees below zero during the winter." The Mayor said. "Don't waste your time with empty dreams. I have very specific desires. A lot of paper, that's all."

"If we had some means of transport. . . ." Oleg ladled out syrup onto the mixture. "Even a small flitter . . ."

"Before we learn to fly we're going to have to learn to walk," The Mayor answered seriously, "or at least invent the wheel first."

"We really don't have any need for wheels." Oleg answered. "There are no roads in the forest. Of course if there were two settlements. . . ."

"We already have the wheel, and we have a cart." The Mayor said. "Now you want it steam driven. . . ."

"Sergeyev and I will make a cauldron." Oleg said. "We've already figured out how to do it. From glue."

"And after the steam cauldron comes the aerial balloon." The Mayor laughed.

"And why not a balloon? I've actually considered it a number of times. What's wrong with a balloon?" Oleg asked.

"You are speaking from imagination and ignorance. You have never been involved in the construction of a balloon." The Mayor said. "Even to displace enough air to be able to lift but a single person the bag of the balloon would have to be enormous."

"How enormous?"

"At least thirty meters high. I can do the calculations. And the balloon would have to be filled with helium or hydrogen. Where would you get it?"

"You yourself told me how the Mongol brothers. . . ."

"Mon-gol-fi-er. With a silent letter, t."

"The Montgolfier brothers flew over Paris in a balloon filled with nothing but hot air."

Oleg went over to the stove and threw some grease onto the fire. Fire flared and shot sparks into the air.

"They had a special burner. And fuel."

"What kind?" Oleg asked.

"Whatever it was, it wasn't wood."

"I'm going to lay down." His mother said. "Help me, Oleg."

The Mayor went over to Irina and helped her to the bed, then covered her with the blankets

"We can work on the fuel." Oleg said, looking at the fire. "And we can make a burner."

"Have you thought this through seriously?"

"Completely." Oleg said. "If we can get up to the mountain pass in a balloon we'll save on time, and our strength. If . . . But perhaps we'll get down as well. Or make two balloons, or three. One for people, the other for cargo."

"Stop that nonsense!" Irina had become frightened. "It will simply drift on the wind and crash."

"Don't be afraid, Irina, it's only a dream." The Mayor said.

"We'll do it." Oleg said. He turned and hurried from the hut. His mother's "Put on your coat!" drifted after him but he did not hear her.

The street outside had grown cold. Snow had fallen, wet and thick. A fine spray splattered the puddles and rolled along the slippery ground. A wind was rising, from the north and the mountains.

It had grown dark just a moment before; twilight flickered through the chinks in the gate. The lantern rocked back and forth, light falling on Gote's erect comb, shiny and wet. Oleg could make out Gote's indistinct form by the gate; she was waiting for her cavalier.

Oleg jumped over a puddle and cut across the road toward Sergeyev's hut. A small lamp's weak light broke through the muzdang bladder stretched tightly across the window.

Oleg knocked and went in immediately, quickly shutting the door behind him to keep in the warmth.

"Pardon me, Sergeyev." Oleg said without preamble. "I have an idea."

Sergeyev was sitting at the table, drinking the tea they made from boiling some of the crushed, wild grasses. Opposite him at the table sat Linda Hind, Thomas's widow. Marianna stood mysterious at the corner of the room in the half darkness.

"Sit down."

Linda nodded in greeting, although she must have seen Oleg at least five times that day already, all the more so as it was Linda who brought Sergeyev his lunch in the workshop. She was seeing Sergeyev all the more frequently recently, and this surprised no one. Everyone expected Linda would soon move in with Sergeyev. Oleg's mother even said the faster the better — Linda was quite unbearable without her husband, there were two children — Irina had long experience with feminine loneliness

"I've decided to build an aerial balloon." Oleg said.

"Why?" Sergeyev asked.

Sergeyev was the strongest and most useful of the men in the village, the most Alpha male of their small human pack. "Still strong, and relatively hale." Oleg's mother said. He was missing two fingers on his right hand. He resembled his daughter Marianna only in the eyes — both had long gray eyelashes that caught the light and made you notice them. But Sergeyev's face was blocky, heavy, and certainly far from pretty if you looked on him for the first time. But his face bore a stamp of competence, and he could be trusted. Earlier the Mayor had been Oleg's idol, the one who knew everything, who was the Teacher. But after the return from the starship in the mountain pass Oleg found himself going to Sergeyev again and again. He was not a teacher, but he was a craftsman, and what Oleg had to learn Sergeyev knew.

"We can construct a large aerial balloon." Oleg said. "And fly to the ship in it. You understand."

"Well sit down anyway. Marianna, make our guest some tea."

"I've had some already, thank you." Oleg said. But he sat down.

Linda got to her feet and said it was time for her to leave, or else the children would never go to sleep.

To Oleg it always appeared that Linda was cold to him, after all, it was because of him her husband had died in the mountains. And there was no way she could forgive him for that loss. Oleg wanted to go to her and say it wasn't his fault, that he remembered absolutely nothing, that a snow flee had bitten him. But the boy had never been able to make himself go to the woman and speak what was in his heart. She had turned grey overnight when she heard of Thomas's death.

Sergeyev followed after Linda with his eyes. Marianna's eyes followed the woman as well, and Oleg imagined Marianna did not want Linda to take the place of the mother Marianna had lost long ago, although everyone knew Linda was quiet and good.

"Continue." Sergeyev's words cut through Oleg's musings.

"If we make a large aerial balloon and wait until we have the right wind we can fly right up to the mountains, perhaps even fly to the *PolarStar* itself. You can imagine the time and energy it will save."

"Certainly." Sergeyev said. He never argued until he could solve the problem himself. "A large aerial balloon. And if we can catch a wind going the other way, then we can make the return to the lowlands in it as well."

"We could make the flight to the starship in it five times. You understand, five times!"

Sergeyev whistled, or laughed, or did both as though coughing.

"You're certain, five?"

"I'm certain." Oleg was already convinced he had found an ally, that, for all practical intents and purposes, they were already airborne.

"You don't mind if I think aloud, do you?" Sergeyev asked.

Oleg wanted to answer: *Don't. Everything is going to come crashing down in flames.* Sergeyev was not the Mayor to criticize in general terms; Sergeyev would find the weak points in his plan for real.

"If we do construct an aerial balloon," Sergeyev said, "and it does fly, that would be very useful. However, first of all aerial balloons cannot be directed. Let us suppose we do get it aloft, the wind is favorable, and we head toward the mountains. Then the wind changes, and carries us toward the glacier covered heights where none of us has ever been before. We will either crash and be killed or land, but then we will be unable to find our way back home. How can we compel the winds to carry us to precisely the valley we want?"

Oleg was glancing at Marianna. She had pushed a cup of tea in his direction. Marianna was supporting him.

Oleg suddenly felt he was sitting down at one of the Mayor's exams. Over the past year the Mayor had scheduled exams for him, Marianna, and Dick, because they were finally grown and finished with school. The exams had even been made the centerpiece of a declared public holiday, where everyone, even the smallest children, had gathered under the awning that covered the calender posts to watch. The Mayor had asked them questions, as had Vaitkus and Luiza, the other members of the Board of Education.

Oleg had thought the questions inflicted upon him had been noticeably harder than those inflicted upon Marianna and Dick, and he had been somewhat annoyed at the Mayor for the apparent unfairness of it all — and then he had understood the reasons behind it; the Mayor had prepared questions he had expected each of them should be able to answer. Oleg felt now the same as he had felt then; that he was on a hunt facing down a zhakal, and all his thoughts were clear and precise.

"If the wind changes unexpectedly, then we'll have to provide some means for the balloon to deflate and descend rapidly." Oleg answered quickly. "That way it won't be able to carry us far off. We'll simply land en route and continue further on foot or wait for the right wind."

"Reasonable." Sergeyev nodded his head. "Assuming, of course, we manage to land on level ground and not on a sheer rock face or the top of a peak."

"We would only have to make it to the plateau." Oleg said. "That's where the cliffs end. The ground is fairly level."

"Will you take me with you?" Marianna asked, looking at Oleg steadily.

"I don't know." Oleg said.

"A second aspect to the problem, of course, is *how* are we to make the balloon." Sergeyev said. "I certainly don't know how."

"I don't either. We'll think of something."

"It will have to be large. Enormous. Where are we going to find such material."

"But what if we tie together lots of muzdang bladders?" Marianna asked. "Would a bunch of them work as an aerial balloon? Like a bunch of grapes."

"No." Her father said. "The balloons will remain on the ground. The muzdangs fill their bladders with hydrogen they generate rapidly from their own bodies; how they get into the air."

"Right." Oleg agreed. "That means we'll have to take a great many muzdang bladders and fit them together into one enormous balloon."

"With thread?"

"With glue." Oleg said. "We have Spytter."

"Okay." Sergeyev agreed. "We'll work on this proposal first. But how are we going to suspend the gondola?"

"The what?" Oleg had never heard the word before.

"The cab, the bucket where the people will sit."

"How did they do it on Earth?" Oleg asked. "I suppose we could tie it onto the lower end of the balloon. Doesn't there have to be a hole at the bottom in order to fill the bag with hot air?"

"No. That won't do. That would just tear the muzdang hides. We have to spread the stress, the weight of the gondola, out over the entire envelope of the gas bag." Sergeyev's eyes clouded over in memory. "The way they did it in the illustration in a Jules Verne novel, they covered it with a net, and the box was hung at the bottom from the net."

"So, we'll make an enormous net." Oleg said.

"And how are we to heat the air?"

"Like the Montgolfier brothers." Oleg said, feeling he had already won. "We'll make a stove. . . . We'll think of something?"

"Maybe, something or other." Sergeyev asked.

Then Gote started a continuous bellow from the gate; something was happening. If a real danger were threatening the settlement the gote would have shrieked twice as loud, so no one was very alarmed. But whatever it was it would have to be checked. Sergeyev looked at Oleg expectantly. Oleg said,

"I'll take a look."

"All right." Sergeyev said. "And I've done enough thinking for tonight. The two of us will work on plans for the balloon tomorrow."

Oleg said good-bye and headed toward the gates. Marianna went with him.

"That's a good idea." She said

The two of them skirted the edge of the long puddle. The sky was a dim glow and their eyes quickly got used to the darkness. The huts' windows were burning yellow — small lamps were alight everywhere. No one had gone outside, although the gote had continued to plead for reinforcements. Everyone knew it was nothing dangerous.

Marianna shivered a little and held onto Oleg's hand. She had strong fingers. Oleg glanced at her profile; she had a finely chiseled nose and full lips. Oleg found himself thinking, *Is she really beautiful?* His mother said Marianna was an ugly duckling who was not destined to become a swan. An eternal teenager. His mother thought Liz was prettier. Perhaps she said that because Oleg didn't care for Liz, but he did like Marianna. Oleg was unable to explain to himself why he liked her so much — he found himself feeling that only in negative thoughts. For example, if Marianna went alone with Dick into the forest. Certainly, although he was unable to formulate the thought, it wasn't so much jealousy as envy for Dick. Because Dick was taller, braver, stronger, and so much the better hunter. Oleg envied Dick's ability to shoot a cross-bow and throw a knife, his ability to track and kill even the strongest animals, his cold recklessness and, chiefly, his complete indifference to Oleg's accomplishments and dreams. Dick found Oleg's achievements inaccessible — he had never even glanced in the communications text books and had only a vague understanding of logarithms. All this was unfair and shameful. It caused the value of Oleg's knowledge and wisdom to fall, and he was forced to convince himself that *someday* he would show Dick the usefulness of his knowledge, although in reality what he wanted to do was show Dick his non-existent superiority in hunting zhakals.

Sometimes Oleg found himself becoming annoyed and angry whenever he was not near Marianna; he wanted to hear her voice or meet her persistent, grey eyes with his own. But in the past few months the two of them had almost never been alone together; Oleg was constantly busy and at the end of the short, overcast days, he was exhausted. Everyone in the village was busy all the time, even the children, and everyone was exhausted, except for blind Kristina, and Liz who had no real liking for work. Oleg found himself having to learn and understand everything written in the communications text books they had brought back from the starship. He had to get back up to the crashed starship and inform Earth they were here.

Gote was running back and forth in front of the gates, bleating, trying to get at a single zhakal sitting on the other side, white coat on end, its black muzzle flaring wide. Gote could have dealt with the zhakal all on its own if someone would have let it out through the fence, she was twice as large and twice as strong, therefore the zhakal just stretched out on the cold ground and groomed itself. But Gote stamped all six feet in frustration, wanting to sink hooves into the predator's hide. It was an empty gesture.

"Quit making a racket." Oleg told Gote. "Go to bed."

Marianna chased Gote off toward the gotery and locked her

in. Oleg picked up a stone from the pile they kept ready by the gate and threw it at the zhakal. The zhakal got through its dim brain it had no business being there and darted off toward the forest.

It was very quiet. Snow drifted down silently, borne on the breeze. Oleg suddenly became very cold.

"Good night." He told Marianna. She had finished latching the gotery's gate "I'll go inside before I freeze."

"Good night." Marianna said. Her voice was sad, but Oleg wasn't listening to the intonation. Slipping in the mud he ran off toward his own hut to invent aeronautics.

CHAPTER SIX

Within the settlement the balloon soon became the cause of arguments and conflict. On the face of it, the idea seemed insane and completely unworkable. To even begin such a project would demand that every man, woman and child sacrifice his or her own time and effort, the work needed for their day-to-day survival, for the sake of a childish speculation which everyone knew would, in the end, come to nothing.

But Oleg had allies.

The first and most important was Sergeyev himself. The man avoided the arguments which flared about them, but he agreed to design and develop a burner. He succeeded. The fuel, in the end, came from the same pieces of wood which heated their houses — almost half the wood's weight consisted of a fatty resin. The logs burned with a hot violet flame, leaving almost nothing behind in the way of ash, a fact long noted in passing but had never before had it proved useful otherwise. Sergeyev made a press to extract the oil from the wood at an enormous savings in weight. Then the Mayor, with considerable lamentation and tears, handed over his old and useless microscope. He had the new one Oleg had brought back from the *PolarStar*, but he still treasured the old one, lenses lost, from the ship himself.

Oleg's second ally was Kazik.

The boy saw the aerial balloon as a great adventure. An adventure that linked them with Earth. Only on Earth itself had people flown in aerial balloons. Kazik asked all the adults, one after the other, quietly and politely, but again and again until they spoke to him merely to drive him away, to describe whatever memories or impressions remained in their minds of the old Jules Verne novel *Five Weeks In A Balloon*.

Kazik had concluded that all of them had read the novel at one time or another, but long ago, as children, and they had forgotten most of the details. But if he spoke long enough with each of them, having each retell the plot and events of the novel, he was able to piece together a more or less complete picture. He even managed to extract the names of the heroes from the story tellers and had the Mayor draw an aerial balloon.

The Mayor was often drawing pictures of life on Earth for the children; the first cohort of students, Dick, Liz, Marianna and Oleg, had been forced to content themselves with coarse illustrations on the ground or charcoal drawings on the bark of oaks. Over the past year the children had gotten luckier — paper had made its appearance and the Mayor, overcome with euphoria and, over the course of a single night, like an enriched pauper, wasted much of the hoard on pictures, crude, naive, but the most real pictures. The Eiffel Tower, the Moscow Kremlin, an elephant, the Luna City domes, the first steam ship, a caravel from the time of Columbus. They had collected the pictures into a large folio and they could be looked at and studied after every lesson.

And there were pictures made at Kazik's request of aerial balloons. Some of these pictures carried corrections made by Kazik himself; the boy could hardly draw, but he knew more about balloons than even the Mayor. In one of the pictures the balloon floated above the African savannah and elephants and giraffes chased after it.

This was the picture Kazik brought to Oleg when the older boy decided to build an aerial balloon.

"Try this." Kazik looked up at Oleg. "It has all the details you'll need."

Oleg took the picture and examined it. He noticed a rope with an anchor at its end hung beneath the bag and realized they would have to make such an anchor.

But for Kazik the fate of the balloon would have been literally up in the air. The spring passed, and the muzdangs, not suspecting what uses Oleg now had for their air bladders, were still hibernating. Finding their nests was difficult and Kazik, and his faithful sister Fumiko, must have gone twenty times or more into the forest until they found the muzdangs' winter lair, in a large burrow in the oke wood. The soft, mobile roots shielded them from the snow and frosts.

Subsequently there arose the problem of the net which would enclose the gas bag itself and from which the gondola would hang. Marianna and Thomas's daughter Ruth collected water vines to make the cordage. The hands of both girls grew swollen from the cold, and finally Linda forbade her daughter to go crawling about in the swamp, and Oleg was forced to abandon his other work and spend his time collecting the plants himself. In fact he was helped by the twins who lived with the Mayor, and Vaitkus's children, but they quickly tired of the work and evaporated with the morning dew.

In the mornings, soon after dawn, Oleg and Marianna hurried around the graveyard on the well trodden path toward the swamp. With each passing day they were forced to go ever further; they waded out from the marshy shore, up to their knees in icy water that seeped even through their waterproof fish hide pants. The water plants had rooted themselves firmly for the winter, forcing Oleg and Marianna to cut them. The tough white strings of the water hairs twisted and turned and tried to crawl out of their fingers, and they had to cut them almost at the roots to get strands long enough to be of use. Their feet slipped in the mud; greedy but still weak leeches crawled all over their pants' legs. When a many-eyed grabbe approached them unawares they panicked and rushed for shore; it swam up, and they were forced to retreat from the water and wait until the creature went back into the mud.

Oleg tried to do more than Marianna, but all the same found himself gathering less than the girl, and it appeared he could never collect water plants with such devilish devotion. Then they had to carry their loads all the way back to the barn and lay them out on the floor to be dried, and drying took forever in the cold, damp air.

Oleg's mother was against it from the start. The thought of her son in the air supported by nothing but hot air in a fragile balloon was terrifying.

"This is suicide." Irina kept repeating to Sergeyev. "You're actually permitting this, going along with it. If it were your own child you'd never allow it."

His mother's words made Oleg angry. "I'm almost twenty." He answered tiredly.

Oleg was exhausted, more tired than he had ever been before in his life, because Sergeyev had not cut back on his electronics studies, as though the time he spent working in the foundry were not enough.

That was the day Oleg exploded. Vaitkus had come up to the boy and asked him when something would be finished.

"Am I doing less? I am getting the mill ready, aren't I? You do want the plough, don't you? Am I forcing you to do something you don't want to do? If I have to build the balloon all on my own, I'll get it done anyway. Didn't everyone tell the Montgolfier brothers they were wasting their time? If they hadn't been the first then we'd never have built starships. It had to begin with something."

"If we hadn't built starships we'd be sitting at home nice and warm." Vaitkus started to laugh from out of the middle of his enormous red beard.

"I'm not joking."

"Too bad. It would be better if you had a sense of humor."

"What good would a sense of humor do me? My mother is crying all the time. Luiza says 'the flame isn't worth the candle,' whatever that means, the Mayor keeps saying that the risk is too great, and the rest of you seem to think I'm just playing some sort of game. Why don't you understand?"

"But you are playing, in a sense." Vaitkus said. "It's a very good game, but it's still unfamiliar to the rest of us simple mortals."

"Don't you want to get off this planet?"

"Of course I do. A lot more than you do. I *know* what it is I'm missing, what my kids have never seen. For you it's just a guess. But even in such an odd settlement like ours we seem to keep repeating the same type of social and personal relationships everyone else has developed, over and over again. And they're little different from what goes on in a large city. To walk to the ship, well that's understood, everyone's done it. Kill an animal, that's understood. That's how we survive. But fly to the mountains in a hot air balloon, that's madness. Typical childish risk-taking. That's Kazik's dream, not something we expect from an adult the settlement depends on. We really expected something different from you."

"Getting there on foot has own dangers all its own."

"But your chances of getting there on foot are still ten times greater than by air. You already know the route. We can equip you far better than we could a year ago. You've been through it before and know what to expect. No, I'm for the traditional route, even if it means we have to go back year after year. Too much has already been put on the map."

Oleg did not bother to reply, but with the exception of Sergeyev, who in the very first days had calculated how large the gas bag would have to be and how much heat the stove would have to produce to warm enough air, and came to the conclusion the balloon, might, indeed fly, the others hoped, were even convinced, nothing would come from the debacle with the balloon.

Dick just ignored Oleg, as he always did. In his own realm he was the unchallenged leader; no one else could even come close to him as a hunter and tracker. He might very well have flown in the balloon, but his destination would not have been north to the starship, but south toward the unknown forests and rivers hidden beyond the small ranges of hills. That was where game and adventure lay. Dick did want to see the world from on high, like a bird, but he never saw any reason to tell anyone of this. So Oleg was surprised when Dick joined the muzdang hunt and brought back whole bags of air bladders to the settlement.

Liz had quite unexpectedly raised her voice against the flight. Oleg was avoiding her, as much as anyone could avoid anyone else in their tiny settlement. When Liz approached him Oleg sought an excuse to go to the workshop or go visit the Mayor to find a place to study where he didn't have to listen to her. This surprised his mother — she and Liz began to speak, seemingly with real interest and affection, about trivial things Oleg didn't even think were worth talking about. At first they talked about all kinds of recipes, how to prepare dishes here on this world and how it had been done on earth, and the differences between the two, and did soups taste better with dried nuts or fresh, and it was a harmless waste of time that kept both women occupied and away from him. But then they started to talk about other people. Oleg found himself listening to their conversations as much as he tried to get away from them — their voices carried through the partition. He knew, for example, that Linda was doing a bad job of raising Ruth, because she was too busy catching Sergeyev, that Luiza was simply starving poor Kazik, he was so small, and that Marianna was getting worse all the time — poor child, there was something wrong with her metabolism (the word was his mother's; Liz didn't understand it but immediately agreed anyway.) Such a totally undeveloped child! Seventeen years old, but she hardly looked like she'd gone through puberty.

Oleg found himself coughing from time to time, just to let them know he could hear everything, and for some reason Liz started to laugh in a high voice. And he immediately found himself thinking of Liz although she was the last thing he wanted to think about. Liz was the fattest person among the young generation. Or rather, she was not fat per se, but there were parts of her body that were. Oleg suspected there was a word for it not yet taught to him — her chest was fat and her hips were fat. Liz often smiled when Oleg or Dick spoke to her, and once Oleg caught sight of Dick's face when he was looking at Liz as if she were a game animal he was going to bring back slung over his shoulder.

Once, after Liz had left, and Oleg returned from the Mayor's side of their hut and started to get ready for bed, Oleg's mother asked him if it wasn't time he thought about starting a family. Oleg didn't understand what she was talking about at all.

"Get married." she explained.

Oleg broke out laughing. He asked,

"You mean, marry Liz?"

"Life goes on." His mother said. "Even in this wilderness. Look, if you don't catch the girl, she'll go chasing after Dick."

"Then wish him luck." Oleg answered.

"You don't have any choice."

"I can go to Earth and solve all my problems."

"Idiot." His mother became angry. "Falling for that starveling will be the death of you!"

"Marianna's thin, but she's not a fool." Oleg turned toward the wall.

***

The slow spring came early and warm. Sergeyev, who kept accounts not only of the calendar but of the weather patterns, said the summer, too, should be warm.

At first the rains washed away the remains of the snow, which held on for a while only in the depths of the forest, then the rains came less frequently and, day by day, the air grew so hot despite the clouds the children threw off their heavy skin garments and ran about almost naked. The sun lifted so high it could be distinguished as an unclear if bright point of light through the eternal clouds. Gote had survived her latest romantic escapade and now grew quiet, spending her time pacing back and forth in front of the palisade, waiting for new additions to her family. The zhakals returned from the south where they had wintered, the first birds perched on the palisade, loudly flapping their membranous wings, hoards of midges and flies put in an appearance, and when the women and children worked in the fenced in garden they were forced to light smokey fires. A snow flee bit one of the Mayor's twins who bit himself on the tongue so hard during the temporary madness he drew blood.

Summer had just started, but Oleg all the more felt an inner disquiet, impatience and even fear, that *too* little time remained. He had accomplished nothing. In fact he had not accomplished everything that was needed if he was to get to the starship and work on the subspace radio. Now he often was freed from common work — he had just stopped going hunting, and they never called him to work in the garden. Even in the workshop Sergeyev told him not to get underfoot, but in the evenings severely questioned him on what he had studied, learned, understood; as a result of which Oleg saw Sergeyev's annoyance as well. Sergeyev himself did not truly understand everything he was trying to teach the boy.

But the balloon was real now. The opposition had been overcome, point by point, in a continuous battle. It had been turned into objective reality. When the rains came Kazik and Fumiko fed Spytter worms until the animal was almost torpid, and it began to produce so much gluey spit glassy lakes formed around the cage set under the awnings between the workshop and the abbal orchard. Oleg and Marianna started to cut and glue the gas bag out of the air bladders of the muzdangs they had taken.

At first, with Sergeyev's help, they sketched the outline of a segment of the gas bag on the ground similar to a flower with sharp petals; it was so big Fumiko would have had trouble throwing a stone from one end to the other. One hundred and twenty paces. After that Oleg and Marianna started to glue together segments of the sphere, the petals themselves. The gas bladders, so many at the start, immediately proved too few. Kazik and Dick were forced to go out hunting for muzdangs again.

The attitude in the settlement toward the balloon slowly turned like the coming summer. It was there. It was seen. And people got used to it. Even Oleg's mother stopped her incessant crying. Liz came a few times to help cut and glue together the bladders. And then together with Kristina, who had suddenly found a talent for knotting the nets, — she wove the lines. Vaitkus and his wife Egli constructed the basket, weaving it together out of thin branches. But no one took the balloon quite as seriously as Oleg. Not even Marianna. That left, of course, Kazik, but he was too small, a wild person, who believed in the depths of his soul the balloon would take him to India, despite everything he had been taught about stars and planets, atmospheric density gradients, vacuum, starships and subspace. A number of times when everyone else in the settlement was sleeping, and the cold black sky had almost started to turn grey, an impatient Oleg would leave the hut and go out quietly into the cold and spread shining, petal shaped bladders out on the ground, and Kazik would appear beside him as an unheard shadow, forest Mowgli. He would run to the cage to wake up Spytter and help Oleg without saying a word.

Then they had to glue the petals along their edges in order to produce what in the end would be a sphere, what the Mayor termed a giant pear shape hung upside down. No matter what care they took the glue fell on their hands, their fingers became glassy and stiff. During the mornings they had to beware of willowwasp globes, which rose in the air in search of baers they could seed with their spores to continue their own life cycle.

In the end the balloon was finished.

At last the net was ready. And even the rope with the anchor they would need to hold it to the ground. Sergeyev finished the burner and the children filled container after container with the thick, fatty resin they would use as fuel. And the basket was made, a strong, flexible basket. It was time to put the pieces together and go to work.

The Mayor demanded the balloon first be tested without occupants. It should be filled and sent aloft and then allowed to return to the ground. Oleg opposed this plan and Sergeyev supported him. It wasn't only the envelope of the balloon they would have to test, but the burner; they would have to find out if their balloon could be made to obey a person.

"Make the rope a little shorter." Oleg's mother said.

Oleg just laughed. Liz and Kristina had woven the rope. He himself had helped them with it, although he had been short of time for everything else. Oleg understood Liz was doing it only to please him. He had gone to the house where Liz and Kristina lived, had listened to Kristina always complaining and waiting for her death, and they had woven together that endless rope. Liz kept looking at him, glancing away and back and trying to find an excuse to touch his hand. Oleg endured it, listened to words he found empty, and tried to think of something else, and then he could not stand it any more and ran away to the workshop.

Oleg knew he would be the first one to go up in the balloon, and no one ever disputed the balloon was Oleg's creation, without him it would have come to nothing. Kazik had spent the last few days walking around after Oleg and could not come to terms with the thought his own ascent in the balloon would have to be put off. He was hoping for some miracle which would force them to let him take the first flight.

Oleg found himself overcome with thoughts of a malicious delight: *None of you believed we* could *build it. We did. It exists. It's mine. We did it together, but it's mine . . . I'm going to fly. . . .*

Perhaps someone might have guessed Oleg's thoughts, but no one spoke it aloud until the morning when the balloon was to be launched, and the Mayor said:

"What does it feel like to be a Napoleon?" The Mayor asked.

"What do you mean?" Oleg asked. "I've never seen Napoleon. I've never even seen pictures of him. And I don't even know what he did."

"You know perfectly well." The Mayor answered, looking his student over.

The Mayor still wanted to tousle the boy's hair, but during the winter Oleg had finished growing, his shoulders had broadened, his hair had darkened. And his face had grown more bony, losing its childish softness. It was an adult's face. Perhaps insufficiently strong, but the straight chin and sharp bones of the skull displayed the internal persistence. A pleasant face.

"Of course I know." Oleg laughed. "He conquered half of Europe."

He pulled on his boots and checked to make certain they covered the cuffs of his pants. Vaitkus said it would be cold higher up. The same as in the morning.

"Are you sure it's enough?" The Mayor asked.

The twins ran in; they were the Mayor's wards, small creatures who inclined to continual laughter and thoughtless pranks. They, like all of the settlement, felt today should be a holiday. And Oleg, the very same every day Oleg who lived on the other side of the hanging partition and who had a really horrible mother, was flying off today into the sky.

"This is all too simple," Oleg said, "As though it were a mathematical formula. Alexander the Great conquered half the known world. Napoleon conquered half of Europe. Hitler tried to conquer all of Europe. Julius Caesar also conquered, Egypt, I think. All those people are dead, gone, buried, and what they did really doesn't mean anything. But you see it otherwise. You've seen their portraits, you've read about them in books. For you they're extraordinary, for me they are ordinary. I've never even seen Europe."

"Well now, they shouldn't be called ordinary." The Mayor spoke up. "They're extraordinary because they've implanted themselves so firmly in human memory. Good, bad, or vile, but always extraordinary."

"For you, yes. But how am I supposed to judge them? I cannot. When I was twelve years old this problem suddenly started to trouble me. What does 'conquer' and 'overcome' mean? I even asked it in class; was there another Napoleon who had conquered not half of Europe, but a quarter of it? And you answered me the difference between the various conquerors was only the duration of their successes. There wasn't one of them who achieved all the goals he had sought."

"I remember." The old man said. "And I also told you the names of those who failed at the start are often unknown to us because in every battle there is a losing side. And waiting for every

Napoleon is a Waterloo if he doesn't succeed in getting himself killed first. I remember."

"So do I." Oleg said, jumping in place and twisting his body to make certain his cold weather gear was on tight. Then he took a water flask and slung it across his shoulder. "And all I can say is, from what you've taught us, conquest is the typical activity of conquerors. And they are all unique. And I really don't understand or see what it has to do with us here on this planet. Like business and merchandising and interstellar finance and trade regulations. For me what is unusual is what is done for the first time."

"In the literal sense you're right." The Mayor agreed. "But I called you Napoleon not because I wanted to compare you with the conqueror. The analogy is somewhat different. The whole town has come out into the street, all at once, together, because you're going to launch the balloon today."

"I'm not the only one."

"Don't you understand? What we're doing today, we're doing out of obedience to your will. I've never seen anything like it myself, but unlike you I can picture it. Early morning. Somewhere in Austria or Prussia at the beginning of the nineteenth century. Napoleon has spent the night in a small, tidy little hotel smelling of vanilla. He awakens from the noise beneath his window, and still hasn't fully come to his senses. He goes to the window and throws it open. The whole road and the village square is cluttered with carriages, caravans of sutlers and cannons going to the front. People are walking about, horses neigh, there's a babble of voices. And suddenly Napoleon understands the utter madness and futility of this general chaos — someone is responsible, it has grown out of someone's wishes — that slowly increases in strength... And these soldiers are waiting for their breakfasts by the field kitchens not because they like eating military rations, and the cannons are not lined up on the road because the cannoneers have nothing better to do, this moment has come about, these lives and fates have converged here, because he, Napoleon Bonaparte, willed it. And because he, Napoleon, had a tooth ache during the night, he suddenly wants to shout at them through the open window: "Go home, all of you!"

"And does he shout it?" Oleg asked.

"You manifest one of the essential qualities of a Great Man." The Mayor clucked with displeasure. "The absolute lack of a sense of humor."

Kazik's head peered in through the door. The scrawny child was tense. He had never been able to reconcile himself with not going up in the balloon today. But he wanted the balloon to go up, today, and again and again, even if it was without him. If the balloon went up today, Kazik knew someday it would take him too. The next time. Perhaps.

"I'm coming." Oleg said. He was ready.

The three of them left the house, the Mayor trailing a little behind. The old man was leaning heavily on his cane. The cane was new and probably harmless. The previous cane had been carved of red wood, with silvery streaks; Dick had cut it from wood he'd found in the whispering grove. But at the start of spring the walking stick had, one fine day, extended a mass of sticky shoots and feelers and started to crawl out of the house while the Mayor was conducting a lesson. The entire class had charged after the walking stick, and then, catching it, let it go. The stick had made its way to the palisade where it had sunk roots and turned itself into a large, leafy bush. The Mayor had sometimes heard how the children had gathered to go fishing and had agreed to meet 'by the stick,' and had guessed what they had in mind.

Oleg, already in the clearing, turned and looked on the stumbling old man, and suddenly felt very sorry for him. And for himself. The Mayor was going to die soon. He was having a great deal of difficulty walking and his body was in enormous pain; it had even become hard for him to conduct classes in school. He was forgetting everything. If the children were going to fly off to Earth it had better be soon. The Mayor had done a great deal. If it were not for his school, none of the other adults could have taught the children all the sciences.

In the field, on the other side of the barn, the aerial balloon lay like an unpleasant mound, like an allyfant about to go on its nightly hunt. The burner hissed and warm air was rushing upwards to fill the balloon envelope. But it was only working at a quarter power; Sergeyev, who was in charge of the balloon, wanted to take no risks.

The balloon was slowly taking shape; back at dawn the balloon had simply been a large pile of rags, the bag and the net that covered it separate. Everything had changed. Now the net clutched at the skin of the envelope. The balloon was coming alive.

Gote was huddled with her young off to the side in fright. She had no liking for allyfants, especially inside the palisade.

Oleg approached. Sergeyev, who was standing by the wicker bag, asked him,

"Should I turn up the flame?"

Sergeyev was treating Oleg as an equal now. He also recognized the balloon was Oleg's property, like the mirror was Marianna's. But this did not mean the mirror did not belong to everyone. Would the idea have ever occurred to Marianna to refuse anyone who wanted to look at themselves in the mirror?

"When are you going to take us up?" Ruth called out to them.

All the faces seemed very tiny, as though Oleg was looking at them across a magnifying glass. Suddenly Marianna ran by with a can of glue — she had noticed a broken seam letting hot air escape.

Off to the side stood Luiza, an enormous fat woman with an swollen face, checking the anchor rope attached to the cords that gathered the lines of the netting into a knot between the balloon and the basket.

The balloon shuddered. As though it were sighing; suddenly it took on a far rounder shape.

Oleg bent down to check that the balloon was carefully tied to the ground.

The ropes were connected to stakes rammed deep into the ground at an angle. Next to the balloon's gondola on the ground was a large bent pin made out of ironwood, forced hard and fast into the ground as well, the anchor. Beside it the rope had been curled into neat spirals.

The balloon shuddered again. Now it had grown nearly round and touched the ground at only on one spot.

"Shall I climb into the basket?" Oleg asked Sergeyev, and his voice unexpectedly broke.

Oleg was frightened the others would notice his fears and laugh. He thought to himself: *I am not Napoleon. I'm doing something very ordinary. I'm not a conqueror. I don't want people eating out of field kitchens and being shot at by cannons because of me. People will move not because I want them to, but if this makes things better for us, then I'll be happy.*

"Still too early for it to take off." Sergeyev said. He wasn't laughing.

The balloon suddenly jumped with a gust of wind and just as suddenly sank back down again, shaking the attached basket. The heavy netting seemed to cut into the body of the envelope, like sections of a round fruit.

"It would be better if the material were a little stronger." Vaitkus said. "In the future we can learn from the experience of the dirigible."

"What experience?" Oleg suddenly realized the word 'dirigible' meant nothing to him.

"If we smear the balloon with a thin layer of glue we can strengthen it." Vaitkus stroked his beard.

"Why didn't someone mention this earlier?" Oleg thought the idea was beautiful, and he was angry at Vaitkus for having kept hidden such an elegant idea from him.

"I just thought of it now." Vaitkus said.

"It would increase the weight of the balloon too much!" Sergeyev shook his head.

At that moment the balloon finally eased itself off the ground and rose erect at an angle to the basket.

Oleg couldn't wait any longer. He put his leg over the edge of the basket and stood up inside it, holding onto the sides tightly with his hands.

The basket was small, about a meter and a half in diameter and only about waist high. The supply of fuel and several bags of sand for ballast had been packed in the middle.

The balloon slowly moved back and forth over their heads; you could reach to the lower edge of it with your hand. The burner was still filling it with hot air. Oleg reached up and held onto the ropes above him.

The basket still stood on the ground; you could jump over the side and stand on the soft, new grass, but Oleg felt a certain detachment from everything that stood around here, as though all the other people were already far below.

Then the basket was dangling; the balloon pulled at the ropes, trying to lift it up into the air.

"Fly, fly away!" Ruth started to shout.

"Quiet." Sergeyev cut her off. "It's too soon."

Oleg bent his head and looked upward at the balloon. It was so large it covered half the sky. It was an ugly patchwork, the edges uneven, some bladders seemed ready to pop out of the sides, a bloated quilt of muzdang bladders tethered uncomfortably to the ground by ropes. The half transparent whitish envelope reflected the grass and the settlement's tottering little houses. And at the same time this absurd enormity radiated strength in its slow, insistent attempts to rise, to break away from the ground, tugging constantly at the ropes holding onto the basket. The belly of the balloon above caught the dull hissing of the burner and cast it back at him, increasing the sound tenfold.

Now the balloon was directly over their heads, and the ropes were taunt. Oleg drew back, looking at the balloon, and did not immediately see Sergeyev give the signal or his helpers bend down over the stakes where the ropes were tied.

"All set, Oleg." Sergeyev said. "We're letting go now. Hold on tight; it might jump."

"Let it. Don't worry." Oleg shouted, looking at Vaitkus bent over the line and leaning with all his weight on the line until his back was against the ground, untying the knot.

At that moment Oleg was almost tossed from the balloon.

Sergeyev had tried to ensure his helpers released all the ropes simultaneously, but the strength of his assorted helpers were hardly equal to the task. Vaitkus had already untied his line and was holding onto it tightly. Dick stood up, almost laughing and clearly displaying his view that he was taking part in a less than serious undertaking. He was holding onto his rope rather loosely, as though the balloon, despite its size, presented him with no challenge. On the other side of the basket Luiza and Egli almost got in each others' ways untying the knots. It was as though the balloon had been waiting for this moment. Dick was about to cast the rope away when he saw Vaitkus still holding onto his rope while Egli and Luiza's had ripped from their hands and flapped free. . . .

Vaitkus felt the rope jerk and, being ready for it, hung all his body weight on the rope, but the other rope flew upwards, torn from Dick's hand and whipping the boy in turn, tossing him back to the ground. Dick was on his feet a moment later, jumping up and clutching at the rope, but it was too late; the basket jerked to the side and almost turned over. Oleg fell, hitting the cans with the fuel and a moment later the bags with ballast fell on him. The basket brushed even enormous Luiza aside, struck Egli; the balloon rocked back and forth as it heaved itself upwards, not forgetting to strike Vaitkus as he tried to free the remaining ropes from the stakes in the ground. It dragged itself into the air and rose upward sharply.

The basket hung below, swinging from the ropes in tune to the balloon's uncertain rhythms.

All this took but a few seconds; the air was filled with shouts, screams, cries of fear and the creaking of ropes.

And then everyone fell silent, except for Fumiko who cried because she was afraid for Oleg.

Everyone else was silent, even Egli, whose arm had been badly bruised by the basket, and Luiza, who still lay on the ground, and Sergeyev, and Vaitkus, and even the children.

Oleg's mother was the only one of them still standing, staring intently at the basket, filled with fears of the body of her son dropping from the basket and falling, arms outstretched, to the ground.

For Oleg everything happened far too quickly; in one second he had fallen inside the basket and the bags of ballast had covered him. And the next moment he realized he was flying, that there was nothing beneath him, that the ground was somewhere far below; the basket rocked back and forth freely, and through the spaces in the weave he could see the world.

Carefully, almost overcome with fear of the height, he got up on all fours, sensing at the same time the basket's rocking motions were slowly subsiding, and the balloon had stopped its wild gyrations.

As Oleg got to his feet he found his senses coming alive again; the burner whistled, sending a plume of hot air up into the balloon above him, the ropes creaked, they crawled like thin muscles over the envelope, the wattled branches of the basket on which he stood cracked but held firm. And there was a child crying from below.

Finally Oleg was ready to stand. He gripped the edge of the basket tightly and was about to stand up straight, but went down on all fours when the basket jerked upward sharply one last time and almost sent him flying. And he did not immediately guess all the ropes had been released and they had come to the end of the ropes connecting the balloon to the anchor.

The upward movement of the balloon had stopped, but it continued its attempts to escape; the basket twisted and reeled about in the air.

To the people on the ground below it appeared a great deal of time had passed. For almost a minute they all looked upwards and were silent. The balloon had ascended to about three hundred feet — the last rope would not let it ascend further — and started to move slowly toward the forest, as though attempting to deceive the rope that still clutched it tightly.

They could see nothing at all of Oleg.

On the other hand, he was still in the basket.

Sergeyev came to his senses before the others and was about to shout to Vaitkus and Dick to help him pull the balloon down, when he realized the burner would have to be closed off first; the buoyancy of the balloon was too great and those on the ground could not overcome it.

And then Irina started to shout.

"Oleg! Boy!" She shouted, disrupting the silent festivity of the flight "Oleg, are you all right? Oleg!"

Oleg heard his mother and became ashamed she was calling to him as though he were a little boy, but then the thought flashed through his head Napoleon, certainly, had a mother as well, and he stuck his head above the edge of the basket, held onto the ropes for support, and called out below:

"Everything's okay!"

Everyone on the ground saw Oleg's small, dark silhouette, and they all shouted; the children started to jump up and down, but Irina began to sob and weep bitterly at the top of her lungs.

The balloon slowly moved over their heads — it had become a real aerial ship that could fly off into the sky.

The Mayor helped Vaitkus get to his feet and said,

"Today balloons, tomorrow air traffic controllers."

Vaitkus laughed.

"Lower the flame in the burner!" Sergeyev shouted up to Oleg. "You have to cut down on the lift! Can you hear me?"

"I hear you fine!" Oleg called back; his head nodded up and down.

Oleg turned to the burner and carefully lowered the volume of the flame. But not much. Now everything had turned out so well he had no desire to descend too soon.

He looked over the side of the balloon again and waved his hand:

"Everything's all right!"

And then he looked at the settlement below him. He could see everything at once. The muddy river of street where the tiny huts formed tight banks, the curved roofs of the barns and workshop nestled behind the palisade. The small scatter of humanity, some of them standing directly beneath the balloon, some of them waving their hands, the children jumping up and down in a wild dance.

Oleg saw Kristina sitting on the porch of his own hut. Perhaps she had not wanted to be at the launching, or maybe they had forgotten about her in the excitement.

Then he noticed Gote's uplifted green snout. She hadn't seen flying allyfants before.

Oleg's view slowly slid further around him; beyond the fence, to the narrow band of the clearing and then the beginning of the forest. He had never seen the forest from above. The wave and twist of whitish bare branches, the occasional patches and green spots of hunting vynes and kreepers, were a jumble stretching all the way to the swamp. From on high the swamp, so vast, seemed rather small, and beyond it began the scrub brush, and again more forest, thick enough to keep a ray of light from reaching the ground, vanishing into the curling mists.

Oleg carefully moved himself to the other side of the basket. Now he could see the start of the path leading back to the mountains and the *PolarStar*. Again more forest, then waste ground and reddish cliffs rising above the trees.

Two more steps to the right. Again forest. Only it cut off, ended abruptly in the plains where they went to hunt dyr, and the dark wall of an even greater forest where the hunters and gatherers rarely ventured. There were no game animals, and carnivorous flowers and hunting vynes hid in the moist darkness.

The wind came up; it was trying to snatch the balloon away. The basket started to hum.

Oleg realized he would have to lower the flame in the burner even more. The people below were waiting for him to descend.

But he could not tear himself away from the vastness now opened up below him. He had ceased to be a fly crawling along the branches; he had flown up over the world like the birds, and the utterly different scales of this world had infused Oleg with a free and ticklish feeling of power and confidence in himself and in those small human beings who were waiting for him down below. This feeling was somehow akin to that which had taken hold of him when, for the first time, he had looked across the mountain pass at the high valley where the enormous lens of the fallen starship lay in the snow. But the starship was only a memory of the powers human beings had achieved. This flight was something he had contrived for himself. And Oleg realized his greatest desire was to cut the anchor rope once and for all and head toward the clouds, seeing everywhere, soaring over the forests, not cowering in them. Fearing nothing.

Oleg thought for a moment even the Montgolfier brothers could not compare with him; they had ascended over their native city where nothing was threatening them with death. They had only the winds to fear. Oleg had to overcome an entire planet that wanted to kill him,

His present height wasn't all that great; it was hardly much colder up here than it had been on the ground, but Oleg found himself becoming chilly. Certainly, he was excited. When he finally reached up to the burner to close it, his fingers were trembling.

The balloon gradually lost strength and its desire to depart for the clouds. It sagged. Below him Sergeyev and Dick had caught at their ropes and had begun to haul the balloon in for landing.

The world around him began to grow smaller; the horizon nearer.

***

At the beginning of summer the preparations for the trip to the starship came to an abrupt halt. The two principals, Oleg and

Sergeyev, were constantly being diverted to other tasks. Oleg continued to go up in the balloon whenever he could; having invented it he wanted to master it, and he contrived to take it aloft nearly every day, sometimes twice a day. Sergeyev now had other concerns; despite everything, Linda Hind had married him.

There was no great wedding celebration; the adults all went to visit them, sat, remembered Thomas and Sergeyev's late wife, drank tea, and wished Linda and Sergeyev the good luck of an eventual return to Earth. And they dispersed.

There were few adults left in the settlement, and some of them were in very bad condition. The Mayor was growing weaker all the time, big Luiza was constantly wracked by pain, and blind Kristina kept saying she was not long for this planet, and good riddance to it, over and over again. Oleg's mother was suffering from arthritis and spent the better part of the day in bed, with the result the garden was tended primarily by Vaitkus, Linda and Egli, while Sergeyev was in the workshop. Naturally, more and more of the responsibility for keeping the settlement going fell to the children. That summer hunting had become Dick's responsibility completely; Dick took Kazik with him, and some times Patrick Vaitkus. It was already hard to speak of the last two as children — teenagers was a better description, competent and quick, awkward. They had stopped going to school; even the Mayor realized he had nothing more to give them. His past was, for them, the future, they hoped, something imminent, obtainable; now everyone believed in the balloon and were even inclined to overestimate its possibilities. It was as though they could fly to the starship in the balloon whenever they wanted, as often as they liked.

Oleg understood better than the others that his creation was unreliable and capricious. He had already developed a feeling for the airship and realized how easily it would move under the influence of the slightest breeze, how the winds could carry it wherever they wished, beyond the powers of the passengers to control it.

On his second ascent Oleg took Kazik with him. It was only fair. Kazik had exhausted himself gathering wood for fuel and had worked the presses constantly to reduce the wood to oil. Kazik had gone hunting muzdangs to repair and patch up the balloon.

Oleg had — not all at once, certainly — noticed how the reactions of the others to the balloon had differed, depending on their own interests, fears and desires. Those who wanted to fly in the balloon had honestly helped launch it, had held onto the ropes, helped empty the inflated bag and then tucked it away beneath the shed when the flight had ended. But after they themselves had gone up into the air their interest in the balloon had fallen. The majority of those who flew with Oleg were enchanted by the flight. There was a moment of terror when the balloon left the ground, then their interest heightened — to see the forest and the settlement from on high. That was all.

That was the way with Linda and Liz, who had put off their turn three times because they were fearful, then gathered up the courage to get into the basket, and when the balloon rose squeaked from terror that the children who were looking from below would die from laughing.

Vaitkus, when he went up into the air, carefully looked over the countryside, and then said they should land on the other side of the swamp; he had seen abbal groves in the thicket on the other side.

The Mayor took his flight in silence. For about twenty minutes. Then he said, "Thank you. We can go down now."

Egli looked down at the settlement, then wiped her eyes, perhaps from the wind, perhaps a mote of dust had caught in her eye. And she said, "You could go mad, such squalor."

Oleg's mother refused to go up in the balloon at all. He was relieved. But every time Oleg was getting ready for the next flight she came out into the square and personally checked the balloon's ropes.

Kazik and Fumiko shortened the ropes. A little more than twenty meters. More wasn't necessary. They had turned out to be so heavy they pulled the balloon downward, and the knots began to tear under the weight of the rope itself, giving the Mayor the chance for a fine lecture on tensile strength and the square cube law.

Dick went up into the air once. For several days after the first flight he had avoided Oleg; he thought it was his fault the flight had almost ended in disaster. Oleg had to hunt him down and ask him if he wanted to go up. Dick agreed.

On the day they ascended a light rain had rolled through; tiny drops splattered as mist against the balloon and made visibility difficult. As the ground fell away Oleg felt Dick grow timid; the other boy was in a strange situation, and Dick was always lost in strange situations. Oleg remembered what Dick had been like at the *PolarStar*. The other boy stood up straight the whole flight, holding onto the ropes on his side of the basket, unwilling to walk around the hanging stove to look at the ground on the other side. Dick had taken his cross-bow with him on the flight and even tucked the blaster from the starship in his belt. Oleg pretended he hadn't noticed.

Unexpectedly, Dick said,

"This summer I have to make it to the great plains. I think it must begin right over there."

And he pointed south, where the forest merged with the clouds.

"There should be a lot of dyr."

And Oleg realized Dick would, all the same, have remained with his feet on the ground.

But he was wrong. Dick felt uncertain in the fragile, almost transparent wicker of the basket. The cause of Dick's uncertainty was totally different; for the first time in his life Dick envied Oleg.

While Oleg busied himself with work necessary for the settlement, but not all that necessary in Dick's point of view, Dick didn't really care. He had his forest and the satisfaction of the hunt. Only now, looking at the forest and watching the zhakals prowling among the branches and legged sneaqs crawling through the trees, the silvery bodies of the young payns swelling with spring juices, seeing the world for the first time with such a precise and clear view so different from Oleg's, Dick recognized the incomparable power and freedom which the control of the balloon afforded. In Dick it awakened a sharp desire to fly with the winds to new forests, chase herds of animals, descend for the night beside mysterious streams. . . .

Oleg was surprised to see Dick reach for his blaster.

"What are you doing?" he asked.

"Quiet." Dick said.

A thread of green light stretched from the balloon to the trees on the edge of the swamp where Oleg had seen nothing a moment before. And suddenly there was movement; an enormous animal roared and thrashed in the thicket and then the heavy body collapsed into a clearing.

"I've never seen anything like it before." Dick said, holstering the blaster. "Let's get down. I want to see what I killed."

Oleg went up with Marianna on a quiet, warm day.

"It's beautiful up here." Marianna said. "You don't really want to go down, do you?"

Oleg looked at her. He was like the generous host showing off his place to a guest, accepting her compliments as were his due. And he was pleased Marianna, of all people. appreciated the beauty of the flight.

"And it's so quiet." Marianna said.

"Thank you." Oleg said.

"Why?" Marianna turned to him and looked him over carefully, as though she were looking at him for the first time. Why thanks?

Oleg stretched out his hand and touched her fingers on the basket. The basket almost rocked, but Marianna wasn't frightened.

"You understand everything." Oleg said.

Marianna lifted her hand from the basket rim and placed her fingers in Oleg's hand.

It was so natural, and his palm was already awaiting her touch. The basket jumped again, and Marianna made a step forward so as not to lose her balance. She was so close Oleg kissed her cheek. He had wanted to kiss her on the lips, but he missed and kissed her on the cheek at the edge of her mouth. And Marianna drew close to him and froze, like a baby animal. There was nothing else in the world around them that mattered, not the sky nor the balloon or the hissing and sputtering stove, and that was fine with both of them.

"Hey," Kazik started to shout from below. "You two okay?"

Marianna raised her head to look into Oleg's eyes and laughed.

"What?" Oleg didn't understand.

"Let's come up here every day." She said. And laughed.

"Let's." Oleg laughed as well. "We can come up in the morning and come down at night."

"Only Kazik would mind. Do you think we should take him with us?"

"No way." Oleg said quietly, suddenly fearing they could be heard on the ground. "No way."

"Hey!" Kazik shouted. "Get down here! Weather's turning!"

Oleg took his time closing off the burner.

While the balloon dawdled downward he held onto Marianna's hand.

They made it to ground only at the last moment—a strong gust of wind caught the balloon and sent it careening toward the line of houses at the end of its tether and almost broke the rope. Kazik was alone at the landing field; after the third flight they had decided it wasn't necessary to attach the balloon to the ground on a line, but this time the landing almost ended in disaster. It was already raining. As the wind blew about them, they jumped up and down on the balloon envelope to deflate it faster so they could carry it beneath the awning. Dick came running to help, then Sergeyev. They were all soaked through, exhausted, and cursing out Oleg for having taken his sweet time with the descent.

"I shouted and shouted at you!" Kazik repeated. "What happened, are you deaf?"

Oleg didn't answer. He wanted — how could he admit this publicly — to go up in the air again, as high as the balloon would go, and let the wild wind carry him wherever it might.

Oleg looked at Marianna. There was a feeling of immense satisfaction and importance that she look at him. And once or twice he was able to catch her eye, But suddenly he was struck with a horrible suspicion: what if she had been joking? What if she didn't feel toward him as he felt toward her?

And when they were already in the barn and the balloon was safely tucked away, Marianna glanced at Dick and Sergeyev, who were standing beside the open doors, enduring the rain, and whispered to him,

"It was a great flight, wasn't it?"

Her voice held a degree of uncertainty as well, as though she were thinking the same as he. It was delightful.

Oleg answered,

"It was a great flight. It was."

***

Sergeyev went with Oleg on the day they first decided to go up without the tether.

They had waited forever it seemed, until finally there had come a day almost entirely without wind; as high as they could see the clouds above them were motionless.

The balloon rose confidently. Oleg was already used to the balloon and knew every tiny idiosyncracy. When the balloon rose as high as the former limit Oleg turned back down and waved his hands at the people below. The whole settlement was down there now, the same as on the day of their first flight. Oleg searched for Marianna with his eyes. He waved to her; no one but Marianna would have guessed.

The balloon rose lazily, but insistently, and faster than ever before, and Oleg felt himself waiting for the basket to tug and for the rope to bring the ascent to a stop.

But the flight continued, and the horizon slowly and imperceptibly widened — the edges of the world were hidden in mist.

The settlement became a mouldy patch in the endless sea of forest.

Suddenly it grew darker; a descending tongue of cloud from above had blocked the horizon. The rise of the balloon slowed.

"Want to descend?" Sergeyev asked.

"No." Oleg said.

Sergeyev's question surprised him, because they had wanted to pierce the clouds and see the sky from the very first. Sergeyev said nothing.

It grew very quiet. Oleg had never experienced such a degree of quiet in his life before.

There was no sensation of lift, but the balloon was indeed rising; they could see clumps of thick cloud slowly descending before their eyes.

It was far colder here than on the ground. The edge of the basket grew wet.

"I'd say we've stopped rising." Sergeyev said.

Oleg went to the burner and increased the flame.

It grew even darker. And terror began to creep into their thoughts. Oleg looked at Sergeyev and thought, *He's lucky he's not afraid of anything. But I don't know where we're going and if we'll ever even get out of the clouds.* He didn't know Sergeyev was even more fearful than he was; this was only Sergeyev's second time up in the balloon, but the older man feared an unexpected whirlwind might catch at the balloon and carry it away, perhaps to be dashed against the ground, or into the high mountains.

"Should I throw out the ballast?" Oleg asked.

The question was rhetorical; they had decided long ago on the ground Oleg would be commander of the balloon in the air. The bags filled with ballast had been brought along to be emptied over the side.

Sergeyev helped Oleg empty the ballast bags over the side. Each time the sand was released the balloon jerked upwards like a tired swimmer desperate to get to the surface of the water to gasp for air.

And suddenly it grew light. The light was odd, alien. And Oleg guessed they would soon exit the clouds.

They came out of the clouds at the lower cloud layer. Around them was grey cotton, but over their heads were stars. And Oleg saw what an unexpected blow this vision was to Sergeyev, who hadn't seen the stars for decades.

Sergeyev froze looking upward. The balloon circled around, reflecting the clouds, but between its side and the clouds was a band of sky so blue it made the eyes ache, and a multitude of stars. To the right the sun was a fiery cauldron, but at the same time it was freezing cold, the same cold freshness of the infinite sky of the mountains, yet their faces and exposed hands were hot where the sun touched them.

But the balloon continued to rise imperceptibly, leaving the clouds which appeared soft, but so flat and firm one could just step across the side of the basket and walk on them.

Sergeyev came to his senses first and said,

"Close off the burner or the wind will carry us away."

Oleg obeyed.

The two of them looked at the sky and clouds in silence. Neither wanted to go back down again, although they were freezing.

Then Oleg saw something very strange.

A black point was moving quickly across the sky in a straight line.

It appeared first at the periphery of his vision, and what caught Oleg's attention first was not the point itself but the straight white tail it trailed far behind, stretching from the horizon.

"Sergeyev." Oleg pointed. "What type of animal is that?"

Sergeyev had been looking to the other side and turned. The point was approaching the side of the balloon which covered half the sky and was almost hidden from view.

Sergeyev said,

"It can't be?"

"What?" Oleg caught the unbelievable astonishment in Sergeyev's voice.

"It's . . . an aircraft. Or a rocket. Or . . . It's man-made."

The black point vanished, and Sergeyev hurried to the other side of the basket. The basket listed to one side.

Ignoring the cold they waited for the black point to emerge from behind the balloon. It did. It sped directly away from them, trailing a long tail behind.

"What man made it?" Oleg asked almost timidly. "There's no one else here. Don't you mean it's a bird?"

"Considering the speed and the height, it can't be anything but a probe." Sergeyev said.

"A what?"

"An atmospheric exploratory scout. It moves at a speed of about two thousand kilometers an hour at a height of ten to fifteen kilometers. Planetary survey expeditions use them all the time."

"You mean, there's someone else here?"

"I mean there is someone else here." Sergeyev said.

The older man looked at the sun, determining the scout's direction.

The scout had started to descend. They could see it dropping down and losing speed.

The contrail vanished not far from the layer of clouds.

And that was all. All that was left was the trail of torn white mist in the blue sky.

"Let's go down." Sergeyev said.

"Right." Oleg agreed. "I'm almost frozen now."

They landed in the lake. The whole settlement had to come out to drag the balloon back before it grew dark. At the end everyone was filthy and soaking wet. And no one cared.

There were people on the planet. Other people.

CHAPTER SEVEN

The planet had no name.

It did have a numerical code. Any library computer in the Galaxy could have provided information about it on that basis, never suspecting human beings would have been more comfortable if the planet had a name. More familiar.

But that happens with a lot of distant planets when they're discovered; most are so far away all they get is a number in a list of discoveries.

The planet had been found a number of years ago. Then, as is usual, a WorldScout station was sent there. The automated station went into orbit, sent down scouts, photographed the planet's surface, dispatched probes to the aforementioned surface to gather samples of the air and soil. Then the WorldScout station gathered together all its servants and headed off to the nearest space lane where it waited for the next starship. On the starship a junior graduate student named Kirejko scanned the material, made a number of qualified choices, and sent all materials on the planet to the archives to await their turn.

The junior graduate student — a previous era would have termed his post "work study" — could have noticed the planet presented special interest because of the existence of autochthonous sophonts, because the non-sapient biota was highly unusual, because there was a marvelous climate and conditions ideal for human colonization, or, finally, because of the wealth and diversity of mineral riches the planet exhibited.

The junior graduate student named Kirejko noticed absolutely nothing of the sort.

The planet was lacking in native intelligent life. The higher latitudes were occupied by ice covered mountains, the lower covered by an eternally cloud-shrouded layer of primeval forest, while a burning desert stretched over thousands of kilometers of the equatorial areas. The orbital inclination was negligible, the local year lasted a little longer than a thousand days. Nothing out of the ordinary.

In principle, the middle latitudes, the cloud covered forests and the somewhat hotter prairie were suitable for human beings, but the planet's distance from the established space lanes and a lack of free Ecosurvey teams in this distant sector of the Galaxy condemned the planet to partial oblivion.

In as much as there was no intelligent life on the planet and little chance of it developing for a few geological eras at least, it was honestly felt the planet had no great need for a name.

"At the very least we could baptize the planet at our own discretion." Pavlysh said to no one in particular. He was trying to oversee the erection of his work desk and failing. "Exploration groups do have that right. For example Violet, if for no other reason that there is no other planet named 'Violet' in the *Galactic Guide to Planets and Bodies* already."

The table refused to erect itself. The flat package had opened up all right and the component elements began to seek out their proper positions, but one of the drawers seemed to be a size too large, as though some work-robot had packed it all wrong in the factory. Pavlysh tried to maneuver it into place manually with his field knife and felt like he was working with screws and screw drivers. Finally he worked the waste basket into place.

Claudia was observing the battle and was displeased. Claudia was unable to stand disorder no matter what the source.

Pavlysh arranged the table and lamp so the grey twilight fell to the left. He preferred not to work with the light shining directly in his face.

Claudia arranged her own work table to ensure she faced the light.

Claudia's own work table was complete in its grey travel case; she had packed it herself after completing her last assignment rather than requisitioning one from ship's stores. When she finished, the woman began to lay out her instruments on the table, precisely and neatly, although some of them had already spent time on half a dozen planets far more complicated than this one.

The third work table, belonging to Sally Hoskins, remained, for the moment, in storage while Sally oversaw the erection of the station. Microbots were indispensable for construction, but a single glitch could cost their lives.

The station's complement was supposed to have been all female.

Claudia Sun's team.

Claudia Sun was the team leader and geologist. Sally Hoskins the technician and cook. Srebrina Taleva the biologist.

Together they had already worked on four planets.

The Center for Space Research preferred not to introduce unnecessary complications into small research parties and tried to find crews composed either of married couples or all the same sex. The station domes were small, shower and toilet facilities separated from the common work rooms by plastic curtains, and the barriers between the sleeping cubicles hardly up to human eye level.

But Srebrina Taleva had succeeded in breaking her leg the day before landing.

The captain of the *Magellan* was Vyacheslav Pavlysh's old friend, Gleb Bauer. He called the doctor to the bridge and gave him a look that begged for sympathy.

"The Sun team is our last drop off, you understand.... The others are already in place."

"Srebrina Taleva will be out of commission for at least a month. A beautifully compounded fracture." Pavlysh, the ship's doctor, answered.

"That's not what I mean. I'd like your opinion on how the absence of a biologist will affect their work."

"Badly." That was evident.

"You understand we are preparing to land them for a four month stay?"

"Why else are we here?"

"We have a responsibility . . ." Bauer made it clear, in his view, the responsibility lay with Pavlysh.

"A leg transplant is certainly possible. but it would be very clumsy because of the size difference. And I'd want my own leg back. . . ."

"Slava, this is no joking matter."

It is remarkable how quickly captains begin to take themselves seriously after promotion. One would have thought it had been decades since Bauer had stood watch as second navigator on the *Seryozha*. Pavlysh had been ship's doctor then, and a ship's doctor he remained.

"What, exactly, do you propose?" Pavlysh asked. "The Captain should have all the solutions."

Bauer chose not to acknowledge the irony.

"Look, Slava, you've been after me a thousand times asking for leave to go exploring. 'I'm tired of sitting in this tin can.' Isn't that a direct quote?" Bauer's voice dropped from that of Captain to Friend.

"You actually want me to become Srebrina Taleva?"

"I'm asking you, if you wouldn't want to help out the survey team."

"I don't."

"Why?"

"I can't imagine how I'll work in an all-female team."

"I can guarantee you, if you agree, the team's composition will be thirty-three and a third percent male."

"Claudia Sun will eat me alive. Don't you know her reputation?"

"I've dealt with Claudia personally. She's one of the most reasonable people this side of the Sol system. I can guarantee . . ."

"You certainly have a right to your own opinion. I asked you to let me off when we landed the Sato team. That was a rather interesting planet and I knew the people fairly well."

"Are you afraid of a single woman, or are you afraid to work?"

"Of the single woman, thank you. And anyway, she would never agree."

"Then everything's settled. Sun is willing to take the devil himself so long as we can land her team on the planet."

Evidently, Claudia had already agreed to take Pavlysh. Otherwise she would have been forced to return to Earth — there were no other trained biologists on board. In fact she was rather dubious about the solution, and as often happens, Pavlysh immediately went out of his way to prove her very worst preconceptions. During unloading he managed to break the infrascope, which theoretically should have been dropable from the top of a ten story building without suffering a scratch. But here and now he couldn't accomplish the most simple tasks, such as overseeing microbots as they went about their programmed tasks.

In any herd, including the human kind, a table of ranks – called by the sociologists a "pecking order" and the ethologists and anthropologists a "dominance hierarchy" – arises out of necessity. Pavlysh, with his entry into the team, had altered a complicated set of arrangements that had taken years to work out. Everything would have been simpler, had but Claudia Sun been a middle aged, masculine woman with a thunderous voice and abrupt mannerisms. But Claudia Sun did not produce the impression of a space wolf and leader of the survey team. She was young and beautiful with the features of a classic porcelain doll, with straight black hair divided into a pair of braids and tied into a tight knot in back.

Claudia Sun was one of those women who wordlessly and immediately take command in any feminine environment, but ordinarily retreat before large men, seeking shelter behind a mask of hostility and impertinence. Worse of all, Claudia's sense of humor had failed her, and she ignored her internal timidity where Pavlysh was concerned and strengthened her external opposition the moment she realized a male cuckoo had been dropped into her well organized, all-female nest.

Vyacheslav Pavlysh should have inherited the ecological niche formerly occupied by Srebrina Taleva, a woman with a romantic nature inclined toward unexpected mood swings; open, cheerful, but luckless, hardly the sort of person who would ordinarily accomplish the fracturing of her leg in the closed confines and controlled environment of a starship. But Claudia immediately began to contrast, albeit unfairly, the clumsy and inadequate Pavlysh with that "ideal worker, that paragon of productivity, Srebrina." As though he were some sort of anti-Srebrina.

But Pavlysh was able to find advantages in his position. He was going to spend four months on a completely unexplored planet — a situation for which thousands of scientists could only dream. He now had the opportunity to make his mark in science, discover new families of bacteria or new types of symbiosis. *And why not? What could possibly be better than to break free of the overworked routines of shipboard life and throw yourself into an adventure?* Had he really asked Bauer to keep him out of the group? Of course he had asked. Read the guide books and instructions and you will convince yourself that a real research station functions routinely, without adventure; that well organized work permits no failures, and that any adventure or adversity is no more than a sumptuous failure to think far enough ahead . . .

In the end, however, Starship Surgeon Vyacheslav Pavlysh, now in his forties, both capable and curious, not excessively vain, had not lost his taste for life; he had jumped ship — if with the Captain's permission — ploughed the cosmic sea and more or less voluntarily landed on the shores of this uninhabited island in the society of two attractive women. One of them at least, Sally Hoskins, was a damsel now into her second divorce. Now all that remained to be determined was if the uninhabited island held coconut palms, tigers, and Men Fridays to be saved from cannibals.

At that moment in his musings the wobbly body of the half-constructed work table chose to collapse, spilling everything Pavlysh had managed to place on it in a heap on the floor.

Claudia watched her new biologist on his hands and knees searching for his property with a certain annoyance. Sally peeped out from the kitchen compartment; torn between pity for Pavlysh and a superficial caution in dealing with Claudia, and said,

"We can always support the top with crates on the sides, can't we?"

"Evidently he will have to." Claudia answered dryly, not looking at her subordinates, and returned her interest to the view screen showing the cloud-wrapped forest. "Not worth dragging any of the local microflora into the station."

"'And one little boy dragged home a crocodile that bit off his grandfather's little finger.'" Pavlysh found himself repeating an old children's rhyme. Claudia's tone of voice had brought it back to mind. A moment later he regretted it.

"My husband . . ." Claudia Sun said unexpectedly, then pursed her lips and fell silent.

"Don't, Claudia." Sally said.

"Why not. Let him find out."

Claudia looked Pavlysh in the eyes.

Lord, thought Pavlysh. *Don't tell me. Her husband died on some godforsaken planet . . .*

"My husband," Claudia repeated, "from whom it has been my privilege to be separated these seven years now, almost succeeded in wiping out the expedition to the Corrac'h system when he carelessly introduced a local life-form into the station."

And after that we divorced, Pavlysh couldn't help finishing with his thoughts, *because I could simply not abide such a scandalous violation of standing orders.* Aloud, he said:

"I promise you, Claudia, I will never bring any local life forms into the station."

Claudia sighed with a certain relief, evidently, she had decided to accept this jest as a serious promise.

Pavlysh grabbed one of the crates Sally had already emptied and placed it under the table's short leg.

***

Pavlysh sat down at the table. The chair obediently embraced him. *Anything for your comfort sir?* He looked to his right. The transparency in front of him had grown dark. Pavlysh wiped it, but was unable to examine the near-by forest because the barrage of wet snow was crawling down the curved side of the dome and the grey trunks of the trees had started to wave back and forth, surrendering to the wind and the streams of rain.

"We should instruct the computer to grow a wiper for the window." Pavlysh advised Claudia. "Without it well have trouble admiring the landscape."

"I thought about that some time ago." Claudia said. "Back on our last mission. But never had time for it."

Pavlysh sighed. Ill fortune had provided him with a serious leader.

The snow came down all the heavier. Snowflakes danced on the window, and the trees finally vanished in the gloom.

"They never sent the weather report." Pavlysh said.

"They didn't?" Claudia was surprised. Then she thought again: "Don't speak nonsense."

"But I haven't the slightest idea what to wear when I go out for a walk."

"You'll wear a full biosuit with helmet and internal air supply." Claudia saw nothing to joke about. "And you will never, *never* take it off outside the confines of this station."

"That was why they never sent the weather report." Pavlysh suddenly realized what he was doing but couldn't bring himself to stop. He wanted to annoy Claudia.

Sally broke out laughing and immediately suppressed it. "I'll get milk and cookies, children." She said.

"We have different temperaments." Claudia told Pavlysh. "The impulse to constantly joke leads to bravado and bravado leads to unjustifiable risk taking. Risks, here, are very dangerous. The fate of the entire station may very well hang on one of your unsuccessful jokes."

"I'll be serious." Pavlysh sighed.

A buzzing at the Com station ended the conversation. Sally asked Claudia to take her place at the stove and she herself hurried to the transmitter. The *Magellan* was calling. It was far enough away from the system's center of mass its engines could stress space and make the jump to the next planet. The team was about to go out of contact with the rest of the galaxy, and would remain isolated for at least four months. Subspace communication from the bottom of a planetary gravity well was only possible for large ships and major colonies; the equipment was too massive for survey stations and planetary cutters. There is an element of risk in this. You had to get used to it. The hypergrav generator of a subspace transmitter would have occupied the entire dome.

For emergencies there was the beacon in orbit well beyond the depths of the planetary gravity well. If necessary they could get to it in the lifeboat now sitting outside their dome on the tough green grass.

From this moment on communication was limited to the unhurried, ancient means. In the case of an emergency a signal would be sent at the ordinary speed of radio waves, up to the beacon, and from there through subspace to Earth-14. Any cry for help would take at least six weeks to get a reply.

At the end of the message Bauer sent his regards. "And remember Slava, don't get bored."

"'til we meet again . . ." In several hours the starship *Magellan* would vanish from this part of space and emerge elsewhere, several parsecs distant.

Pavlysh listened to Sally acknowledge their call and bid them a fond adieu, noting down the final instructions. He walked closer to the window and looked out at the sky. There was nothing much to see. Just a mixture of gloom and greyness.

Pavlysh knew the station had been landed where it was the end of spring, in the northern hemisphere, in the temperate zone. That meant one could count on the weather getting better with every day. This spot had been chosen because of data collected by the earlier automated probes. This was the optimal climate for the investigators: to the north began the mountain ranges, empty and bleak, with only naked tundra beyond. To the south were oceans, and on the other side of the waters the land was desert scorched by the type F star. The latitudes chosen for work were the most active biologically and a significant part of their work would be carried out in the neighborhood of the dome itself.

On the other side of the scanner Pavlysh could see the rounded tunnel leading to the smaller dome of the bioscout lab. There were three auxiliary domes attached by airlocks to the station. One, with the bioscouts, was Pavlysh's domain. The second, with the geological equipment, was Claudia's. The third was the supply shed and garage where the all terrain vehicle was kept. The teardrop shape of the lifeboat stood on three inadequate looking legs some distance off. The legs served it quite well.

"If my help isn't needed now," Pavlysh said, "I'll go off to the store room. I have things to sort out."

"Go." Claudia said. "You can ready the bioscouts after supper. We start the research program tomorrow."

"I know." Pavlysh said.

Pavlysh headed down the tunnel into the supply dome. Containers with tools and instruments and supplies were packed away in precise order. Claudia had supervised the loading herself — they said she made the robots tremble. The air was stuffy and Pavlysh went to the life support controls and turned them on. The dome began to breath. Pavlysh could hear the machinery drawing in outside air and selectively filtering out the non-terrestrial organisms, turning the cold, living air from outside into the warm, sterile, breathable mixture identical to that found on any starship.

Then the most complicated part of Pavlysh's work began: he had to search out in this ordered mess the crates containing the twenty-three numbers which matched the bioscouts, analyzers, surgical kit, the lab, diagnosticon, field recorders and film packs and who knew what else had been loaded.

Pavlysh sighed, looked over the printout list of tools in his hand, and realized at the very least three of the four months would be spent in searching for his own equipment.

Mostly Pavlysh wanted to find the containers where he'd stowed away his microbooks and reader. Pavlysh was afraid Claudia had discarded his precious hoard of mysteries and old space operas while checking over the loading of their supplies. He knew the microbooks were in container Sixteen, which, as luck would have it, had found its way to the bottom of the pile. But it couldn't wait until Sally activated the servorobots; so the good doctor got some exercise.

Trying not to make too much noise Pavlysh dragged the container with the holy grail into an empty corner. He opened it. His very worst fears were confirmed. And he came to hate Claudia Sun. No doubt she had found the box with pulp fiction and in its place inserted something far more necessary for their research. His annoyance, although it was not unexpected, was deep and painful. Pavlysh realized there was no way he would be able to stand the society of this prig for a month without the mental anodyne of Hercule Poirot and Kimball Kinnison, Blackie Duquesne and Miss Marple.

Pavlysh sat down on the container and told himself he was lucky; now he would be able to spend more time on useful work and his chances of making a valuable contribution to science had been sharply increased.

But Pavlysh was unable to convince himself of any such thing, and he began to compose an emotional limerick about the departure of the ship and the sadistic cruelty inflicted by the station head on her crew.

Then the door opened; Sally entered. She was a tall, full bodied woman with light brown hair, with wise green eyes, and a full mouth inclined to grins.

ing across the plast window. They moved so fast they merged into a greenish blur. The face closed its maw.

"Pavlysh realized Sally was holding his hand.

"Frightened?" Pavlysh asked.

Sally took away her hand.

"There go the walks in the woods." She sighed. "And I was hoping to be able to get out and around here."

"Here's my first paper for *Annals of the Royal Society of Extraplanetary Zoology.*" Pavlysh said. "The peculiarities of symbiotic creatures on the planet . . . what's it called, by the way? The planet."

"You can think of the most irrelevant things." Sally said. "You're very cold blooded. Slava. I nearly died of fright."

"Just think how repulsive we must be to that."

The white, eyeless muzzle vanished. The worms became even more agitated; evidently they were afraid their residence had departed. Sally called Claudia.

Claudia threw only one glance at the worms and immediately reached for her camera. She cast Pavlysh a bitter rebuke.

A black whip struck at the plast, squashing one of the worms; the innards flowed yellow over the clear surface. The remaining worms froze. The whip slowly crawled, expanded, until it turned into a band about ten centimeters in width. The band curled into a tube and the worms began to crawl into it obediently. After a few seconds the plast had become clear, all that remained were a few yellow streaks to remind them to the little tragedy they had just witnessed.

"Up to now we haven't even turned on the outside cameras." Claudia said. "We don't even know what's going on outside."

"Thanks for not forgetting my murder mysteries." Pavlysh said.

"Don't mention it." Claudia said. "Just don't forget about your work."

"I'll remember. I even remember my Latin. I can bestow all of the creatures we've seen outside the window with the appropriate terminology. Deformis, foedus, odiosus, invisus, horrendus,

"I think I can assuage your grief." Sally's smile widened. She went over to the pile of containers and said, "Help me, Slava."

They pulled out the second container from the top marked Fifty-Seven, which indicated it belonged to the geology section, Sally opened it and pulled out the treasure chest box with the microbooks.

"You did it?" Pavlysh said joyfully, almost having to stop himself from embracing the Faerie Queen, the fair Gloriana. "She pulled it out and you put it back in?"

"No that simple." Sally answered. "Claudia would never have decided to leave something belonging to someone else, especially if it wasn't broken. We repacked everything and her microborer didn't fit. I had to rearrange things."

"All the same, thanks." Pavlysh said.

"But I prefer classics." Sally said.

"And Claudia prefers geological journals?"

"The journals and *Anna Karenina*. She carries a hardcopy *Anna Karenina* with her everywhere. As soon as things start to go bad she starts reading. Look, just don't send her into it today, all right? Think of what she has to deal with?"

"You mean me?"

"She thinks you're laughing at her. All the time."

"No, of course not, certainly not all the time." Pavlysh answered, which caused Sally to start to laugh.

The lighting in the supply section was meager, coming from only one window. When the face covered it the dome darkened. Both Pavlysh and Sally felt the change in illumination.

The face was nearly white, and if it had eyes they were hidden beneath a mass of tangled fur. But it did have long, jagged fangs and when it opened its snout the face tested the strength of the plast window. Pavlysh could see the fangs were brown and thought the face never brushed them. Between teeth like the crenelations of an ancient fortress sat shining tiny creatures similar to immature worms. The worms also had teeth. The worms burst out of their fortress and clutched somehow at the smooth surface, hunt-

horribilis, will serve excellently in the naming of new genera. The opportunities are endless."

Claudia turned and left.

Sally looked after her and said,

"When you decide to name something after me, I'd rather the fangs were short and not too many eyes, please."

"Your name shall only be bestowed upon the butterflies." Pavlysh said.

The sound of plates rattling came from the living section. Claudia was putting out the dishes.

"Do you think there's intelligent life here?" Sally asked.

"Not very likely. The automated probes didn't observe anything, and the native life forms they did observe weren't all that high on the evolutionary ladder."

"And what if?"

"What if, we can say when we leave."

"I love new planets." Sally said. "At first the new world is completely dark. As though you were only just born. And then you find yourself coming alive in the new world. And it becomes light."

Pavlysh walked over to the window again. Small insects were crawling across the plast around the yellow scraps. The snow had stopped. The forest was empty, watching and waiting.

We're the aliens here. Pavlysh thought. *Small bits of protoplasm in a plastic cover. Will this world accept us? Will it reject us? Or won't it even notice our passage.*

"The nearest other people are trillions of kilometers away from here." He said aloud.

"What does it matter?" Sally retorted. "And why are you able to read my thoughts."

"But trillions of kilometers isn't that much." Pavlysh said. "Our existence is registered everywhere it has to be. At Space Fleet Headquarters, on Earth 14, in Survey's records, at the Central Institute of Cosmological Studies. In the paymaster's computers where we're earning on-planet bonuses. If something does happen to us, someone will raise such a ruckus we'll have rescue cruisers heading here from all parts of the galaxy."

"And if they're late?"

"They'd better not be." Pavlysh said. "We should behave ourselves and listen to aunt Claudia. And nothing bad will happen. Most importantly we should wash our hands before supper."

"I guessed," Sally said, "You are lonely, and you're already sorry you came with us."

"Not in the least."

Pavlysh continued to look out on the forest. He was hoping to catch sight of some sort of movement, some sort of life. Just for a second as the light vanished he thought the trees began to waive their branches slowly, like somnambulant dancers, obedient to some common rhythm born of a distant unseen drum.

***

The research station had been landed the edge of an enormous forest.

After the first two days' furious activity, the erection of the dome, the unloading of supplies, there was only silence.

No one had left the station, and the thin double walls dampened any sound that might have come from inside.

Slowly, the forest got used to the aliens beside it. The motionless dome disturbed nothing.

Pavlysh, although he was extremely busy, finally had the satisfaction of observing a research station begin operations on a new world. With the powering on of the external cameras and recorders, the setting up of the meteorological station and the release of borers into the ground beneath Claudia's geosurvey dome, which industriously set about to tunnel their way through the soil of the planet, an objective understanding of the forest and forest's world had begun, with the probes' data flowing directly to the computers.

The information being returned would confirm first and foremost what the team knew already: all planets are composed of the same elements which form the same compounds wherever they are in the universe, and evolve into life which obeys common laws of genetics and consists of identical cells, anywhere in the Galaxy.

The differences the team expected to find were not in the biological principles but in the exterior peculiarities. Therefore Pavlysh was continually facing a total lack of satisfaction from the contrast between the accumulation of objective knowledge and his complete sense of ignorance.

Pavlysh understood it was madness to go outside into the living, unsterilized air, take in his hand a leaf from a tree, or pull up a handful of grass and smell it. He knew that behind the serenity of the surrounding forest were hidden powers hostile to human beings, not because they were directed against human beings per se, but because they were totally alien, did not know him, and fled as soon as attempts were made to contact them.

On the morning of the third day Pavlysh prepared to launch his first bioscout. In all he had three bioscouts — they were programmed to examine the atmosphere, registering chemical and biological constituents at various heights. Claudia had virtually identical scouts, but they were intended to provide a geological map of the planet. The difference was that, in the case of emergency, Claudia could land her scouts and use them to carry out long distance coring. Pavlysh's scouts were simple information collectors although he downloaded the information when they returned. Afterwards Pavlysh would search through the data the scout brought back, examine the photographs, and determine which areas he should check in person.

Pavlysh went through the airlock and down the low, oval corridor into his lab.

The scouts were waiting for him, laying on high pedestals. Pavlysh, following the program developed long ago and now standard operating procedure, should have been in the first stage of sending the scouts out in search daisies. Every flight corresponded to a petal of the daisy. The length of a "petal" was five hundred kilometers, the heights varying. The ellipse of the first 'petal' reached the height of thirteen kilometers, all the rest would be carried out lower. This way they would investigate a cylinder of atmosphere to thirteen kilometers in height with a diameter of a thousand kilometers in all directions.

The launch procedure itself was fairly simple. Having fed in the program, Pavlysh just pushed the launch button, and the rest followed without his participation.

The scout gave him a green light; it was ready. The pedestal started to move, carrying the scout to the top of the dome and the overhead lock. Pavlysh, raising his head, saw a grey cloudy sky. A drop of rain fell on his helmet. Pavlysh wiped it with his glove.

The launch trembled. The scout slowly rose from the pedestal and confidently headed toward the hole in the roof. It lifted, lowly humming, like a fat beetle flying out for a hunt.

The opening in the dome's roof closed.

"Why not?" Pavlysh thought aloud. "The work day's begun."

He touched his com button and said,

"Claudia, I just launched the first scout. I'm going outside now."

"That's dangerous." Claudia said; her voice, almost distorted in his helmet phone, seemed like a girl's and almost soft. "You haven't forgotten your hand blaster?"

"No, my angel." Pavlysh said. "What's more I've taken emergency food rations, the sleeping bag and a large stick. Consequently I am informing you I will be going the enormous distance of approximately ten meters from the dome.

"Slava, stop joking." Claudia said. "This is the first time you've gone outside here."

"In point of fact my second." Pavlysh said. "You might remember when we were landed here we had to spend about an hour in the open."

"Protected by the ship's forcefield." Claudia corrected him, "With about ten other members of the crew around."

"Thank you." Pavlysh said. "I'll be careful. Don't worry. And anyway I have to test the stunner."

Pavlysh pulled the pistol from the pocket of his overalls. The pistol was small but heavy. The handle fit into his palm snugly. The weapon was designed especially for expeditions; it could immobilize any aggressor, from a snake to an elephant, but the effect was relative, depending both on the mass of the target and the predator's metabolism. What would be enough to make one animal sleep peacefully for a week would make another drowsy, yet might kill a third. Thus part of Pavlysh's reason for going out was to test the weapon on local creatures, to obtain laboratory specimens and determine the action of the anaesthetizer. If, in fact, those would-be lab specimens did not object too much.

The outside lock dilated open.

For a few minutes Pavlysh stood just outside the dome, looking around and waiting to see how the local fauna would react to his presence.

The fauna did not react at all.

Pavlysh sauntered across the sparse grass toward the landing boat, looking up at his reflection in its curved side above his head. Then he looked through the window into the geological lab. As to be expected Claudia was standing by the window and looking as if to make certain her child were about to cross the street only on the green light.

Pavlysh waved to Claudia, who raised her hand in answer, but she didn't leave the window.

"You should have children." Pavlysh said. "Five, at a minimum."

Then he was horrified he might have left his com on. No, it wasn't and she hadn't heard. Otherwise she would have been embarrassed.

Now to take his time looking around.

The steep dome of the station with its finger-like corridors leading to the small domes of the labs stood about two hundred meters from the edge of the forest. This was the side on which the window on which Pavlysh's desk looked out.

In order to circumnavigate the station Pavlysh had to walk in a broad circle that led him nearer the lake. The slope was covered with grass and sharp rocks.

The lake itself was grey, flat, quiet; in fact the entire world gave the impression of peaceful greyness. Only the impression. Pavlysh realized this greyness covered passions and tragedies, primitive yes, and because of that all the more cruel as it put on its best face to newcomers.

Pavlysh bent his head back and looked upward. For the last three days the clouds had not once parted, the sun had not shone down for a minute. It was the same grey color as the lake, and so featureless he could not tell if they were moving or hanging motionless over his head.

Something was shining in front of him.

Pavlysh carefully headed down the slope and stopped a few steps from a shining creature, which was busily digging into the ground. The creature paid no attention to the human whatsoever. Pavlysh walked a little closer, holding the stunner at the ready. The creature's shiny round metallic back was almost entirely hidden below the ground. Pavlysh squatted down and started to carefully pull the dirt away from the hole. Then he clutched the being and, with a jerk, pulled him out of the ground.

It didn't fight back or complain. Something in it cracked. Pavlysh saw a long probe drop to the dirt.

He raised the ball in his hand and realized he had managed to grab the rarest 'animal' in these parts — one of Claudia's mobile borers, and now Claudia was going to burn his ears off for this and he deserved it.

Since the borer was going to have to be fixed anyway Pavlysh decided to carry it with him, pulling the thin probe out of the ground and packing it all in his sample container. Then, as much as he did not want to do it, he pressed the com button and called Claudia.

"All your borers working?"

"One just this moment went off line." Claudia said. "I was about to ask you to check to see if something has happened to it?"

"You needn't ask." Pavlysh said. "I went hunting and just caught it. I'll bring it to Sally so she can fix it."

"But the borer was metal! Round! How could anyone mistake it. . . ."

"As you can see, terror has great eyes." Pavlysh said. "Ignorance leads to the silliest mistakes."

Pavlysh switched off again. He was angry with himself. No ordinary biologist would have mistaken a test instrument for a living being. And Pavlysh, over the years, had worked on achieving a reputation as a more-or-less normal person and even a scientist.

This was the danger of an alien world and one's own watchfulness. A remarkable coincidence — he was exhibiting an almost paranoid watchfulness together with a complete lack of danger.

The only reason I went after this ball was because I knew my helmet is strong and no teeth can puncture it, my paralyzer can fell any predator, because I can run back to the dome and even run back to space in the landing boat if worst comes to worst and wait there until they pick us up. I have no reasons to fear this planet, if it doesn't want to inflict some sort of cataclysm on us. And at the same time I don't trust it. I fear it and am taking all measures to avoid coming into contact with it while studying it. What would happen if I found myself here without the dome, the helmet, naked and without protection? Would I still look on the forest and lake as so picturesque? If the forest hid death for me, and the lake hid death, and the air itself threatened me with death?

These were empty speculations leading him nowhere. The best thing to do was to go down to the lake and take water samples. Of course one of the scouts could have done it for him just as well, but he couldn't surrender all the joys of field research to the automated machinery. The robots had no imaginations, and Pavlysh had one that was very well developed indeed.

Pavlysh avoided the scatterings of bushes, keeping to the open areas.

It was apparent the locality was deficient in fauna, although the plant life throve. It was perfectly reasonable a world would exist dominated by flowers, storied for its man-eating mushrooms!

Suddenly he saw an insect — something black and quick darted between his legs, extended gossamer wings and flew off into the bushes.

So, Pavlysh thought satisfied. *Our first neighbor.*

Pavlysh went down to the edge of the water. He stood a while on the bank. The lake's water was clear, the shore itself was covered with thin ice. The thin hairs of water plants were frozen into the ice below. A thin snake about a finger length long flitted between the stones and went off into the depths.

The lake's long shore vanished into the roiling gray mists; you could only guess hills rose beyond it if you'd seen them during the landing.

Pavlysh smashed the surface of the ice and gathered some water into a test bottle, then turned over the next stone hoping to see something else alive. But the ground below was unoccupied.

Far off, about a hundred meters from the shore, the water bubbled and foamed. Something dark, like the shell of an enormous turtle, lifted above the surface, then plunged below and the water whirled about and sent ripples toward him.

Pavlysh stood up, holding the test bottle in his hand. The water quieted down, the lake grew silent. It was waiting for Pavlysh to do something. He looked around involuntarily — it was pretty far to the domes. The water was agitated again, but differently this time; he caught sight of a speeding wake as whatever it was in the water, not wanting to show itself to the human, quickly headed toward the other shore.

And then it was dead quiet around him again — even the wind had died down.

Pavlysh began to feel an unexplainable, irrational terror that something unseen and unheard was heading for him. He made a step back from the bank, then another, not looking where he was stepping and stumbled on a stone, hardly keeping his balance and unexpectedly found himself running a little ways back up the slope, not turning around, and trying to give the impression he was merely tired of walking along the shore.

"Pavlysh?" He heard Claudia's voice. "Has anything happened?"

The woman really did have intuition. And, perhaps, experience.

"Nothing. Nothing at all." Pavlysh tried to get control of his breathing.

He quickened his pace, throwing a glance back over his shoulder at the lake.

The lake was undisturbed and quiet again. Idyllic.

From far off the snow storm was an approaching grey wall, and the lake water before it grew pockmarked.

"No bother." Pavlysh said. "I'm coming back now. Rather boring lake."

The dome was a comfortable, welcome vision. Inside it was warm, the monsters that ruled outside were barred entrance.

Sally Hoskins was outside, standing beside the landing boat, her orange biosuit gleaming from the moisture. She waved to Pavlysh.

"I discovered you had gone for a walk." She said. "And decided to tag along. So long as you don't mind."

"But won't Claudia be angry?"

"Certainly not. Standing instructions are that dangerous and unfamiliar areas should be studied only in groups."

"And where's the dangerous place around here?"

"Don't go too far." Claudia's voice came over their coms.

"We're only going to the forest and back." Sally answered.

The sparse grass covering the fields vanished altogether three steps from the first trees. Here the ground itself was bare except for spots of grey-blue moss.

The boles of the tress were whitish, some with red, others with yellow tints. 'Boles' was a convenient tag; they were more like underground roots which for some reason had decided to come up for light than the trunks of true trees. Along the ground the roots had twisted themselves into complicated knots, as though they feared someone would drag them back below the ground and had taken measures against that.

The trees had no leaves, in the usual meaning of the term. The roots grew thinner, turning into gray hairs which hung like tassels and hardly moved despite the breezes, giving the forest an ominous, haunted appearance.

The ground beneath their feet was damp, flat cakes of snow lay everywhere, a tossed salad of orange lichens and leaves and blue mounds of moss like ragged mops.

"Out of a nasty fairy tale." Sally said.

She stretched out her hand and carefully touched her fingers to a tree. The seemingly hard surface gave way and pulled back, as though it were made of rubber and the hairs on the tree's head started to shiver. Sally gave a start and pulled back her hand. Pavlysh almost laughed. The ominous atmosphere of the forest was palpable.

"What happened?" Claudia asked sharply.

"Everything's okay." Answered Pavlysh. "We'll get used to it."

They went forward a few more steps; a small hemisphere stuck out from the moss on the ground, like a button mushroom.

Pavlysh bent low pick up one of the mushrooms, but Sally said,

"A moment, I have a probe."

She reached out to the mushroom with the small probe; at the touch of the metal the plant suddenly vanished, darting back beneath the ground.

"Curious." Sally said, and extended her probe toward another.

But then a thin root, sticking out from the tree and laying on the ground, the same color as the tree and therefore obviously safe, approached the probe and grabbed it, twisting the metal; as Sally tried to hold on to the probe the root almost pulled her from her feet such was its strength.

Pavlysh acted almost instinctively. He pulled out the stunner and sent a shot into the plant. The root immediately jerked erect, frozen.

Sally was standing with the probe clutched to her chest, as though she feared something else might try to grab it away from her.

"Sorry." She said.

"They don't like us here." Pavlysh said,

The forest had grown dark. The snow storm, from the direction of the lake, had covered the forest with a greasy layer of snow.

"Lets go home." Sally said.

"I agree."

The snow filled the air and they could see no more than three feet ahead. Because of their brief contra temps with the root they had lost their orientation; they found themselves walking fifteen meters through the forest but the mass of trees never ended. The trees just became thicker, the trunks fatter and whiter.

"Claudia." Pavlysh finally said. "Can you give us directions."

"Got lost, eh?" Claudia said.

The directional beacon began to buzz in their ears.

They made their way back slowly, avoiding the spots of moss and lichens. One time, in fact, Pavlysh stepped on an orange slime and it glued itself to his boots and began to crawl up his leg. Pavlysh bent down to wipe the lichen away but the wort immediately attached itself to his gloves.

"Oh well." Pavlysh said. "You can say we're bringing back a sample."

"What are you carrying?" Claudia asked.

"One very unpleasant forest." Pavlysh said. "I don't want to get lost here."

"I'd put the tea out now." Sally said.

"Superb idea." Pavlysh agreed.

Through the last trees they could see the domes of the station through broken streams of rain and the snow storm. Then they stopped and stood motionless, hoping not to be seen.

There was an animal between the forest and the dome, waiting for them.

Pavlysh had never conceived of such an animal even in his most fevered nightmares. Six thin legs carried a heavy body covered in long greenish fur similar to the water plants; a long line of armored plates decorated his crest. A terrible, fanged muzzle slowly opened and closed as though the monster were already smacking his lips at the thought of tasting them.

On seeing the people the animal gave out a strange, bleating sound, which Pavlysh heard as threat and challenge, and started to prance about, causing the Stegasauroid plates on his back to shake and crash together, beating out a fierce war drone.

Still bleating, the monster rushed at them.

Pavlysh pushed Sally aside and shot it with the stunner.

The monster howled and started to circle in place, as though it had lost sight of its quarry, small red eyes burning with anger. Pavlysh shot it again, and again without affect. It simply reminded the monster where they were standing.

It was Claudia who resolved the impasse. The green light of the station's defensive laser reached out from the top of the dome. It struck the grass and moved to the monster, and the creature collapsed to the ground.

"That's it." Pavlysh said, trying to laugh.

He turned to Sally.

Sally was silent. She was trying to extricate herself from the embrace of a tree. In backing away from the monster she had walked into one of the trees, which had spread wide and opened to envelop her, as though it wanted to swallow her whole.

Pavlysh drained the charge of the stunner against the tree. It worked on the tree. The bole shrank away and turned black, and Sally made three steps forward to fall into Pavlysh's hand.

"Why didn't you say something?" Pavlysh asked.

"I didn't want to alarm Claudia." Sally answered quietly.

Supporting Sally, Pavlysh walked over to the fallen monster — the three meter long body lay stretched out on the ground.

"Everything here wants to have us for dinner." He said.

He took Sally's probe and carefully opened the monster's maw to examine the teeth. In place of jagged canines and the equivalent of shearing carnassials were the flat plates of a herbivore.

Claudia had come out of the dome and joined them.

"First lesson." She said. "The stunner doesn't work against the local large predators. Or the effect remains insufficiently effective."

"This isn't a predator." Pavlysh said. "These type of plates are designed to crush and grind plant food, Although if this had managed to run us down we would never have learned that, and it would hardly have mattered. Thanks, Claudia."

"I was watching you all the time." She said.

"My knees are still shaking." Sally added.

"Just as well it happened now." Claudia continued. "As an object lesson."

"I don't understand."

"An object lesson in caution. You were walking around this planet like you would back on Earth. You won't do it again."

"Perhaps you're right." Pavlysh sighed. "Can you help me cart the carcass into the lab."

"I'll activate the servos." Claudia said.

As though it had heard her words one of the servos emerged through a lock and began to trudge toward the monster's corpse.

"What do you have on your leg?" Claudia asked.

The orange lichen had covered the overalls of the space suit nearly to his knee with a think crawling layer. Pavlysh scraped some of the moss into a test tube and headed off for disinfection.

CHAPTER EIGHT

The rain had turned into a snow squall, as though winter had decided to return, so everyone crowded into the Mayor's class room. It barely held them all. The children were sitting on the floor; the adults wanted to throw them out, but no one left, not even the youngest.

It seemed to Oleg that all the adults had only one aim ; argue with Sergeyev, show him up to be a liar, or at least delirious. But they simply didn't pay any attention to Oleg. Oleg did not understand this came about from a superstitious fear — everyone was so desperate to believe Sergeyev really had seen a bioprobe they came up with the most desperate arguments against it. Even stupid ones, from Oleg's point of view.

For example, for some reason, Oleg's mother insisted it was only an automatic satellite left behind by old researchers.

"In the atmosphere?" Sergeyev answered. "In atmosphere so dense it left a contrail? On the first such orbit a satellite would just burn up."

"But the height? You're certain of the height?" Vaitkus asked. He face had grown redder than his beard.

"Oleg, repeat what you saw."

Oleg repeated for the fifth time, at least, that he had seen a dark object; that object had moved quickly and had left behind it a misty white trail.

"Height up to about ten kilometers." Sergeyev said.

The room was stuffy, but no one bothered to open the door because blind Kristina was sick again and was coughing.

"Not positive proof." Luiza said. "We do know there are some very fast birds on this planet. Incredibly fast birds."

"Flying at a thousand kilometers an hour?" Sergeyev asked patiently.

Oleg was astonished at the older man's even temper. For what seemed like hours now the younger man had wanted to shout: *No, that wasn't a bird, it wasn't a satellite! Why are we sitting here wasting precious time in empty talk?*

"You're certain it's too small for an orbit boat?" Vaitkus asked.

"Just your ordinary, everyday bioprobe." Sergeyev answered. "I've seen hundreds of them in my life. I've launched them myself."

"Do you mean it photographed us?" Marianna asked.

"I don't think so." The Mayor said. "The previous expedition would have taken photo maps of the planet when it orbited a WorldScout satellite. It would be a bioscout or geoprobe."

"Well at least you believe me." Sergeyev said.

"Perhaps I want to believe you." The Mayor answered.

"Does that mean they might not spot us?" Marianna asked.

"They might not." Sergeyev agreed. "But they might."

"Just be careful to avoid this optimism I hear." Kristina said. "No one is going to notice us. For them to notice us, they'd have to be looking for us. Can you imagine what a tiny, insignificant speck we are on the face of this planet. Insignificant because the amount of metal we have in one spot is so small any sensors will just count us a part of the forest. No one is going to find us."

"Not even by accident?"

"Scouts carry out tests of the biosphere, air, soil, they are not used for producing maps." The Mayor said. "Kristina is right. The chances they will find us are nil. Never forget we are always beneath the clouds."

"They might find the ship?" Oleg said. "There's no cloud cover there."

"Chances a little better." Sergeyev said. "But not too great either."

That's all, thought Oleg, *they're starting to come to an agreement. They're allowing themselves to convince each other. As though they were doing each other a favor.* He suddenly wanted to say loud enough for them all to hear him that if it weren't for his balloon they would never have even seen the scout; perhaps the expedition which had launched the scout had been sitting around on the planet for the allotted half a year and is already getting ready to depart. Oleg had in his mind the clear image of a starship so much like the *PolarStar*, but intact, and people walking around inside who were washed and dressed in fine uniforms or space suits — they're closing the last of the containers with their specimens now and telling each other: "That's all; there's nothing interesting on this planet except for bleating gotes and zhakals."

The room had suddenly become very quiet.

And then Kazik's voice broke the silence. Kazik was sitting on the floor with the other small children; Fumiko lay across his outstretched legs.

"What if they've already leaving?"

"Who leave?" Kristina asked in a high pitched voice. "Why do you conclude that? They'll never leave."

A gust of wind hurled a blast of snow across the roof; the roof shuddered.

The light penetrating through the stretched muzdang bladders across the small windows was so wan the details of the people's faces scattered in the twilight, turning them into individual grey spots, masking the expressions.

"Then we have to go to them." Dick said. "If we just sit here nothing will get done. We have to find them and let them know we're here."

"Good for you, Dick." Marianna said, and put her hand on his shoulder.

Idiot Oleg cursed himself. *I should have said that. Why did I wait for Dick to speak up?*

"And where are you going to go to find them?" Oleg's mother asked. "What if the scout was moving in a circle or arc? Did if fly to the right or to the left after Sergeyev lost sight of it? It may well have landed in the other hemisphere."

"And what do you propose?" The Mayor asked the boy.
"We have to make some sort of signal."
"And how are we to do that?"
"I thought about it." Sergeyev said. "In my judgement the situation is not nearly as hopeless as it seems. We know the precise direction the scout was headed. And from my own experience I can confirm scouts rarely move in circles. Bioscouts are sent out from a central location and return there."

"If it was a bioscout." Oleg's mother said,

Oleg realized his mother was objecting not because she did not in fact believe Sergeyev and considered any attempt to find the expedition senseless. She was simply afraid they would send Oleg off in search of the explorers. Rather than speak of it she was searching for other reasons.

"It was flying in a very flat arc." Sergeyev said. "And then it descended below the clouds."

"Why didn't you say that before?" The Mayor got angry.

"You didn't want to believe I saw what I did in the first place." Sergeyev answered. "And that's a detail."

"Not *just* a detail!" Vaitkus started to laugh in a loud, bellowing voice, and Oleg's mother shouted at him to stop.

"But how far is it? Where would it have landed?"

"I can determine the direction of the base." Sergeyev said. He pointed with his hand.

"South-west." The Mayor said.

"The clouds were everywhere and covered everything, making precise judgements impossible." Sergeyev continued. Vaitkus stopped laughing. "So I could not tell for how long the scout flew after dropping beneath them."

"But the range! The range!" Luiza said.

"Tens of kilometers." Sergeyev said. "Certainly no more than a hundred."

"That would be pure luck." Vaitkus said.

He's never gone walking in the forest. Oleg thought. *He hasn't the slightest idea of what a hundred kilometers here is like. There's none of* us who's walked that far. Not even Dick. No, we've only gone to the ship in the mountains. The south-west is all thick forest. And swamp. Dick once made it to the river and back. Before we even get there, there's the swamp.

"One can consider it luck." Sergeyev agreed. "At the very least it is possible to reach it."

"Difficult." Dick said.

"But certainly possible, isn't it." A questioning tone appeared in Vaitkus's voice. Vaitkus understood it would not be he who went there. It would have to be Dick. And Oleg.

"They've already left." Oleg's mother said. "When you find their camp they'll have already left."

"We can't lose this chance." The Mayor said. "If I have to I'll go myself."

"You'd never make it." Dick told him. "It's too difficult."

"But we can do it." Kazik spoke up. "We'll make a raft."

"What about the swamp?" Dick asked. "I've tried to get through there myself and couldn't."

"We can go around it." Kazik said. "It does have an end."

"In the final analysis," Oleg said, because it appeared likely others would be going, and not him, "We made it to the mountain pass. And this is more difficult."

"Five, six days' travel." Vaitkus said. "I can go with you."

"This will be far more hazardous than going to the mountain pass." Sergeyev said.

Beyond the windows it had grown dark, and the light started to play on their faces, making them impalpable and cruel.

Someone moved beside Oleg, drew near, her soft hand touched his neck. Vaitkus and Sergeyev were arguing about the regions to the south-west, as though they had actually been there. Oleg turned, hoping it was Marianna's hand, but he knew it was not; Marianna's hand was dry and ridged with scars and calluses. It was Liz.

She put her lips close to Oleg's ear and whispered,

"Don't go there. Stay here. I'm afraid for you."

Despite her whisper they were packed too tightly into the

cabin Oleg was afraid everyone would hear her words and laugh. And he turned his head to free himself from her touch and said nothing. The blood was pounding in his ears and he had difficulty understanding what the Mayor was saying about the raft.

"For a raft we'll need logs, and logs have to be cut." He said. "We have one axe and the saw is more a nail file these days. And we don't know for certain if the trunks of the trees that grow here will even float."

"If there were no river we could get there in about five days." Dick said.

"We'll need bladders." Oleg said. "Bladders for swimming. The kids always swim on bladders. Like the balloon, only smaller. And we can swim across."

"That's the idea." The Mayor said.

"Wait, wait." Marianna suddenly spoke up, as though she feared that they would cut her off or someone else would guess what she wanted to say before she could herself. "Oleg said that the bladders were like the balloon. But we don't have any reason to swim across the river or walk through the swamp. We have the balloon!"

"The balloon!" Oleg heard his own voice. "And we were talking. . . ."

"How then are we going to fly to the ship?" Sergeyev asked.

"But why?" Oleg was surprised. "Now we don't need the ship."

A general commotion followed; everyone was interrupting each other because the balloon was the solution to their problem of making contact with the previously unknown survey expedition, the launchers of bioscouts; an elegant solution to a decades' long dilemma. To sit in the balloon and fly for one day, perhaps even less. Someone mentioned that the winds here were constant, if it grew warmer toward evening and the barometer dropped, that the winds necessarily blew to the south. Even Oleg's mother suddenly quieted down and started to speak in her son's ear, telling him to be sure he dressed warm.

But then Kristina started to groan and said it was stuffy in the room, she was feeling bad, and she asked to be led to her house. And Liz asked Oleg to help her with Kristina, because she could not deal with her alone.

Oleg didn't want to leave; they were now about to discuss what was most important to him.

Fortunately, Sergeyev then chose to get to his feet.

"Time for a break." He said. "Kristina's right — I can't breath in here either. I propose we all have something to eat and then we continue the discussion on full stomachs. Put the kids to bed and we can talk some more. This has gotten to be serious business."

Oleg didn't understand what was so serious about it all, but he was grateful to Sergeyev for cutting off the discussion.

They led Kristina back to her house. Liz hardly helped Oleg at all; she just walked alongside him. Nor did Oleg need her aid. Kristina was light, almost weightless; he could have carried her.

"I'm dreaming I'm stuck in a sweet nightmare." Kristina said. "Will I ever finally see real people again? I suppose they could cure my blindness immediately, perhaps even at their base. It can't be that hard an operation, can it?"

"Of course they can cure you." Oleg agreed. While they spoke he could almost feel Liz looking at him.

"I'm bored without you, Oleg." Liz said. "You never come to visit us."

"Who needs us?" Kristina started to sing her sad refrain again. "Even if they can return my sight there's still no way they can return my youth. Never. And maybe it might be better not to open my eyes again — what pleasure would it be to see my deformed monstrosity in a mirror?"

But Oleg did not believe Kristina was really thinking what she said. *Really, she's thinking: It's been twenty years; things will have changed enormously out in the Galaxy. People no longer die any more. They can return my youth. If people have many places to live — habitable planets seemed to be the statistical norm around main sequence stars — then there are places for everyone.* Nature, as the Mayor had taught Oleg back in school, considers the life of the individual as a defense against the extinction of the species. This general law applies to every biological species: the individual members of a species only live long enough for parents to provide their offspring with the aid they need to survive to adult-hood. Fish, which lay eggs, may perish immediately after spawning because the fry are so many, but the young of mammals must be cared for, kept warm, fed, and taught how to avoid predators and what to eat, and how to build starships.

Once upon a time people lived only to twenty or thirty years. And then human beings began to deceive nature, and created civilization, and with modern medicine and regen techniques the individual members of the species was freed from most diseases and lived to a hundred years or more back in civilization. It was not important to the survival of the human species that its individual members could live to a hundred or a hundred fifty, but it was to the individuals. And where does this idea lead? The Mayor, when Oleg began to put this idea to him, said Oleg was a natural determinist. Oleg didn't try to argue. He was already firmly convinced he was right. He was right individuals do not live a hundred fifty by accident. Nature was doing something here as well. Nature was driven to seed the Galaxy with mankind, to fill all those planets that failed to develop indigenous intelligent life. And old people were needed because they conserve experience and wisdom. And they were needed on the new planets more, perhaps, than on Earth. Without the Mayor and Thomas the village long ago would have died out or gone feral. Perhaps the scientists have discovered eternal youth. And immortality. And in the end human civilization would have to accomplish still one more leap, to other Galaxies.

"Why don't you come visit me." Liz repeated, and Oleg realized she had been speaking all this time, alone and patiently. "I'll wait for you. When we lay down to sleep you can come to me. Kristina won't say anything."

"I certainly will." Kristina said. "You'd be keeping me up. You're still children. It's too early for you to be thinking about such things."

"But we weren't thinking about anything." Oleg said.

They reached her house. Oleg stopped Kristina and said,

"Liz, you can take her. I have to be going."

"I'll wait." Liz said. "I'll always wait for you."

"Good night." Oleg said.

Oleg had not been paying much attention to her words; he thought it was strange Liz should be speaking like that to him now. He did not realize Liz was terrified he would be leaving again and again she would have to wait for him never knowing if he would return or not. Liz could not manage on her own and she was thinking of Oleg all the time and even went outside her house at night, walking to his and standing outside the thin wall to listen to him talking late at night with the Mayor or with his mother. And then she listened to him sleeping, and fought with the burning desire to quietly enter his house and lay down beside him to embrace him, warm and comforting.

But Oleg returned to Sergeyev's hut where he found the Mayor and Vaitkus already there. They hadn't summoned Oleg, but they were not going to throw him out, like from a Town Council meeting. And now Dick went off to sleep, although the conversation touched on him as well. Marianna and Linda were there; there was nowhere else for them to go. But Kazik had come too, although he hadn't entered the hut; he was standing out in the street, shaking beside the wall, listening. Oleg said to him,

"Go inside, why don't you."

But Kazik just waved him away. He knew better than Oleg what he could get away with and what he could not.

"Can I sit in?" Oleg said asked when he entered the room.

No one said anything, but no one raised any objections. Sergeyev was summing up what he had said earlier:

". . . . so I don't see any reason to change my opinion; the order of our priorities should remain firm."

Everyone was silent.

What order of priorities?" Oleg thought. He'd have to wait. Someone would say something and he could make sense of the conversation.

"Sergeyev is right." The Mayor said. He held a cup of tea in his only hand. He blew on it.

Marianna placed another cup in front of Oleg.

"It's a fairly old problem." The Mayor continued. "Cranes and blue tits. We just can't say for certain if there is an expedition on-planet or if Sergeyev and Oleg both suffered from an optical delusion."

"No." Oleg said. "We did not."

"Don't interrupt. We do not know if the scout was descending to return to base or to take a sample at a test site. We do not know if the expedition is about to leave now, and we can't exclude the possibility we merely observed an automatic station. We do not really *know* anything. So we have a bird that is not quite in the hand. Certainly the idea of finding people here is enticing, alluring, but I fear the odds are against us. Yet we do have a very real bird in the hand. The *PolarStar*. It is reachable. Oleg, I hope, hasn't spent the winter in vain. I tested him, and so have you, Sergeyev. His knowledge is insufficient, of course, but what there is, is solid and can serve as the basis for making informed judgments. And there is the hope the two of you might be able to do something with the transmitter. That's it."

The Mayor started to sip his tea, and Oleg didn't understand what he had been driving at. Would he be unable to fly in search of the expedition?

"But it wasn't a delusion of any kind, optical or otherwise." Oleg protested. "I'm certain it wasn't."

"There is another problem." Vaitkus said. "That of the goat, the cabbage and the wolf."

Oleg knew it. But again he didn't understand what Vaitkus was driving at. The rest did. Sergeyev smiled and looked at Oleg.

"Would you explain." Oleg said. "You're just talking riddles."

"Not riddles." Sergeyev said. "Problems."

Marianna sat down beside Oleg; he looked at her; he kept looking at her even when Sergeyev spoke.

"You accept that to go in search of the expedition we will have to fly?"

"Yes of course. There's no other way. We'll have to use the balloon." Oleg agreed.

"Then we are all in agreement. To continue the problem further — who will fly in it?"

"Me of course. Marianna and me. Or Dick and me." Oleg said. "We're the ones with the experience."

"Except we cannot let *you* go on the balloon."

"What?"

"The problem is elementary. You just heard us mention the crane flying in the air and all I have to do to catch it is let go of the titmouse in my hand. But the crane might get away, and if I release my grip the titmouse certainly will escape, and I risk being without a bird in the hand at all. The settlement is very small; there aren't that many people. To survive we must minimize our risks."

"I don't understand."

"You will have to go to the *PolarStar*. It's necessary. And you'll have to go fast. Summer's only now starting."

"But we can fly in search of the expedition and return if there's no one there we can fly to the *PolarStar*. . . . It's that simple."

"It is not that simple!" The Mayor almost shouted and struck the table with his fist hard enough to send one of the cups bouncing toward the edge. Marianna just managed to catch it before it fell to the floor.

"We do not know how long the flight in search of the expedition will take. We do not know where it – the expedition – is located. We do not really know anything. The best we can hope for is that the balloon will carry our people across the river and swamp. I do not believe the balloon can land in the forest and take off again. Most likely, once it is on the ground, the balloon will have to be abandoned. We have to assume the search for the expedition will take a great deal of time."

Oleg heard a moment at the door. Kazik had entered silently; he couldn't contain his curiosity, or perhaps he had been freezing out on the street. He was standing beside the door, motionless like a wild animal.

"But we do know we can make it to the ship." The Mayor continued. "We know the way, how to dress; the trip is difficult but not extraordinary. And we need you for that. You can go there with Sergeyev. Is everything clear?"

"And who will be flying in my balloon." Oleg asked, involuntarily stressing the possessive pronoun.

"I spent as much time building as you did, Oleg." Marianna said, as though embarrassed.

"Dick and Marianna will go on the balloon." The Mayor said. "They have the best chance of surviving in the forest."

"And me." Kazik said quietly.

"Go to bed, Kazik." Vaitkus said. "It's too late for you now."

Kazik remained standing by the door, and in his unmoving pose there was such obstinacy Vaitkus decided it was best just to ignore the boy.

"So this is how it turns out." Oleg said angrily. "I developed the balloon, I can fly it better than anyone. I should fly in it to the ship, and you want to take it away from me?"

"And who would you send in your place?" The Mayor asked. "Stop thinking just of yourself; think of the entire settlement!"

"As if we didn't know." Sergeyev laughed.

"I'd go in the balloon with Marianna. And Sergeyev could go to the ship. He knows more about communications equipment than I do."

Oleg realized he could not stand the idea of Dick and Marianna flying off so far without him — to the swamps, to the river, and he would be sitting here for most of the summer until the snow in the heights had melted. And therefore he threw out still one more obstacle.

"Why do you think the balloon won't be able to land and take off again in the forest? We've flown and returned. At the very least we returned without the balloon. And we'll make another one. Spytter will help, and there are still muzdangs to be caught."

"The muzdangs have left their dens for the summer." Kazik said quietly. "There's no way we could catch so many again."

"Well it's not that important." Oleg angrily ignored the problem. "We'll have lots of time to get to the ship. The summer's long."

No one contradicted him, They were all silent and not looking at him. The Mayor finished drinking his tea. Vaitkus was twisting the hairs of his beard idly with his fingers, and Sergeyev had dragged out his knife and started to cut off a twig that had started to sprout on the table.

Oleg stopped speaking and it appeared they all agreed with him. They were saying nothing, which meant they agreed, which meant he had convinced them. And then Marianna spoke up.

"They're right, Oleg." She said. "They're just afraid to say aloud what has to be said."

"What?" Oleg was surprised by the way she spoke. They all knew something he didn't, something that was evident . . . What?

"What they mean is, we, those of us who go looking for the expedition, we might not come back. Not for a long time. Perhaps not ever. That's why you have to remain behind and make it to the ship."

"You've gone crazy!" Oleg shouted. "How can you talk like that?"

The adults were silent because they agreed with Marianna and from the very beginning had entertained the unacceptable, unpronounceable thought Marianna might not come back.

"I thought it was all very clear." Marianna said. "Do you want some more tea?"

"I don't want to say anything more to any of you at all!" Oleg said and rushed out the door; Kazik had to dart to get out of his way.

Oleg ran a few steps down the street, stepped into a cold puddle, and nearly tripped. He slowed his pace and walked along the filthy road toward the palisade, thin ice snapping beneath his boots. He ignored the cold.

The boy stopped by the settlement wall, looking out toward dark forest alive with flashing blue glow worms, listening to the creaking of the stoop in front of Sergeyev's house as Vaitkus and the Mayor came out. He heard Vaitkus's ask,

"What's gotten into him? Can he really be that worried about a balloon?"

"That too." The Mayor answered. "But he has other reasons too."

For whatever the reasons were Oleg could not hear them; the Mayor dropped his voice into a whisper.

"Odd." Vaitkus said. "You have to be right of course, but I didn't see the signs. They really are adults, almost. And things that would be obvious and natural on Earth, I didn't even notice . . ."

"I'm sorry for the boy." The Mayor said.

"I don't see any alternative that makes sense." Vaitkus said.

"Oleg will understand it's for the best." The Mayor raised his voice and Oleg realized with spite the Mayor did it because the old man knew he was listening, and Oleg wanted to shout in answer to him: *Never! I don't want to understand!*

Then Vaitkus and the Mayor went their separate ways.

The door creaked again. Someone else had left Sergeyev's house. Oleg told himself it had to be Sergeyev come to convince him everything was for the best, but he hoped it was someone else.

"Oleg." He heard Marianna's voice. She was looking for him.

Oleg was ready to reply; he was overjoyed Marianna had come looking for him, although he himself could not have explained why. No, he could; she was now going to try to convince him just like the others. She had already agreed to fly in his balloon, she had already agreed it was best he be left behind. But she of all people should have understood they couldn't listen to their overcautious Mayor and elders! The old people feared everything. They feared dying here; they feared to take risks, and he was sick of them. They were glad to throw him into a pit if they thought it was for the good of the settlement. And just what was the good of the settlement? They were thinking of themselves, every one of them. The "good of the settlement" were empty words. Surely the people on Earth who started wars or enslaved other people also spoke about the good of their settlements. He had to ignore the lot of them, pay them no attention at all. In the morning he'd find a way to go up in the balloon himself, alone, and fly away. He knew the direction to take; he could go there on his own and find the expedition! And really, what could prevent him from leaving at dawn? Where was the balloon?

The balloon was deflated, folded up, and packed away beneath the awning. There was no way Oleg could drag it out or inflate it by himself.

Oleg resolved to try anyway, while everyone else was still asleep. At that moment he was not thinking of the winds that might carry the balloon away. He turned and headed for the barn. He had all the night ahead of him.

Then Marianna caught sight of him. She had not gone back inside; she was certain Oleg was somewhere close by. She didn't call out, but walked up to him under the awning.

"What are you trying to do?" She whispered.

Oleg sighed, as though a zhakal had fallen on him.

"What are you doing here?" He spoke in a whisper as well.

Marianna hadn't dressed properly for the night; she had run out into the street, the drizzling snow had caught in the short braids of her hair.

"I was afraid something might happen to you."

"Go back to bed." Oleg said. "I can take care of myself."

"You want to go off on your own. That's stupid." The girl said,

"I'm the stupidest person in the village." Oleg said. "You're all so smart and I'm a fool. That's why I'm going to sit here and wait."

"You've been studying for the ship all winter. Everything's depending on you."

"If I had known how it was all going to turn out I would have thrown the books away."

"I love you, because you're the smartest . . ."

"No one loves me. They just want to use me. Like a machine. And no one gives a damn about what I think."

"Don't be worried about me. I'll be with Dick. You know perfectly well nothing is going to happen."

"If nothing's going to happen then we can go together."

"And if it does?"

"All the better."

"Oleg, don't. You're rebelling because they're right. And you know they are. While we're going there in the balloon you'll have to prepare for the trek to the ship."

"If there is an expedition on this planet then there's no reason for me to go to the ship. It's a lie."

"No, it's just the way the adults think."

"They only think of themselves."

"That's stupid. And it's odd to hear it from you, Oleg. They're thinking the same way I am. About the kids who are already almost grown and who should be gotten home so they can go to school. So Kristina can get cloned eyes and Vaitkus a new pair of lungs. And about you too."

"Then come with me to the mountains."

"And who will go in the balloon?"

"Kazik and Dick. They can cope."

"Don't you ever mention it to anyone. Or I'll never speak to you again. Aren't you in the least bit ashamed to hang on to me just so I can sit beside you? Why? To look at you and admire you? Your mother will do that."

"They can get along without you."

"I'm the only one who knows all the plants and herbal medicines. I'm needed there."

"I need you."

"Why?"

"You know why. I love you."

A door creaked, loud.

"That's dad." Marianna said. "We'd both better get some sleep. And if you really love me like you say, you'll understand it all."

The dark figure of Sergeyev was approaching across the snow-dusted ground.

Marianna started to pull Oleg by the hand toward the houses. He started to pull away.

Oleg's head was whirling so badly he himself didn't know what to think.

"I was beginning to get worried." Sergeyev said.

"We were just talking, dad." Marianna said.

"Okay." Sergeyev said, laying a heavy hand on Oleg's shoulder. "If I were in your place I'd be confused and angry too. I understand. But you have to understand us as well, Oleg. The decision was very difficult. We've lived here too long, side by side with death. You're simply too young to feel the way we feel. Do you actually think I'm not terrified to send Marianna out? Or that I wasn't just as afraid last year when you went to the ship? Think about that a moment."

***

The next day they started to ready the balloon for a long distance journey. Oleg went up three times with Dick and Marianna, and once Kazik went with them. No one wanted to send Kazik along, but eventually they all had to agree there was no way they could stop the younger boy from going. No matter what they did or said or wanted he would be on the balloon. Dick and Marianna did not object; Kazik was no burden.

Oleg went up together with Dick, showing him how to get the fire in the burner going and the best way to cast out the ballast. Dick was silent for once and listened to everything. The other boy completely lost his sense of confidence in the air. The two of them said nothing to each other beyond what they had to say.

Then they ascended above the first layer of clouds. On this time they had gone too high and too far, it seemed, for the clouds never came to an end and ice started to form on the basket. Oleg wanted to go back down, but then he waited longer, because it had been decided they would try to take the balloon above the clouds with each ascent, the same as they had on the day they first caught sight of the probe.

But on the first two ascents they saw nothing.

Oleg was looking at Dick. All his life he had been forced to admit Dick was better than he was, in the forest and in the settlement, because Dick was stronger and swifter. True, there had been the time on the starship, when Oleg had proven himself more useful than Dick. But that was a year ago and forgotten. But now, seeing how hesitantly Dick's fingers gripped the side of the basket, Oleg felt himself in charge again. And he considered bringing the balloon down. If Dick had asked for the balloon to descend, Oleg would have agreed with him. But Dick said nothing; the knuckles of his fingers were white, from the cold and from tension.

But the clouds above them did not end. The sea of featureless grey stretched above and below to the ends of the world. There was no sensation of wind and there could not be, because the balloon moved with the winds, but the cold clawed at them terribly.

We have to descend, Oleg told himself, not moving his eyes from Dick's frozen fingers. *It could carry us too far.*

Dick lifted his head, hoping to see an end to the clouds, and asked unexpectedly,

"You're certain we're not going up?"

"No, we are descending." Oleg said, although he wasn't certain of it at all, and in any case he had emptied the last bag of sand overboard.

The balloon just held there.

Dick was silent again.

And then Oleg reached out to the burner to lower the flame. At that moment the clouds came to an end and the painfully blue sky broke through to them.

They remained aloft, above the clouds, for as short a time as possible; they were frozen and the ascent had taken forever. But

Oleg was almost overjoyed. It was difficult to explain why that was. Perhaps it was because they had almost reached the sky.

"It's a good thing this balloon you built." Dick said.

And Oleg was grateful to Dick for these words. If Dick hadn't spoken first Oleg would not have said,

"Listen, Dick, I have to tell you something . . ."

"Me?"

"Only just don't laugh. I'm in love with Marianna."

"Marianna? You love her?" Dick didn't immediately understand what the words meant. "What are you talking about?"

"For real. Like in the novel. I want to marry her."

Dick grunted. He didn't know what to say.

"I have to ask you . . . Take care of her, will you? You understand she's just a girl . . ."

"Idiot." Dick said. "How does that change anything? What am I supposed to do? Carry her? In the forest we're all on our own."

"I know that. All the same I'm asking."

"Then let her stay here." Dick said. "Kazik and I can go it alone."

"No. She's going. There's no way to talk her out of it." Oleg said.

Dick didn't say anything. It was as though he was displeased with Oleg's words. At the very least, they weren't what he wanted to hear.

"I guess we're not going to see a probe today." Oleg said. "I'll get us down before we freeze."

Oleg lowered the fire and the balloon sank heavily into the cloud layer.

Dick was silent.

They proceeded to descend without a single word. Only when the clouds came to an end and they could see the world below them again did Oleg say,

"Don't tell anyone what I said . . ."

"Who'd care?" Dick answered, thinking of something of his own.

Under them was the sparse forest. They had been carried some distance, fortunately to the north where there were wide open spaces. They brought the balloon down into one of the clearings. Sometime far in the past they had walked through here with Thomas on their way to the *PolarStar*.

The wind rose, the gas bag dragged on the ground, and by the time they could tame it they were exhausted.

"I'm afraid it's going to be a one way trip in this thing." Dick said when they were sitting on the ground, waving away the flies, exhausted. The balloon's shining hide lay in a heap around them. "I can't see us lifting up from the forest."

"It might be best to return in it." Oleg said. "That's why I asked them to send me with you. I can pilot it better."

"It's not that hard." Dick said ingenuously. "You didn't take long to learn."

They heard shouts — the kids from the settlement were running to meet them. Kazik was in the lead. They had seen the balloon being carried toward the waste.

Despite working as fast as they could was another ten days before the balloon was ready to rise into the sky and head for the south-west. The last four days were spent waiting for the right wind.

The aeronauts — so the Mayor had called them — were dressed as warmly as possible in clothing gathered from the whole settlement. And they waited.

On these days Oleg was very tired — every day he had to prepare the balloon, launch it, go up in it, then be dragged back down, clean the burner, fix anything that had gone wrong, and Sergeyev still insisted Oleg study the hyperspace com manuals. And he did. Perhaps Sergeyev was doing it to impress on the boy the importance of his own work, and so he would have less time to regret he was not going in the balloon.

Marianna was also busy. There was little food in the settlement; the summer had only just begun, there was still snow everywhere, almost no muzhrumes had sprouted and the older stores were nearly exhausted, and the settlement had little enough to eat. Three times Marianna went with Kazik and Fumiko into the forest to the places they knew in search of colonies of young muzhrumes which were still hiding in the ground and it was only possible to search for them by smell and by the squeaks of the small, stinging midges that hunted them as well.

A madness had descended upon the settlement. Everyone hurried somewhere, everyone found something that had to be done, and there was the palpable sensation that not only were the three of them going in the balloon, but that all of them were gathering their things and prepared to depart. The mood had infected everyone. Even Gote felt it; she tripped not so softly after people, almost barging her way into Kristina's house. The great male had ceased to come calling and the gote waited fruitlessly by the palisade gates calling after him. She did not know, nor would she ever learn, that her fine stallion had been killed by Pavlysh, for that had taken place far from the settlement and no one in the settlement had ever heard of Pavlysh.

Oleg and Marianna saw each other and spoke, but it somehow turned out it was awkward to get together with everyone's eyes constantly upon them. Oleg couldn't even go with Marianna into the forest. Only on the last evening before the wind finally changed did Oleg search out Marianna under the awning where they ground grain to keep it from rotting. He was surprised she was alone. The two of them had gone up that day in the balloon, but Dick had been with them, and with Dick present there was nothing either wanted to say. Marianna did not know what Oleg had told Dick, and now he was ashamed he had said anything, and did not even understand how he could have spoken about it at all.

"Aren't you tired." Oleg asked.

"No." She said. "You'll have a harder time walking."

"Doesn't matter." Oleg said. "But I wanted to know, if, you know, how you felt . . . ?"

"The same." Marianna said. "Exactly the same."

Oleg drew closer to Marianna. She was squatting and did not

get up when he approached, but she stopped pounding the grain, frozen. Oleg stretched out his hand and touched her face. Marianna lifted her head and looked at him. His hand touched her cheek. The cheek was hot. The sensation was like a blow, everything tangled into a knot beneath his ribs.

And then like a leaf on a breeze Marianna drifted away. Luiza had taken that moment to come up on them under the awning, carrying a basket of dried muzhrumes, the remains of the fall's harvest. That had to be loaded too.

***

From early morning the dry wind had been blowing from the north and Oleg began to inflate the balloon. Kazik was in the basket, tying down the sand bags so they were out of the way until it was time to throw them out — the three of them were going to be cramped for space. Kazik didn't want to get out of the balloon; he was afraid they might forget him. Then Dick arrived carrying a bag with supplies, checked out his cross-bow, and tested the lighter. Sergeyev had given the boy his own lighter — it was the best in the settlement, producing a spark every time, even in the worst weather. It had a cover which kept the rain off.

"Look," Oleg asked Sergeyev. "Isn't there any way you can send me?"

Sergeyev did not answer. Oleg hadn't expected an answer.

The Mayor hurried the aeronauts, fearing the wind might change. And when you hurry there is less time for nervousness.

Toward noon the entire settlement gathered in the field. Only Liz and Kristina hadn't come. Kristina was coughing again, and Liz preferred to remain at home.

Oleg stood beside the basket.

Marianna was looking at Oleg, but she was far from him, on the other side of the basket. Oleg paced his way around the basket, examined it, checking that everything was in order. He stood beside Marianna, separated by the wicker basket wall. But neither reached out to touch the other; there were simply too many people around them.

"Come back soon." Oleg said. "If you're not back after a week I'm coming after you."

"No." Marianna said. "Wait for us. Don't go off on foot. We'll be back. But maybe not so soon."

"Your attention!" The Mayor shouted. "Where's Oleg? Time to cast off."

Oleg didn't want to hear the words, but Marianna said, "Go on."

So Oleg ran to the anchor rope — he was responsible for that rope.

The others started to untie the cords which held down the balloon.

The balloon shot upward. It was fully inflated, ponderous and very large. As though it understood its time had come.

The balloon dropped away into the sky. Vaitkus helped Oleg get the rope free. Marianna rushed to the side of the basket from where she could look down on her father and waved goodbye.

The rope dragged, the anchor crawled along the ground, and Oleg had to jump back to keep from being struck.

"Pull it up!" He shouted. "Pull up the rope!"

The anchor vanished upward in jerks.

The balloon began to shrink in size.

"Lower the fire!" Oleg shouted.

The balloon, clutched by the wind, quickly hurried toward the forest; it had never flown so swiftly before, but over the forest the wind, evidently, weakened, and the balloon just hung there and even began to descend. Oleg could see the heads of Marianna, Dick and Kazik as black spots over the edge of the basket. Dick was feeding the fire. The balloon traveled further and after a few minutes vanished over the tops of the trees into the grey mist which separated the trees from the grey clouds.

"That's all." Sergeyev said to Oleg. "Just us orphans left here now."

***

Pavlysh awoke while it was still pitch black outside. At first he didn't realize where he was, and when he did he was even more disturbed over the question of what had awakened him. Then he heard a cry and understood it was Claudia. She sometimes cried or spoke in her sleep, and once even shouted. But she never remembered any of it later.

If Pavlysh had been allowed he would have moved himself and his belongings into the lab section a week ago. He had even tried to convince Claudia it would be for the best, although he feared she might take offense, but Claudia explained to him, in a cold tone, as though she had considered the possibility earlier and prepared an answer, that the lab sections were not sufficiently secure biologically. Despite the airlocks they were literally filled with bacteria and viruses which Pavlysh had tracked in from outside. Had Pavlysh bothered to occupy himself with the necessary precautions in using the airlocks leading from the main dome to the lab it would have been far better and far safer for the station.

She had not given him to understand with a single word his request to move had offended her in any way. She didn't even ask why he wanted to move to the lab.

In fact Claudia's nightly nightmares were not the cause of Pavlysh's desire to move to the lab. More precisely, it was a small contributing factor. Had the planet been less threatening and inhospitable, if it had been possible to simply take quiet walks outside, to experience new impressions, Pavlysh would not have felt growing cabin fever and claustrophobia. Pavlysh had dreamed of getting off the *Magellan* for some time now; dreamed of the skies of new worlds. Now the starship appeared positively spacious. You could dive in the pool, sit with others in the hydroponic gardens, play music in the crew's lounge . . .

Here the planet not only rejected them, it extended insidious fingers inside the station as well. There had been the orange mold which had clutched at his space suit's overalls; water would not get rid of it. Pavlysh had to virtually scrape it off after the achievements of modern chemistry failed. The mold not only successfully resisted him, but when Pavlysh had the poor sense to touch it with his bare index finger it struck back, burning him with acid. Now his singed finger was wrapped with a band-aid and Claudia was forced to consider amputating the digit; had she decided to use the scalpel she would have done so without asking his opinion of the subject, and she would have been within her rights.

Otherwise nothing untoward, or remarkable, or for that matter entirely unexpected had happened with either the planet or the expedition. It had been expected the planet would throw surprises at them; that was, in fact, the purpose of such expeditions. Their daily round was sufficiently banal Pavlysh had time to brood over a burned finger. Nor was this planet all that dangerous, nor its life forms notably aggressive, compared to some other worlds, Except for their encounter with the monster, which turned out far worse for the monster than for the human explorers, nothing any of them considered at all serious had taken place.

And not merely because Claudia Sun enforced strict discipline. Neither Sally nor Pavlysh were children to be coddled; both knew the world on which they had landed was far more dangerous to them than the wilds of Africa their remote ancestors had left a million years before. And they could deal with their emotions.

They were already into planning their big trip — such a trip was clearly called for in the expedition protocols. To sit in an All Terrain Vehicle and see how this world lives beyond the boundary of the field where they had landed. All the more as they had finished the initial data gathering with the launching of probes; there were certain interesting results, although nothing extraordinary had been found. So far. Just like in an archaeological expedition where the explorers accumulate a mountain of broken pots and rusty nails representing enormous interest for science, but simple trash to the average man who walks past the glass cases with projectile points and decorated clay pots. The average man wants to see the fabled beauty of the Venus de Milo or at least Priam's Treasury.

Any professional archaeologist will loudly and piously proclaim that the goal of his science is not merely finding and hoarding Priam's Treasury, but the collection as many pot shards and beads as possible to determine consumption patterns, migration routes, the level of material culture, and social structure. However, no matter how straight faced and fulsomely the archaeologist proclaims his noble intentions, you may be certain the archaeologist is lying. In the depths of his soul, in his nightly dreams, the pits he digs into the ground yield gold crowns studded with emeralds and rubies and carved jade statues. He longs for that unexpected flash amid the soil and roots that signals the rare find, the contempt for which forms so much of the basis of his professional pride.

Living worlds do not conceal their biological treasures; they stand in the open waiting to be identified, and Pavlysh was intent on finding at least one. A small piece of the planet was gradually opening to him; it was trifling compared to the rest of a world that demanded more than a few expeditions and a few more Pavlyshes before it could be even more or less explored and understood.

Pavlysh recognized he had neither knowledge nor understanding of the planet yet. But his intuition was constantly cautioning him against this world, and Pavlysh was used to trusting his intuition.

Pavlysh had already prepared the All Terrain Vehicle for the trip when Sally came out of the service dome. She had wanted to accompany Pavlysh but Claudia had overruled her, because she herself needed an assistant at the time. She had promised to take Sally with her the next day to an interesting morphological feature geoscouts had discovered on the other side of the lake.

"If you find any flowers, real flowers, bring me back a small bouquet." Sally said.

"And Claudia?"

"No animals worse than a cat."

"Gradually, I have to admit, I am becoming inclined to the view that she's right."

"You? The untamed mutineer?"

"All a game, Sally. And now I have a belly ache this morning . . ."

"It's clear to me you cannot continue this way." Sally said. "Three days ago I had a fever. And then chills. And I began to suspect this cowardly planet had succeeded in sending its bacilli through our impenetrable walls."

"Unfortunately the old dreams that we would encounter some totally unbelievable forms of life somewhere still haven't been fulfilled. Yet. The laws of nature are the same everywhere. The same chemicals combine to form chromosomes, and identical principles of life account for even the most extreme external differences. And nearly everywhere we observe microorganisms capable of dining well on human beings, if not feasting on us."

"Sally, are you free?" Claudia's voice came over the com.

Both of them heard her.

"I'm coming." Sally said.

One might even think Claudia was jealous, although Pavlysh would not have considered saying it aloud.

Pavlysh drove the ATV out of the dome and headed down the slope along the shore of the lake so as not to get lost in the forest. He wasn't in any hurry. He was looking to the sides, peacefully triggering the cameras every so often; the analyzers clicked from time to time telling him they were at work. The ATV mostly drove itself, only occasionally paying heed to its passenger.

Pavlysh would have liked to have found real flowers, but he expected not to. There were few higher plants on this world, and from what he had seen of the local flora he would have expected any flowers to have eaten any insects or birds that tried to take nectar, which limited the usefulness of flowers in spreading pollen.

The day was warm, steaming, only the depths of the forest held any snow. The ground was soaked with water, and the surrounding forest had become noticeably alive over the last few days. The planet's long, gloomy summer had begun. Pavlysh saw no large stretches of snow — the large patches had vanished with the end of spring. On the other hand, he knew he would have to make a trip into the mountains where there were glaciers and permanent snow cover. Too bad they had selected this gloomiest of all places for their work; further south by the ocean it was true desert, and at least dry . . .

Something very strange caught Pavlysh's attention. He brought the machine to a stop to get a good look at enormous insects that, however odd the thought resounded in his head, resembled nothing so much as horses. A herd of them had come down to the water to drink and had unexpectedly encountered the ATV. The insects froze for an instant, then immediately turned tail and ran; flashing and turning all the colors of the rainbow they began to inflate translucent bladders. The herd swarmed along the shore, and the bladders became larger than the creatures themselves, reaching about three meters in diameter. Every step turned into an extended jump of several meters length — the insects flowed like an exotic, graceful cloud over the land. Then the entire herd turned toward the lake and threw themselves into the water. Only the bladders and the narrow black heads with white, saucer-like eyes stuck out above the surface of the lake.

The herd did not swim very far. Unexpectedly the water in front of the lead animal erupted and a snake-like head with a gaping, fang-filled maw snatched at the shining bladder; the bladder collapsed and the black muzzle sank below the water. The snake head followed it down. The remaining swimmers abruptly turned toward the shore.

Pavlysh made certain the camera was working; it would be worth running through this scene when he got back to the domes in the evening. Claudia would say something banal on the order of 'the cruel struggle for existence.' Sally would be astonished, perhaps even feel sorry for the critter, or perhaps see it as somehow entertaining — probably not; how could there be anything entertaining on this humorless world?

Pavlysh drove the machine further along the shore, trying to decide what, if anything, by the criteria of a civilized world, might serve as a sense of humor. Even monkeys can laugh, but you need a sufficiently developed language to relate an anecdote and see the laughing faces of your neighbors. There was simply nothing humorous about this world.

Pavlysh was soon forced to slow down again — hills, overgrown with sparse, bleached white, and somehow frail looking bushes sloped down toward the shore. But among the bushes he could see spots of overturned earth. The spots were perfectly circular as though drawn with a compass.

Pavlysh stopped the machine at the edge of one of the circles. He just stood there a little while. Nothing interesting happened. Then he extended the probe. The long, flexible rod emerged from the body of the ATV and began to scoop up dirt. He continued to extend the scoop closer to the center of the circle. And, suddenly, after Pavlysh had decided the circles were harmless, the ground trembled, something white and formless stuck out from under the ground — it was part tentacle, part soft, shapeless being — it enveloped the scoop and dragged it toward its underground lair with such force the scoop broke off. The tentacle vanished, the ground again took on a flat, circular appearance. Pavlysh was annoyed he had lost the scoop, and said to the predator morosely:

"Return my scoop! I swear I'll strangle you!"

He moved the ATV through the bushes to one side, closer to the slope of the hill.

That's when he saw the flower. Or something he thought was a flower.

Scarlet, palm-sized petals surrounded a dusty yellow center. It was magnificent. The long, graceful stems were almost waving at him, bending under the weight of the petals.

Pavlysh looked around carefully. As far as he could tell there was nothing threatening in the area. In any case his, armored biosuit would protect him.

He exited from the ATV and started to walk toward the flower. Sally would be delighted when he presented it to her.

But at the moment when Pavlysh's gloved hand touched the stem, the flower bent away from him, as though terrified of his touch, folded its petals, and crawled along the ground. Only a narrow hole indicated the spot where the flower had been growing.

Pavlysh decided to play it smart with the second flower. He grabbed it quickly, as though he were snatching a buzzing fly from the air, and held it fast.

The flower twisted and turned in his hand furiously, trying to dart away underground, but Pavlysh's grip was firm. The struggle lasted all of a minute until the flower surrendered and hung lifeless in Pavlysh's hands. Pavlysh tried to open the petals, but these weren't petals but slimy balls of red protoplasm.

Pavlysh threw the flower away; it landed on the ground and came alive once more; the stem, a moment before soft and lifeless, began to search over the ground for its former hole or another in which to plant itself. After several attempts it was unsuccessful, and it crawled away like a worm, hiding in the red flock of flowers.

"Good riddance!" Pavlysh said, not hiding his disgust. "I won't go picking any more flowers."

To Pavlysh's right was a stand of bushes somewhat brighter in color than the rest of the underbrush. The leaves on the bushes were needle sharp, as though young pines had withered in the hot wind. Something oily-looking was hiding in the mass of twisted branches.

In order to allay his feeling of foreboding Pavlysh moved a little closer to the bushes. But he was unable to get close enough to touch them — as he approached the bushes unsheathed long needles, and the next moment the needles were being whipped at Pavlysh, needles so thin, sharp and strong hundreds of them were able to stick to the biosuit's impenetrable fabric, and Pavlysh almost lost his balance from the simultaneous blow of hundreds of needles.

Pavlysh jumped back, cursing the bushes, and took several minutes cleaning the mass of unbelievably strong and sharp needles from his biosuit before he was able to return to the ATV.

Several hundred meters further on he was forced to stop again. The line of hills marched down to the shore; sharp rocks stuck out of the water, warning that swimming in the lake might be dangerous. Then Pavlysh took the ATV into the air and headed off over the tops of the trees.

It was difficult to make out what was going on in the depths of the forest through the thick blue and green leaves; all the worse when the rain started again and everything clouded over.

Pavlysh tried to convince himself this world was fascinating; that, as a biologist, and a traveler, what he was seeing today no human being had ever before witnessed, that he was this world's Columbus and had every reason to be satisfied with his first trip outside the dome. But at the same time his mood was venomous, and all he could think of was how he had torn a slippery living stem from the ground, and how the flower had turned into a mass of red slime.

Perhaps he should go back? Pavlysh saw himself entering the confined space of the dome filled with clean domestic smells, how Claudia would look at him with resigned sternness and declare he had failed to completely disinfect himself on entry, and Sally would busy herself at the stove, surrendering to a feminine impulse to feed the brave hunter upon his return.

The forest was cut off by an enormous, swift-flowing river which fed into the lake. The forest stretched to the river flat and thick, without a single clearing or piece of bare ground; the trees dipped their tall white boles in the water like swimmers unsure of the current, undecided whether to dive in and swim, arms tight around the chest, hands in their arm pits, about to dart back to the towel stretched out on the shore behind them.

On the further shore Pavlysh saw a small cape, overgrown with grass and edged with a band of pebbles. He piloted the ATV there, decided this cape would be the furthest point of his travels today.

When Pavlysh cycled through the airlock out of the ATV it was quiet around him. The only sounds came from the current of water flowing around the stones. It was as though he had entered a room where only a moment before a delicate conversation had been going full swing, but at the unexpected guest's appearance everyone falls silent and casts hostile looks in his direction, waiting for him to leave.

"It's boring here!" Pavlysh shouted at the river; the only answer was silence.

Turning away from his sad musings Pavlysh started to look further. The forest began not far away, in general the trees grew lower and stunted; further away from the shore they grew taller, their crowns darker. And still further, where the forest vanished in a screen of rain, Pavlysh caught sight of a colossal, abrupt cliff . . . *No, not quite cliffs.* He thought. They looked more like massive columns, two, three, four. The columns vanished into the clouds. *That looks more interesting.* The desire to return to the domes lessened.

Pavlysh lifted the machine into the air and flew further. Five minutes after he had first seen them he drew close to the columns and could make out the details that had escaped him from the distance and the rain.

More than anything else, Pavlysh realized, it resembled boles of trees. But boles several tens of meters in diameter and looking as though they were twisted out of a great many ropes, each more than a meter thick. The twisting had to be accidental, unsystematic; and at some places the trunks widened and became enormously knobby, broadening and flattening; this creation was covered with bushes, vines; small trees grew out of the branches. In one spot Pavlysh even made out a small lake surrounded by thick reeds nestled in a crook of wood. Then he saw the cavity; it had to be large enough to fit a three story house, and the temptation grew in him to enter the cave in the ATV, but then Pavlysh imagined what sort of vile character the inhabitants might exhibit, and thought better.

Circling around the tree, Pavlysh slowly lifted the machine, and each succeeding circle was ever larger because at the height of two hundred meters rough branches began to unfold from the trunk and the trunk stretched ever upwards until he lost sight of it and only then did Pavlysh realize the tree vanished into the lower clouds.

Pavlysh turned on the floodlights. The strong ray won through the mist and Pavlysh was just able to make out the interdigitated branches crossing in front of him. When he drew about five meters closer to the tree he saw the unmoving red eyes of some sort of creature reflecting the light; it was looking at the ATV, waiting for it to come closer before deciding whether to add Pavlysh and his machine to its diet or not.

Suddenly the machine halted and Pavlysh struck his fist against the control panel. He did not immediately realize, with his hand on the control wand, the ATV's proximity sensors had stopped the machine and turned it aside to avoid an enormous horizontal branch — a ten meter wide overpass vanishing off into the mist toward the next tree.

Pavlysh was unable to see anything else; he would have to return here when the weather was a little better, he decided. And anyway, if this were not Priam's Treasure, at the very least it was a silver necklace. He had found the biggest tree in the entire Galaxy. At least it was some sort of discovery.

And Pavlysh guided the machine upwards on auto pilot, trusting the machine more than his own senses.

He rose slowly; about ten minutes passed before the ATV broke free of the clouds.

The light was very bright; after a week in twilight the little white sun was unpleasantly bright.

Over his head the sky was an electric blue infinity, darker in shade than Earth's sky; some near-by stars were of such magnitude they were visible during the day-time. Beneath the ATV the clouds were a mass of cotton padding stretching to the horizon, unbroken, quiet, white and clean.

That meant the tops of the trees were hidden somewhere inside the mass of clouds.

Doesn't matter. We'll sort it out at home. And I can get a radar image of the tree anyway. Pavlysh turned the ATV and set his course back to the base, but he kept above the clouds.

Pavlysh was sorry he hadn't decided to come here earlier. He had launched his bioscouts into the clean sky and hadn't considered the best psychotherapy for a man depressed by an eternally soggy, endless forest was empty sky over eternally moving clouds.

Where you can really breathe ...

The effect was purely psychosomatic — the air in the space suit Pavlysh was breathing was the same air he had been breathing since they landed on this planet.

"Excellent." He said aloud. "Now, as soon as it becomes tedious, I can fly up here."

"Where?" Claudia's voice answered.

Pavlysh looked — the communicator was on send, and that meant that Claudia had been listening to his deep breathing, swears, and the conversations he had with himself since he had left the dome.

"I'm returning now." Pavlysh said.

"How was the flight?" Claudia asked.

"Very interesting." Pavlysh answered honestly. "And the sky is gorgeous."

***

They dined extremely well. Fortunately (it should have been a consolation) Sally had chosen and packed the stores and Claudia was a superb master of Chinese haute cuisine; Sally informed Pavlysh their group was renowned throughout the Survey Service for its culinary refinement. But such diversity and ingenuity in the feeding of a Survey mission was a special ostentation, not achievable even on a large ship because ship's cooks usually take the path of least resistance, obeying the instructions written on the cans and pouches of concentrates and other factory produced foods. One has to have both the desire and an imagination to turn condensed mushroom soup into a marvelous sauce for a three inch steak, not to mention that the steak itself is a work of art; a moment too soon, or a moment too late, and the steak is nothing more than the standard piece of vat grown meat found on any ship and base.

Pavlysh idly pushed away the pudding uneaten — more his soul could not stand, and said,

"Now I am determined to treat you, my beauteous ladies, with marvelous sights unequaled and unseen elsewhere in the Galaxy."

He turned on the 3V.

On the screen insects, supported by air bladders, slowly flew by. Then they turned toward the water and dove in, the air bladders sparkling in the water.

Sally sat on the floor, her arms around her knees.

"Too bad I wasn't with you." She whispered.

Sally drew close to Pavlysh for the first time since they had landed on this world.

Claudia continued to work. A flat tray divided into cells for separate specimens lay in front of her on her work table. She was taking spectrograms, whistling something almost inaudible, some strands of her long straight hair had broken away from her too strict coiffeur. The work lamp cast a round circle of light on her table. To Pavlysh it seemed that, in continuing to work, Claudia was reproaching him for entertaining himself with amateurish films and deflecting Sally away from her duties. He was wrong. Claudia glanced a moment at the screen and suddenly said,

"Interesting; this snake knows to go directly for the bladders and punctures them. That means the equidic insects must swim in the lake on a regular basis, and the snake must hunt them on a regular basis."

Pavlysh said,

"And here I lost the probe."

Circles of flying dirt appeared on the screen.

Sally gasped.

"A reasonable enough way to hunt prey." Claudia said. "The method isn't unknown to other predators elsewhere in the Galaxy."

"Even women do it." Pavlysh tried to joke and failed.

He waited for the affront, but nothing followed. Claudia just laughed.

"Don't be too much afraid of us, Pavlysh." She said. "Would you have preferred we sent in a probe first to test your reaction?"

Finally they came to the immense trees.

On the screen the trees did not appear as immense as they were in life. Pavlysh almost wanted to ask the women whether or not they believed what they were seeing. Grey branching trunks drowned in the clouds, branches streamed down from above, small lakes and forests where the branches widened into glades as they bifurcated . . .

"The camera's field of vision is limited, it can't turn its eyes like I could," Pavlysh said. "Our imaginations are fed by the illogic of the movement of the eyes."

"No," Claudia said. "The sight truly is impressive."

"Were there many such trees?" Sally said.

"I'd say three or four. at least as far as I could see. Further on there could be a whole forest."

"Properly speaking those aren't trees." Claudia said. "I'd say it's more a form of symbiotic organism that has taken the form of a forest. Examine it more closely. You can see that every bole is connected to hundreds of other boles, like a rope from fibers. Structurally, it resembles something Buckminster Fuller might have designed."

"And every such tree is a whole world." Sally said. "There must be organisms there which don't even suspect there is a world beyond the boundaries of the tree."

"We should make a point of spending time at the trees studying their ecosystem." Pavlysh said. "Might take several days."

"At the expense of the rest of our studies, you mean?" Claudia asked.

"Do you wish to deprive me of the discoveries that will make my name resound down the ages along with . . ."

"Slava, never jest about sensationalism." Claudia failed to respond to his display of humor. "Take a look at this." She handed him a lump of dark ore, shiny on one side. A wide golden band stretched through the rock. "This is a vein of gold." Claudia continued. "My geological probes have discovered whole mountains literally threaded with gold ore. A rather rare phenomenon. A romantic like you would immediately write a trenchant article, and the worthy minions of the press would exhaust you with hundreds of interviews, imagine, someone who discovered the gold mountain. But all it really is, is one more relatively minor notation in the general geomorphological map of the planet."

Sally's fingers touched Pavlysh's hand, as though she were afraid he'd say something caustic and anger Claudia. Her palm was warm and soft. Claudia cut off her monologue, and Pavlysh realized she disapproved of Sally's open display of affection. Sally also realized it and jerked away her hand. A moment after Sally broke off an awkward silence engulfed them.

"I'd like some tea. Anyone else want some?"

"With pleasure." Pavlysh said.

Pavlysh turned off the 3V. Claudia bent down again over her work table. She turned the piece of ore containing the veins of gold over and over in her hand without really seeing it.

After tea Claudia suddenly decided to busy herself with cleaning. She declared that, over the last few days, because of Pavlysh's carelessness, the station had ceased to be hygienic. Pavlysh was not invited to join in the hunt for microbes, but rather than do nothing, and because, if he stayed in the dome, he would have had to watch the women, he headed for the laboratory and sat down with the book-reader in his hands. He wasn't in the mood for working.

Beyond the lab's windows it had already grown dark; the air was almost blue. It was possible to imagine he was sitting in a cottage on Earth and, at any moment, might get up and go outside for a walk. His reading, for some reason, wasn't going all that well; there was no way he could get himself lost in the plot.

Pavlysh got to his feet and turned on the external sound monitors. The forest was quiet, but the silence was incomplete, as though it were composed of a multiplicity of threatening sounds. Branches snapped, then something rustled the grass not far from the ship. A hollow sound came from far off, muted, almost inaudible, but clearly produced by something enormous, then it started to champ, as though someone in swamp boots was walking near-by, pulling its feet from the muck with difficulty. . . .

Our problem is we're trying to get rid of all the risks. Pavlysh thought. *Wherever we go. The ships Columbus sailed were little toy boats against the storms and winds, every reef could have gutted them, every sudden squall capsize . . . But the explorers went out, again and again, down to the sea, or in caravans across inhospitable deserts and mountains — it wasn't just the passion for gold and spices leading them on. To fall asleep with mountains like strange tents over their heads, to listen to a new and strange city come awake in the morning, to see palms of the shores on an undiscovered island . . .*

So we've become somewhat more rational. We're trying to adapt the Universe to our everyday needs, lay it all out and analyze it on our work benches and we even become annoyed or angry if something doesn't fit into our neat boxes right on the shelf where we want it to be. The ancient travelers believed in the Hyberboreans and people with dogs' heads, and it didn't frighten them. We're so convinced the genetic code is the same throughout the Universe, a man with a dog's head wouldn't make us blink, we'd just count his chromosomes . . .

When Pavlysh had read Robinson Crusoe as a child he had been overwhelmed by the Englishman's naivete, by his proud loneliness, by his human defiance and mastery of his fate. As he grew older he learned Crusoe had problems of his own — Robinson Crusoe is already a rationalist. He can never make peace with nature, he never expects to meet the dog-headed men, he just lists his supplies of grain in his account books or sews himself clothing from goats' hides. This means the old boy should be banned — here he is, the source of all our woes. Daniel Defoe lay down the basis of our own rationalism.

Realizing this, Pavlysh began to search his mind for an alternative and came to the conclusion that, spiritually, he was more at home with Sinbad the sailor. True, the fellow was a merchant, and assumed the Roc belonged to both the natural and the fairy tale worlds. So Pavlysh began to plan in his mind a tree climbing expedition. He even convinced himself it was necessary to understand the planet fully. His desire for danger and risk and the unexpected had nothing to do with it . . .

They had been on-world three weeks now and had learned nothing at all but the planet's reciprocal hostility. The gold mountain was faceless and boring. It could be found on an airless asteroid, let alone any geologically active planet. Claudia's realm was the inanimate world and she could have remained here a century doing her work and remained a stranger in a strange land. Understanding the planet as a mass of interconnecting living organisms was Pavlysh's function. And there was no way he was going to understand anything by hiding away in the station's domes.

Pavlysh argued internally with Claudia; naturally, as is the case with such solitary arguments he hardly gave her right of reply. All Claudia's imaginary responses were as unconvincing as Pavlysh's were overwhelming.

A wild, high pitched scream cut through Pavlysh's ears to his brain. The doctor jumped to his feet and it was several seconds before he realized the call had originated in the forest outside the station. The same forest that contrived to live and to go about its own business as though Pavlysh, with all the technology and power available to him, did not exist.

Pavlysh turned to the window. A mass of bodies twisted and rolled on the ground in the lights of the slowly rotating spot lamps. A number of predators — in the confusion Pavlysh could not determine what they were — were tearing a fat, unmoving animal to pieces. Pavlysh turned off the sound and walked away from the window; the primitive cruelty and fight to the death was enormously depressing, and Pavlysh realized he would depart from this world with what was formally a vast store of observations and scientific research, yet learning and understanding nothing.

The doctor had completely lost the desire to sit down and read, but he hesitated over returning to the living quarters. By now the women would be getting ready to go to bed in their own little kennels. Claudia the cleaning woman had been in the shower for at least half an hour, but Sally had already endured five games of solitaire — not the most apropos game for the valiant explorer. Pavlysh found himself wishing Sally would throw down her cards for the last time and drop by. Because she was bored, because she was tired of the sound of Claudia whistling beneath the spouting water . . .

"I'm not bothering you, am I?" Sally asked.

"No not at all." Pavlysh said far too quickly.

"What was all that racket? I thought I heard someone scream . . ."

"I had the outside microphone on; some of the locals were engaged in meaningful personal relationships . . ."

Sally walked over to the window.

"We're empty." She said. "No one lives here. They just come by to try to frighten us away. Are they frightening us?"

"No of course not. Certainly not."

"Ever think of settling down permanently here?"

"With you, in an instant. Yes." Pavlysh said.

"I'm serious."

"Wherever there aren't any people! Here, at least, we can breathe the air and rain falls from the sky."

Pavlysh approached Sally and placed his hand on her shoulder.

"You don't like it here. It's boring and you're sorry you ever came on this expedition. And I am just part of the entertainment."

Pavlysh took his hand away.

"If we were on Earth . . ."

"If we were on Earth you wouldn't even notice me." Sally said. "I just do not know how to flirt. There's nothing out of the ordinary about me."

She turned and looked him in the eyes.

"Maybe I feel the same way you do. And ordinarily I wouldn't even notice you. There's nothing wrong with that, is there?"

"No."

Sally pressed her body to his, took his head in her hands, brought their foreheads together and kissed him on the cheek and the corner of his mouth.

"Thank you." Pavlysh said.

"That's a stupid answer, but it will do." Sally laughed. She stepped away from him to one side and Pavlysh saw they were not alone; a white furred, gape-mawed muzzle was looking in from the forest outside.

"Go away." Pavlysh told the animal.

Sally turned and started to laugh.

"Claudia would ask why you haven't turned on the camera." Sally said.

"I've given you no reason to laugh at me behind my back!" Claudia said sharply.

Claudia Sun was standing by the open door at the entrance to the lab dome, dressed in her night shirt, her wet hair wrapped in a towel.

Pavlysh could feel himself turning red, like a child caught with his hand in the cookie jar.

Neither had any idea how long Claudia had been standing there.

"I never laugh at you behind your back." Sally said. "And you know that."

"We have to get up early tomorrow." Claudia said.

And the children are sent off to their separate beds.

Pavlysh did not speak his thoughts aloud; he wanted to avoid provoking Claudia.

"We get up early tomorrow." He agreed.

CHAPTER NINE

As Dick, Marianna, and Kazik watched, the settlement grew ever smaller, the houses became toys like Vaitkus modeled for the children.

Then the village vanished into the clouds and the people who were standing in the pasture, and Gote — who could not understand why her beloved Marianna was leaving, and the small hill where the graveyard lay — were all gone. Below them passed forest, an unending sameness of trees.

The aerial balloon flew evenly, as though it were hanging on a rope, but the three passengers could tell they were moving only because of the backward motion of the trees below. The basket was silent; they could feel no wind.

All three of them had gone up in the balloon before and knew what to do, but this was the balloon's first real flight, not just an ascent to the clouds, but an actual voyage.

Kazik stood at the burner, keeping the fire even and maintaining their height. He did it without being told. Kazik had spent no more time in the air than the others, and in most things he was still a child, small even by local standards. But here, in the balloon's basket, he had been transformed from a timid and silent being into a person sure of himself, as though he had been preparing to pilot an aerial balloon all of his life. His confidence was so evident Marianna and Dick both deferred to him without saying a word; both of the older youngsters were still unsure of themselves in the air.

Marianna watched the dark forest below them to the last moment, still thinking she could see Oleg, who had summoned up his courage and hid his fear for the girl and his envy of those who were departing. Marianna had no fears for herself — the idea would not have occurred to her. She only wanted one thing: to go off and return as quickly as possible. As for the expedition from Earth, she did not entirely believe in it, as earlier she had difficulty in believing the existence of the Ship until she had reached out her hand and stroked its side. But if the ship had always existed, if only in the words and memories of her father, the Mayor, and the other adults, the appearance on the planet of a Survey team was more on the order of a dream. This was some sort of unreal expedition, and their inability to find the settlement now and rescue them had only deepened this feeling. So Marianna only feared they might get lost if they flew too far. She wanted to be able to return to the settlement before the day Oleg was to set out for the *PolarStar,* to go along with him.

For Dick their expedition also lacked a certain degree of reality. It was something outside the well established cosmogony by which he had ordered his mind. It was true last year's march to the *PolarStar* had changed this picture, but it had not destroyed it. The *PolarStar* was a part of the settlement, and at the same time its source, but it was dead. Dick had never imagined a life for himself away from the planet, away from the forest. The constant battle with the forest, their need to vanquish the animals and trees, was attractive to his vanity. He never imagined life on another world, let alone the life there might be different; the Earth would simply be another forest with different animals and threats.

Of the three only Kazik had ever imagined himself on Earth. If the inhabitants of the settlement were familiar with aerial balloons for the simple reason it was here and a part of their world, Kazik had imagined it far earlier than the others. Kazik knew everything there was to know about aerial balloons intuitively. Already in his first flights with Oleg he understood the balloon's temperament better than Oleg himself, but had said nothing of this to anyone. Kazik himself did not think he knew how to pilot the balloon better than Oleg, and in the first minutes, while both

Marianna and Dick still remained on the ground in their minds, Kazik used that time to set about storing the ballast bags and food to achieve maximal balance, or, as he explained it to himself, so the balloon could carry them more comfortably. He thought of the balloon much like a living being, which was heavy or light, happy and even uncomfortable, and he wanted to make it more comfortable.

Dick kept looking down. He was trying to make out the paths and glades he knew in the forest, but from above what he saw was a twisted mass of unfamiliar trees, as though he had not tramped the length and breadth of the wilderness. Suddenly he recognized a meadow. The year before there he had cornered a large baer and the baer had left him with three parallel scars on his hand — trophies of the hunt. Dick looked at the scars, and then back down. The meadow was gone from sight.

The wind grew quiet. Kazik fussed beside the burner, increasing the flame because he felt the balloon was beginning to drop. Visibility was becoming worse, even the trees below were covered with mist.

"Want to go lower?" Kazik asked.

These were his first words since they had left the ground; and they sounded awfully loud to him,

"Lower?" Dick didn't understand the import of the question immediately. The flight certainly hadn't come to an end. "Have we come to the river?"

"I can't see where we're going." Kazik said.

"We're on course." Marianna said. "We're almost at the first swamp."

The balloon drifted in the air, hanging far above the clouds. A barrage of rain struck from above. They could hear the drops pounding the thin envelope. The basket started to rock. Dick held onto the edge tighter and Marianna sat down — she thought the side of the basket was too low and the rocking might throw her over the side.

"I'm going back up." Kazik said. "We can find a wind that will carry us back to the settlement."

"We can't go back." Dick said. "They'd just laugh at us." The thought someone might laugh at him was unbearable.

Kazik heaved a bag of sand over the side and loosened the draw string, sending the sand far below. The bag he kept. The bag was still valuable.

The balloon immediately shot upwards — they could see the trees grow smaller and sink into the mist.

"Hey, great! I fed him and he listened to me." Kazik said joyfully, but no one answered him.

The balloon terrified the others. It was unreliable and capricious. Both Dick and Marianna felt they were prisoners of the balloon and subject to its whims, whether it wanted to be carried into the sky or to crash into the ground. Unlike Kazik they had no empathy for their conveyance and enjoyed nothing of their journey.

For a number of seconds the constant clouds hid even the gas bag from them; beyond the bag were only the impenetrable clouds in which they were lost. The world and whatever it contained — cliffs, flying creatures, the frights of their imagination — remained beyond the mist.

"And now I don't know what's happening at all." Kazik admitted aloud. "If we're going up, where we're going, I just don't know."

"Then let's go up." Dick said. "We can get above the clouds, like we did with Oleg."

"Not enough ballast this time." Kazik said. "We might need it later."

"Then increase the flame." Marianna said.

"Oleg said not to inflate the balloon too much." Kazik said. "If the envelope breaks, we'll drop like a rock."

Kazik was feeling his power over his elders; he realized he feared nothing; he could ascend above the clouds or just hang over the world and watch the forest pass below him, but the others were terrified.

"Go up." Dick commanded; the older boy tempting Kazik

into rebellion, but the boy shrugged his narrow shoulders and fed fuel to the fire.

The air grew colder, first dew formed on the flat slats of wood, then fat drops of rain struck against the balloon's envelope and trickled from the lower rim.

Kazik wanted to burst out singing, but he was too embarrassed to do that in the presence of the others. Not here and now. He sang silently, his lips clenched tightly.

For Dick the feeling of desperation and helplessness was overwhelming. The clouds were never going to end. They were lost. They should never have even begun this madness. Had they gone on foot they could have gotten across the river *somehow*. It wasn't anything special. But now there was neither river nor village . . .

Then light exploded about them; the balloon had burst through into an gap between the clouds. Another layer still stretched over their heads, and they were headed toward an enormous black cloud which stood like a wall before them, a gaping mouth in the sky big enough to swallow them. Sparks of lightning flashed through the blackness like clashing fangs waiting to rend the balloon's tender flesh.

"That's gorgeous." Kazik said. "We're in for a real ride!"

"Get us lower!" Dick said. "Get us below it; don't you realize what that is?"

"Too bad." Kazik put his hand on the burner control and lowered the fire. "I've never seen anything like that. It won't be so interesting from below."

"I'm not interested it in at all." Marianna said.

For some reason the balloon did not descend; but continued to fly toward the storm cloud, and the thunder issued from it almost uninterrupted, as though someone was beating an enormous stick across an enormous fence, reverberated against the gas bag's fabric.

Dick pushed Kazik aside and cut off the burner himself.

"This isn't your toy!" The younger boy said.

The gusts of head winds struck and the balloon was blown

about between the clouds and would not descend.

"Don't put the fire so low!" Kazik shouted at Dick. "You're fools!"

"Quiet." Dick said. "I've had enough."

Dick was covering his own terror; he wasn't willing to admit to himself he could feel so much fear.

The balloon suddenly started to shake violently, fell into the aerial whirlwind and began to plummet downward.

"Turn it back on." Kazik shouted. "You don't understand it — now the air's getting cold."

"We've got time." Dick said. "We'll get lower first."

"We can't go down so fast. Where's the lighter?"

Dick had the lighter; he held it away from Kazik's reaching hands, because he did not believe the boy that anything threatened the balloon below. He only wanted one thing — to get away from the menacing cloud as fast as possible.

"Can't you see the balloon's shrinking!" Kazik pointed upward, but he was the only one who could tell the balloon had lost buoyancy and the speed of its deflation was increasing.

"Now!" The insistent tone in Kazik's voice carried enough fright. Dick handed the boy the lighter.

The lighter popped, cracked; the boy struck the iron to the flint again and again but it just did not want to produce flame.

They were all cold and went; the rain had soaked them through. The lighter's iron had also managed to get wet; had Kazik known Dick might put out the fire he would have gotten it into his hands and kept it dry.

There were clouds around them again; it was half dark and the thunder still came from the storm cloud. Now it was over their heads.

"You're doing a fine job." Dick said, excusing himself. He was watching Kazik click the steel again and again out of the corner of his eyes.

"Give it here." Dick snatched the lighter from Kazik's exhausted fingers. The lighter obeyed him no better than it had Kazik. Kazik stood to one side and looked on the sparks that flew away from the flint. They were cold and small.

"It has gotten smaller." Marianna was frightened. She was looking upwards; the ropes forming the net holding the balloon cut into the once round shape of the envelope all the deeper.

Dick held the lighter in his palm and tried to wipe the wick. Now it was clear to everyone they were falling far too fast.

"Can we close the hole?" Marianna asked, but she didn't expect an answer. She realized there was no way to tie off the hole at the bottom of the balloon.

"What about your lighter?" Kazik suddenly shouted at the girl. "You have it with you, don't you?"

"Of course." Marianna answered, as though she had just remembered. "I have it."

"Give it to me!"

"Where did I put it . . ."

"In the bag around your neck?" Kazik guessed.

Marianna quickly untied the medicine bundle hanging from her neck and pulled out her lighter.

Kazik grabbed it from her, pushed Dick aside and started to strike the fire.

But the burner would not light.

"Open it up." Kazik shouted to Dick. "You closed it!"

The basket rocked again. Dick lost his balance and nearly went overboard.

Kazik opened the burner, almost breaking off the little wheel that controlled the flow of fuel, and caught the unpleasant scent of gas coming from the pipe.

The second lighter, fortunately did not die, and the end of the pipe burst into violet flame. Kazik quickly turned up the fire and the flame vanished a moment, then burned bright and confidently.

Kazik looked into the aperture of the balloon above them. The hot air was moving upward in the half-light.

They burst through the lower layer of clouds.

"We're still falling." Marianna whispered.

The wind was not strong, but came in gusts; the balloon sank lower in jolts.

"Too late." Dick said. "Hold on."

Dick had calmed down. The forest was familiar to him; he could not quite bring himself to believe it could or would smash him to tiny bits, no matter how hard it tried, no matter how great the height from which he fell.

"The bags!" Marianna shouted and broke the charm trapping them.

The girl bent down to the bag laying next to her feet and with difficulty heaved it over the side of the basket, almost following it overboard at the same time.

The balloon had reached the tops of the trees; they could see the leaves, and Kazik, who had remembered about the ballast only with Marianna's shout, looked spellbound at the approaching ground, fearing less for himself than for the beautiful balloon which must inevitably be shattered.

The tops of the trees suddenly passed beneath the balloon and the land drew back as if with regret. . . .

At the last moment everything came alive. Dick grabbed a sack as well. Kazik had taken a third bag, but he did not throw it over the side like Marianna but emptied out the sand, pleased with himself he had thought to save the sack even at such a moment. He said.

"We have to keep the bags."

But no one was listening to him. Marianna and Dick were looking downward at the tree tops sailing away into the mists. They continued to look even when Kazik quietly went about his business. No one was in a hurry to rush back to the clouds, and there wasn't any ballast left anyway. Kazik adjusted the flame and the balloon hung levelly in the air; the storm winds still wanted to play with the gas bag and were not going to die down anytime soon. The balloon continued to dangle like a soap bubble in the misty expanse between the clouds and the forest.

"Well," Dick said. "Whatever were we afraid of?"

It was difficult to stand in the balloon's basket; they had thrown out so much ballast it had lost stability and rocked from side to side. The clouds spat hisses at them, the balloon swayed, tilting the basket as though it wanted to cast all its passengers out and they huddled on the floor, clutching at the wattle sides, and the ropes, and surviving until the wind died away and the torrent ended, to be replaced by a strong and even shower of rain as a sign the madness was over.

"We're still here." Dick said, getting up from the floor and looking over the side. "But we don't even know we're the wind's carrying us."

"We were flying in the right direction right from the start." Kazik said. "Right up to when we ascended. We flew south for almost an hour, and then it shook us for about ten minutes."

There were no clocks in the settlement, but the understanding of hours, minutes and even seconds remained. And Kazik had an almost perfect sense of time. They believed him.

"Does that mean we're on the right side of the river now?" Marianna asked.

"No way to be sure." Kazik shook his head.

They were soaked through by the storm and half frozen. Even the jackets and fish hide boots hadn't saved them. But for now all they understood was that they were only frozen, and not smashed on the ground.

"Let's see what we can on the ground." Marianna said. "You're hunters."

"We should be able to see the river." Kazik said. "And the swamp before it."

"If we didn't cross it while we were above the clouds." Dick said.

"No, the wind wasn't that fast. It would take us five days to reach the river if we were going on foot."

A steady breeze had taken hold of the balloon and was slowly carrying it south.

"The rain's ended." Kazik said. "And we can go back upstairs."

"Why?" Dick asked,

"To look at the sun." Kazik said. "And find out our direction."

"There aren't any shadows. We can't see anything."

"Better to land and search on foot." Dick said uncertainly.

Not the best solution, he knew; if they found themselves in an unfamiliar spot it would be even more difficult to tell the direction from the ground. But he didn't want to go back above the clouds a second time.

"Are you cold?" Marianna asked.

"No." Kazik said.

But Marianna pulled some sweetgrass bread from the pack, smeared it with muzhrume paste, and the boys started to chew it, looking downward in the hope of catching sight of something familiar. Once Dick swore he recognized a hill sticking out of the forest, but Kazik said it was a different hill.

Time passed. The rain never ended, but the rumble of thunder drew further away and threatened them less.

Another hour and a half passed. Marianna, to get warm, sat huddled in the basket, although she wasn't tired. But she could not get warm and just collapsed from exhaustion. Dick squatted down on the floor and set about to polish his cross-bow. Kazik warmed his hands by the burner and called to Marianna to join him and warm herself. They were all exhausted from uncertainty. It felt like they had been flying for so long away from the settlement they would never be able to return.

The rain ended, and with it the sound of raindrops beating against the basket and envelope. A warm current carried the balloon higher.

Kazik spent most of his time looking ahead. Suddenly he said, "Take a look at that!"

There was a bright band visible on the horizon in the gathering early sunset ahead of them.

Dick took a look and said,

"Has to be a river."

"Perhaps it's the end of the forest." Marianna said.

The girl was standing on the other side of the balloon and could make out a gleaming line on the horizon as well. For a moment they did not understand, then it became clear; they were looking at two rivers.

After they had drifted in the air for another half an hour they were convinced a river really did lie ahead of them, the dark shore on the other side could be made out as well. The bright brand of light to the right was wide and stretched along the horizon, but the river linked up with it.

"It's really big. It has to be a different river." Dick said.

"Wouldn't it be great if it was a sea?" Kazik imagined.

"A sea?" Marianna knew the word, but she had never imagined there was a sea on this world, or it might be so close.

"Or a really big lake." Kazik said. "But I'd rather it was the sea. Then we can build a ship and go sailing in her."

"Only if the balloon isn't carried out to sea." Dick said.

They were all staring ahead, trying to tell if this was the river they needed. In the past, some years back, Dick and some of the adult men had tried to get as far as the river, but had to turn back before he reached the shore because of swamps swarming with every sort of creature. Their food had become exhausted and hunting was terrible. They were forced to return. Dick remembered the hills and the rivers, but there was nothing he even thought he recognized visible below them now.

They decided to raise the balloon somewhat, bring it closer to the clouds in search of a stronger wind. The balloon hardly lifted at all; it was sluggish and hesitant, as tired of flying as the passengers.

The wind was stronger here, but it was not blowing in the direction where they wanted to go. Then a rain squall struck again. They had all had enough; a recalcitrant balloon, the cold, the damp, and what was even more frustrating was they were almost at their goal; all they had to do was fly across the river, land, find a place to spend the night and go in search for the new people.

Several of the large sky dwelling birds, ones that lived so high they were hardly ever seen from the ground, approached the balloon. They emitted shrill cries and flapped membranous wings; they started to circle the balloon, displeased at the unwanted intruders in their domain.

One of the birds even managed to clutch the ropes with its claws and several times pecked hard at the balloon envelope.

"I wouldn't do that if I were you." Dick raised his cross-bow and fired.

The bolt struck the bird in the chest; it continued to beat its wings slowly, pulling against the taut sphere, then flew past the basket in expanding circles toward the forest below. Dick even tried to grab it as it fell; Marianna held onto his body to keep him from tipping out of the basket.

"Too bad. That could have been lunch."

He shot at another bird, but missed.

The birds continued to follow the balloon for some time, but were lost in a curtain of rain.

They could now make out more of the river below them. It was broad, dark grey colors reflecting the perpetual clouds, and it flowed straight with hardly a bend, unlike the small streams they were used to.

"If we fly across it we'll have a hell of a time getting back." Dick said.

"Perhaps we can land for the night." Marianna said. "In the morning we can wait for a wind and fly further."

"That would be fine," Kazik said with uncertainty. "It would give us a chance to gather more ballast. Only thing is, there's no place to land down there."

None of them spoke; they were listening to the silence reigning over the world. Only the constant patter of raindrops against the balloon envelope broke the silence. And then, ahead of them, they saw the grey wall.

Marianna gasped; she was the first to see the enormous, uneven wall lifting skyward ahead of them. A gust of wind clutched at the balloon and carried it ever faster, as though the balloon itself wanted to take revenge on its occupants for having made it fly for so long.

"Kazik!" Marianna shouted.

Kazik had seen the wall swimming toward them out of the rain as well. Before anyone could say anything else he opened the burner on full and shouted,

"Overboard! Throw everything over the side!"

They had almost no ballast left, just a few small bags. Dick heaved them over the side. Marianna snatched up a bag of food but hesitated.

"Faster!" Kazik shouted. Dick snatched the bag of food from Marianna's hands and tossed it out as well, then he bent down and began to throw out of the gondola anything he could find, without hesitation.

The balloon held back for a few moments, then started to rise.

Frozen in astonishment the aeronauts watched the grey wall pass below them.

It was a tree, an unbelievably gigantic tree. They saw the twenty meter thick branch emerging from the thick trunk to stretch out almost horizontally. The balloon was flying beside the bough close enough for them to reach out and touch it. Higher up the branches clustered all the thicker and it was only by a miracle the balloon did not collide with them.

No one knew how many minutes their ascent lasted, but suddenly it grew darker and the trunk of the tree vanished from their eyes — the balloon had passed into a cloud.

The tree was still beside them; they had yet to pass over it; the tree stretched out grey toward the balloon.

A gust of wind caught at them; it tossed the balloon against the giant's side.

"Hold on!" Dick shouted. He dropped to the floor and pulled Marianna down with him. Kazik fell on top of them.

It was just in time.

They heard an enormous crash; the balloon's basket was thrust forward, then it landed on some obstacle, the basket tossed and jumped up again like a bird fallen into a trap, something fell with a crash over their heads, the balloon made several convulsions as it lost hot air, the death throes.

Then everything was silent again. Nor could they see anything.

The basket hung at a sharp angle, swinging back and forth gently.

"That's it." Kazik said sadly. "That's the end of the balloon."

"What matters is we're alive." Dick spoke sharply. "With nothing broken. That's what matters."

***

They sat in the bottom of the basket, trying not to rock it lest it turn over and spill them out. Tongues of cloud curled around and inside the basket, for a moment hiding the dark gaps of the balloon's mortal wounds, dispersing and letting them carefully look upward to glance into the mysterious depths. But none of them had managed to figure out what had happened to them. The light was creeping up so slowly it seemed day would never come. The swirls of cloud were brighter than the air, but gradually the air took on the same color, and everything became a monotonous grey.

The aeronauts dozed in an extended dream just at the edge of sleep, which tied their tongues and chained their hands and legs but which never turned to true sleep; the cold and the feeling of hopelessness kept gnawing them to wakefulness.

"I never imagined such trees could exist." Kazik said.

"Certainly there's nothing like them on Earth." Marianna said.

"The trees are even bigger on Earth." Kazik said with certainty. "For example, the sequoia. They grow in the Rocky Mountains."

"Maybe it's not a tree?" Dick said. "Could there be a cliff that high?"

"With branches?" Marianna asked,

"Did you really get a look?"

"But we're hanging. . . ."

"Could be we're hanging from a projection." Dick said. "If it is a tree, so much the worse for us."

Marianna carefully turned and looked around in the hope they hadn't thrown out all the food. But the basket was empty.

"It didn't make any sense to throw out the fuel." Kazik said.

"We're not doing any more flying." Dick said with certainty. "I've had enough. Better to go on foot."

"Then we'll have to get down to the ground." Marianna said. "And look for the food bags. But by then they'll have been found and eaten."

"Well, no one's going to eat the fuel."

Dick crawled to the edge of the basket and started to peer out into the mist.

Marianna started to cry. She had stretched out her leg and needles of pain lanced her whole body. Dick sighed. The basket started to rock.

"I think the balloon's caught on something overhead and deflated." Dick said. "If we shake the basket it might come loose. It's a long way to the ground."

A small breeze sent streams of cloud away, and in the gaps between the mist they could make out the branches of a tree, a wall grey with dark gaps and holes. The balloon above them was still hidden in the mist.

"We have to get out of here." Dick said uncertainly.

He pulled a bolt with a heavy point out of his quiver and tossed it down.

There was silence. Kazik counted beneath his breath. He reached twenty. They heard nothing.

"Maybe it fell on the tree." Kazik said. "Or on moss. I'll go out."

"How?" Marianna asked.

"Up the ropes. There's no reason to wait here, is there? I'll call down when I get there."

"Okay." Dick said. "You are the lightest."

Kazik made certain his knife was secure, then grabbed the rope and carefully edged himself over the top of the basket.

"It's not that bad." He told them. "I can't see anything anyway."

Kazik held onto the rope with both hands and wrapped his legs around it as well. Marianna and Dick froze motionless on the other side of the basket. The basket rocked back and forth.

"I'll keep talking so you know what's going on."

Kazik crawled his way upward quickly; he was used to climbing on vines in the forest. After half a minute he was lost to sight, but the basket rocked back and forth in time with his movements.

"How is it?" Dick called.

"I'm still climbing." Kazik said. "I can see the bag hanging down deflated, like a rag."

After a while the basket stopped jerking.

"What happened? Are you there?" Dick called.

"Nothing happened. I'm just resting." Kazik said. "I'm almost there."

Waiting is always hard, especially when you don't know how things will end. Marianna thought. *But for some reason we're always waiting for something. Never getting on with living. Most of us are waiting for when we return to Earth, and I'm waiting for when I get back to Oleg. Dick's waiting for when he returns to the forest. Now we're waiting to see if the balloon will fall or not. Very stupid to wait, it's the most ordinary and most improper occupation. We'll have to find a way to live without waiting. . . .*

The basket again began to rock from side to side. They heard the sound of fabric tearing and wood breaking. Marianna realized it was the envelope of the balloon tearing. The basket dropped with a jerk for half a meter and hung.

"Careful!" Dick called.

"A moment . . ." Kazik called; his voice was muffled, as though the cloud had swallowed him whole.

The rocking of the basket became even worse. Dick and

Marianna held onto the wood and the ropes.

"Made it!" Kazik shouted down to them. "You've nothing to worry about; all the balloon's ropes are really hung up good here. It's a big branch, about as thick as I am. And a lot of smaller branches. Nothing to be afraid of. Come on up. I'll wait for you."

"Well, go on." Dick told Marianna. He got up and slung his crossbow around his back to leave his hands free. He trusted Kazik's judgement and knew there was no reason to fear the balloon suddenly falling. "If you get tired, stop and rest. And don't look down."

"It's just as well there's nothing to see." Marianna said. "Don't worry about me."

"Take your time. Don't hurry." Dick repeated. "I'd be right behind you but the single rope might not be able to support us both."

Marianna climbed up on the edge of the basket, her hands grasping the rope tightly. The rope was wet and slippery, but Marianna wasn't afraid; she'd been climbing up and down trees all her life.

Some minutes later she found herself standing beside Kazik on a wide road hanging suspended high above the ground; that was what the branch seemed to be to her. The balloon was twisted and caught on sharp twigs sticking out from the main branch, tangled and torn on leaves like knives, but the ropes still held.

***

Finally it grew bright; now that the worst of the fear was behind them the three had become terribly hungry. But if they were going to have anything to eat they would have to climb down to the ground and hunt for the bags of food they had thrown overboard.

"Let's get going." Dick said. He had the cross-bow in his hands to be ready for the unexpected. "Marianna you keep the middle . . ."

"No." Kazik said.

"What do you mean?"

"You've forgotten — we have to go down."

"What of it?"

"I have to get rope."

Dick stopped. Kazik was right.

The problem presented itself immediately; how to get enough rope. The cords they had spent so much time manufacturing back in the settlement were so tightly spliced together they were able to untwist none of them. Dragging the entire balloon upwards was equally impossible — the basket was too heavy and their feet slipped on the enormous branch's slanting spines.

"Wait a moment." Kazik said finally; before Dick could say a word the boy had already climbed back down the rope and vanished into the mist. About five minutes later he returned, exhausted but pleased with himself, with the end of the rope he had climbed down on tied around his waist. The rope was strong and long. It was heavy for him, but he gave no hint of it.

While Kazik had clambered down to cut the rope free from the balloon Dick had gone ahead to the spot where the enormous branch grew into the main trunk of the tree. He encountered nothing dangerous. Marianna also lost no time; she squatted down and cut a small piece from the branch. It was wood, real wood, with a hard thick bark, slippery and smooth on top, but somewhat more crumbly and amenable to the knife deeper inside, so if you walked along the branch for any length it almost seemed to spring back beneath your feet.

They headed for the thickest trunk. Marianna saw Kazik bending beneath the weight of the rope and realized the boy would never agree to let anyone else carry it. So she said,

"Kazik, why carry the rope without aid? I think we should tie ourselves together with the rope and if someone should accidentally fall then the rest of us can catch him."

"Great." Kazik was delighted. "Like the mountain climbers who went up to the top of Everest."

Neither Dick nor Marianna had the slightest idea what or where Everest was, and could not really understand why climbers would want to go up to the top of mountains, but they didn't ask the boy to explain.

They tied themselves together with the rope; it was so long it did not interfere with their walking.

Tied together, they made it to the end where the branch it grew out of the trunk. Then it became clear this branch was really one of the gigantic vines from which all of the local trees were in fact woven. Only it bent away nearly at a right angle. The branch did not grow out of the trunk like an ordinary tree but continued further on inside the trunk itself, separating into adjoining strands, like the plaits of a little girl's hair, one of whose locks stuck out further than the rest. Where the plaits came together overhead they vanished into a small cave, a tunnel filled with mist, dark and gloomy, the walls overgrown with long quivering moss and hunting vynes.

The three of them stopped in front of the tunnel, not knowing what to do next. They either had to enter the tunnel, or search for another way down.

Marianna shook the moss carefully. She was familiar with it from elsewhere. The greenish mass took fright at her touch, pressing itself to the bark. Such an easily frightened moss. It could be found often in the trees in the depths of the forest and was quite inedible because of its bitter taste. But from time to time you found nuts in them, as parasitic growths, hard, crunchy, almost tasteless. Usually only the small children went after them because there was so little nutrition in them. But now not even small nuts were something to be ignored.

While Marianna silently hunted through the moss for nuts Dick carefully explored inside the tunnel as far as the rope would let him. With every step the gigantic vine became steeper, rolling like a waterfall inside the tree trunk. Dick slipped and fell on his stomach to prevent himself from sliding down into an endless black gullet, carrying the others down with him. Then he crawled back to them. "We'll go down on the outside." Dick said. "Find anything?"

"No." Marianna said.

"I'm thirsty." Dick said.

They untied the rope and attached the end around one of the small branches that grew like bushes out of the great branch itself. Kazik, having fixed the other end to his belt, started to descend down the side of the trunk, clutching the uneven surface of the bark and the plants that had taken root there with his fingers.

Dick stood guard as best he could from above. He was just hoping the winds would stay calm, but he expected at any moment to feel a sharp jerk at the other end as the winds pushed the boy away from the slanting trunk and he was forced to support Kazik's entire weight himself, despite his uncertain perch on the branch's slippery surface.

And Kazik descended very slowly; he too was being careful. He looked about below him as far as he could in the mist, trying to see if there were another branch or flat surface below him. The boy imagined himself a terrestrial mountain climber.

Suddenly he saw a small, sharp branch sticking out of the side of the tree directly in his way; he reached out a hand to grab on to it, but just at the moment he touched it the branch divided into two fanged knives and only Kazik's quick reflexes saved his hand. He was able to pull his fingers away, but not before the living blades had raked them. Above him they could feel the rope tug and Dick grabbed at it more tightly and shouted down:

"What are you doing?"

Kazik did not answer immediately. Blood flowed from his palm where the knives had cut him, and he could see the knives were really the jaws of an enormous insect which hid in a hole cut into the bark of the tree, and waited for prey while pretending to be a harmless branch.

There was no way to bind his injury now. Kazik shouted back to the others,

"Nothing much, I'm just cut. There's a critter sitting here. Took a bite."

"Be more careful!" Dick answered. "You badly hurt?"

"Not very. I'm going further down."

But the smell of blood had awakened the critter's desire for breakfast and it started to crawl slowly out of the hole. The jaws continued to open and close; they were followed by a segmented body flowing like an endless sneaq out from its hole in the tree.

"O-ho." Kazik said.

"What's the matter?" Dick asked.

"A long one!"

Kazik, holding onto the rope with his uninjured hand, pulled out his knife with the other; when the critter, now an enormous-headed, iridescent sneaq crawling along on a myriad of tiny, prehensile blades, came at him, Kazik brought the knife up in a steady motion and cut off the head. The body of the sneaq continued its urgent but aimless clamber down the side of the tree trunk, but the head fell downward for about three meters before another set of tongs darted out of the tree, grabbed the head of its conspecific, and dragged it inside.

Kazik's hand was hurting; probably from venom. Kazik said, "We have to go down carefully here. The bark is infested with critters just waiting for something tasty to come by."

"Should I pull you up?" Dick asked.

"No way. I'll go down a little faster and I won't touch the bole of the tree. There's something below me."

Ignoring the pain in his hand Kazik grabbed the rope with both hands and continued down.

The holes in the bark exploded outward with sharp razor jaws that reached toward Kazik, but never touched him.

Unexpectedly a gust of wind blew the white mass of clouds below to one side and Kazik could make out the end of the rope; it lay in water. But even as the hope that the tree was smaller than they believed, and he was looking at the ground could take root, he realized it was only a gigantic puddle formed where two enormous vines had grown together. The puddle was long and narrow; bushes grew beside it as well as two medium sized payns.

Kazik started to move faster but when he was about three meters above the surface of the water the pain in his hand became too great and he let go, falling with a splash into the water that proved to be over his head.

Kazik pulled himself from the pond and sat on a bark shore overgrown with grass, and immediately the pain returned to his hand. He ignored the pain and shouted upward he had found a lake and when Dick and Marianna came down they should avoid touching the tree trunk.

"I'll burn them out." Dick said. "Remember, I have the blaster."

"Don't bother." Kazik said. "We still need the blaster and there are just too many critters here. If you come down fast enough, they can't bite you."

***

The water in the little lake was dark and muddy, filled with small darting creatures. After Marianna had covered Kazik's injury with antiseptic lotion and bound it tightly, she gave each of them one of the tablets Oleg had brought back from the starship; unfamiliar standing water could give them dysentery or poison them, but it was the only water to be had.

They drank and satisfied their thirst, but that only made them think of their empty stomachs.

Marianna hurried over to the payns. The payns growing here were tiny. The windblown spores had taken root in soft bark. On the land below they always found muzhrumes growing beneath payns, and Marianna was uncertain what she would find as there was no dirt here for muzhrumes to burrow underground. But she was lucky — in the dust at the base of the payns she found a number of muzhrumes, although small. Their color was unfamiliar and they might even be poisonous; sometimes poisonous muzhrumes imitated the real ones.

She bit into one — it was real all right, somewhat sweetish; it would be better to boil or cook them, because they nibbled back at her, but there was no way to make a fire here and they were all starving. So Marianna simply gathered up the two dozen or so muzhrumes growing there and brought them back to the boys; they parceled them out and ate.

By now Kazik's hand had swelled so much it was thicker than his foot, and it turned black. It wasn't all that bad because it hurt less. He was not shivering and did not feel sick, which was fine since it meant the poison in the critter's fangs hadn't been strong. But for now Kazik's hand was useless and he would have trouble going down the rope, which they would all have to do anyway; the ground was still below them somewhere, lost in clouds.

It grew somewhat warmer; they were at the lower edge of the clouds, and during the day the cloud layer rose higher. When they finished eating they found they had clear visibility below them and could even make out the ground.

The ground seemed incredibly far away. As though they were still flying in the balloon. They had some difficulty in making it out because the supporting trunks expanded and doubled in number with every tier below them and the vines spread out into a labyrinth of tunnels. In one spot about a hundred meters below them vines and branches came together to form a wide field with a forest and scattered streams of swamp. Through gaps in the branches there they could make out the ground at least a mile below, or more.

The travelers' hearts sank.

"It would be better if we couldn't see." Marianna said. "Then we could convince ourselves it wasn't so far."

"By now our food bags have been gotten to." Kazik said. The boy was still famished.

"There has to be some sort of game around here." Dick said. He was holding onto the trunk of a small payn, resilient and soft, and looking down at the woods nestled in the juncture of vines and branches. "We just have to get down there."

"Too bad Oleg didn't make parachutes." Kazik said. "I told him to make parachutes so we could jump from the balloon, but he said he'd do it later."

"Oleg would think of something." Marianna said; Dick heard

her words as a reproach.

"He has a lot of time to think in the village." Dick said. "But now we have to act."

"Oleg wanted to come with us." Marianna said. "They wouldn't let him."

"Then there's nothing to be sorry about." Dick said.

In fact Dick wasn't angry with Oleg; it was just habit, their accustomed roles in village life. All that really mattered now was to get down from the tree.

Kazik had gone out further onto the branch, beyond the small lake, to get a better look at the distant world.

And, having looked, he shouted:

"Come quick! Take a look at that!"

The other two ran over to him.

Kazik pushed aside a mass of leaves larger than himself hanging from above and made a window through which they could see a wide river, seemingly close by. They could even see the water rippling in the wind. Further on the river split into a number of tributaries and flowed into a lake. They realized it was a lake rather than the sea because on the far end of the enormous mirror rose a line of blue hills, marked with a dark border of forest. In the river delta a herd of muzdangs roamed along a sand spit. Something must have spooked them; they inflated their swim bladders and hurried toward the water.

On the other side of the river the forest was different; it was dark in color, sky purple, it rose over low hillocks and vanished into rounded hills like the frozen waves of a blue sea. It was beautiful.

They could not see the expedition's camp; it was still twenty kilometers from them and hidden by the waves of hills. They wanted very much to see it; and they lost track of time looking over the forest on the other side of the river.

"That's shining!" Kazik suddenly shouted, pointing toward the forest.

A shining point of something lifted over the forest, like a spark against a background of grey clouds, and vanished.

The spark vanished too quickly into the clouds for the others to see. But they believed Kazik; they wanted to believe him. The spot from which the spark had risen was not far from the shore of the lake. Dick said,

"We'll cross the river as close as we can to the lake; the streams aren't as wide there so it should be easier to get across. And then go along the bank."

"Right." Kazik said. "The forest isn't as thick at the edge of the lake."

They still stood for a long time and watched the spot, hoping to see somewhat else. But at that moment Claudia would launch only one geoscout. She had planned to launch a second but decided she had enough work to do already. She was in a very bad mood and she did not want to admit to herself that the cause was what she has seen the evening before in the laboratory. In fact she had seen nothing, but she had felt the awkwardness of both Pavlysh and Sally as the two of them stood close to each other, as though they were united in a secret which they were not willing to share with her. It was a shameful betrayal on Sally's part.

Pavlysh suspected nothing. He had become engrossed in thoughts of the flight to the mountains. The doctor was quite fed up with preparing specimens of the noxious local critters and categorizing the endless species of bacteria. He wanted to stand beneath a blue sky in the fresh snow, where nothing crawled, crept, where you had to guard against nothing, where no stinking dampness rose from the endless swamps, where you could take off your helmet and walk about without thinking of diseases, where there was only fresh snow, frost, and a blue sky.

So at the moment when the kids were looking down from the enormous trees into the forest surrounding the station, Pavlysh was talking with Sally, performing routine maintenance on the orbit boat. And Sally had asked Pavlysh to take her along; the damp forest had succeeded in depressing her as well, and she was delighted Pavlysh felt the same way she did.

***

The travelers spent the next night in the aerial forest where the network of branches and vines grew together to form an enormous vale. It was a true forest, in which grew not only payns but the more predatory bushes as well. True, if you caught sight of them in time there was no danger. The bushes could sense warmth and if some incautious animal drew close to them they cast long, sharp needles into it. The needles were sharp enough to penetrate the hide of a gote or a baer. They had learned how to deal with them quickly; all you had to do was throw something warm at them so long as you got no closer than about ten paces. You could even take off your jacket and throw it; the bushes quickly exhausted all their needles, and then you could move in closer. Their needles were soon expended and the young shoots were very tasty.

When she saw the bushes Marianna was overjoyed. She grabbed the branches and they ate them for more than an hour until there were none left. All that was left was a sweet aftertaste in the mouth. Their hunger was not satisfied, only suspended, and they really wanted to eat something a bit more solid.

Dick went about the forest hunting for game; he was convinced there was something nesting here. He walked through the wood for a whole hour, but other than some inedible sneaqs and birds which flew away as soon as they noticed him, found nothing.

But they had to delay their descent to the forest floor. The weather again turned bad, and although it was warmer than usual the clouds had gathered below them. Even worse was Kazik's injured hand; there was no way he could make the climb down to the next stage clutching the rope with only one hand.

***

The same evening, before it became dark, Pavlysh decided to take the ATV along the shore of the lake; not in the direction of the river but away from it, where he had not been before.

After he had driven for about ten kilometers along the shore he reached a small, swift stream flowing into the lake. He turned his back on the broader water and went along the stream for a few more kilometers. Then he saw a strange and somehow attractive, slow moving creature a little larger than a dog. The creature was covered with thick, long strands of sea weed reaching to the ground. It was roaming among the low bushes, paying no attention to the ATV, sometimes clawing at the ground with long claws, searching for food. But then something so unexpected happened that only after he had returned to the lab and reexamined the tape did Pavlysh realize that, as this small green baer drew close to a harmless looking bush overgrown with thorns — one of the same bushes that had spat needles at Pavlysh earlier — the bush immediately shot out needles at the baer. The baer, turned into a porcupine, fell down dead.

Pavlysh found the bush's aggressiveness perplexing; the baer had done nothing to threaten the plant. Later he removed a number of needles from the baer's hide and examined them under the lab microscope. It turned out the ends of the needles carried microscopic spores. The spores, finding themselves in the baer's blood, immediately began to germinate, turning the body of the dead baer into another bush.

***

In the morning Kazik woke up before the others. He chewed on the remains of the shoots and made his way over to his observation point silently, in order not to awaken the others. An endlessly long mass of cloud covered the lake and shore. It was easy to imagine it was the Pacific Ocean, and he was Francis Drake who had climbed with an Indian guide to the top of a tall tree growing on the Isthmus of Panama to take a look at the vast ocean which he was determined to cross on his ship the Golden Hind. Somewhere off in the vastness of the Pacific awaited atolls on which rocked the fuzzy tops (for that was what the line drawings looked like) of coconut palms, an encounter with the Spanish silver galleons, the scent of nutmeg on the Spice Islands and the mysterious shores of Africa. . . . The world was alive with color, romance, and open for him, the great adventurer and explorer . . .

From a dark green leaf, which might very well have covered a whole house, a train of small, two-tailed sneaqs descended, their combs sparkling — on their way to the morning hunt. Fat, bluish-grey aphyds swarmed over the leaves; the insects quivered and shook, sensing the danger. A striped flie was carried from the stem by the wind; as Kazik watched it turned into a flying strand of hair and went off on its own business, a white bird chasing after it flapping its wings. A swarm of flies hovered over head. Kazik felt certain something poisonous was going to crawl out now from the trunk of the nearest payn. Therefore he, averting his eyes and not interrupting the stream of sweet day-dreams jammed his knife into an aperture in the bark and forced the critter backwards. It wouldn't stick out its stinger before nightfall now.

"Kazik, where are you?" The boy heard Marianna's voice.

"Here!"

"How's your hand?"

"Better."

There was a small gust of smoke; Marianna had started a fire to heat up what was left of yesterday's harvest of shoots and whatever muzhrumes had climbed out of the moss during the night.

Kazik pulled himself away from the illusion of the Pacific Ocean and commanded the 'Indians' awaiting him bellow to carry him back to the Golden Hind. Walking at the edge of the branch, along the slope, holding onto the thin vines, he reached the grey wall of the main trunk and crossed over on a small bridge formed from a dried out branch to the next vale. Here he was lucky and managed to catch sight of an old vine about half a meter thick which spiraled around the trunk and crawled down about thirty meters lower to the entrance to a cavity about the size of Sergeyev's workshop. Kazik dragged out his knife again and carefully edged his way into the black abyss. He stood there until his eyes grew accustomed to the darkness. Then he threw a nut ahead of him. The nut bounced up and down along the floor of the abyss, softly clattering along until it ended with a splash. So there was water there. And if there was water, there was no way out, otherwise the water would have found it. Then, as if in answer to the splash, Kazik heard a growl — evidently he had awakened the dweller in the abyss. He could wait for the dweller to come forth; but he had no idea what it was. As an inhabitant of the forest world Kazik preferred the better part of valor and retreated.

Kazik returned to the older kids. When they had finished eating they all went down to the chasm and tried to get a good look at the tree trunk, silently, without awakening the unknown resident, searching for some way down. There had to be a way down; they were determined not to die on this tree.

"We can always cut steps in the bark if we have to." Dick said finally. "That's one way we can go down."

"You know how many we'd have to cut!" Marianna was shocked. "It would take a whole year!"

"We'll try." Dick said. "There's nothing better to do anyway."

**

After dinner Pavlysh told Claudia he was going exploring and would be taking Sally along; the motor on the ATV was making odd noises and he wanted Sally to get a chance to examine it in operation.

"All right." Claudia said. "But don't go very far."

"Thanks." Sally said after they were airborne. "Now can you show me that tree?"

"Certainly. I can hardly wait to take a good look at it again. I still have trouble believing such a thing could even exist."

The ATV flew across the river, and when Sally saw the mass of tree trunks woven from gigantic ropes rising up into the clouds she had trouble holding back her delight at the view.

"It is not possible." She said. "It has to be a dream."

"I'd like to get rid of the clouds somehow." Pavlysh said. "So I could photograph it in all its glory."

"Claudia should drop by here." Sally said. "She'd love it."

"She never leaves the station." Pavlysh said. "Remarkable — she loathes the planet she's studying more than we do."

"And you just love this place, Slava?"

"Obviously, I would not apply such standards to a planet . . ."

"Obviously one would never apply such standards even to a living being. Subjectivism in an investigator is dangerous . . . Sorry, Claudia's gotten me to memorizing her lines. But that's not the issue, the issue is none of us like this planet. We've been spoiled by civilization. We bring our own world along with us, including the champagne bottles ready to be uncorked, and we examine this world through the very necessary windows of the ATV. Like a microscope lens."

"Does that mean you do not agree with Claudia?"

"What's there to agree with or disagree with? Claudia is the same as I am, a victim of high tech civilization. Moreover, she has a highly overdeveloped sense of duty. She has converted the subscripts and amendments thought out in air conditioned offices. . . ."

"Who have never once left their own planet . . ."

" . . . by the wise and all-knowing laboratory staff on Earth-14 into hard and fast moral obligations. . . ."

"And who would like the explorers to return without suffering needless casualties. All the more so as contact with an unknown world, red of tooth and claw and all that, tends to be rather more dangerous to the inhabitants of the savage wilderness than for us. So far we're all hale and healthy and alive. A substantial number of the local critters aren't."

"From fright." Pavlysh laughed.

"In general, we both recognize the people who wrote the instructions are completely correct. We have to recognize just what it is we're doing and then get the job done. We're the price — not just us but other people as well who will come here after us, and those with whom we come into contact when we return home. The last thing any of us want to do is bring back some uncontrolled virus, or introduce one."

"But doesn't the fact the planet doesn't like us at all help?" Pavlysh concluded.

"Maybe." Sally agreed. "Let's go get a look at this mountain of a tree."

"I've been dreaming of this for two days." Pavlysh said.

The ATV rose higher, about two hundred meters, to the lowest layer of clouds. The branches wove together to form hanging gardens; in a wide vale formed by vines and branches nestled a small lake surrounded by small trees.

"Idyllic corner of the universe, a spot for a picnic." Pavlysh said.

"Don't tease." Sally said, placing her hand on Pavlysh's. "You do not know how much I've wanted to go off on a picnic with you. But not here. Here there be dragons, or at least scorpions."

"We're in space suits."

"What sort of picnic can you have in space suits?"

Pavlysh took the controls and the ATV rose even higher. From an enormous horizontal branch stretching along the lower layer of clouds like a viaduct from some forgotten civilization hung an enormous torn rag entangled by veins and intestines, with a smaller body, almost like a woven basket large enough to carry several people, hanging out over emptiness. Pavlysh turned the camera on the bag and said,

"Imagine that; nature here's thought up the aerial balloon."

"Not at all similar." Sally said.

"I'd say this creature resembled an enormous balloon when it was alive and filled with air. I've seen similar creatures, only much smaller; when they sense danger they inflate the bladders on their backs — you remember that tape? And here's one that flies off to the clouds. If people ever inhabit his planet I can see teenagers joyriding on them!"

CHAPTER TEN

Oleg, the Mayor, and Sergeyev were sitting in Sergeyev's workshop. From where they sat they could see Vaitkus and his wife working in the garden, digging out the weeds that wanted to crowd out or eat their own vegetables; the children were carrying the leafy tops of the weeds and piling them beside the fence. Gote was on guard there; she had brought her own young along and they were rooting through the green pile.

The weather had grown warm; it almost felt like the end of summer. Three days had passed since the balloon had vanished into the clouds. The settlement was waiting, wondering if the next moment might bring a visitor from Earth.

"Bad." Sergeyev said. He had even grown thinner over the last three days. "Under optimal circumstances they should have reached their destination in two days at most. We should have had guests here today."

Oleg was looking from time to time in the direction of the gates, without wanting. He had been looking that way a great deal for the last two days, thinking, imagining a Survey Service ATV, mostly shiny but with a few dents, crawling out of the forest toward them, and how they would all rush up to greet them and how real explorers would get out of the ATV and how they would be astonished: How could you possibly survive on a planet like this? And even plant gardens?

The forest, as ever, was silent.

"We cannot exclude the possibility they landed the balloon somewhere in the forest and can't find the expedition's camp." The Mayor said. "It would be difficult to find it on the ground."

"I've gone over all the possible explanations in my mind." Sergeyev mourned.

Luiza stuck her head into the workshop, asking if Sergeyev had fixed the shovel. He handed it to her. Oleg found himself angry with the woman that she could thinking about a shovel when they didn't know if Marianna were alive or dead.

The Mayor noticed the look on Oleg's face and said, suddenly:

"Once upon a time Leo Tolstoy, yes, unless I'm mistaken it was Leo Tolstoy, went into a hut where one of his peasants, the sole support of his family, had just died of cholera. The dead man's wife was sitting in the hut eating borscht. That's beet soup. And some of the people who were with Tolstoy became indignant — how could this woman eat soup at this tragic moment? And the old woman answered: 'It would get cold.'

"Maybe I'm not recounting it properly, but you are wrong, Oleg. Luiza is as worried as you are. But she understands the settlement has to live, we just can't stand here and mope. . . . We've gone through worse times here and we've kept going. Otherwise none of us would be alive now."

"I wasn't thinking anything." Oleg said.

"Now that *that* is settled," Sergeyev said, "what do we do?"

"Logically, we'll have to go out into the forest." The Mayor said. "If they landed — we know the direction of the balloon. We'll find them."

"Right." Oleg said. "I'm going."

"Wrong. That's nonsense." Sergeyev cut him off. "Think a moment. The wind could have changed. They could have been carried the wrong way. A long ways off too."

"What if they had to make an emergency landing?" Oleg had difficulty speaking his thoughts aloud, but he forced himself to say, "What if they crashed, they're hurt and need help?"

"And just where do we find them to help them?" Sergeyev's words were cold metal. "Show me."

"We can go as far as the river, along the path the balloon should have taken. It will only take four or five days."

"And who will go on this trip?" Sergeyev asked.

For some reason Sergeyev's voice was filled with bitterness. And Oleg did not understand the anger and rage came from the man's recognition of his own helplessness. All Oleg's thoughts and Sergeyev's intentions and hopes for the last few days had risen, drifted off, and now crashed; he would have preferred to go after the aeronauts now and search for them in the endless forest too. Anything so as not to sit and wait.

"I'm going." Oleg said. "With you. And we can take Fumiko as well. She's almost as good in the forest as Kazik."

"It will be a very long, and very exhausting trip." Sergeyev said. "Not even Dick would go out in unknown territory for so long. We don't have enough food stored now to let us . . . the whole settlement's already half starved . . ."

The beginning of summer was Oleg's least favorite time of the year; there was never enough food and they were always hungry. The migratory animals had yet to come through, the muzhrumes were few and small, the native plants had only just now started to turn green, their bodies manufacturing carbohydrates and sugars.

"This means you can take with you almost nothing in the way of supplies; what there was we sent with the balloon. Remember?" The Mayor asked.

"We can hunt something in the forest . . . we won't get lost . . . how can we think about such things now?"

"Thinking is generally useful, as a rule."

Oleg looked at the Mayor, searching for support. The old man was silent.

"But we're talking about our. . . . can it really be bad?"

"We've always lived close to death." Sergeyev said. "Sending you or anyone else out into the forest without any hope of success, because we were worried about the fate of our loved ones, might doom the settlement. And the settlement — that isn't Boris and me. Or you. It's the kids who depend on us. Fine, so we go off into the forest . . . Who's left to guard the settlement?"

"A lot of people." Oleg said. "The Mayor, and Vaitkus, and the women and Liz. A lot of people."

"Vaitkus is sick and can hardly move. Boris is a little better. There would not be anyone left in the settlement to defend it, you realize that? No one!"

"You're wrong . . ." The Mayor said. "If we have to we can still relive our past."

"If Dick and Kazik can't cope with the forest," Sergeyev ignored the Mayor and spoke to Oleg, "you and I won't be finding them. And that lowers our chance of making it to the ship. Or have you forgotten the ship?"

"The ship can wait." Oleg insisted.

"Aren't you forgetting why we wouldn't let you go on the balloon? You have to get to the ship."

"And if I go to the ship who will defend the settlement?" Oleg was searching for weak spots in Sergeyev's arguments and clutched at straws. "Who? You yourself said it. Now what are we supposed to do, sit and wait?"

"Since we crashed on this planet we've lived with the knowledge we might die of starvation, a plague might kill us, a storm, wild animals. . . . We have remained human because we always think."

"And now we're not doing anything to help Marianna!"

"Would you just be quiet a moment." The Mayor grew irritated. "Do you think Sergeyev even wants to imagine his daughter might be. . . . You're already grown, you're our heir. The inheritor to our little kingdom here. All our hopes are on you, and here you're arguing with us like a small child. Of course you're in love with Marianna. . . ."

"What do you mean?" Oleg was truly offended. "Nothing of the sort!"

"It's obvious." The Mayor laughed. "Even if you yourself haven't guessed it. And of course you have because you're embarrassed. . . ."

"This arguing is tedious." Sergeyev said, getting to his feet. "You'll wake up the entire settlement."

Oleg turned away from them. In love or not in love — it was a ugly word, stupid, it had nothing to do with him. He already knew he was going to run away from the settlement tonight and find them himself. Even if it took five days, or ten days, no matter what sort of monsters he'd have to face in the forest, but he'd find Marianna and Kazik, and Dick as well. Only now he had to get control of himself and not argue with the older men. There was no balloon for him to fly on and he wasn't going to waste his time arguing with them. But when he went off into the forest no one was going to stop him.

"I'm counting on your common sense." Sergeyev said. "You've shown enough of it in the past." Oleg didn't want to listen to him, but there was no way to stop the man from speaking. "We know the route to the ship, and it's relatively safe. I said *relatively*. And that's the way you'll have to go, Oleg. The fate of the entire settlement, of all of us, depends on it. If a tragedy has happened to my daughter (*He said 'my daughter' deliberately so I would understand,* Oleg thought,) and if we cannot contact the expedition and no one finds us, we have to be ready for the worst, then the ship is left. And so are you. Do you understand?"

"I understand." Oleg said it like a school lesson.

"He doesn't understand one whit." The Mayor said. "He doesn't understand he doesn't belong to himself, or there are moments in life when the fate of the whole world depends on you . . ." The old man shook his head.

***

When it grew dark in the evening and Oleg's mother was visiting with Linda and sewing, Oleg put together a small bag of supplies. He pulled down the boxes on the shelf with the flour and sweet roots; there was nothing else left in the house. Then he sat down to sharpen his knife. He knew he should take his crossbow, but the cross-bow was heavy and cumbersome and he was going to have to move as fast as he could, and he knew he could run from nearly all the predators in the forest.

Oleg was infatuated with his own stubbornness. He realized he was not right in what he was doing; the Mayor and Sergeyev had cautioned him to do the most sensible thing, but their authority and self assurance was a cold cruelty that left Oleg no peace of mind.

He was not refusing to go to the ship, but he would go *after*, but not while the others were possibly injured in the forest while everyone just sat around and talked. He had already worked out his route in his mind: straight to the swamps, then to the river. He wasn't at all afraid, although if anyone had said to him earlier he would be walking at night in the forest, not knowing where he was going, alone, Oleg would have been terrified. But now only one thing mattered: get out of the settlement without being noticed and get so far from here they could not chase after him and bring him back. All that mattered was that he find Marianna and return.

The evening stretched on horribly slowly. Oleg lit a candle, adjusted the light and opened the text book. He had already read it three times so far and Sergeyev had modeled the communication center's controls from clay so he could see what he should be doing; he had to prove to himself his flight was not a refusal to go to the ship. He was just putting it off for a while.

***

"You're not sleeping?" Liz came into the hut.

Oleg tore himself away from the pages. Without realizing it he had entered into the text and, in his thoughts, was standing beside the communications console on the starship.

"I can't sleep."

"Are you busy? Am I disturbing you?"

"No, it's nothing. My mother's not in; she's sitting up with Linda."

"It was you I came to see."

"Why?" (He still could not stand Liz!)

"I found this sweet grass." Liz said. "It grows just outside the fence. It smells delightful. I've put some on my hands — here, smell it."

It was stupid to smell someone's hands.

But Oleg never had a chance to say anything because Liz had already placed her palm on his face, almost cutting off his breath, although her touch was soft. Her hands did smell pleasant, but it was nothing unusual; Marianna often used the herbs to make an ointment for burns.

"It smells fine, doesn't it. I found it myself."

"Marianna has a whole bag of it somewhere." Oleg said.

Liz said nothing. She may have been ashamed, or she may have been thinking what else to say. She was sitting next to Oleg on the bench so close the boy could feel the warmth of her body. Liz's hair was unbound and flowed across her shoulders. She had gorgeous hair such as you saw on no one else in the village, thick gold plaits. When Liz had been younger Kristina had plaited her hair into braids and Oleg had pulled on them in the class room, but that had been so long ago it might as well have been on another world.

"You're worried about them, aren't you?" Liz asked.

"You're not?"

"Of course I am. I'm always worried about everyone." Liz said sincerely. "Whenever anyone goes off into the forest I'm afraid. You couldn't drag me out there, no matter what."

"I know." Oleg said.

"But your hair has grown out rather long enough to be braided. If you want I can cut it for you?"

"No need; my mother's going to do it."

"I want to do it." Liz said.

"Why?"

"I don't know."

"You should get some sleep." Oleg said.

"It's too early. And I'm bored. All my work is done, and all I have to do is sit with Kristina, and she's mad. I got bored and went looking for you. And I'm still worried about Dick. And for Marianna and Kazik of course. They're in the forest somewhere, aren't they? Or could they have found the expedition already? What do you think?"

"If they found them, they could have flown back here."

"But I was thinking, what if they only just found them now? And they're giving them supper. Don't you think the people from Earth brought all kinds of foods? Things we've never eaten before?"

"Maybe. They hardly need to go hunting."

"I mean what you ate on the ship?"

"Aren't you forgetting what we brought back?"

"You brought back condensed milk, but Linda grabbed it all to give to the children when they got sick; I don't get sick and got to taste one spoonful."

"You live an uninteresting life." Oleg said. He chased away the comforting thought that Marianna might very well be out of danger now; they simply might not hurry to return while the Earth people asked them questions about everything.

"Who can possibly have an interesting life here?" Liz was amazed. "You of all people know how bored I am, even if you don't want to bother with me."

"I'm not really interested in you." Oleg said.

"But you are in her?"

"Yes."

"I think we're having a rather childish conversation." Liz said. She got up off the bench and sat down on the bed.

"It's much softer here."

"Why childish?"

"Because we should be thinking about the future. But you can't. It must be because I'm older than you."

"Not by much."

"You don't understand, Oleg; you're still almost a boy. You go off running about in the forest, you build aerial balloons. You're already grown up, but you let them treat you like a child."

"And what would you know?"

"I don't know much, but I can sense everything."

"It's all in your head." Oleg suddenly felt rather uncomfortable with the way she was talking to him. "It doesn't have anything to do with me."

"Too bad." Liz said and grew silent.

The silence seemed to last an eternity. Oleg pretended to read, because Liz was sitting with her legs beneath her on his bed, everything had changed in the room and something might happen although he was determined nothing would.

"Come sit over here." Liz said. "I don't want to have to shout across the whole room."

"I can hear you." Oleg said. "The room's not that big. And my mother hasn't come back yet"

"What do you mean?"

"Just that she'd be surprised."

"She wouldn't be at all surprised. In her place I'd be surprised you're still a virgin."

The silence descended between them again. Oleg kept his place at the table, hoping Liz would leave quickly, but Liz gave no sign of departing.

Finally, Oleg said:

"Time for you to go to bed."

"I know." Liz said. "You want me to leave. Why? Are you afraid of me?"

"I'm not afraid of anything."

"Then come over by me. I'm freezing. Your mother isn't going to come. She'll be sitting up with Linda until midnight — I dropped by before I came here. Linda's crying and your mother is minding her and the kids. And the Mayor isn't going to come either; he's playing chess with Vaitkus. I know all about everything."

"I have to leave."

"You? At night?"

Oleg didn't answer.

"I should have known." Liz said. "Lord — I should have guessed right away. Our brave boy is running off into the forest to look for his unfortunate friends, who are so busy with the Earth people they've forgotten all about us. Am I right?"

"Shut up."

"Why should I? I don't want you to go into the forest. You'd just die there, and I'd never get over it. Honest . . ." And suddenly Liz burst into tears. "I'm not good for anything here." She whispered. "And you don't want anything to do with me. . . ."

She sat down on the bench, slumped her shoulders and began to sag.

Oleg started to feel sorry for her. He walked over to the bed, stopped, stretched out his hand and stroked Liz on the shoulder.

"Don't cry like that." He said. "Everyone here likes you."

"No one needs me." Liz sobbed. "You're the only one who needs me. You just don't understand, you've never experienced real life and you've never known what it means not to be needed."

She reached out and drew Oleg closer to her. He obeyed; he couldn't pull himself away.

Liz was hot, as though she had a fever and a high temperature. She immediately embraced Oleg and started to caress him and clutch him to her, not strongly but very tenderly. She was so defenseless and tender Oleg found himself caressing her head and shoulders, but he consoled her and said not to worry, everything would be all right . . . We're going to get back to Earth . . . everything will be all right. . . . It was just that the others were missing, that the balloon was down and they might get lost in the forest.

And Liz said she understood everything, she understood how Oleg felt because he was so brave and so fine and cared about others. She said he was right in setting out to the forest now, only she could not let Oleg depart alone; she'd go with him, she would defend him, it was better for the two of them to go into the forest together; she had never gone into the forest before because it was terribly frightening, but with dear Oleg there nothing could scare her; she would be with him always, as now . . . in his strong embrace. Without Oleg realizing what was going on Liz placed herself in his embrace, grasped his hands to her and clutched him with all her body. It was almost completely dark. The candle illuminated only the table and he couldn't see the bag he had pushed underneath the table; all he could see was the face of Liz, the flickering reflection of her eyes and hair . . .

"Come to me." Liz whispered hotly. "Come to me my dear one, we'll be together forever, always together, I'll go wherever you want, into the forest, to the edge of the world; you have to believe me; I love you; kiss me, here, kiss me, I ask you don't turn away from me . . . I want to kiss you too. . . ."

By now Oleg no longer understood where he was, because there was nothing else in the world other than the intense heat of Liz. She was all over him, and it was so sweet and pricklish, like the air after an electrical storm . . .

The door started to scrape like a saw through wood, and then his mother's steps made the floor boards creak next to his bed.

Oleg tore himself from Liz's arms; he tore his own fingers away from her as well and jumped up. But Liz sat on the bed and clutched her hands to her breasts. Oleg didn't so much see this in the thick half light as feel it. What he saw was his mother's eyes.

"What are you doing?!" She almost screamed. "What are you doing here? Oleg!"

"It's nothing." Liz said, moving herself away quickly. "I dropped by; Oleg and I were sitting here talking. I'll be going now."

"Well this I never expected from you." His mother said, as though she expected something else, but wasn't about to say just what.

"What do you mean?" Oleg was so embarrassed he immediately became aggressive.

"You know exactly what I mean." His mother said. "And from you, Liz, of all people!"

"I'm sorry." Liz said. "I was so worried for Oleg; he was planning to run off into the forest to look for Marianna and Dick all alone and I was talking him out of...."

"Liz, how could you?" Oleg was aghast.

It was a base betrayal.

"You can be angry with me as much as you want." Liz said. "But I care only about you; if you go out on your own you'll die for certain. You know I wanted to stop him so much I even offered to go into the forest with him. Word of honor."

"An odd way to deflect him." Oleg's mother mused to herself,. and turned to her son. "You really were planning to run off into the woods?"

"She's lying." Oleg said. He was an incompetent liar. Liz, on the other hand, wanted to take his mother's thoughts away from her.

"No, Oleg. I'm not a traitor; I love you and I'm not ashamed; I love you so much I'd rather die than let you go."

Oleg's mother looked around. She knew her son too well. She dragged the bag out from beneath the table.

"And what is this for?" She asked.

Liz had achieved her goal. His mother forgot about her.

The girl got up, slipped on her coat, and looked around for the bag she had brought.

"What is this? You want to kill me. You really want to kill me!" Oleg's mother was shaking, overcome with rage.

"I'll be going." Liz said. But no one paid any attention to her.

The storm scene hadn't yet ended when the Mayor decided to look in on the source of the racket, concluded what the whole affair was about, and said:

"I suspected you might get some such fool notion into your head — forget about it. Get some sleep. Sergeyev and I will spend tonight guarding the fence ourselves. If you try, you'll be seen." He went off, muttering: "Raging hormones . . ."

"It's not stupid . . ."

"It isn't stupidity, it's foolish pride." His mother said.

"I'm not doing it for myself. . . ."

"Of course you are! You want to think of yourself as the brave hero who can carry Marianna back here in your arms with Dick slung over your back as well. . . ."

"You don't understand anything at all!"

Oleg ran out of the house as he was, without pulling on a coat. It was cold; he sat down on a log in the wood pile, not wanting to return, feeling everyone's eyes on him from the huts. Liz, his mother, the Mayor and Sergeyev. And no one believed him.

He knew the others were out there in the forest, needing his help, waiting for him to come rescue them.

The cold wind made his skin burn; he wanted to wrap himself up tightly and hide away, but he didn't go back inside. And his treasonous imagination started to construct a picture of Marianna and Dick sitting in a dome in the forest with the explorers from Earth, laughing and eating odd foods from strange containers, cups of hot liquid, the chocolate he had heard of but never had, in their hands . . . It was the thought Liz had planted in his mind, but it was a very comfortable thought, and it was difficult not to submit to it.

"Oleg!" His mother's voice called from the door to their hut. "Come to bed! You'll catch a cold!" He knew he would have to go back inside; the whole settlement was listening and watching.

Oleg said nothing to his mother. She was just silent.

Oleg lay down on his bed; the bed, alas, stank of Liz, of her body and the grasses she had smeared all over her hands.

Oleg wanted only to think of Marianna and he managed to form her image in his mind. It was delicious, but when he fell off to sleep he dreamed he was in Liz's arms, and there was nothing he could do about his dreams, as much as he felt ashamed.

**

On the next day Kazik started to cut out steps and handholds in the bark of the tree. It was tiring and boring work, all the more so since Kazik, and Dick who spelled him, were famished.

On the first day Kazik managed to cut out steps leading almost twenty meters down to the remains of a broken branch that still stuck out of the side of the trunk. Kazik cut a trench into the bark to let them tie their ropes to the branch.

On the second day they used the smaller branch to cut out steps and hand holds another thirty meters downward. Dick was able to go down like Kazik on the steps but Marianna needed the security of the rope.

Marianna told them to leave her in the tree and go down without them; she could wait until they came back with help, but Dick wouldn't think of it. He said it might turn out there was no expedition, or the expedition might have already left when they found the remains of the camp. At which point they would have to go home, which meant Marianna would have to stay alone in the tree for as long as ten days or two weeks. While Dick spoke Marianna turned into a skeptic. He was right; Marianna stopped arguing with him. While she had argued with the other kids to leave her behind, she was afraid they would actually agree with her and she would have to remain behind, and might die of terror and loneliness.

Kazik discovered a small hole in the tree trunk and chased out the occupant, a poisonous sneaq. Now they had one more station, a spot where they could tie the rope. He estimated they would need at least three or four such waystations before they reached the ground, it was so far below them.

On the fourth day Dick climbed back up to the remains of the balloon in the clouds and brought down another rope. On the way he hunted and killed a tree dwelling ribbit and the three of them managed to quiet their hunger for a time; they were so worn out they slept for ten hours. It felt like an eternity had passed since they had left the settlement, and their destination was as far from them now as it was the first day.

When they awoke the weather was very good and they could see to the ends of the world. Kazik sharpened his knife before he descended to continue his work; the metal blade had shrunk to half the original size while they had been in the tree from continuous use and re-sharpening, then Marianna smeared the remains of her oils on his hands. Kazik's fingers were bloody and swollen; the knife was still good enough to bite him back.

Kazik went out to his observation point to look to the side where he expected he should see the camp of the expedition from Earth. He sat there for almost half an hour but neither of the others bothered him; they knew the boy was working hardest of all. He kept his vigil until he saw a shiny tear drop shape flashing through the trees, not knowing it was Pavlysh flying in the ATV to the other side of the lake. Now they had no doubt they were going somewhere, and they knew where it was they had to go.

With the second rope in place Kazik's work went all the faster. That day he was able to continue the stairway down another fifty meters or so. At this rate it would take them two more days to reach the ground.

The two days passed. Marianna spent much of her time at the observation point hoping to see something rise along the shore of the lake. She watched as Pavlysh flew Claudia Sun across the lake to the gold mountain. It was Claudia's first trip on the surface of the planet. The geologist was tense and came alive only when she saw the ores washed out of the mountain by the stream, and the thick, shiny veins and tendons of gold and quartz. The sight impressed Pavlysh as well; he wanted to forge a gold bracelet for Sally, only he lacked the instruments. When they returned to the dome Claudia made him go through the disinfection process twice — Pavlysh grumbled, taking comfort only in the ore samples with branching veins of gold they used to decorate their quarters. A second flight to the mountain had to be put off, but it remained a possibility. Pavlysh subconsciously found himself more work and more reasons to put it off. The flight to the mountains was a holiday, something they could look forward to; afterwards they would have to get back to everyday concerns. So he never found the time or the place to be alone with Sally.

Claudia never let the two of them out of her sight. Sally found the situation rather humorous, all the more so as Claudia was her dear friend as well as colleague and the Englishwoman didn't want to annoy her.

Then Pavlysh looked at their calendar and discovered — if one assumed simultaneity and a certain twisting of known physical laws — it was his birthday. Sally and Claudia set a banquet table with a cake and candles; Pavlysh was overwhelmed.

***

After two days Kazik had finally reached the spot on the tree where, at fifty meters from the ground, the tree trunks spread out into a pyramid. It would still be difficult to descend without a rope, but it was no longer a sheer drop.

Kazik shouted up to the others so they wouldn't worry and finished his crawl down to the ground.

The boy was delighted; he could walk where he wanted. The ground was soft — you could jump up and down, run on it without a chance of falling through. Kazik went for a quick run around the base of the tree on the off chance he might find the bag with their supply of food they had thrown out a week earlier in the hope of lightening the balloon enough to avoid crashing into the tree. He didn't find it; either it had already been found and finished off by some animal, or else was lost in the underforest.

Kazik was so unused to life on the ground he almost ran into the claws of a zhakal, but he darted away from the creature in time. Kazik would have preferred not to run away from the predator, but there was nothing else to do; all that was left of his knife was so dull it wouldn't even scratch the animal's hide. The boy was able to gather some muzhrumes and he brought those back up to the others on the level where they had made Marianna remain while the boys had constructed their exit.

On the following morning they began the descent to the ground together.

Dick had tied the rope above them to the trunk of the tree, then Marianna, holding onto the rope and resting her feet on the narrow steps let herself down as far as the broken branch and stopped there. Kazik was already below her, on the next level. Then Dick untied the rope and crawled by hand down the steps to Marianna. After a brief rest Marianna continued her descent downward, toward Kazik. Their progress was very slow; Marianna was exhausted, and a rest over the abyss helped little if at all. With every meter her fingers grew weaker and her legs hurt; she wasn't used to this; but that was obvious to everyone.

A rain storm struck at them again out of the sky and through the tree. Streams of water battered their hands and heads, trying to wash the human flies away from the side of the tree, and there was nowhere to hide from it. The rope quickly became wet and swelled with water, becoming heavy and slippery, finding safe holes for their feet in the cut steps was all the harder.

They still had two stations left to go before they reached the ground.

Dick shouted down for Marianna to stop and not try going any further down now, but there was no way for her to stop; the continuous torrent was driving her with it, and she could let herself be carried away once and for all by the water or use what purchase the rope and steps gave her to slow her descent. She passed their way station, thirty or forty meters remained to the ground, and then she was where the bowl of the tree began to spread out and the descent became much easier.

Kazik, while he had gone down to the ground and had come back up, had never been able to attach a rope, and without it Marianna slipped and slid, her feet groping for holds and clutching with her scratched body to the slippery, uneven bark. Kazik tried to go down not far from her; he was afraid she was going to fall off altogether, although he understood if she did there was no way he could hold onto her. But he did hold himself closer and advise her where to put her feet.

Marianna did make it to the spot where the tree started to

spread out, and realized there was no longer just an empty drop below her but a sharp slope.

Kazik sighed in relief; they had made it. Covering his eyes from the rain with his palm he looked upward again to watch Dick's descent.

He heard the short cry — and past him, brushing him and almost grabbing him after, flew Marianna, twisting and sliding down the abruptly inclined slope of the tree, unable to get a grip anywhere on the wood. Kazik watched in horror as she fell.

Later, Kazik didn't recall how he got down to the ground himself; he may have ignored the steps as well and clambered down like a giant insect. Kazik got down very quickly and ran to where the girl lay with her arms extended. He was calling her name but received no answer. He placed his ear to her chest and for a long time was unable to hear the beating of her heart. Then Dick ran up to him. He pushed Kazik aside and had him place his jacket over Marianna's head to keep the rain off her face.

Kazik was cold and the rain pounded hard enough to hurt.

"She's alive." Dick said. He ran his hands over her body to see what was broken; at her twisted legs Marianna groaned without opening her eyes. "She has a broken leg. It's bad. "

Dick ran off into the forest and cut down a number of thin reeds.

Marianna was semi-conscious; evidently when she struck the ground she had lost consciousness, but when Dick had to straighten her leg she screamed in pain; the girl started to cry and came to. Dick did not hear her cry, although Kazik asked him to stop and not hurt Marianna. But Dick started to wrap her leg to make it immobile anyway.

The two of them carefully carried Marianna into the forest where a thick cover of leaves shielded them from the fierceness of the downpour. Marianna had already come to her senses again and was in pain, but she was able to stand it.

"That was dumb." Marianna said. "I let you down."

"Shut up." Dick said. He was trying to light a fire; he had sent

Kazik off to find a large empty nut so they could boil water. "There's nothing we can do about it." He said. "And anyway, we're all down now."

Marianna was so tired she fell asleep and slept until morning despite the pain. But Dick and Kazik just sat by the fire and thought how they could continue; everything had become very complicated now.

They could, in theory, send Kazik back to the settlement. But on foot in the forest would take at least five days, if not longer, and going would be difficult: they had passed over swamp and thick forest, the worst places. And leaving Dick alone with Marianna would be dangerous. Someone would have to go hunting, or after fire wood, and leave Marianna alone and defenseless. Nothing defenseless lasted long in the forest. And even if they left her with the blaster sneaqs might always crawl up unnoticed.

"Too bad." Dick shrugged in the end. "It means we'll have to make a stretcher and carry Marianna to the river."

"Right." Kazik immediately agreed. "First thing we'll do is get her across the river, or if we can't one of us will get across and go find the other people and bring them. Right?"

"That's what we'll do." Dick said. "To the river will take us at least half a day. We can find a way to cross when we get there."

"So long as they haven't left already, so long as they're still there." Kazik said with fervor, as though he were praying. "They can't leave; they have to know we're dead here without their help. But they're from Earth; they have to know everything. . . ."

"Get some sleep." Dick told him. "Sleep and I'll sit guard. I'll wake you later. We'll start for the river tomorrow."

"Tomorrow. . . ." Kazik muttered. "We don't have all that far to go." The rain struck the leaves, then after a while died down and fat drops of water rolled from the branches and dropped onto the moss.

***

They did not make it to the river on the next day, no matter how close the water had seemed from the tree's heights. Their road first had to cross a swamp which cost them more time, and they had to make a sledge for Marianna. Dick cut down poles for the sledge, but they could not find the thin vines they needed to tie it together.

Marianna became worse from the pain which stayed with her, and from the concussion. Neither of the boys knew what it was called, but they knew she was sick; her head hurt and she had trouble recognizing the two of them. The bruises on her cheek, her breasts and across her thighs turned black.

With nightfall the storm rose up again; it came with winds and little rain. Lightning danced along the branches of the tree and twisted to the ground as sneaqs of fire. Dick was thankful they had made it down in time, any way.

The fury of the storm ripped the remains of their balloon from the upper branches. They saw it falling and everyone realized at once in the darkness what had happened: lightning lit the skinny black envelope as it fluttered to the ground.

In the morning Kazik came upon an previously unknown creature, lifeless and harmless not far from them, and realized that it was their old balloon. It looked nothing like a balloon any longer; it was even difficult to imagine the tattered skins and ropes could have risen into the sky and ridden currents of air. All that was left of the envelope were a few enormous, torn scraps; only splinters remained of the basket.

But the ropes were intact, and the old muzdang bladders were still useful, and out of them and the poles Dick and Kazik constructed a litter for Marianna and even fashioned an overhead canopy for her to keep the river flies that swarmed as black clouds near the water away.

So on the next day they headed for the river crossing through a swamp filled with sneaqs and were forced to spend the night on a small island comprised of water plants and reeds nestled against the bank in the river.

Marianna grew delirious; her fever rose and there were no medicines to give her; it didn't help that she was the only one of them who really knew which plants were useful as medicines.

The islet almost rocked — the river current had under-cut it and if you were not careful where you put your feet they would go through. During the night Kazik killed a large sneaq that had wanted to wait out the darkness with them on the islet as well.

To Kazik they had left the settlement a horribly long time ago, perhaps a year, and since then they had been walking, stumbling, crawling and swimming somewhere or other and it was never going to end. To keep his mind off their situation he let his imagination draw pictures of their meeting with real earth people, and then he started to recite from memory the names of all terrestrial mountains with an altitude greater than seven kilometers. The words meant really little to Kazik, they were an invocation, that thread connected him with Earth.

In the morning they cooked and ate the sneaq and then hunted for poles suitable to make a raft, and exhausted themselves moving through the swampy shoreline, along a sandbar and through a thicket of brushes.

They could not leave Marianna alone for a second, all the worse because the spot was unfamiliar and dangerous. There were swamp critters and varieties of sneaqs they had never seen before. A short ways upriver, in the depths of the swamp, there was something, a cluster of creatures — if you stuck a pole into the water you could see the water seethe as if the inhabitants had become even angrier.

Only toward evening did Dick find two suitably heavy trees; but where they lay in the swamp was awkward and it wasn't clear how to get them and tie them. Kazik realized if they cut the roots which held their riverside floating island to the side of the river they could float it over to the trees. And then they tied the trees to the island and produced a boat — dry, unexpected, almost unnavigable, but it did float.

They made a bed for Marianna out of heaps of dry grass and branches they covered with pieces of muzdang bladder from the balloon — she would stay dry. Marianna came through it without screaming once; she only groaned a few times. Her leg was inflamed and swollen. And she had difficulty performing her normal bodily functions; despite the pain she was shy, and she didn't want to eat anything, so Dick went away and Kazik helped her, as he had helped Luiza when the big woman had been sick during the winter. Dick felt terrified, more afraid than any time in the forest.

On the next day Dick cut long poles; they weren't very strong and they bent but they were as long as he could get.

Kazik dubbed their new boat *The Golden Hind*. Both boys pushed away from the bank with their poles as hard as they could and the island ship broke loose from the shore and floated free.

The current carried it gently downstream; this current was but the first of three or four streams within the greater river they would have to overcome, and it was gentle and slow. The long poles reached down to the river bottom even in midstream.

Their voyage did not prove difficult, and the three became cheerful. Marianna sat up on her elbows and watched the two boys work.

They had never before had the chance to sail over a large expanse of water and found it interesting. When they looked down through the transparent water they saw the sandy bottom; water plants floated up toward them and, from time to time, even fish. A flock of unknown birds circled over them — the birds were small and noisy and suddenly one of them made a quick dive into the water and emerged a moment later with a small fish in its talons.

The sandbar that broke above water was narrow and low, a narrow band of small stones rolled round and smoothed by the currents. They had to drag their island boat across the rocks. This took them the better part of three hours and Kazik and Dick were both exhausted, and the island boat was showing signs of wear of its own. From the band of stones they saw a wide and fast river bed, and after it a third, even larger. Between the second and third river beds was a long hill overgrown with grass, and it made absolutely no sense to drag their boat out of the water to cross it, so they decided to let the current carry their makeshift boat further down stream, closer to the lake where all the currents flowed together.

They were forced to spend the night on the far shore almost at the entrance to the lake — the currents had carried them so far down stream. But they had made it to the other side.

With the coming of the next day would begin the most difficult part of their crossing.

Kazik had been asleep; Marianna had been sleeping and awoke in fits, and Dick, to avoid waking Kazik up, and to get Marianna something to drink, had boiled water in an empty nut over a fire himself. Dick was a firm believer in the medicinal properties of hot water. Then he, as much as he wanted to get some sleep, crawled through the bushes in search of other branches or large twigs they could use to repair their isleboat.

During the night it drizzled again, but the rain was warm and not unpleasant. Dick had covered everyone with the tent. Marianna wasn't sleeping; her leg hurt too much. It felt like someone was hitting her with a hammer fast enough to match the beating of her heart. She just wanted to cut away the damned, heavy, useless leg. Through a hole in the tent she looked up at the black sky. The weather had turned warm and stuffy; Dick coughed in his sleep next to her, barking orders and arguing with Kazik over something. Marianna tried to think about Oleg; he must have already set off for the starship after they decided she had died. Oleg must be suffering a great deal with her loss, and she was happy he was suffering in vain. She was alive and was going to return to him. And then Marianna suddenly began to weep, soundlessly in order not to awaken the others. Marianna was crying because she imagined they were going to have to cut off her leg, and Oleg would stop loving her and abandon her. What did it matter if he was going back to Earth; she'd remain here in the settlement. The settlement would be almost empty because only blind Kristina and Marianna would be left and Marianna would look after Kristina and feed Gote. . . .

***

All of them gathered there, except for the smallest children. Of the small children only Fumiko, Kazik's stepsister had come. She hadn't been playing with anyone for days, but she hadn't been crying. It made no sense to cry over Kazik. She went around like an automaton, not hearing or seeing anything. The Mayor wasn't there either; the Mayor had a cold again and hadn't been out of his bed for three days.

There was room enough in Sergeyev's small house — three were absent — too many for such a small settlement. You could feel their absences, sense the empty places.

"We're going." Sergeyev said. "Oleg and I will be departing in the morning; we can't wait."

"Still too early." Vaitkus said. "I don't have enough food for you."

"The kids are collecting muzhrumes." Sergeyev said. "The summer's warm this year so far, but there's no guarantee it will stay that way. You remember two years ago when it was hot for months, and then we had snow? We might get that again. But at the moment we've had warm weather for more than a week and the snow in the mountain pass should have melted."

"It'll just be the two of us this time." Oleg said. "We won't need a lot of food."

"Oleg's right." Sergeyev said.

"And what will this change?" Oleg's mother suddenly spoke up.

Oleg realized his mother would now think of arguments against this trip; he had expected she would start to speak them aloud. She thought if she were just to speak wisely and convincingly they would understand her, listen to her, and Oleg would remain.

"There's no guarantee you'll be able to repair the communication system." She said.

"Mother, we've gone through that before." Oleg said. The others said nothing; they realized it would have to be Oleg who spoke to his mother.

"Twenty years ago there was no time to do anything. The ship was dead, cold, both communications specialists were dead; you of all people remember, and the Captain had died, everyone who had been on the bridge was dead. Back then the only way to survive, you all knew and you were right, was to get out and get out fast, or you would die of radiation poisoning and freeze at the same time."

"True." Vaitkus said. "If our people are lost, if they've crashed on an island, there's no way they can return. Our only hope is the starship."

"Don't speak nonsense." His mother said. "The ship's in the mountains."

"Mother," Oleg said, "We've discussed this for years now. If we can get to the starship and fix the com system we can transmit distress signals. Don't you understand? While this expedition is here, we have a chance they'll hear our signals."

"There's no chance at all!." His mother insisted. "The *PolarStar's* interstellar communications system uses gravigrams. The expedition will only have access to in-system methods of communication. Radio signals. Why do you foster unrealizable hopes?"

Irina's eyes were moist; she could hardly hold back the tears, which made her face angry and tense.

"Which is why we'll ignore the hyperwave communication." Sergeyev said. "We'll concentrate on the radio wave transmitter."

"You'll never fix it."

"Fixing it will be easier than fixing the hypewave, which is why we're going now, Mother, right away." Oleg said. "When we realized what we could do I almost jumped from joy."

"And you said nothing?" Irina asked.

"Vaitkus knows." Sergeyev said. "And the Mayor too. But we didn't want to talk about it earlier."

"Stupid secrets." Linda said. "No one needs secrets."

She didn't want Sergeyev to leave either.

Oleg looked at the adults. Everything was decided.

Now the fate of the settlement was in his hands. And in Sergeyev's. And they would have to hurry.

The door of the hut slammed wide, almost tearing the ropes holding it in place.

The Mayor grew in the opening as a cumbersome silhouette.

He didn't enter the room; he just stood there and slowly looked over the people sitting at the table.

"Boris, this is too much!" The Mayor's appearance gave Irina the chance to focus her rage, even her hate, against the people whose mad ideas threatened Oleg's life, on him. "You're still sick! Are you mad too? Come in right now!"

The Mayor burst out laughing. It was very odd. The time was not appropriate for laughter.

"Idiots!" He said happily. "And I'm the chief idiot!"

"Sit down." Linda said, getting up to help the Mayor. Perhaps she was thinking the Mayor was delirious.

"Just listen to me." The Mayor said. He tottered over to the table, reached out his one hand and leaned on it; the oil lamp's glow was reflected in his eyes. "We were talking about ways to repair the *PolarStar*'s in-system communication system, am I remembering correctly?"

"Right." Sergeyev said.

"Only total fools would waste their time on that." The Mayor said gleefully. "Because there's no need to fix it."

"Why?" Vaitkus asked.

"Because all you have to do is turn it on!"

"What exactly are you talking about?" Sergeyev asked, realizing the Mayor was not delirious. The Mayor had thought of something.

"Who can tell me where, other than in the com center, there is a transmitter on board the ship?"

"You're right." Sergeyev said almost immediately. "We really are total foo ls."

"Where?" Oleg asked. "What are you talking about?"

"Quite simply, there is a transmitter on the landing boat." Sergeyev said. "The one we couldn't launch after the crash."

The Mayor said, "As far as I know the boat's transmitter is intact. We never thought of it because we never thought there would be anyone on this damn planet we could communicate with."

It became very quiet, as though the Mayor had spoken his words in an incomprehensible language. And everyone was translating them for themselves.

"Oho!" Luiza's bass cut through the darkness. "This changes everything."

This changes everything, Oleg repeated in his mind. In the minutes before the Mayor's words the trip to the starship had been a sacrifice, underlined by the cold and reasonable necessity. Every step to the ship carried him away from Marianna and increased the likelihood she and the others would be lost forever. A minute ago Oleg, already obeying the hated Necessity, had been cursing the trip and those who were forcing him to go to the *PolarStar* rather than rush out into the forest, all were his enemies because they were willing to accept Marianna's death. . . .

Sergeyev's ideas as much as they gave a slight shadow of hope, did not promise immediate hope. . . . What a fine, kind face the Mayor has. How wise and knowledgeable he is. Why can't I be the same? And then the blow fell, the feeling of shame, the realization that he, Oleg, should have thought of the transmitter on the landing boat. There was no need for the balloon's flight to the river, no need to put Marianna and the others in danger; ten days ago, two weeks ago, they should have flown the balloon to the *PolarStar* and contacted the expedition from Earth . . .

"I should have thought about this earlier." Sergeyev said. The man's eyes sank; as Marianna's father he was thinking the same as Oleg. It was the first time Oleg actually felt any kinship for Sergeyev — after all, they both loved Marianna.

"Why are we standing here?" Oleg heard the words before he

realized he had shouted them himself. "We have to get going now."

"At least wait long enough for us to pack your supplies." Vaitkus said. "It wouldn't do for you to starve before you got there."

***

"You're leaving in the morning?" Liz asked Oleg when the crowd dispersed.

Liz hadn't approached Oleg for days now; she kept silent, just looked at him from afar intently and pathetically. Oleg's mother hadn't spoken of that night to him since then either. Oleg sort of understood he himself was to blame — Liz could not be blamed, and then he would not have become a deceiver, even though he found it hard to think of himself as a scoundrel who would kiss a girl when another, the one he loved, might be dying in the wilds of the forest. Oleg just tried to avoid thinking about it at all; all he thought about really was Marianna and the trip to the ship. It had to be said things had actually turned out quite well; it was as though Liz weren't even in the settlement. And, therefore, when she came up to him, Oleg instantly remembered and felt his guilt, and he came to hate Liz. He even hated the scent of the grass she had rubbed on her skin again. And, certainly, he would have said something unfair and shameful, but at that moment he was already in the mountains, already switching on the radio . . .

"As soon as it's light." Oleg said. "There's no reason to worry about me. Everything's all right."

"I'm glad, really I am. I've been awfully worried about you. I don't expect anything from you, you understand, I just don't want you to be angry when you remember me."

"Okay." Oleg said, glancing around to see if anyone was listening to their conversation. "I'll remember. No need to worry."

"Then let's go for a walk this evening." Liz almost whispered.

"Walk?"

"Outside the fence. Not very far."

"How could I?" Oleg was actually surprised. "I'll be getting ready all night; we really are leaving at dawn."

"For a little while?" Liz said. "You're not coming back."

"We'll see." Oleg said.

Oleg again felt sorry for the girl, and his lips and hands lived the shameful, but indelible memory of the touch of her skin and lips, and he realized he could never go walking anywhere with her . . .

Oleg headed off for the workshop to help Sergeyev finish the grapnels, the iron claws to help them crawl over ice and rock. And he forgot about Liz.

But she stood for a long time by the fence not far from the gate, in the shadows, waiting, even though she really didn't believe he would come. Then, cold and shivering, she made her way to bed well before Sergeyev kicked Oleg out of the workshop so he could get some sleep before they left.

And only when he lay down did Oleg remember about Liz and think in relief, *Just as well I forgot.*

CHAPTER ELEVEN

On this occasion they made no ceremony of the departure. No one was in the mood for it.

It was very early. The children were still sleeping; only the adults gathered by the gate, although Fumiko ran up at the last moment hoping they would take her. She had overheard Oleg would be talking to the people who were going to save Kazik and wanted to be there when it happened, but no matter how hard she tried she could not convince them to take her into the mountains: she was too small and would just be a burden.

Liz hurried out to them from her own hut; she carried a small bag. Liz hadn't slept, she had fretted, and delayed, and worried, looking for something tasty to give to Oleg. She was like a mouse, always hiding away tasty things, but afterwards forgetting about them. But now she had rooted around in her belongings and found sweet roots, lumps of sugar from last year, and the pitiful remains of her own attempts to bake pies during the winter. Liz had wanted to tie everything into a pretty bundle but in her hurry did not succeed and simply threw everything into an ordinary bag for carrying muzhrumes and ran off for the gate.

Oleg took the bag; he thought everyone was laughing at him. Liz was standing two steps away from him and looking at him as though she wanted to drag him to her.

Oleg's mother stepped between the two of them and started to straighten the collar of her son's jacket. Oleg didn't object.

"Too bad there's no time to waste." The Mayor said.

"Today we have to get everyone to weeding." Vaitkus said.

Vaitkus's voice was hoarse and Oleg thought the man was getting worse — everyone was going and they were leaving him with the women and children. But Vaitkus's lungs were weak and his heart wouldn't let him walk very far. Despite that he was responsible for their garden and all the agriculture.

Linda started to weep; she didn't say a word but she cried. A year ago she had said good-bye to Thomas, and Thomas had never returned. And now she was here with Sergeyev and he was leaving as well.

Oleg and Sergeyev fixed their packs on their backs and quickly headed toward the mountains. The mist was flowing along the ground and rising like steam — the day promised to be warm. Oleg hurried; he recognized the landmarks of their journey of a year before. Sergeyev followed after him, trusting the boy's memory. They spoke only when they had to.

The Giant Muzhrume was in the same spot as the last year; it had grown considerably during the winter. They didn't stop near it; it was almost dark and Oleg wanted to make it to the cave, or go even further if they could. He was determined that every day they should walk further than the year before.

***

Dick, Kazik and Marianna wanted to begin the crossing of the wide tributary at dawn, but the knots and ropes holding their little island together had become undone during the night and they set about fixing them. Marianna fell asleep. She had not managed to get any sleep during the night, and now it had finally grown warm she dozed off. Dick and Kazik didn't want to awaken her; they walked a short distance along the shore and waited.

"You tired?" Dick asked.

Kazik was surprised. Dick had never asked about such things before. If someone was tired, that was his problem. If you were really exhausted Dick might take your pack or the game you were carrying; he didn't bother to say anything, he just took it. *Maybe he's tired too?* Kazik thought. Aloud, he said,

"Doesn't matter; we don't have all that far to go."

Dick tapped Kazik on the shoulder with his palm. Kazik thought, *Here we're sitting together and he doesn't know I love him. I love him more than anyone else, even Marianna or Aunt Luiza because I want to be like him, strong and silent. When we get back to Earth will we still be friends? I'll have to grow up fast and also become an adult, but he'll still be relatively young. We may together set out on a long journey.*

"Maybe we can climb Everest." Kazik said aloud.

"Forget about Everest." Dick said; he realized the boy was thinking about Earth again.

"Or go hunting." Kazik said.

"There's no hunting there." Dick said. "I asked the Mayor. They don't hunt on Earth. I don't want to go there."

"You don't even want to see it?"

"See it, maybe." Dick said. "I just don't want to stay there. I'd be bored silly. You can't do this, you can't do that . . . They sit around in antiseptic houses and fear microbes might attack them, I guess. . . ."

"If they were afraid then we'd never have flown here." Kazik said, trying to reason with him.

"And just why are we here?"

"Because we're the same as they are. We're exactly the same as they are. Where are we going? To them. That is, to ourselves. I understand it that way. It's as though we were lost in the forest and now we want to get out. They're all stronger than we are, more beautiful, like in the photos."

"They'll just find us dirty." Dick said.

Kazik didn't argue; he realized why Dick said what he did. It did not lessen his love for Dick; the understanding of the weaknesses of a beloved person even makes him closer. Dick feared the Earth people because he envied them.

"We're not going to be totally useless there." Kazik said.,

"Where?"

"On Earth. They'll be able to put our talents to use. We can become explorers with the Survey Service."

"If they take us, they'll have to teach us from the cradle." Dick betrayed his fears.

"Boys, why aren't we moving?" Marianna suddenly called out.

"You woke up?" Dick got to his feet. "It got hard to row and we decided to take a short break. How's your leg; does it still hurt?"

"It's better now." Marianna said.

"Want something to drink?"

"Yes."

Dick brought the girl water in a shell. He supported her head so she could swallow; Marianna's forehead felt hot to his touch. Dick was afraid for the girl; they simply didn't have any medicines to give her. Dick had always liked Marianna more than anyone else in the settlement but he understood everything between Marianna and Oleg and felt there was something unfair in it. Not that he was going to take offense at it; it was their business what they did.

They collided with a small island in the water and started to push away from it with the poles against the soft bottom. The poles kept getting stuck, and pushing them became difficult because they kept sinking deeper and deeper. The shore they had left was now very far away, but the other shore seemed no nearer; the river had gotten all the wider as it prepared to flow into the lake.

The poles no longer reached the bottom and Dick and Kazik had to paddle with large branches thick with rigid leaves they had found that morning on the riverbank. The current was strong, and they could not tell if their rowing was making any difference. Most likely it was not.

They were all sweaty and tired. Marianna was angry with herself because she could not help. One of the logs started to drift away and they lost even more time tying their raft back together again. The wind and the currents carried them even further down stream.

To the right was the lake, gray and smooth; little dark points that were small islands lifted above the surface to form the river delta; the far shore was invisible beyond it, lost in the grey mist.

The current carried them over the shoals but they were unable to stop at them because Dick pushed too strongly with his pole and the pole got stuck in the muddy bottom and stayed behind, almost dragging Dick into the water. Besides which their islet, the mass of dirt and roots tied to the logs, was pulling apart at all the knots. The raft trailed branches and water plants behind it in the river.

The shores suddenly split apart to distant sides, the wind came up — a fresh clean wind devoid of the cloying scents of the forest — it rocked them and the movement of the boat slowed to a halt. The river and currents were behind them.

"What happened?" Marianna asked.

"Nothing." Dick said. "We row from here."

"Just as well." Kazik said. "The current is slower here. We'll be able to row our way out of it."

But there still was a current and it stretched even further from the shores, until it ran up against the shoals which stuck out of the water as flat, low lying sandbars.

But for the presence of the insignificant arc of sand they felt they were already inside the lake. The river mouth was so wide the low growth along the shores were no more than fur trimmings on a grey hide, it was so far. And in as much as they began the crossing late, in the second half of the day, it had already started to grow dark. They made a fire in the dirt that held the wood of the raft together to warm water for Marianna. Dick and Kazik drank straight from the lake; they drank a lot, on purpose, to fill their stomachs and kill their hunger, but it really didn't help.

In the evening Dick tried to catch fish — he still had a few bolts left. But he'd never shot at fish with his crossbow before, and just missed. He hoarded the blaster; he didn't know how much of a charge was left it in and was afraid it would soon be useless.

The night on the sandbar proved difficult; the wind rose and the water began to toss their little island about. The small boat rocked back and forth, and they were constantly forced to pole it back into the shallows. And when the waves became too big Dick and Kazik climbed down into the cold water and held the raft in place. Marianna didn't get any sleep either.

***

Oleg and Sergeyev had an easy walk; they went fast, and generally the hike to the starship was different from the last time. Their relationship to the road had changed. The year before it had been an almost impossible trip, made as much in desperation as anything else. The death of Thomas had been the unavoidable price for the attainment of an impossible goal, and the *PolarStar* itself had seemed a mysterious, distant memory, the reality of which was doubtful.

Now they were walking along a difficult road toward a definite goal with concrete objectives. What mattered was they reach the ship as soon as possible and get in contact with the expedition from Earth.

Sergeyev let the younger Oleg take the lead, not trying to underline the difference in years and experience. Oleg silently recognized this difference. This was a trip of two adult men.

The two had just passed the gigantic muzhrume and were walking along the rocky slope when Sergeyev asked:

"Then you really do love my daughter?"

"I think so." Oleg answered. He was thinking Sergeyev would prefer a less than categorical answer.

Sergeyev ignored Oleg's attempt at diplomacy.

"None of us have ever thought we might live to see the younger generation grown up, let alone married."

"Marianna and I never spoke about marriage." Oleg blushed. He was remembering Liz, and he wanted to bury the memory and incident so deep Sergeyev would never find out.

"If we're successful in this, the settlement will never see a marriage." Sergeyev said. "There won't be a settlement. The forest will take it."

"I won't be sorry!" Oleg said.

Oleg turned. For a moment he thought there was an allyfant passing by them some ways off. It had already started to grow dark, and gusts of snow had fettered the world with a grey darkness.

"But I will be." Sergeyev answered. The older man was walking easily, relying upon Oleg's feel for the path. "I've spent almost half my life here, and all my life as an adult."

"You mean you don't want to go home?"

"That has nothing to do with it. We've lived long years in poverty and helplessness; someone from the Earth who took a look at us, you and me, might decide we were funny looking monkeys. And I am certain if we do return home, what will remain in our memories are victories and moments of triumph which you have never even noticed."

"You mean I was too young?"

"You think it natural we remained people, that you went to school and eat with a fork. But do you know how we celebrated when I made the first fork?"

Oleg grabbed Sergeyev by the sleeve sharply, pulling him off his feet so fast the man only had a chance to grunt from pain.

A black flock passed over their heads. *The Horsemen of the Apocalypse.* Sergeyev thought, looking up at the swift and efficient movement of the black shadows.

"What was that?" The older man asked.

"I don't know." Oleg said. "I saw them once, a long time ago, but I haven't the slightest idea what they are. You were talking about the fork?"

"Back then it was still funny." Sergeyev said. "We were often laughing. A lot more than now. Now we're just tired."

The pair had passed the cave where Oleg remembered spending the terrible night the year before. Perhaps it would be worth it to spend the night in its shelter, but it was still light and they had no idea what the weather would be like tomorrow. The stubbornness with which the wet snow covered the ground was ominous. Sergeyev didn't argue with Oleg, although he was far more tired than the boy. An hour later Oleg was already regretting they had bypassed the cave's shelter. The snow grew thicker and Oleg was afraid he had lost the path. They set up the tent and huddled inside what shelter it gave. Sergeyev talked until he fell asleep. Marianna's mother had never loved him, and had wanted to leave him, but had only stayed with him because of their daughter. Oleg found the ideas involved perplexing: how could someone *leave* someone else in the settlement?

The wind rose and fell, casting handfuls of snow against the side of the small tent.

They got up when it was light enough for them to see the ground beneath their feet. More properly, a ragged towel of wet snow; a few small stones and occasional bushes stuck out through the holes.

The snow died away, but the wind was as strong as before, wet and foul. Oleg watched Sergeyev shivering with every gust, wiping long strands of salt and pepper hair away from his forehead with treebark hands. And suddenly Oleg realized he was afraid. He was afraid because in the last trip the responsibility had not been his. Dick was a better hunter and had found their path; Thomas remembered the first trip so many years ago; Marianna knew which plants to use if they got sick. Oleg's one responsibility had been to get there, somehow. And now what would he do if they lost the path? If they could not find the canyon with the ice-covered stream? Return home? *That would be the worst. . . . Anything but return . . .*

"It's boiling now." Sergeyev said.

Oleg threw a handful of muzhrumes into the can; they quickly swelled and floated to the surface. Oleg and Sergeyev took their turns burning their fingers to snatch the slippery soft balls out of the hot water, blow on them, then pop them into their mouths. Oleg didn't really want to eat; it was a necessity, a duty he had to fulfill, or he wouldn't be strong enough to walk. The settlement had always had trouble getting salt; earlier they'd had to depend on the plants, but then Vaitkus had found a salt lick in the swamp, and suddenly they could shovel it into bags and take it home. True it was more bitter than salty, and Vaitkus had to concentrate it by evaporation, cleverly separating it into fractions. The muzhrumes they were chewing were only slightly salted, but enough to kill the bothersome taste.

"Shall we be going?" Sergeyev asked.

Oleg hadn't noticed the older man had already gotten up and started to take down the large roll of fish hides they used as a tent.

Oleg checked his crossbow. The bow string had dried out, and it would have to be restrung.

They walked a little further, heading up the slope. Oleg recognized nothing he saw and angrily cursed himself: *We could have left markers! I should have thought of it. We went through here twice and could have left markers!*

"I suspect my black mood arises from my contemplation of my total uselessness on Earth." Sergeyev started to speak after they had gone another kilometer. "All my training is twenty years out of date. My flight up the career path has crashed. My value back on Earth is equal to zero. I suspect they'll just offer me retirement."

"Why? You're not old, and you're still strong." Oleg asked.

"There's no way I can just insert myself into a world that's been changing for twenty years; at best I have a future giving lectures as a modern Robinson Crusoe, the worst is I'll be an object of sympathy. Ah, I'll have to write my memoirs!"

"Memoirs? About what?"

"About us . . . I'm joking a little. Actually I won't have time to write my memoirs; I'll be too busy playing nursemaid to the grandchildren. You and Marianna aren't going to have it easy. You do understand that everyone else your age has been plugged into a learning center almost since the day they were born?"

"So I'll study."

"So you will. You still won't have it easy."

Sergeyev didn't understand that for Oleg, the problems to be faced on Earth were not fortified with remembered images and prior experience. Earth was still the Promised Land on the other side of the sea of space. If Oleg had to learn something, he would learn it. The disappointments would only come later.

Oleg was becoming all the more disturbed with the unfamiliarity of the areas through which they walked. The rivulet should have trickled down through canyon walls long ago; the cliffs around them were strange and unremembered.

Sergeyev could feel Oleg's fears.

"Have we lost our way?" He asked.

"It's all different from the way it was then." Oleg said. "It's because of the snow."

"Don't worry." Sergeyev said. "We can't be too far off. We still know the general direction to take; so long as we're going uphill there's not much to worry about."

"Wait a moment." Oleg said. His ears clutched at the sound of running water.

A gust of snow struck at them again. They reached the stream after several minutes and walked uphill along its course, but it was hopeless. The last time when they had found a stream the walls of the ravine were already around them. How many streams must flow through these hills. . . .

They walked until evening, almost without stopping. They had no adventures. Oleg shot at a ribbit but missed. The occasional snowfalls did not let up. The snow clung to their clothing. It wasn't cold but with every step it became more difficult to knock the snow from their boots.

As it was growing dark they found themselves entering a gorge, but it was a different gorge from the last time. It was more like a wide ravine. They spent the night there. Both understood they had missed the right path, but to go back now and find it would take too much time. If there wasn't all that much snow in the heights then there was still a chance they would make it to the mountain pass. But neither of them wanted to speak of it. Oleg split the last of the muzhrumes into three parts. They had been saving on fuel and, as soon as the water in the can had grown warm, they put out the fire and put the coals in a bag.

They slept beneath an overhang; the night air was ice and the winds danced down the ravine like a current of newly melted water.

***

In the morning Pavlysh got ready to go into the mountains.

He had invited Sally to go along, as the two of them had discussed earlier, but Claudia objected because Sally was scheduled to carry out the required biosecurity procedures today to ensure no native life forms had penetrated the domes. That was her job. Pavlysh tried to convince Claudia the prophylactic procedures could be put off for another day, but the station head was unbending. She was profoundly convinced she was motivated purely by a high sense of duty and only by a sense of duty. She knew no other feelings.

"Dear god, Claudia," Pavlysh said, "If you don't want Sally to come with me, then why don't *you* come instead?"

Pavlysh thought Sally, who had heard his offer, was laughing, but he didn't dare turn his eyes in her direction.

"You've gone out of your mind." Claudia said, unexpectedly turning red. Pavlysh hadn't even suspected Claudia could blush. "Do you assume I am the chief layabout on this station?"

"I had absolutely nothing improper in mind." Pavlysh said quickly. "I merely thought sooner or later you are going to fly to the mountains. You'd be in your element."

"My element is the whole planet." Claudia said. "The mountains have already been explored by the scouts. The orogenous system to the north of the forest is comparatively young, without active weathering. If there is something out of the ordinary there, then deep coring is demanded. . . ."

"And it's my business to invite you. There remains a place in the ATV."

"Thank you for the invitation, but some other time. . . ."

Sally had prepared a number of sandwiches for Pavlysh and handed him a coffee thermos as he exited.

"Don't get angry." She said when Claudia had departed for her lab. "I really do have work to get done today. I'll go with you the next time."

"I don't know when that will be." Pavlysh said. "Tomorrow we'll have a million more things to do."

"We'll think of something. Today you can go scout the landscape and find out what's really worth seeing, right?"

Sally went up on her toes and kissed Pavlysh on the forehead.

"I know what to do." Pavlysh said. "It just came to me."

"What?"

"I'll move into the laboratory. You can join me."

"I can?"

"Yes. We can set up housekeeping there. We can put in an extra door. Why should we have to dissemble and pretend we're not attracted to each other?"

"There's no reason to pretend anything."

"Exactly! Whatever happens, Claudia won't like it."

"Obviously. A clear transgression of the accepted norms of behavior. Despite her being a geologist she knows perfectly well the sources of small children, if you leave out storks and cabbage patches. But she's used to having Srebrina Taleva in your place on expeditions. Our relationship is incorrect, unexpected, and there's no way she can get used to it; we're irritated because we can't get used to it. For example, this planet irritates us."

"There's no need to philosophize." Pavlysh said. "We'll present it to her as a *fait accompli.*"

"No, we won't. There's no way I can keep the laboratory sterile. Claudia would rather die than let anyone live in there."

They were never able to finish the conversation; Claudia returned. She was carrying a yellow print-out sheet.

"Three days ago one of my scouts registered a metallic anomaly in this quadrant." She said. "The telemetry must have been fouled

— I haven't been able to determine the cause. If you're going to fly there anyway, take a look in this valley. The anomaly seems to be on the surface, which makes it even odder."

"With pleasure." Pavlysh gritted his teeth.

***

Pavlysh made a wide circle over the station; the weather was good and he had visibility clear to the horizon. The cliffs of overcast had lifted; the boles of gigantic trees rose into the clouds. Steep waves ran along the lake surface near the shore; further out they curled into whitecaps. On Earth Pavlysh would long ago have taken an inflatable boat out onto the lake and might have gone diving in his free time. Anyway, they would have to check out the life at the bottom of the lake, but that would be next week.

Then Pavlysh took the ATV higher, cutting through the clouds.

A flock of birds flew out of the clouds — Pavlysh had already seen the species before; strange creatures, more insect than avian, he would have to catch a specimen for the expedition. The creatures were engaged in a desperate aerial battle — they wove their motions into an enormous web, flew apart, then rushed against each other again.

The heights of the mountains, still far away, cut the meringue blanket below him. Closer at hand the mountains were black and snowless, further on they were covered with snow; massive, quiet, familiar. Mountains are the same everywhere, on any planet.

Pavlysh piloted the ATV to the mountains. Now he was able to make out the design of the mountain system. Much like India and the Himalayas really, or Italy and the Alps; one northward moving continental plate had struck another, and mountains rose as ledges from the lowland valleys, turning into the first, comparatively low and gentle range. Beyond stretched even higher mountain valleys in which even now, in summer, the snow had yet to melt. After the valleys even higher mountains rose, stretched out in a long chain, already respectable giants of more than five kilometers height. Further on — Pavlysh knew about it from the orbital maps but it was difficult to make out from within the atmosphere — a truly enormous pattern of mountain tops burst from the crust, the highest on the planet, and the highest mountain was more than eleven kilometers above sea level. Some day someone would have to name it. Something fitting.

At the moment Pavlysh wasn't headed there. At least not yet.

He landed the machine on a gentle slope in the second mountain chain. For a while he just sat in the cabin,

His outside sound pickups were on. It was very quiet. A gorgeous quiet as yet unbroken by human voices.

After a while Pavlysh turned on the com and asked how things were going at the station.

Claudia answered. Everything was just fine, and please don't be late for supper. With him out of her way she was in an excellent mood. She reminded Pavlysh to check on that valley where the anomaly had registered.

"Certainly." He answered. "I'll be heading there shortly."

Pavlysh cycled through the airlock and went outside. There was no wind. His legs sank to his knees in the snow covered with a hard layer where the surface had melted and then refroze into a scab during the night, but below the crust was a dry white powder ideal for skiing; Pavlysh hadn't seen anything so white and shiny on this planet before.

Pavlysh took a handful of snow and crushed it in his glove; the snow scattered like talc and drifted down on the windless air.

Then Pavlysh committed a crime against set procedure and standing orders. He did it because, as a biologist, he knew he had nothing to fear here. He took off his helmet.

The cold air burned at his cheeks; for a second Pavlysh even held his breath to keep the cold out of his lungs. When he finally did inhale all his expectations came true — the air was crystal, primordial, wonderful air.

Holding his helmet in his hand Pavlysh walked a little, sinking up to his knees in the snow. He didn't hurry. There was only one sound; the crunch and shatter of the ice crust. Here, on the heights, his lungs caught at the air, dragging it in slowly until they were full, then let go; after all he was more than four kilometers above sea level.

A white bird flew past far in the distance. That meant there was some sort of life up here as well. There was no reason for there not to be — the air was normal.

Pavlysh's ears froze. He was annoyed he hadn't taken along a warm hat — he had an old knitted hat stored away somewhere in his bags.

Pavlysh returned the helmet to his head and turned on the heater.

He didn't want to leave. He was standing, slowly turning his head and looking around at the tops of the mountains one after the other, all so similar and all so gloriously different; it was the special, glorious and perfect architecture only grand mountains exhibit. The distant, bright white sun swam in the heavens above them, but the sky was somewhat darker than Earth's and some of the near-by stars were bright enough to shine through at daytime.

Pavlysh returned to the ATV, lifted it again and headed for an enormous but distant range. He flew along the chain of mountains, taking in the details of the giants: the rocky precipices two kilometers high, the narrow crests overhung with snowy eaves, noting the cracks in the storm tossed ice of glaciers vanishing into blue infinity.... Some people love to watch a campfire, others the sea. Pavlysh's ideal of fun was to look at mountains.

Pavlysh realized he was beginning to feel tired and his stomach was growling. He reached for the sandwiches, drank the coffee, called the station again and again heard Claudia's admonition to check out the anomalous valley.

Therefore Pavlysh, before he returned to the lowlands, changed his course in the necessary direction. During the short flight he sipped the coffee peacefully, indulging in the soothing condition of a man whose highest expectations had been fulfilled.

He landed the ATV in a sloping valley cut into a half bowl by a now melted cirque glacier.

"Well, where exactly is this anomaly?" Pavlysh said aloud and turned on the scanner.

On one side nothing was visible — it was a white slope rising to a naked granite peak.

He turned in the other direction, below.

Then he said,

"Oh, yes."

Out of all the unexpected sights which could befall the duty of a man to see, his was the most unbelievable.

Below, in the valley, in the arena of an icy circus ring, quite small from here far above it, lay a starship.

At first glance it appeared to be completely intact, and for a moment he thought *Another expedition.* . . . Then he realized the ship had died.

The disk lay at an angle, one edge to the snowy field. A cap of snow and ice covered part of it.

Pavlysh quickly got the ATV into the air and headed for the ship.

Only after he had landed again and gotten out of the ATV did he remember he had failed to inform the station, which was another violation of the sacred standing orders, but then he forgot about orders altogether.

On the side of the starship, still visible in paint more dazzling than the snow, was the name *PolarStar*.

***

The ship didn't want to let Pavlysh aboard.

The passenger airlock was slightly ajar, he could see, but there was no way to get up to it; it was three meters above the ground. There was no way to lower the stairway. The cargo lock had been wedged shut when the ship crashed. Having walked around the wreck and realizing he found himself in the position of a cat who wanted to drink from a jug with a narrow neck, Pavlysh stamped about in the snow, slowly wandered around the *PolarStar* and suddenly realized he was in no hurry to break into the ship; he had no great desire to find himself face to face with the spectacle of unexpected, long frozen death.

At the same time there was the faint hope . . . Of what? And suddenly the answer came to him; something might still be alive, jump into the space boat and leave . . .

The stupidity of such a thought caused him to frown bitterly. Pavlysh knew too much. He knew about the ship, he knew it had been lost more than twenty years before. The *PolarStar* had made its last communication as it had been about to jump. The ship hadn't arrived at its destination. It had vanished without a trace, an act of extreme rarity and notoriety which occurred on average about once a decade.

Evidently the ship had emerged from hyperspace only to crash helplessly in these frozen mountains. And, just as evidently, no one had been saved, for the simple reason that if they had been able to launch the boat they might have made it to an inhabited planet, and everyone would have heard about it. This hadn't happened.

Pavlysh returned went back to the ATV; he had been out of communication for so long Claudia might be going out of her mind from panic.

If Claudia had been out of her mind with fright she exhibited enormous self-control when he did make contact.

"What's happened?" Claudia asked coldly when she heard Pavlysh's voice.

"I'm not certain how to tell you. . . ."

Claudia was silent. The com was working perfectly. Pavlysh could hear her rapid breathing on the other end.

"I found the *PolarStar.*" Pavlysh said.

"Which polar star?"

"Remember the anomaly you mentioned. There is no anomaly. What we have is Starship *PolarStar*, lost some twenty years ago; you might recall the incident."

"Oh!" He heard Sally's voice on the other end now; she must have been standing right next to Claudia, worried about what Pavlysh had gotten himself into. "What about the people . . ."

"It's dead. Crashed." Pavlysh said. "I'm trying to find a way inside her now."

"Wait up." Claudia said, "We don't know the cause . . ."

"It crashed." Pavlysh repeated. "Twenty years ago."

"Then there's no reason to hurry." Claudia said. "We can wait and fly up there with you. Standing rules prohibit you from entering alone."

"I'm in a space suit." Pavlysh said.

"Slava's going inside." He heard Sally say. "I would too."

"I am completely against this . . ." Claudia said.

"Sorry." Pavlysh answered and broke the connection.

The revolution had been declared. Insurrection. Mutiny.

Pavlysh opened the cabinet with the survival tools. In the expedition's space boat there should he primitive things — ropes, grapnels. Sometimes a good stretch of rope is worth more than all the technology of the space age.

Pavlysh found the ideal tool for entering a dead starship — the emergency laser cutter.

***

Inside the starship everything was perfectly preserved, as though it had been entombed in an ice vault.

Pavlysh slowly walked down the ship's corridors, looking into the cabins. His goal was the bridge where he expected to find the ship's logs.

The cabins were empty. It was odd; even if the majority of the ship's company had been in the stasis chambers, the watch crew on a starship this size should have numbered no less than a hundred men and women.

In the cabins everything was left just the same or nearly the same as at the moment the ship had died. Things were in their expected places. There was not a single corpse.

The ship had been carrying families. In one cabin — Pavlysh remembered the '44' on the door — he suddenly found himself face to face with one such a frozen moment. There was a child's cradle, inside it a half-filled milk bottle. There were toys in the cradle.

Pavlysh was already convinced the crash had left survivors. And he expected to find out what had happened to them soon enough.

Pavlysh found the navigation room. It had been badly damaged. Numerous instruments had been smashed and broken. It was a miracle one instrument was picking up the automatic navigation beacon from Earth and flashing in the dead chaos. Pavlysh turned the green light off in disgust.

Pavlysh found no bodies in the navigation room or any of the other service areas on the *PolarStar*. There were no people even in the engine room, which had suffered most of all. Finally, Pavlysh made his way to the stasis chambers. The door there was locked. Pavlysh was ready. He had carried the laser cutter with him from the hole he had burned in the hull.

The lock surrendered to him fairly easily. Inside the stasis chamber it was dark — the walls here had never been covered with phosphorescent paint. Pavlysh turned on his helmet light.

Then he understood everything.

The people in the stasis chambers had died with the ship. The accident had destroyed the power plant, and those still alive hadn't been able to activate the revivification system, although they had tried, judging from what he saw. A number of the individual chambers had been opened, but their efforts had proven fruitless.

And then the liquid baths in the individual chambers froze, and the chillsleepers found themselves buried in transparent blocks of ice.

Right away Pavlysh found those who had died during the crash; someone had dragged their bodies here and placed them in the aisles between the individual chambers.

Pavlysh had no desire to remain in the icy graveyard the stasis chamber had become. He found it terrifying. One may be howsoever rational, sober and even courageous, and still shudder inside when you hear slow, imagined footsteps behind you in the icy silence, or suddenly see one of the figures who had died in the frozen stasis chambers twenty years before flutter his eyelid or smile as the uneven light of Pavlysh's head lamp flickered over them.

Pavlysh backed out of the stasis chamber, unable to turn his back to the *PolarStar's* graveyard. And when he closed the section door he pressed his back to the corridor wall and just stood stock still for several minutes until the damn weakness in his legs had passed.

Pavlysh headed for the exit, which proved to be very far off. Pavlysh hurried and stopped only once when he caught a glimpse of an opened door to some storage area or other, because he saw the devastation that ruled there — as though savages of some sort, or wild animals, had broken into the containers and packages, tossing them about the floor, opening some cans and boxes with either stones or claws, testing some things and then tossing them aside when they did not prove satisfactory.

This was not something the ship's crew and passengers would have done, even at a moment of extreme need — how could they have forgotten how to open cans? This meant someone had entered the ship after the last people had died or departed. There was no explanation for it; an explanation would have demanded the existence on the planet of animals or primitive intelligent beings developed sufficiently to figure out how to enter the ship. But Pavlysh, as a biologist, was completely convinced there was no intelligent life on the planet. And only after he had left the devastated storage area behind did a simple and convincing reason enter his head. It had been growing in his subconscious for some time: the survivors had died on the frozen starship gradually, one after the other, and the last ones, or the last, overwhelmed by hopelessness and fear, had gone mad. And the dying madman, not knowing what he was doing, had found his way to the storeroom because death was more merciful to him. . . .

Sooner out of here the better! Pavlysh wanted the sun and fresh air. The sooner he got out of this lifeless graveyard, inhabited by the frozen shadows of yesterday, the hard facts of the tragedy for all to see, the better.

***

The three were so exhausted and soaked during the night that by dawn, when the waves died down and the islet ceased to be in danger of capsizing, they collapsed and slept as if dead.

Dick and Kazik embraced Marianna from either side, keeping her warm, but even in their sleep they tried not to move about to avoid aggravating Marianna's injuries, and Marianna, who was awake all the time, could not get warm; every so often she shivered, and she had to control herself, but Oleg never came. He went away and she called to him, running after him, but her broken leg refused to obey her, then she no longer had legs at all, but Oleg didn't even turn around and her hands could not reach him. . . . The ground shook from an earthquake and then the roof over her head began its long, slow fall . . .

Marianna woke up. The awning had fallen onto her face and was blocking her breath. Marianna pushed it aside. Dick and Kazik lay on either side of her and she remembered how last year they had lain in the snow and frozen, and the boys had put her in the middle to keep her warm. And then she hadn't known she would have to freeze again so far from home, but just two steps from the scientific station from Earth — was that true, just two steps?

The islet was rocking her to sleep. . . . But it shouldn't be doing that.

"Dick," Marianna asked, "Are we floating free?"

"What?" He asked half asleep, then after several seconds woke up, sat up, pushed the awning back from overhead and said, "This really is too much."

Kazik was unable to get any more sleep, what with the shaking and groaning. Skin and bone was the best description of him, from what the older women in the settlement said; just as we'll they weren't looking at him now.

Marianna tried to sit up. Her elbows disappeared into the bedding, and her leg had almost stopped hurting today.

Dick stood up and crashed down through their boat into the water up to his knees; leaning on his palms he pulled his leg out from between the branches and began to look around. Kazik was fully awake.

"We lucked out." Dick said. "It could have been a lot worse."

While they were sleeping the currents had carried the boat away from the sandbar. But the wind had been on their side and they were closer to the far shore of the river than they had been the night before.

They began to row toward the shore, using the passing branches, rowing with their hands; even Marianna edged up to the side, hung over a branch and used her hand as a paddle.

They pushed, their lungs heaving, that damned heavy raft, as if it were alive, opposed them. And suddenly Dick felt his foot touch bottom. He pushed the boat with greater strength forward. Kazik lost his balance. He almost foundered and would have drowned in the deep water if Dick had not reached out and grabbed the boy, pulling him off the sandy bottom; the pair swam hurriedly after the raft toward the shore. They walked, half swam through the water without hurrying, just giving the raft a push every so often when it slowed, and after several minutes they carried Marianna up onto low, flat ground and placed her under a canopy of short, whitish oaks.

The ground under the oaks smelled of muzhrumes; insects were running about on the moss; the bushes smelled the humans and began to chitter.

Their journey was not over yet. Not quite.

***

On his return flight Pavlysh was forced to answer endless questions from Claudia and Sally. Never before had a Survey expedition happened upon the wreckage of a space ship. Especially a starship whose disappearance all of the members of the team remembered.

"That ship shouldn't even be in this sector." Claudia said as though Pavlysh had imported the *PolarStar* from elsewhere just to vex her.

"An accident during jump could have left them anywhere. Even here."

"Yes, but the Stellar Commission concluded they hadn't even come out of hyperspace."

"You are certain no one survived." Sally asked.

"I am certain of absolutely nothing." Pavlysh said. "But I believe at least some of them did not die immediately."

"If any of them survived the crash they could certainly not be alive now." Claudia said.

"When exactly did it happen?" Sally asked. "In local terms."

"I couldn't access the log. But there's frost even during summer up there. At night it gets down to 40 below. At other times of the year conditions are even worse."

"There was nowhere for them to go." Claudia said.

"We can check the surrounding mountains." Pavlysh said.

"There were a lot of people involved." Claudia said.

"And kids." Sally added. "An expedition, and colonists."

The women had prepared supper for Pavlysh's arrival, but he hadn't any stomach for it. He immediately began to rerun the tapes.

.... The starship in a circle of snow.

The same scene closer up, the still shining hull in overhang. The enormous view — the dulled, wind-torn and snow-torn and scratched surface of the hull. One of the ship's corridors. The bright circle of light from the light on Pavlysh's helmet, The bridge, the dead and lifeless instruments . . . The wreckage from the explosion in the engine room. . . . The cold neglect of death.

They were drinking coffee and sitting in the station's small, warm, and clean sitting rom, each of them imagining the dead cold of space, the dead cold of the mountains and the dead cold of the starship *PolarStar.*

"Want to see the rest of the tape?" Pavlysh asked.

"Not now." Claudia said. "Tomorrow. We have to figure out what we should do."

"What do you mean 'should do?'" Pavlysh realized no one had ever encountered such a situation before. But there were rules for everything, on how to go through an air lock and on behavior on meeting intelligent natives. It was possible even the most unlikely and unforeseeable situations would have rules somewhere on the books describing how to behave.

"Is there anything there we can use?" Claudia asked.

"Use how?"

"Is the landing boat intact?"

"The boat's slightly damaged. The hangar was right at the point of impact."

Claudia took out her hand terminal and went into her database. Text appeared on the screen, small, bold, confident letters which allowed for no argument. Claudia read the text aloud.

"'During evacuation from an investigated planet the expedition will ascertain that no examples or other evidence of terrestrial origin remains on the planet with the exception of instruments left behind deliberately with the aim of their later removal.'"

"This is a very different case." Pavlysh said. "That's the bureaucrats telling us we can't throw away our used tooth brushes here."

"Tooth brushes?"

"I haven't been able to find mine for three days." Pavlysh said. "The brush's probably worked its way into a crack and a million years from now, when civilization arises here, they'll dig it up and conclude there were aliens on their planet once."

"This isn't the time for jokes." Claudia said, bending back down and bringing up the index. "There should be something else here as well. I remember . . . Here!"

Again the screen flooded with information. "'In case of the discovery of terrestrial instruments or equipment left on the investigated planet, either through carelessness on the part of a previous expedition, or as a result of accident, the expedition is required to remove them; should this prove unfeasible they are required to destroy them.'

"As I said." Claudia repeated. She was pleased that memory had not failed her.

"No matter what that says there were people there." Sally said.

"The people died twenty years ago."

"There's no need to hurry." Pavlysh said. "We're not due to be picked up for some time."

"The sooner done the better." Claudia said. She went back to the index.

Pavlysh did not understand Claudia had declared war on him. He had completely forgotten about his little revolt in going into the *PolarStar* against her categorical orders, or that Claudia might be forced to demonstrate her authority.

"The reasons are somewhere in the footnotes." She said. She held it up to him. "Read this."

"I don't understand." Sally said. "Why the need for immediate action?"

"I may err in the precise formulation but the intent of the orders is obvious." Claudia said. "It should be equally obvious to you. The ship crashed on this planet. It is a source of likely terrestrial microorganisms. It could easily cause an ecological catastrophe here, which would be our fault if we did nothing about it."

"The microbes are dead." Pavlysh said. "The ship would have undergone normal disinfection procedures before leaving Earth orbit, and anything that survived would have either died in the radiation from the accident or frozen."

"Can you guarantee it? As a biologist?" Claudia asked.

"No. No, I can't." Pavlysh had to agree.

He understood what Claudia wanted to say. Pavlysh had gone into the ship. If there were alien microorganisms or viruses dangerous to this world inside, Pavlysh had offered them the chance to get out. At the moment it wasn't terribly cold even in the high mountains, and they had no way of knowing if there was anything there or not. Most likely there was not, but some terrestrial microorganisms were adapted to such diverse environments as volcanic hot pools and the cold deserts of Antarctica while some could subsist on boiling sulfuric acid.

And of course the standing orders and accepted procedure had been compiled by wise and foresighted people whose judgement was never to be second guessed. . . .

"Oh the other hand," Sally said, "Isn't it a sort of grave marker. . . ." She stopped short.

"People didn't go out into space to leave grave markers capable of exterminating other life forms. We are not sources of infection." Claudia said. "We have a moral duty to leave this planet as we found it, not with an ecosystem devastated by our refuse."

Claudia's high toned words filled her eyes with the light of a zealot.

If they had thrown you into the fires in the Middle Ages the flames themselves would have drawn back. Pavlysh thought.

Sally got up and left the room to get more tea.

She stopped a moment in the doorway and turned, "You always convince yourself you're right. . . ."

Claudia didn't answer.

***

After the three of them had a chance to rest Kazik, prepared to head for the station.

Marianna told him, "Wait a while, get warm. At least dry out."

"I can dry out on my way." Kazik said. "While I'm running."

Dick handed the boy his own knife — Kazik's was worthless now — and wanted him to take the blaster, but Kazik refused. He didn't trust the blaster. He said,

"You need it more than I do. I'll be moving; you have to sit and wait."

Kazik walked until twilight, but on the way came to a river; the current was too swift for him to risk swimming across; he walked up stream in search of a place to cross but came instead to a thick bog.

It was already dark by the time he made it back to the camp.

"It's me!" Kazik shouted when he saw the fire Dick had lit.

"You didn't find them?" Dick got to his feet.

"I'll head out tomorrow. Now I know the way." Kazik said.

Marianna lay with her eyes open and said nothing. She was in pain, but it wasn't just her foot; her entire body was racked with a dull, slow pain that came in waves.

***

The station awoke when the morning mist had cleared. The mist departed, flowing away like jelly into the lake and sinking down to hide in the forest. Among the wisps of cloud was the smoke from the fire Dick had lit to heat water. Pavlysh, departing with Sally toward the *PolarStar*, didn't see the smoke for the mist. Had he even noticed it he would have taken it for dissipating fog, but Kazik had been looking up into the sky right at the moment the boat flashed over the trees.

"There they are!" Kazik shouted. "They're flying away!"

"You saw them?" Marianna asked.

"Yes. A small ship."

"Probably going off on a scouting trip." Dick suggested.

"I'd rather they hadn't." Kazik said. "Do you think there are many of them at their base?"

"Does it really matter?"

"If there are a lot they might have another ship with them to pick up Marianna." Kazik said. "I might as well be off then."

The boy was excited. Contact with the Earth was so close at hand.

"Wait a minute and finish your tea."

Dick would have preferred to have the boy remain with Marianna and push on to the station himself, but he said nothing further. Anyone alone in the forest was in danger. A person who is at least moving often finds himself in less danger than someone who is guarding a helpless girl. Also, he understood what a joy it was for the boy — he would see real Earth people. Dick would experience no such pleasure. He was just worried about Marianna; today she was really bad. Dick made Kazik drink down the last of the hot water and said,

"Okay, off with you."

At least he knew no one else on the planet could move through the forest as fast as Mowgli.

***

Claudia Sun had not slept very much that night.

In the evening her dispute with Pavlysh had exploded again: Claudia had insisted he take measures for the liquidation of the crashed starship in the morning. She used the word 'liquidation' in relation to the *PolarStar*, as a way of reducing the actions she insisted Pavlysh perform into an abstraction; it helped her not to see the ship as Pavlysh saw it. The crashed ship was a mere tool, a tool that threatened the planet's indigenous life forms. Instructions and rules existed which demanded the liquidation of dangerous tools. The *PolarStar* had not existed as a starship for more than a human generation. And this entirely reasonable act of liquidating it she ordered Pavlysh perform, as though it made a distinction between the events of twenty years ago and his own actions.

Claudia herself pulled out the container with the implosive; it would insure the radius of destruction was confined, no debris was scattered to spread contamination with the winds and damage the local balance of nature, and carried the heavy container to the lounge and issued Pavlysh his instructions in a voice that left no room for appeal: tomorrow, having made a full hologram of the starship for the records and later study by the Stellar Commission, he would do thus and so. . . . If necessary, she agreed with Sally's demand, Pavlysh might remove from the PolarStar items and materials which might prove valuable for the investigation or which might have sentimental meaning to the relatives of those who died.

After this Claudia withstood a furious, unorganized and far too emotional reaction from Pavlysh, who categorically refused to destroy the ship.

"We are on a Remote Survey outpost." Claudia said quietly and reasonably. "When you agreed to assist in this expedition, Doctor Pavlysh, you knew perfectly well that in extreme situations command devolves to the head of the expedition. In instances where members refuse direct orders, those guilty, I assure you, never work in space again. You may dispute my decision, you may consider me unreasonable. But I and I alone bear the responsibility for my decisions. However, you are obligated to obey my decisions. You will find these rules provide no exceptions. In many circumstances this has saved the lives of the expedition members."

"Claudia, you know this isn't such a case." Sally said. "There is nothing threatening the survey. And you can delay the decision to destroy the ship until just before our departure. There's a lot of time . . ."

"We cannot put off the decision until departure. The danger of infecting this planet increases with every second."

Pavlysh said nothing.

There is a logic in iron certainty. Claudia had been overcome by some sort of hypnotic effect. Possibly, he could have continued to argue and search for reasons to delay; Pavlysh had not been raised in the Deepspace Fleet, where the authority of the Captain or the head of the expedition was unquestionable and often the main element of upbringing. Claudia was right — under certain circumstances the Commander of a starship or the head of an expedition had the right and even duty to make decisions which no one else could refuse. The element of error inherent in such a system was always less than the risks of anarchy. Mankind may very well have reached the stars, attained near universal prosperity, people might travel in time and subjugate distant galaxies. But all the same they still remained the human beings who had been born when the savannas had dried up on the Eastern edge of the Great Rift valley in Africa and forced their ancestors down from the trees to begin the five million years of evolution that led to research laboratories and starships. Some thirsted for glory, others for peace and quiet, people found themselves friends and lovers but enemies and competitors as well. Ideal human beings are no more attainable than ideal societies, fortunately, or the human race would have been frozen into unending nirvana and sunk into self-satisfied immobility. The result was that the rule of law operated in space. Conceived by moral human beings, insufficiently complete, fraught with error, but the same for all and unbreakable.

This law now depersonalized Claudia Sun, a short, direct woman as sure of the rightness of her position as Pavlysh was. And Pavlysh would have to back down.

"Better if I had never found the thing." were Pavlysh's last words on the matter.

And the man suddenly realized he was deathly tired after the events of the day and wanted to see no one. Neither the self-assured Claudia nor the friendly Sally. They had become alien to him. He had been to court and lost, and now had to pay the fine . . .

Claudia got no sleep that night; the nightmares came again and again. She had not been on the ship, but she had seen the tapes Pavlysh had made. Her imagination was more than sufficiently developed to bring it alive in her mind.

It forced her awake, just as the dead ship came alive and people she had doomed to a second death descended on her, drawing near, their gaping mouths opening and closing again and again but making no sounds. She had tried to argue with them, convince them she was only performing her duty, but they did not understand her and threatened her, although she could not see their faces . . . She tried, but they had no faces. . . . In terror Claudia awoke and determined not to fall asleep again, but then the dead from the ship came after her again, if only to prove that she was asleep. . . .

Toward morning the endless battle with the *PolarStar's* passengers and crew had exhausted her so much that she understood there was no way to convince them of anything and force them to leave her in peace. The thought eased her so much Claudia fell into a deep, dreamless sleep. When she finally awoke it was almost ten in the morning and the station was empty. Pavlysh and Sally had gone off to the crashed ship without bothering to awaken her.

Claudia got up. Her head hurt. She tried to reconstruct her nightmares but they remained formless and somehow stupid. She realized she hadn't ordered Sally to go with Pavlysh, but, obviously, there was nothing wrong in the two of them going . . .

Claudia took a cold shower and performed her morning exercises and the ritualized acts of preparing and drinking a cup of coffee; these actions did not repair the low, nasty taste remaining in her mouth, but the hot black liquid flushed the nightmares from her mind completely. She thought of Pavlysh in the flyer sitting next to Sally, and the two of them laughing, remembering the arguments of the night before, perhaps even laughing about her. Obviously laughing; with Sally readily nodding her head, agreeing . . . Claudia didn't bother to call the ATV; the order had been given. It should be completed, or tomorrow anarchy would reign at the station.

In the final analysis this was a minor incident, just a footnote to history. A long crashed starship, long dead people . . . The exploration of space had never been without sacrifices and victims, and if discipline were ignored there would be ever more sacrifices and ever more victims.

Claudia put down her cup of coffee, got up from the table, and prepared to do her work.

***

Kazik hurried; now he knew the direction he would have to take; he cut across a range of hills to avoid the swamp, and then cut down a hollow to the spot where the river broke into ten thousand tiny streams over a mass of rocks and became fordable.

He stopped at the river for a moment, looking for water that was clear as the glass of a mirror. Not as fine as the mirror Marianna had left back in the settlement, but still enough for him to look himself over. He surprised even himself — his face had become so thin and dark only the whites of his eyes weren't smeared with grime. His hair was a muddy mess.

There was no time to make himself presentable really, but Kazik took about five minutes to wash himself in silty water. He understood the earth people would find him repulsive looking — Kazik never really looked after himself, despite Aunt Luiza constantly chasing after him.

Kazik forded the river; at one spot it was almost up to his belt, and his teeth chattered in the cold so badly he ran through the forest until he grew warm again. The forest was sparse, okes at arms's length, their light blue boles bent away from him fearing the noise of his passage; the hunting vynes that snatched at him Kazik cut with the knife — it was a good knife, which was why Dick had given it to him, or else Kazik would have been defenseless... He'd have to ask the earth people for a book on geography. The first thing, after the furor had settled down, would be to ask them for a book with colored pictures. The Mayor had said there were books called holos that wrapped themselves around you with moving pictures. What more could you ask for?

***

Oleg was not cold. The fallen snow was thick and even, at the first it had plucked at the tent with cruel fingers, and then, after it turned the tent into a little hill and died down, as though it was satisfied with establishing the cleanness and whiteness of the mountain valley, it became heavy, suffocating, and warm.

Oleg was tired; he wanted to sleep but his thoughts raced ahead lazily and unwillingly. Yesterday they had walked the whole day; they tried to ensure they always went uphill. Now they knew they were lost, but they hadn't stopped hoping they would come out at the mountain pass, it didn't matter if they were right on target, just so long as they got above the clouds and out of the constant snow storms.

Both men were exhausted well before darkness came; they didn't have enough strength to warm the water. In the grey twilight, silent, as though they were performing a ritual, they set up the tent, tied it down so the winds would not carry it away, then wrapped themselves up and lay back resigned, feeling the cover grow heavy above them with a burden of snow.

Oleg woke up during the night — or perhaps he just thought he woke up — filled with a sudden pity for his mother. And he became endlessly sad for his mother because, even if they were found and able to return to Earth, in her thoughts she would remain forever on this world where she had spent her life. And he felt shame for how often he had been angry at her, disobeyed her, or tried to avoid listening to the stories about his father and their old life. Oleg started to cry soundlessly as well, in order not to awaken the heavily breathing Sergeyev, and asked his mother's forgiveness.

***

Claudia Sun sat at her work table fidgeting; she'd gotten nothing done all morning.

After a few minutes she caught herself staring absently out the window. The forest had been changing during the weeks they had been on-planet: the summer had made the leaves on the trees unfurl from rapier-thin needles into draped banners; the moss had shot out fresh feelers which started to flinch whenever one of the insects flew past, trying to seize prey. The lichens had swollen into round balls that extended and collapsed as if slowly breathing. Some larger animals had made their appearance in the thicket; some had come up from the south while others had awakened from their winter hibernation. The forest produced an immense revulsion in Claudia, while at the same time it attracted her. She found herself possessed by a desire as strong as a thirst for water, to go out and walk about the forest without her space suit, fearing nothing.

No, that would be too. . . . Claudia drove the thoughts from her mind and went back to thinking about work.

Why did Pavlysh have to find the crashed starship? That was just too much! It was like finding Tut-Ankh-Amun's tomb. . . .

Claudia took offense easily and was impressionable but she tried to hide it from those surrounding her, because if the psychological fitness boards found out she would be out of the Survey Service. For the past few years she had grown used to suppressing her feelings, which she found shameful, and built a reputation as a human computer, which gained her enormous professional respect but little friendship — as though it were the goal of her life. It was surprising, but Claudia did not guess, that Srebrina and Sally had been working with her from the beginning not at all because Claudia was methodical, industrious and punctual. On the contrary, they preferred the other Claudia, who was now quite hidden even from herself. They had seen, they understood her, and were content to ignore the bland packaging their team head had chosen. The both of them had, on occasion, protected Claudia, like an awkward child who was unloved by his or her schoolmates, the teacher's pet or the new recruit, because they knew that at home when no one was watching he was totally different and spent hours caring for a sick kitten, drawing flowers or carving Medieval castles from pieces of wood.

Claudia had fallen in love with the noisy and most politically incorrect Pavlysh the moment they had met on the ship, before Srebrina had broken her leg and anyone had ever considered adding him to the Survey crew. And, having fallen in love, she became sharp, cold and decidedly hostile to the man. This time she managed not only to deceive herself but the otherwise perceptive Sally too. The moment the fates had willed Pavlysh would be landed with them, Claudia was filled with a raging joy greater than she had known before, so great it overwhelmed her like a wave, because a man like Pavlysh was a danger for a properly balanced Survey crew. But, as Claudia was a professional, she convinced herself the interests of the survey were of greater importance and they would simply have to suffer if the work was going to get done. Gritting her teeth, tormented by her love for Pavlysh, she had accepted him as a team member. When she had observed that Pavlysh and Sally, two grown, intelligent and healthy individuals were attracted to each other and their intimacy was only a matter of time, because it was natural, Claudia found a mass of arguments which forced her, as the person responsible for the expedition, to celebrate this.

Perhaps this was why Claudia found herself in a state of continual excitement; not giving herself a chance to determine the real causes, she let herself be overcome by an active dislike of the planet. All the more so because the planet really was primitive, dangerous, and hostile to human beings. For the first time in her life Claudia Sun wanted only one thing — for the expedition to end so they could return to the normal world of laboratory work and the rat race, a world in which she understood nothing but everyone thought she understood all.

And at the same time that the planet repulsed her, no matter how much it revolted her orderly and efficient and restless soul, this world drew her closer to it, and threatened her.

. . . Claudia got to her feet. She was overcome by terror, by an inexorable desire for action. She could not work any more. She could not even think about working any more.

Claudia walked over to the hot plate, wanting to make some coffee; she poured water into the coffee pot but didn't turn on the hot plate.

Then she went over to the airlock and began to pull on her space suit.

I'm going outside. She thought to herself. *I'm going into the forest for a minute. What reason is there for me to sit cooped up in this jail for weeks on end?*

Had there been anyone else in the station at the time, Claudia would never have allowed herself to go out. But now there was no one close at hand. There was no one to watch her. Now not even the inflexible Claudia Sun was watching. No, Claudia had flown off into the mountains with the others. It wasn't her going outside, but the illegal, unrecognized, and formally non-existent, the real Claudia Sun, over whom she really had no authority at all.

Claudia made certain the airlock was sealed — she knew the drill perfectly after all — and stepped out into the forest

She had been outside before, certainly, while working. She'd had to carry the probe packages out of the scouts, she'd walked back and forth to and from the orbit boat. But not once had she actually been into the forest. And when Pavlysh, half-in-jest, and very carefully, had tried to convince her to go out with him, she had dryly refused, giving him to understand she was not intent on wasting her time with nonessentials.

Claudia walked across the field, looking around. The domes of the station and laboratory watched her depart silently, disapprovingly.

It seemed the wind rocking the streamers of leaves back and forth was fanning her face. She even drew her gloved fingers across the helmet's face plate to make certain it was intact. Everything was in order.

She came to the edge of the forest and stepped into it; she walked into a broad glade, slowly, looking where her feet went to avoid stepping on some sort of monster, because her trip into the forest did not signal a complete peace with it. It was a test of herself; if, instead of the forest, there had been a volcano ahead of her, it is possible, in such a emotional condition, she would have gone down into the crater.

To her own surprise, Claudia noticed something new and astonishing in the forest with every step: a dry leaf here, there a root curved and twisted and bent whimsically; beyond it the splendid movement of a motile, predatory vine attracted her attention with its primordial beauty and naturalness, a flash of color, an unusual form... Claudia stopped; once she even bent down to examine a comically striped beetle on long legs.

The giant beetle, on seeing Claudia, raised up on its hind legs and jumped, and Claudia wasn't frightened, she understood he was similar to a caressed puppy which wants to lick you on the mouth.

The pretty beetle fluttered its wings and offended, began to buzz, and then flew off.

It was fortunate for Claudia she did not know the striped beetle's venom, although not necessarily fatal for human beings, produced a progressive necrosis of the liver and anyone from the settlement who encountered one in the forest would turn and flee without looking back. But the people in the settlement had no space suits, or helmets, or helmet face plates tightly in place.

Laughing after the funny beetle, Claudia watched it depart and might very well have gone back into the station's domes, but then she saw the flower in front of her.

Flowering plants were rare on this planet — simpler forms of life reigned in the plant kingdom. And more often than not what appeared to be flowers were something else entirely.

Claudia had stopped in a small field. The center of the field was occupied by a circle of emerald grass — the blades of grass sparkled as though oiled; closer to the trees, under the canopy of interlacing branches overhead, huddled helpless lumps, dandylyons, but smaller than their terran namesakes and softer.

When Claudia drew close to the dandelions, they began to flutter on thin stems, bending in the wind. These were dandelions for Tom Thumb. Claudia terribly wanted to blow on them. She wanted to see the white dust flutter in the wind.

That was utterly against standing orders.

Claudia even looked around — was someone spying on her; was the criminal being watched?

The forest was silent and empty.

Claudia hit the button to unseal her face plate, raised it a few centimeters, and blew on the dandelions.

A white cloud of snowflakes rose into the wind, curled back and scattered.

A few of the weightless bits of fluff touched her face, and Claudia brushed them away. They were cold to the touch and tickled.

At once she closed her face plate.

The touch of the bits of fluff, although they had been tender and unthreatening, had frightened her and sobered her up. She got to her feet.

The green stems on which the dandelions had rested no more than a few seconds ago had already retreated back into the ground.

Idiot! Claudia thought.

Claudia's nose started to itch — she had been able to catch a whiff of the forest — a cloying, putrid scent.

Her enchantment vanished.

Claudia looked around. The forest stood on all sides of her unmoving, on guard, hostile to outsiders.

She could not decide where to go — there was an unpleasant moment of indecision. Then, she caught sight of the white top of the dome across the glade and realized she had gone all of fifty meters.

She ran back to the dome, entered the airlock and went through the disinfection cycle, then peeled the suit off without touching the outside surface and stepped into the shower.

A hot, medicinally smelling stream of water beat on her body. She washed her face, again and again, feeling ever more ashamed of herself. It seemed that nothing could wash off the delicate touch of the white snowflake.

Not even the smallest child in the settlement would have drawn close to one of the dandylyons; had they seen them from afar they would have run to tell the adults about it, because there was nothing worse to encounter in the forest than the nest of the snow flee. And the adults would set guard over the person who had chanced upon the nest, for most likely he was infected and would certainly, within a half an hour or an hour, lose his sanity in a fit of madness . . . Nearly everyone in the settlement had gone through this at least once, many of them several times. When it had happened to Oleg the local year before in the mountains, Thomas Hind had died.

CHAPTER TWELVE

There was something about this forest that set Kazik on edge. Normally a forest was alive and burbled with sounds; this was summer; but up ahead, where his path lay, it was more quiet. Perhaps the presence of the research station here had driven away the animals? Kazik thought it likely, and hurried along.

He had to make his way through a mass of fallen and decaying trees; there must have been an enormous storm here some time in the recent past to tear up the trees like this. Kazik carried his knife ready for use if need be, but he passed through the forest silently, trying to attract no more attention than a shadow.

Well before he ran into it Kazik noticed the net stretched across a Spytter nest and ran to one side. That was when he caught the scent of the zhakals.

They could be smelled from quite far off in the forest; they feared nothing and chased after prey. They preferred to hunt alone, they were tireless and vile, but sometimes they gathered in packs. Such a pack had attacked Dick and Marianna last year in the forest. This was the reason the forest was so silent.

Doesn't matter. Kazik told himself. *I'm faster than you are.*

The zhakals had also caught Kazik's scent. The boy saw the first zhakal as he was cutting through a hollow and had to walk slowly.

The zhakal showed itself above him, on the right hand side; he was watching quietly, as though Kazik really didn't interest him, as though he were simply looking out from the mass of bushes in curiosity and wondered who it was making so much noise.

But Kazik knew it was feigned; now it was his life or the predator's.

Alright if the zhakal's alone.

. . . The second zhakal was lying in wait for the boy further on. As soon as Kazik had gotten through the ravine onto flat ground he caught sight of the zhakal already waiting for him; it was sitting up on its hind paws, the hairs of the white coat on end, the black maw gaping open as if laughing.

"Get out of my way!" Kazik shouted. He knew there was no way to frighten a zhakal, but somehow it made the scene less frightening.

Kazik rushed at the animal barring his path, but the predator did not stir, it merely waited patiently for its mad prey to deliver himself to its teeth. At the shoulders the animal was taller than the boy, and reared on end it was twice as tall.

At the last moment, almost at the zhakal's snout, Kazik slid to one side and jumped several centimeters from the tooth-packed jaws that snapped at him.

Kazik leapt over a moving root and ran ahead; behind him the claws of the zhakal cut the turf as it ran in pursuit, and it could run faster than Kazik. As misfortune would have it, there was nowhere to hide or find a resting place, only payns with soft straight trunks. Of course there was no way to wait out a zhakal; the predator could just sit there for days on end.

Kazik glanced back a moment without slowing down; his bad luck knew no bounds — there were now three of them giving chase.

Kazik began to work his way further to the right, toward the shore of the lake. Perhaps he could make it to the water. Kazik did not know if the zhakals could swim or not, but now he could at least find out. It had to be at least a kilometer or more to the station and the predators were bound to catch him before then.

Kazik threw himself in to the thicket, ignoring the dangers it might hold, but it didn't help; for the zhakals the hunting vynes and predatory leaves of the bushes were like grass.

Ahead of the boy rose a sharp hill. With the last of his strength

Kazik rushed at the stones and clambered upwards. The three zhakals began to circle his refuge.

Kazik's lungs were heaving — he was exhausted. Perhaps if he were near the settlement he might have been able to get away from them, but they were nowhere near the settlement now.

The first of the zhakals began to climb upwards, scattering the stones with splayed claws. It was approaching him slowly, without making any noise, the way the zhakals always approached their prey

When the zhakal's snout was about even with Kazik's feet, the boy struck at the animal's throat with his knife. The throat was the weakest point of the animal's anatomy. The knife penetrated the hide to the bone. The zhakal jumped back, as though he hadn't expected the blow, then it came foreword again. Kazik was able to get in one more strike, successfully, before he had to jump down from the hill and begin running again, because the other zhakals had begun to climb after him.

Now Kazik only had two enemies. But he was whole, unscathed.

Kazik continued to run ahead, but the zhakals again caught up to him beside a large, soft blue tree. Kazik began to climb the tree, but he slipped because he had caught hold of a thick hunting vyne.

The teeth of the first zhakal broke the skin on Kazik's shoulder. He almost screamed from the pain.

Kazik turned and started to strike at the zhakal with his knife, hiding behind the tree which in turn bent and twisted, trying to get out of the way, and the zhakal drew blood once again. Kazik realized his pain and desperation had clouded his judgement — there was no way he could stand and fight. He had to get away. He had to run and save himself.

So he ran, gliding between the trees...

And suddenly he ran out into a broad field.

Standing in the field, confident and quiet and proud, shining silver and impenetrable, stood a real Earth dome.

***

About an hour had passed since Claudia's unsuccessful foray into the forest, but the station chief had been unable to calm down. For some reason she had begun to clean the instruments, then she turned on the washing machine and had dumped in the bed clothes. She didn't want Pavlysh and Sally to return; for some reason she wasn't ready to see them yet. Then she convinced herself she was hungry, pulled out a dinner, set the package to reheat and opened it, but she could not bring herself to begin to eat and threw the contents and the package into the recycler.

She was trying to avoid looking out the windows; to spite her they came at her with every step she took and the forest, hostile and predatory, was watching her every movement.

She was beginning to feel chilly. Claudia did not know this was the first sign of the snow flea's bite, but she instinctively felt something was wrong with her and the wrongness was connected somehow with the forest.

Outside it was getting ready to rain; it was starting to grow dark early. Dark clouds gathered over the station. Her imagination, defeated by the illness, believed the trees were coming closer and closer to the dome. They were going to try to break inside . . .

So when a blood splattered monkey came running out of the forest and battered hands against the dome, leading a pack of disheveled white monsters, she thought it was another attempt by the forest to get inside, and at her.

Claudia immediately ran to the cabinet and pulled out the stunner — it took all of a second, she was acting according to instructions foreseeing the defense of the station from an attack by wild animals. She did it all quickly, mechanically, overcome by terror and revulsion.

The animals that had attacked the station had clustered into a ball. The thought passed through Claudia's head that what she was observing was really none of her business; it was simply the natural order of things on this world, the survival of the fittest, a continuation of the eternal struggle for existence, which, as a result, demanded the monkey's death.

Because the lights inside the station were turned on full Claudia could not make out the details of the furious battle outside. She did have enough sense to know she should turn on the outside cameras, and perhaps she did, but the nausea and fever grew worse and she could not say if she were really behaving oddly or in fact at some moment or other she saw the enormous, desperate, intelligent eyes of the monkey pressing its face against the plast of the window. The dark, scarred, bloody muzzle moved desperate lips as though begging for succor.

Frightened of this monster, frightened of the muzzles of the white animals, which sprang into existence beside the muzzle of the monkey — all of this took but a second — Claudia raised the hand blaster to fire, defending herself, at these monsters, but her reason stopped her — the shot would puncture the wall of the dome and eliminate the hermetic seal, and permit the entry inside of alien microorganisms. The monkey-like creature saw Claudia's raised weapon and moved to one side.

Claudia thought for a moment the monkey had a knife in its paw, or perhaps that was just a long claw. The creature fell, the hunters rushed at him. The monster was repulsive, bloody, typical of this planet, and Claudia did not want to watch, but she did; in the threatening darkness, illuminated by lightning, this being — such an impression that he had no hide, but pieces of leather clothing: what games her imagination was playing with her! — was able to get away from the claws of the white creatures and ran, falling and getting back to his feet again, snarling with his last strength before death as he ran down the hill toward the lake....

***

Racing down the slope toward the lake, his strength failing, Kazik kept seeing the terrified eyes of the Earth woman in front of him. Beautiful, clean, surrounded by shining and intact machinery and instruments and furniture, aiming the blaster at him although this certainly could not have happened, and his hands hurt with overpowering pain from the desperate strength which he had hammered on the dome's window . . .

And the zhakals, tormenting and playing with him, chased their prey toward the grey waters of the lake. . . .

***

In the crashed starship Sally tried not to leave Pavlysh's side.

The doctor had become morose. He hardly spoke, his face looked haggard.

How strange. Sally thought. Typically sanguine. She herself had looked up his personality file. *Inclined to compromises... Willing to abandon his opinions in the face of authority.... Seeks compensation in secondary problems... A mild personality who will never become a leader.*

Sally intuitively understood the final decision to destroy the *PolarStar* came about not from Claudia's personal inflexibility, not from Pavlysh's mutiny, but because she had failed to speak up when she had a chance.

Therefore she got up first, at dawn, and prepared breakfast. Pavlysh had gotten up a short time later and looked into the galley where she was working; he wasn't surprised to see her dressed for travel in a well worn old jacket and narrow pants under her space suit. Normally Sally went around in a jumper or open skirts within the station; highly unfashionable but comfortable and rather domestic. Claudia maintained Sally was the only member of the Survey Service who dressed so oddly.

Sally told Pavlysh not to awaken Claudia. The other woman hadn't slept at all during the night and only now had dropped off to sleep. Pavlysh surrendered to his fate; he understood Sally was motivated not only by pity for the expedition leader but by a lack of desire to explain why she had not asked permission to fly to the mountains with Pavlysh.

Pavlysh kept a morose silence; he couldn't eat what Sally had prepared, and he was silent when they moved the container of implosive to the landing boat. He performed all his actions, as though he did not doubt he was blowing up the *PolarStar*. He was condemned to blow up the *PolarStar*, only Sally was not quite certain he would, and suspected Pavlysh's mutiny needed but a catalyst — Sally's own willingness to go along. But she herself still didn't know whether she would or not. But on the starship she grew bolder. Sally had taken part in many expeditions. She had seen people die; she knew the power of hostile nature and the insignificance of human beings in the face of it. She knew the ship was dead and had died long ago. But there was something very wrong in it all. The ship was deeply injured; it was in a coma, but life remained in it as distinct traces not even the decades of deep freeze and pitiless mountain frosts had been able to chase away.

Sally helped Pavlysh cart the container with the implosive to the ship, but when Pavlysh, instead of distributing the charges as per instructions, made her leave the container at the entrance, she found it easy to obey.

The two of them strolled the starship's corridors. They stopped for a while at the command center, at the navigation department, and looked into the stasis chambers, then Pavlysh led Sally to Cabin 44 where the child's cradle stood. Having led her on the excursion around the ship, Pavlysh did not try to move Sally to his position. He was doing something else. Sally understood Pavlysh was continually searching for something, watchful like a hunting dog.

The doctor lit up the floor not far from the entrance with his helmet light then spent a long time looking over the empty cans, torn packets, and opened containers in the devastated food storage locker; they went down to the hangar where the damaged landing boat lay and went inside, spending a few minutes there. Sally couldn't stand it any longer and called to him:

"Slava, is there something there?"

"I'm going outside."

Then they went toward the open airlock again.

Only the tops of the mountains lifted over the fat grey blanket of clouds that tightly enveloped the valleys and abysses. The blanket twitched, shivered, and moved slowly toward the west as though a capricious giant was dragging it to one side. Sally imagined herself there, beneath the snow blanket waiting for the next storm, and felt the cold reaching through her survival suit. But here, above the clouds, the wind blew evenly, unobstructed, and Pavlysh had opened his helmet faceplate. Sally had followed his example. The frost quickly stung their cheeks, and the cold air tore at their lungs — Sally unexpectedly found herself coughing and covered her mouth with her glove. Even her eyes were cold. But she didn't replace her face plate. As rarified as it was the air was fresh and clean. Pavlysh pulled a flat instrument out from one of the space suit's pockets. Sally had never seen anything like it before.

"I happened to bring along a biosensor." The doctor said. "The two of us are going to check over this valley."

For some reason he didn't doubt Sally was going to willingly help him.

"And . . . . our orders?" Sally wanted to say 'the explosion,' but her tongue disobeyed her.

"And what do you think of them?"

"I think we have no reason to hurry." She said.

"There's no way I'm going to set it off." Pavlysh scowled. like a little boy who refused to give anyone a beetle he's caught.

Sally immediately saw how much he was like a little boy. She laughed involuntarily.

Pavlysh was surprised.

"What are you laughing at?"

"I'm. . . . You do understand Claudia, as much as she might respect you in reality if not in her behavior, will have to report your refusal to carry out orders."

"I will not let her blow it up either." Pavlysh said.

"I'm not talking about that. She'll get you kicked out of the Space Corps."

"I know that!"

Pavlysh sharply got to his feet. The instrument sparkled in his hand.

"You haven't answered if you're ready to give up space?"

"Sally, my dear, don't speak nonsense. It's not a question of giving up anything or agreeing to anything. What would you do?"

"I asked you something, and you replied with a question."

"The container's right here. You can set it off if you want."

"I'd do the same thing you're doing." Sally said.

"Then we'll both be grounded. We'll have to spend the remains of our days on Earth. It's not really something terrible . . ."

"You're a fool, and I love you."

Pavlysh went down the ladder the two of them had brought with them from camp; the two of them had covered the ground with tracks but the wind had quickly obliterated them.

"Close your helmet." Pavlysh shouted from below. "Or you'll get pneumonia!"

Sally jumped. From three meters she broke through the thin layer of ice that formed on the snow banks as the sun warmed the snow and was up to her waist in snow. Pavlysh had to drag her out.

She was delighted. Because there was clarity. Instantaneous and final.

"If they walked away from the ship...." Pavlysh said; he had the instrument in his gloved hand held out before him. "If they were able to evacuate the ship, and I don't doubt it, they would have tried to get out of the mountains. Down the valleys toward the forest. They would never have made it in winter, but they wouldn't have had any other choice. If I am right we'll find some of them. Under the snow."

Sally's cheer vanished.

"Don't."

But Pavlysh was already walking forward with the life sensor, watching the read outs, as though he weren't listening to her.

"Later . . ." Sally said. "Not today. Leave them in peace."

"You don't understand." Pavlysh said. "We have to find out the direction they were heading."

"Why."

Pavlysh noted where the indicators pointed, and slowly moved across the crunching snow in that direction. Sally walked beside him.

"Because some of them might have made it out of the mountains."

"That's naive. There's no way they could have survived."

"Sally, my dear, you are applying your own views and opinions to other people. To you this planet is fatal. You are convinced it is impossible to live here a minute without a biosuit and helmet. You think that because you live in a comfortable surroundings, breathe sterilized air, drink disinfected water. Imagine you had no choice in the matter. Adapt or die."

"Then better to die." Sally said.

"Death is never the better choice."

The indicators flashed and an arrow appeared on the surface of the life sensor pointing to the left.

"It's like a children's game." Sally said suddenly. "Cold, hot, now hotter."

"The range is limited. It will pick up electrical activity in the human central nervous system, or organic breakdown products." Pavlysh explained. "And then only fairly massive ones, of several kilograms at least. It was designed in order to ignore most objects. You know, the life sensor was developed by mountain climbers and Alpine rescue teams. It was first used to search for avalanche victims . . . Here!"

Pavlysh stopped in front of a low rise.

"Wait a moment." He handed the life sensor to Sally and began to break the ice cover with his gloves, then pulled away the soft snow.

Sally forced herself to follow Pavlysh's hands, but then turned away. She didn't want to see what she would see now.

"Now that is odd." Pavlysh said.

His voice was just surprised, not more. Sally turned.

Under the snow she saw a mass of yellowish white fur. Some

sort of enormous animal had been buried by the snow, something like a polar bear.

"When we come back here next time we'll dig it out intact." Pavlysh said.

"Why?"

"For two obvious reasons, my angel." Pavlysh said. "Firstly because this is an animal unknown to science; secondly I think it rather important we find out *how* it died. But we'll need a shovel."

In widening circles they walked around the crashed starship moving further and further away from it. Sally became tired; the re-frozen show wasn't strong enough to support them everywhere and sometimes it collapsed, forcing them to walk through powder. The wind rose in strength and pressed against them, scattering snow everywhere and making it difficult to walk and sometimes it was difficult to see more than three paces ahead.

After two hours of search they had found absolutely nothing. Finally, Pavlysh stopped. He looked on Sally and asked,

"Are you tired?"

"Yes."

"Sorry. I got carried away." He laughed guiltily.

"I'm not angry."

"Then let's go back to the station. After dinner I can return and continue the search."

"What makes you so certain anyone survived?"

"The only corpses on board the ship are those that were dragged to the stasis chamber."

"But even if they got out of the ship alive, they would have died in the mountains."

"And what if they made it to the forest?"

"You of all people know what the forest is like."

"I know. But someone was on board the ship not long ago. Remember the mess in the store-room?"

"That wasn't done by human beings."

"So non-human beings, or animals, got up to the airlock, opened it, walked along the corridors until they reached a food storage locker, and, on leaving, closed the airlock behind them."

"That's your presupposition."

"The implications are sufficiently serious to abandon everything else and go searching!"

The two of them reached the landing boat.

"Claudia must be frightened out of her mind. We've completely forgotten to call her."

"That's not all that terrible." Pavlysh said.

Sally called the station.

Claudia didn't answer.

Pavlysh sealed the landing boat's air lock, and sat down in the pilot's seat.

"There's still no answer." Sally said.

"She could be away from the communicator." Pavlysh said. No one could get very far from the communicator in the close confines of the station.

Pavlysh took the boat directly upwards. The *PolarStar* shrank into a black dot on the valley's broad, white apron. Sally kept trying to get in touch with Claudia. She didn't succeed.

***

Pavlysh made a steep bend and, gathering speed over the lakes, cut through the clouds so that the landing boat came down vertically beside the station.

In the gloom beneath the clouds rain was whipping the land.

Pavlysh landed the ATV beside the laboratory dome and, turning off the engine, lifted a large bag of artifacts he had removed from the *PolarStar*.

"Haven't forgotten anything?" He asked Sally.

Sally shook her head.

They went straight to the entrance. The lights were on, and the station's series of round windows cast a comfortable warm glow through the curling streams of rain.

The station was sealed. Claudia hadn't opened the airlock door when the boat had landed.

Sally pressed her hand to the door buzzer. They could hear it sound outside.

Pavlysh tried to look into the airlock — the streams of water ran down the window and his helmet, masking his vision.

Sally had to punch in her own security code. The airlock door slid to one side and they entered.

"I don't like this at all." Pavlysh said.

The disinfectant mist pounded on their biosuits. Sally turned off the shower and pulled off her helmet. She was the first to rush into the living quarters.

Pavlysh was beginning to work his way out of the biosuit when he heard Sally's shout.

He ran into the next room. The room was brightly lit. In the bright light the picture appeared especially unbelievable.

The crew's quarters were a shambles. It looked like an entire army had run amok. They saw the traces of struggle everywhere, in the overturned furniture, scattered tableware and smashed instruments. In the middle of all this chaos Claudia lay on the floor, a blaster in her outstretched hand.

Sally was bent over the other woman, listening to her heart.

"Let me . . ." Pavlysh moved Sally aside. He raised Claudia's eyelid; her pupil dilated.

"She's alive." He said. "But in extreme shock."

Pavlysh quickly ran his hands over the woman's body, trying to determine the extent of her injuries, but there were no broken bones, open wounds or other serious trauma.

"She emptied the blaster charge." Sally said.

Pavlysh had also noticed the burn marks of the blaster bolts on the furniture and walls.

Claudia's hands were bloody messes — scratched and torn. Pavlysh had no way of knowing that in the fit of madness brought on by the snow flee bite Claudia had found herself battling invisible enemies that attacked through the walls and floors. Pavlysh had to conclude the enemies were real, that someone had broken inside the station and nearly succeeded in killing Claudia.

Pavlysh moved Claudia to the divan, then found the portable diagnosticon — the results he read off it were worthless. They described simply a picture of deep unconsciousness, nervous exhaustion, but no prospects, nor treatment he might give. The data base was empty; the machine had nothing to go on.

All Pavlysh's attempts to awaken Claudia proved fruitless.

Time passed. They had now been inside the station for twenty minutes.

"I think her pulse is weakening." Sally whispered.

Pavlysh glanced at the instruments and shook his head.

"I should have felt something." Sally hovered over Claudia.

"I can't understand it." Pavlysh said. "What we have here is a locked room mystery. The door is closed, the lock is in order, we can find no traces of anything from outside within the station. And at the same time something must have gotten inside . . ."

"And just what do we know about this world!" Sally answered him heatedly. "We've just scratched the surface of this planet! How do we know . . ."

"If anyone had been careful about what she's done it's Claudia!"

"Just tell me what to do. I can't do any more."

"I can see only one solution." Pavlysh said. "We'll have to use the orbit boat."

"You mean the beacon?"

"Yes; at top acceleration we can be at the beacon inside three hours."

The beacon was in open space, where the planet's gravitational field was low enough to permit subspace communication.

"I guess you're right." Sally said.

At the beacon they could establish contact with Galactic Center and log into the medical data bases of a hundred worlds.

The two of them carried Claudia to the landing boat.

Then Pavlysh ran back beneath the dome. They might have to

go to the edge of the system to make rendezvous with a deep space liner and might not return here, if ever.

Pavlysh turned on the recorder — he had about a minute and a half while Sally programmed the lander's computer for the orbital flight — and took pictures of the devastation. The holos might help when Galactic Center was searching for the cause of this drama; were they sufficiently serious, if something inimical could make it through their barriers and threaten explorers inside the dome, then the planet would be put on the list of forbidden worlds and closed for investigation.

The last thing Pavlysh did, as he left, was trigger the station closedown; the microbots would break it down into its component units, load them into containers, and get ready for possible evacuation.

That was all he could do. Pavlysh hurried to the landing boat.
Sally was sitting on the floor, supporting Claudia's head.
Pavlysh carefully lifted the boat and headed for orbit.

***

"Dick," Marianna called him. "Dick . . ."

Dick bent over the girl.

Another storm was coming — the first gusts of rain were hitting the ground around them. Dick rushed to cover Marianna's head with the remains of the tent.

"I thought you were asleep."

"I wasn't sleeping. I was swimming. I was far away . . . Where's Kazik?"

"I'm worried myself. It's been a long time."

"You've got to go after him. There's something wrong! Do you understand?"

"How do you know?"

"I don't know anything; I'm hurting because something's happened to him."

"No, I'm not going to leave you."

"Nothing's going to happen to me. Nothing . . . Go on."

Marianna was speaking insistently, as if casting a spell, as if she weren't looking at Dick or at the forest bracing itself for the storm; she was looking far off, outside of space, and her voice was an order.

"It's raining." Dick said, thinking aloud. "The rain will wipe away his tracks. If I go it has to be now."

"Go as fast as you can." Marianna said. "Or you might be too late; it might be too late already."

Dick obeyed. But first he bent down the tops of three small payns, tied them by their branches and put Marianna in the nest he had made above the ground. It wasn't a very a very comfortable bed, it was scarcely more than a meter above the ground but at least the ground dwelling critters could not reach the girl. Marianna gritted her teeth and just said, "Go on."

"I'm leaving you the blaster." Dick said.

"I don't need it. I'll just hunker down and lay still." Marianna had trouble speaking.

"You fire it by pressing the button. It's easy. You hardly have to press at all." Dick said. "And I have my crossbow — I'm more used to it."

He placed the blaster in Marianna's hand.

The girl said nothing.

"I'm off." Dick said.

"Run."

Dick ran down the trail the boy had left. Although the clouds were scarcely higher than the trees and rain beat the ground Dick noticed first broken leaves, then overturned stones. The ground was wet. But somewhere Dick made out the traces of Kazik's passage — the boy had lost his shoes back in the lake and ran barefoot.

Suddenly Dick froze. He caught the scent of the zhakals. It wasn't fresh, but zhakals had passed by here.

And Kazik had stopped here. Cautiously, walking on tiptoes;

he had smelled the zhakals as well, but the scent would have been fresher then, more immediate, dangerous.

Dick was even more alarmed. If the zhakal had not been alone, Kazik had to hurry all the faster to the earthmen's house — the kid's knife wasn't enough to take on even one zhakal on his own.

Dick passed through a narrow gorge and learned the zhakal had not been alone. The boy had faced three of them.

The hill was a woman's breast of stones. There was blood there, and a zhakal carcass not yet cleaned by scavengers . . .

It was here they had caught up to Mowgli.

Dick could smell the scent of the zhakal's blood. And Kazik's blood as well.

Dick ran even faster; he was terrified, and the forest shrank back, hid itself from him. The forest believed him to be an animal, overcome by rage that made even a helpless gote a thing to be feared if it ran to the aid of its young.

And just like Kazik, Dick ran out into the field in front of the unexpected station.

The domes were weakly illuminated; it was a fairy tale vision, a series of domes connected by rounded, above ground tubes, with rounded windows, and light. The station had to be from the same world that created the *PolarStar*, but Dick had no time to compare and judge. He watched as a darker, teardrop shape rose into the air, and the power of the soundless acceleration froze him into motionlessness.

He watched it fall upward against the clouds, become a glowing point, not knowing it was a landing boat, and not understanding why it might be leaving the station.

Dick ran to the station's door.

The air was heavy, but the rain had almost stopped.

Dick pounded on the door; the door did not give way.

He looked inside through the window. The airlock was empty.

"Hey!" Dick shouted at the top of his lungs. "Open up!"

Nothing called back. Dick wiped one of the windows.

Dick could see there had been a battle inside the enormous,

bright room — everything was overturned, spilled onto the floor and broken. . . . There were traces of blood on the soft carpet. A blaster, different from the one they had brought back from the starship, longer and larger, also lay on the floor.

Dick pounded on the door with his fist. Where was Kazik?

Suddenly he guessed; they had taken Kazik with them in when they had left for the sky, where they must have their starship. Of course Kazik was injured when the zhakals fell upon him, and they were taking him to their ship.

The thought was a great comfort.

Dick's breathing slowed. Now he had to return to Marianna. . . .

But something troubled him. Something was not right. Was it the scent of zhakal? Yes, but it wasn't a fresh scent. The scent of Kazik? Dick looked in the direction of the lake. Kazik's scent led there.

Dick looked down at his feet and noticed Kazik's tracks, covered and mixed with the tracks of two zhakals. That was odd.

Dick slowly followed the tracks, and with every step the scent of Kazik and the scent of the zhakals became all the stronger. Why hadn't Kazik gone inside the earthmen's house? They had certainly been here. They had departed for the sky as Dick had watched.

Kazik, from what he could see, had run, exhausted, stopping, turning back, slashing with his knife — all that Dick could tell from the boy's tracks and the tracks of the animals hunting him — rushing closer and closer toward the water. Dick would have tried to make it to the water in his place.

Dick did not have very far to go.

Kazik had made it to the water, to the stones that lined the shore.

Then he had gone about twenty more paces out into the water and fell there. The zhakals had prowled the shore for a while, then left.

Dick saw Kazik's body, half covered in the water, and reached the boy in several jumps and lifted him up. Lightning flashed, and thunder deafened the world; the sky opened up and water poured over them.

Kazik's head hung limply; Dick carried him to the shore, trying to support the head.

"Are you alive?" Dick asked. "Just tell me you're alive."

Dick placed Kazik down on the ground and bent over him, covering the boy's face from the downpour.

"Sorry." Kazik whispered, but clearly. "I asked, but she wouldn't let me in."

"What are you talking about?" Dick didn't understand.

"They won't let us in." Kazik said quietly. "They're afraid of us. We're wild animals . . ."

Then he was silent. And Dick knew Kazik was dead.

Dick picked up the body and ran some ways up the shore with it in his arms; there still had to be something he could do.

At the dome Dick began striking the round transpan of one of the windows. The window just ignored his fists.

"Damn you!" Dick shouted. "You killed him! Let me in, you cowards!"

Dick realized there was no one inside the station now; the domes were empty, but he continued to batter on the door.

In desperation Dick turned and ran down to the water's edge; he returned carrying the largest stone he could handle, larger than he could have carried under normal circumstances. Hefting it he returned back to the door and with all his strength heaved it against the nearest window.

The transpan and the dome itself were normally invulnerable, but Claudia's firing of the blaster had weakened the metallic frame. Dick's blow was sharp and so strong the transpan popped from the frame and fell clattering to the floor inside without breaking.

Dick crawled through the window, and dragged Kazik inside after him, and tried to rouse the boy by shaking him. There was no response.

Dick ran into the other room, pulling open cabinets; he wanted to find medicines, but he didn't know where to search, let alone what medicine was needed. And how do you give a medicine to someone who's already dead?

"I'll kill them" Dick shouted. "When I get my hands on you I'll kill you all!"

The station was empty; his words echoed hollowly and nothing answered him back.

In a far corridor Dick suddenly noticed movement — a strange metallic creature — a flat platform about the size of a gote's kid was slowly dragging a metallic container. Dick, as much from momentary fear as from rage at the station's inhabitants, struck the platform with his foot. It stopped. He grabbed the metal container — the container was heavy — and struck the platform with it several times until it stopped moving.

"I'll get you all!"

And then he remembered Marianna. Marianna was in the forest. Alone.

The zhakals might get her too.

Dick crawled out the window into the rain and darkness and hurried toward the wet forest.

***

Sally was flying the landing boat, pouring on as much acceleration as the engines would take. At this rate it would take less than three hours to reach the beacon.

Claudia had not returned to consciousness, but Pavlysh, who was monitoring her condition was convinced it had not worsened.

It was all very odd. The oddities had slid together like the images of a kaleidoscope; the pattern was illogical, all the pieces of glass were different colors, but the rhythm was obvious and symmetrical, only the thought behind them incomprehensible.

And Pavlysh now had time to think.

He ran through all the events and images of the planet in his memory in search of the odd, the illogical, and suddenly he remembered the enormous tree whose tops were lost in the clouds and the rag that hung from its branch. . . .

Pavlysh reached for his log — he had grabbed it just as he was leaving the station.

It took a few moments to call up the right images, then they appeared in the space in front of him. An enormous branch; bushes on it and a draped sheet under which a lump hung swaying in the winds. . . . no, not a lump, that wasn't the body of an animal as Pavlysh had convinced himself it was at the time. It was a basket. Pavlysh froze the image and tried to enlarge areas. He twisted the image around and looked inside the basket. It was empty of course. And those were ropes. How had he been so blind as not to see from the start those were ropes!

"Sally, take a look at this." Pavlysh said.

"At what?"

"At — I'd say it's an aerial balloon."

"Looks like it." Sally said without interest. She was still concerned with Claudia and her continued unconsciousness.

And what else is there? Pavlysh thought, not turning off the image of the balloon. There is something else. Aha! He found the image of the looted food store. The image area showed the scattered, opened containers and boxes. A torn plastic package, a smeared scrap of foil . . . But it wasn't just smeared. He enlarged the image, shifted the light to ultraviolet and found the mark of a hand. All five fingers.

"Sally!"

"Quiet. You'll frighten me. What's going on?"

"Tell me what you see."

"A hand. Where could it have come from?"

"They were in the store room. You remember."

"Those look like the hands of a monkey to me."

"Take me at my professional word." Pavlysh said calmly. "The four fingers are stretched because of the plastic, but what you're looking at is the mark of a human thumb. Look how it bends away from the body of the hand at almost a right angle. An opposable thumb. Doctor Pavlysh knows a human hand print when he sees one."

"Then it's obvious what happened." Sally guessed. "They died on the ship but managed to save the children. The adults died and there are only children left. That's why the mess in the food store."

"And the aerial balloon?"

"An aerial balloon? Now that's your hyperactive imagination talking."

***

Dick told nothing to Marianna; he found her and carried her in a blanket he made out of the tent through the forest to the dome, to Kazik. He didn't have any strength left, but he had to do this; he could not leave Kazik and he could not leave Marianna. He was the oldest, the strongest of the three, so it was his responsibility.

Marianna was heavy; she was unconscious and burning from fever.

Dick brought Marianna to the domes and carried her inside.

Kazik lay on the divan beside them.

Only the light in the dome became dimmer, as though the power was dying. And what was strange — two of the small domes had vanished, in their places were large flattish rolls. Some of the things in the large dome had vanished as well.

Dick placed Marianna on a bed which he found on the other side of a curtain.

The bed was covered with very white coverings, but Dick had little use for fine bed sheets.

He sat on the divan at Kazik's feet.

He had been sitting for about five minutes and doing nothing; he was exhausted, and he didn't know what else he could do.

One more metal monster entered the room and started to pull the rug from the floor.

Dick, without getting up, reached for the blaster and put a

shot into the monster. The monster chittered and puffed momentary flame before stopping completely.

"Just come back." Dick said. "Just come back."

Dick sat on the divan beside the dead Kazik and dying Marianna, and there was nothing he could do except swear to himself he would dedicate his life, how ever much he had left, to taking vengeance on the earthmen who had killed Kazik and ran away to let Marianna die.

He would find them; he would find them wherever they might hide themselves, and he'd kill them like he would kill zhakals.

***

"Slava," Sally said, "Look."

Sally was bending low over Claudia. Claudia was breathing deeply. The medical readouts indicated her pulse had speeded up and her breathing had increased. She was coming to her senses.

They were two hours into their flight.

Pavlysh injected Claudia with a cardiac stimulant. Judging from the displays the woman's condition was nearly back to normal. Pavlysh ran over the analysis of the blood sample he had taken from the woman earlier. There were traces of a toxic substance in her blood. Exactly what they were was hard to determine under field conditions; he needed a real lab.

Claudia opened her eyes. She immediately realized she was in the landing boat.

"Sally, why are we here?" She asked.

"Don't move; that could be dangerous." Sally said. "Everything's going to be all right."

"But what happened?" Claudia frowned, trying to remember. "There was the forest, wasn't there? And dandelions. Very pretty dandelions. And that monkey. I chased it away — all the animals were crawling in through the windows. And then what happened?"

"We don't know." Pavlysh said. "We thought you might remember."

"I don't. I remember strange animals at the windows. And then there were nightmares."

"What type of animals were they? Did they frighten you?" Pavlysh asked.

"No, they were just monstrous. This whole world is monstrous. They always pester us when we go into the forest. Everything's that way. . . . No, I wasn't afraid of them. And then I don't remember anything."

"Try and take it from the beginning. What happened?"

"I was in the forest."

"You went into the forest?"

"Yes I went into the forest. I went for a short walk. There were dandelions there. . . . All right, I opened my face plate; I wanted to smell them."

"Did you take off your helmet?"

"I don't remember. I think I just lifted my face plate."

"And then what happened?"

"Then there was a vile sensation. I felt really bad, and there was the monkey clawing at the window and it was fighting with the other animals."

"And then?"

"It ran away; they all ran away, and I felt really lousy . . . I'm sorry if I caused you any . . . discomfort. Why are we in the landing boat?"

"We were on our way to the beacon to tie into the diagnostic data base at Galactic Center. Perhaps, to evacuate the station."

"Then return."

"I still want to tie you into the medical computers — let them check you out. We cannot exclude the possibility of a dangerous, unknown infection."

"I don't want it." Claudia sat up with difficulty; she was pale. "I have no intention of letting my . . . indisposition interrupt the work of the survey."

Pavlysh realized for Claudia to give up would have been unforgivable shame.

"Wait a moment. Did you get a very good look at the monkey?"

"No. Not very."

"You understand of course there's not the slightest chance anything at all humanoid in form would evolve on this planet. What you saw might have been a human being."

"A savage? But if it couldn't be a monkey then where would you get a savage?"

"I said human being." Pavlysh said.

"And where would he come from?"

"The *PolarStar* of course; I assume some of them survived."

"That's nonsense. This planet would kill anyone."

"It killed some of them. There are fifty or so bodies missing from the ship by my count. If there is a colony of people on this planet trying to survive, waiting for us, waiting for rescue. . . ."

"I don't believe it."

"Then look at this." Pavlysh pressed the button on his log again and called forth the scenes with the aerial balloon.

***

Oleg just didn't want to walk. He didn't care any longer.

But Sergeyev, when it had become fairly light and the storm had died a little, forced himself to get up. He never could have gotten to his feet if it hadn't been for the children. Not Marianna and Oleg. He knew if he wasn't able to get up then Oleg and Marianna would never find each other again, never see each other again, never touch. . . . His life had no value if Marianna and Oleg died. Sergeyev was able to convince himself to raise his head, the effort was all he had left in him. Fortunately, in the sharp, convulsive movement Sergeyev struck his head against the snowy roof of their refuge and the fabric there was weak enough to tear. The roof collapsed, letting in icy air and oxygen. The cold air set Sergeyev's face and shoulders on fire, and he immediately woke up.

Sergeyev scrambled out of their shelter and squatted for a long time, until it almost grew dark. He forced himself to dig the bag with wood out of the snow and light a fire. When the water came to a boil he turned Oleg over and poured hot water into him, opening his mouth with filthy, gnarled fingers. Oleg protested weakly, mumbled he just wanted to sleep. Then Sergeyev rubbed the boy, shook him to get him moving, although he was so tired he didn't even notice he had overturned the hot water container in the process. The hot water spilled into the snow, leaving a hole on the ice, a ring of re-frozen grey ice around it.

But then Oleg came to his senses, at least enough that he could light another fire, bring water to a boil again and give it to Sergeyev. Now their roles had changed. Sergeyev, though, did not resist. He understood what had to be done, he was just too tired to do anything.

So the two of them continued walking upwards, through the clouds and mist, enticed only by the unreasonable hope that some miracle would bring them out in the mountains where the *PolarStar* lay.

After another couple of hours they collapsed in the snow. They felt like they had been walking for an eternity, but in reality they had moved less than a kilometer. They pulled together the last of their wood and again drank hot water as though it were a medicine. They said nothing; they were both covered with the frost condensed from their own breath, their toes and fingers were numb. But despite that they got to their feet again, although they had to hold onto each other, supporting each other so that their movement forward slowed even further. But it felt like they were walking. And they expected that suddenly the clouds would open wide and the blue sky unfold above them . . .

***

Dick saw the landing boat descend. In the first instant he was overcome with joy — they had returned!

But then he remembered the promises he had made. He had to kill them. They had caused Kazik's death, and because of them Marianna was dying. And they could have saved them. They just hadn't wanted to help.

Never before in his life had Dick ever had to consider the idea of killing another human being. There were just too few people in the world. People needed each other to survive. The rest of the planet was out to get them.

But these things from the shiny dome; he had already concluded they could not be human beings, not really.

And if they are like that on Earth, we don't need Earth. We don't need white bed sheets and smooth tables. Dick was forcing himself into a mental fury. *You came back because you forgot your things. You want to take it from us because we're dirty and scarred and not pretty to look at, because you're ashamed to think we came from the same world you did! But I won't let you have them. Everything will remain here. The settlement can come and live in the dome. We're never going back to Earth!*

To Dick the station's domes were the prey he had been hunting for the settlement for many days; because of the search Kazik and Marianna had died. The rage he felt toward those who, he thought, wanted to take it away had overcome his reason and the thoughts that arose on seeing the landing boat. *I have to ask them if they can cure Marianna.*

Exhausted and nearly senseless, Dick could no longer think logically. He was in fact a savage, a product of the forest, a zhakal raised on his hind legs lunging after prey . . . But unlike the zhakals Dick had a blaster in his hands.

Pavlysh landed the boat and was the first to exit. The three of them had already discussed a course of action: first the women would launch the probes, but configured this time for a search beneath the cloud layer. The area they would have to examine was comparatively small, limited on the north by the highest mountains where the *PolarStar* lay and on the south by the great lake where the station had been placed. Any human settlement anywhere between these ranges would be found by the scouts in under an hour.

As soon as Pavlysh got the stunner recharged he was going to search the immediate area of the station — whoever or whatever Claudia had seen, or thought she had seen, could not have gotten far.

When he opened the airlock and jumped out onto the grass Pavlysh saw the smaller domes had already been taken down — the station had already begun to pack itself away. In fact that process should have been considerably more advanced, but Pavlysh had no way of knowing Dick had already shot half the robots working on it. He didn't give the repacking a second thought, he was just thinking he should what materials would go best for trapping Claudia's wild man. *Sugar and chocolate from the kitchen . . .*

Pavlysh hadn't made two steps from the landing boat, the women were still cycling through the landing boat's double doors, when he saw the dark silhouette of a man in the window.

From inertia Pavlysh continued walking forward, thinking of what he should say, something just right for the moment that could be recorded and go into the history books: *Hey!* He managed to think. *So you were looking for us too. We managed to get back here in time . . .*

Then he heard a hoarse, low pitched voice:

"Go away!"

"What do you mean?" Pavlysh didn't understand. He just continued walking.

"Go away!" The voice croaked. "Go away or I'll kill you!"

"Hold on . . ." Pavlysh said.

The man stopped. The light inside the station was brighter than the gloom outside and he could make out the figure of a man. The head was enormous — probably because of the mane of hair. His mind made out trifles, details. Pavlysh had no way of knowing what was going to happen.

Where had he seen a similar picture? Long ago, as a child. Yes, in the illustrations to Robinson Crusoe. Robinson on his island, his hair down to his belt, dressed in animal hides. They were lucky; these feral children still remembered how to speak.

"Go away!" Dick repeated. "Go away."

The moment he had spoken and the creature had answered him, Dick had lost the will to fire. He saw a tall figure, taller than even the Mayor, in a space suit. Dick knew what a space suit was. The helmet was a transpan ball that let the occupant look everywhere. The face inside was just that of a human being, but it was shaved, and Dick had never yet seen an adult human being who was shaved. To Dick what stood before him was an enormous child. Dick's own beard had grown out long ago; only Oleg's was little more than wisps of down.

"Go away." Dick repeated, now he was begging. He no longer wanted the stranger to depart, but he could not think of other words. He was overcome with inertia and a strange dullness, like the onset of a fever.

Now there were two women standing beside the giant child. One was almost as tall as the boy, the second small and thin like Marianna. Both were in space suits. There was shock and even fright on both faces. They had seen the blaster in Dick's hands.

"Don't!" The smaller of the women shouted. "It's all my fault. I didn't understand. When you came here I didn't understand!"

She quickly hurried toward the station. The giant boy, or maybe man, tried to hold her back, but the small woman broke away from him and walked in quick, uneven steps, as though she had been sick.

And then Dick threw the blaster on the floor and went back to the far wall, to the divan where Kazik's dead body lay. He just stood there with his hands lowered and waited for what was to happen because now he no longer had any decisions to make and couldn't even think.

Claudia quickly punched in her code to the door and quickly removed her helmet, despite her weakness her hands moved precisely. This situation, despite being out of the ordinary, fell into the category of an emergency, and her mind could find analogies from years of work on expeditions: there had been a disaster and people were in need of immediate aid. Claudia could and did work faster than any other person in the Galaxy,.

Claudia already knew there was more than one stranger in the station while Pavlysh and Sally were still removing their helmets: an emaciated boy with shaggy hair in animal skins, and two others, a small child lay on the divan in the lounge and a very thin, unconscious girl with a badly broken leg.

Claudia told Dick firmly, "Sit down and try and rest. And don't interfere."

Pavlysh came into the lounge; Dick had already sat down in one of the chairs.

"The small boy first." Claudia told Pavlysh. "I think he's still alive."

"No. He's dead." Dick said hoarsely.

"Sally!" Claudia ignored Dick's opinion. "Hot water and disinfectant. Lots of hot water! And tell the station to put itself back up again right away; we're going to need it."

The robots had yet to get around to the wall with the medical equipment — Claudia had already opened the cabinet with the diagnosticon and tossed it to Pavlysh while he was still walking the ten paces to the boy on the assumption the doctor would catch it. She was right.

Dick did not help them. He just watched them moving quickly and self confidently and with every passing minute the boy felt more and more ashamed for behaving like some savage, like a wild animal. The man and the women wanted to help them. There had been some sort of error. People can make mistakes when they do something new. Anyone can make a mistake, especially if they saw an apparition like one of the people from the settlement. They hadn't expected there to be anyone living here. There was no reason to even suspect it. Even Sergeyev had said finding the settlement in the forest would be next to impossible, even with the best of equipment. It was just a part of the forest. Dick wanted to get to his feet and watch what the people from Earth were doing to Kazik and Marianna. The three of them were talking in low voices, and from those of their words he could understand he had no way of telling if they could help the children or if it was too late. But Dick knew if he sat quietly and listened attentively then he would certainly understand. The most important thing was not to interfere because then they would consider him some sort of wildman. *Perhaps they think there are only three of us on the entire planet. Three savages. They must have really been surprised to hear me shout.* Dick just sat there unmoving, trying to figure out what their words meant. He was terribly thirsty and wanted some water, but he didn't ask.

Pavlysh and the women said very little. The small boy's pulse was almost undetectable, but it was still there. He had lost so much blood Pavlysh wasn't sure why he was still alive. Some of the wounds on the child's back were very deep. His peritoneum was ruptured, a number of ribs were broken . . . The diagnosticon spat out the information quickly and Pavlysh considered it in silence. Sally prepared water and disinfectant and pulled out and hydrated the stored plasma supplies. The synthaskin supplies were insufficient for the boy's injuries, and Sally replaced the doctor a minute while he searched for the synthesizer. They paid no attention to Dick at all.

Sally cast a watchful eye at Dick as she moved from room to room, but the savage just sat there stonefaced and silent; he didn't appear likely to explode now. All the same Sally drew the boy a glass of water with a tranquilizer in it and gave it to him. Dick took it but just sat here with the glass in his hand, not drinking until Sally told him to drink it. The water tasted strange, almost bitter, but Dick drank all of it. He had decided he would behave like a civilized person in front of them.

Claudia had taken charge of the young woman. Pavlysh tore himself away from the boy for a moment and examined her quickly. He saw no reason to worry about the girl; her situation was serious but nothing that could not be dealt with quickly. A gangrenous inflammation, extreme dehydration — her condition was unpleasant but nothing life-threatening.

They undressed Marianna; Claudia wiped her body with a sponge. The girl was so thin all her bones stuck out through her skin; so dirty, so thickly covered with scars and scratches it was difficult to determine her age at first. She might have been fifteen years old, she might have been a little older.

After Pavlysh readied the blood transfusion machine Sally brought it to Claudia. Claudia had already prepared Marianna and set up an IV drip with a nutritional solution. Things would have been simpler if the expedition had carried two reanimation kits, but there was only one and the small boy needed it more. The girl would have to heal herself. Pavlysh had already shrouded the boy with data sensors and carefully inserted tubes into the boy's veins. The nanoprobes had already made their way to the chest cavity and had taken control of the heart and were keeping it going. Pavlysh was worried more about brain function — they had dragged the child back from clinical death, restarting the heart and lungs. Again and again he made the diagnosticon tell him the brain was functioning.

Dick listened as the giant boy — or was he a man? — and the enormous woman spoke in the other room beside Marianna. They were speaking very quietly, not thinking he was listening. They didn't realize Dick's hearing was used to the forest, and was twice as good as their own.

At first there were phrases, long medical words. Dick understood they were medical words. From their speaking tone he had already realized they were going to cure Marianna. There was more alarm in their voices when they looked at Kazik. To his own surprise and suspiciously timid joy Dick realized Kazik wasn't dead. Or did these people have the means to revive the dead? Dick hadn't heard about anything like that from the Mayor, just in stories which his mother had told him long ago, before the epidemic . . .

"We should feed him." The large woman said somewhere in the next room.

The small woman went off somewhere.

Dick realized they were talking about him.

"Want something to eat?" The large man said half jokingly; the women had called him Slava.

"Their problems are only beginning." The woman said.

"You mean the Mowgli Syndrome?"

Dick's head shot up — How had they heard about Mowgli? But then he realized they meant the one raised by the wolves in India. As to what a syndrome was, he didn't know. But the familiar name sounded so strange he didn't even take offense at the man's words.

"Interesting — has he seen plates somewhere else?" The woman said.

"I've seen them." Dick shot back. "Also knives and forks."

"Well he certainly can speak," The man said, "Although he's lived here at least twenty years."

"It's some sort of unbelievable mystery." The larger woman said. "How many of them are there, how do they live, and where? How were they able to hang onto human cultural attributes like, clothing, for example."

"Or the aerial balloon." The man said.

"And the mess in the storeroom."

"Slava." The woman said loudly. "She's coming to."

"Dick." He heard Marianna's weak voice. "Dick . . ."

And immediately Dick jumped out of the chair. He forgot all about his pride.

Dick ran into the room. Marianna lay on the divan. Her face was pale; they had undressed her and covered her with a white sheet.

"Marianna," Dick said, bending over her. "How are you?"

"Okay." The girl opened her eyes. "Is Kazik alive?"

Her eyes stopped for a moment on Dick's face, then moved on to Pavlysh's, froze a moment, then met Sally's smile.

"Thank you." Marianna said. "We were so afraid we wouldn't find you."

"Girl," Sally said and suddenly started to cry. "Dear child, your Kazik's alive. He'll even recover."

Claudia appeared in the doorway. She was silent.

"Have you told them, Dick?" Marianna asked.

"No." The boy said. "There wasn't any time. And they didn't ask me."

"A severe misunderstanding." Pavlysh said. "Hopefully our last one."

"Do you have a ship that can fly to the settlement?" Marianna asked. "Our people will be worried about us."

***

Sally flew with Dick to the settlement in the landing boat. Pavlysh and Claudia remained with the injured.

Dick was full, his hunger satisfied for the first time in many days, and it made him worried, but there was no reason to be sorry. Sally was hurrying to the settlement. Before the sedative Pavlysh gave Marianna took effect the girl had said,

"Dick, please, they were so worried . . ."

Dick realized the girl was fearful Oleg had been unable to wait and had gone to the ship. She was afraid for Oleg.

Had Dick not been so troubled he would have imagined the landing boat descending into the village with everyone running out of their houses, he would have seen himself coming out first and saying "This is a woman from Earth. Her name is Sally." But now he really didn't care.

The landing boat had to fly low, below the clouds, almost touching the tops of the trees. Dick knew the precise direction and was certain he wouldn't get lost. From over head the forest was a storm tossed, grey green sea.

They passed over the river in a few seconds. It was difficult to imagine their crossing by boat had taken all of three days. The river wasn't all that wide. To the left the skyforest rose in tier after tier into the clouds.

"We were up there." Dick said. "Way up there."

"Yes." Sally said." "We saw your balloon. But we didn't know what it was at the time. Slava figured out what it was but I didn't believe him."

"Too bad." Dick said. "It would have saved a lot of time."

Dick looked at the woman's hands. Her hands were so white and smooth he couldn't believe it — did she never take off her gloves? Her hands lay on the control stick and small movements of her fingers changed the landing boat's attitude or made it rise higher. Dick had wanted to ask Sally to let him sit in her place and pilot the boat. But in the end he had said nothing.

Sally increased the boat's speed; the green sea below them slid into a blurred mass; it was Sally who made out the clearing below them in the forest and the settlement even before Dick.

She cut their speed, but the boat still overshot the settlement and had to return in a circle, descending over the palisade. It was raining again. The Mayor was on guard at the gate; he pushed back his fish-hide hood and looked up. His eyes were rheumy and his lungs burned whenever he coughed, but some sort of sixth sense made him throw back the hood at the moment when the landing boat cut over the tops of the trees, quite low, and began to make a circle over the village.

The Mayor started to shout wildly and began to beat the warning drum, as though a whole horde of zhakals had erupted from the forest. People erupted from the houses and no one understood why the Mayor was making the noise, shouting and for some reason jumping up and down as though a sneaq had bitten him.

Sally looked down on a circular mud puddle from overhead, surrounded by a long, leaning wall of pointed trees. In some areas of the devastation small vegetable patches grew between a few short bushes; round, flat areas that were rain puddles reflected the grey clouds.

And then Sally made out the houses where the people lived. Narrow shacks, two rows of lean-tos stretched on either side of the the dirt band that was the street. The road bent when it came to the passage in the gates, it branched and one end stretched to two tilting sheds over one of which lifted grey smoke. If an artist had wanted to express the depths of poverty and hopelessness to which human beings could descend he could not have chosen a more fitting and frightening picture.

The landing boat came to ground in the scrub brush beyond the last of the houses.

Sally turned off the engine and looked at Dick.

Dick was silent. Sally looked at him, feeling guilty because she was in her space suit and she couldn't take it off. Dick slowly turned toward her and looked in embarrassment. His eyes burned, but his mouth was tight and seemed bitter. *Lord.* Sally thought. *You need a bath. You need a good washing.* The bluish whiteness of his skin was hardly visible beneath a layer of soot and dirt. The long black hair was matted to his cheeks. Dick had been hot in the landing boat's cabin; he was feeling sick, something he tried not to display in front of the clean woman. And Sally didn't understand him.

Dick began to pull the airlock hatch to one side. Sally bent down and helped him open it.

Dick jumped down from the landing boat. Sally came out after him.

Almost immediately Sally saw the children. They were running in the mud, in the puddles, naked, hair a mess, barefoot. They were shouting and waving their hands.

After them came the adults, running. Three or four women, then a man with a wide spade beard of reddish hair which hid all his face, leaving only the red nose visible, the red nose and blue eyes. One of the woman who wore an overall patched together from pieces of uniforms and leather scraps was fat, which surprised Sally. Then Sally saw a tall, stooped, one handed old man come running, leaning on a crutch, and limping. The door of the nearest house opened and a fair haired girl led out an old blind woman who felt the air in front of her with her free hand, as though she feared bumping into some obstacle.

Sally stood waiting while they all came running; it was terrible to think they might have departed and left these people here.

The people stopped some steps from Sally. No one said anything.

The silence lasted a whole minute.

Sally could see how the heavy woman cried. She was crying silently, swallowing her tears, and her fingers went crawling over her chest as if she were searching for buttons.

Sally looked at the children. There were a great many children for so small a group; it had never occurred to here that the people here, in this filthy emptiness, might breed children.

There was something animal-like in it, humiliating. Sally saw not the continuation of Earth in the settlement, but a dying handful of destitute castaways.

The dragging silence was bought to an end by the blind woman.

"Where are they?" She said loudly. "Are they here. Did they really fly here?"

"Hello." Sally said then. It was always hardest to say the first words. The first word.

"Where is Kazik?" The heavy woman asked. "Has anything happened to him."

"We left him there, Aunt Luiza." Dick said. "He'll recover. They promised."

"Both their lives are out of danger." Sally said.

"But Oleg? Where is Oleg? He went to the mountains!" A thin old woman started to shout. "You have to go after them, please!"

"Wait, Irina." The one handed old man leaned on his crutch and said. "My name is Boris." He continued. "I'm the mayor, here. I'd like to thank you, for all of us . . ."

Dick had moved to one side, toward his house. They let him go. No one was looking at him.

Sally made the acquaintance of each of them in turn. Everyone extended their hand and greeted her, even the small children. The odd ceremony served to diminish the image of destitution. but Sally was glad she had her gloves on.

A strange animal caught Sally's attention — she recognized one of the monsters Pavlysh had killed. It was surrounded by a whole herd of similar but smaller monsters which moved heavily and threateningly toward the group of people who had surrounded the landing boat. Sally wanted to scream for the people to run, but one of the small children bravely ran forward first to head off the monster, shouting,

"Go away, Goat! Don't bother us. We've got visitors! Go away, stupid!"

The monster who bore the strange name suddenly stopped and stamped feet. But one of Gote's kids understood nothing and bleated and howled when a little girl dragged it out of the way by its long ears. Mama Gote did not come to its aid.

Well of course, Sally suddenly understood, *Living conditions have been miserable, but they stayed people, and people domesticate animals, hunt in the forest, tend gardens. What was I expecting?*

"If you're not too tired we'd like you to fly into the mountains." The one-handed old man said. "Oleg and Sergeyev are there. They were headed for the *PolarSta*r to try and make contact with you by radio. But the weather in the mountains is terrible. . . ."

***

Twenty minutes later — there was no time to waste — the landing boat lifted again. Dick was feeling better; he had flown with Sally. He knew the road from the settlement to the *PolarStar* which they had taken the last time.

Many of the people in the settlement wanted to go with her in search of Sergeyev and Oleg, especially the children; Oleg's mother even tried to push her way into the landing boat, but the Mayor stopped her.

"Irina, you can't; they'll manage without you." Boris turned to Sally and asked. "Return as soon as you can. Please."

But he said these ordinary words very seriously, trying to maintain not only his own dignity but settlement's as well. He was standing very straight. Dick had never seen the Mayor stand so straight before. He was leaning on the knob of his walking stick with his only hand. The small children has stopped shouting and running and jumping around the landing boat. Oleg's mother was slowly backing away from them.

"All right, Boris." Sally said. "We'll try to find them as soon as possible."

When the boat was in the air Dick said,

"You see those reddish cliffs? We went through there. There's a cave on the other side of them. We spent the first night there. Don't go too fast or I'll lose my way."

The landing boat flew slowly; it lifted over the gorge where the stream flowed between flanges of ice on either bank. But the gorge was wrapped in low-lying clouds and was filled with snow.

Dick could imagine what a difficult time Oleg and Sergeyev would have had there.

The boat topped the plateau. Dick recognized the spot where he had found the canteen filled with cognac and then the spot where Thomas had died.

"Thomas fell down there." Dick said. "A snow flee bit Oleg; Thomas tried to hold him back from the edge of the cliff and went over himself."

Sally nodded, although this was the first time she had heard of Thomas Hind. She knew she would be hearing the story many times in the future and Thomas would become as familiar as the living.

The boat sailed about a hundred meters above the snow, then Sally descended once more and went slower: the boat had entered a thick layer of clouds and they were afraid of missing the men.

"They should have gotten further along." Dick said. "They should already be at the *PolarStar*. If they made it to the ship there's nothing to worry about because they could just sit there."

Sally almost blurted out: "But we wanted to blow up the wreck."

She held back. Dick would never have understood such a blasphemy. How could you explain such insane instructions to someone who had grown up in the forest?

A few minutes later they exited the cloud bank. Here the sky was purple blue and some of the nearer stars were visible in daylight. They could see to the horizon.

Dick stayed calm. He was waiting for the appearance of the *PolarStar*.

The ship still lay in the saddle of rock and ice, the same as it had a year before. They made a wide circle over the ship. Sergeyev's and Oleg's tracks were nowhere to be seen.

"Maybe they're in the ship. It's really cold." Dick said,.

Sally landed the boat right beside the hatchway. The stairway Pavlysh had forgetfully left behind still hung from the airlock. "Thank God he's forgetful." Sally thought.

She and Dick searched the starship, checking the bridge and the food stores, then went down to the flight deck where the starship's own landing boat still lay in its cradle; Sergeyev and Oleg might be in it trying to establish contact with the station.

The two of them found nothing. They left the *PolarStar*. Dick was morose. Around them the silence as like a forest full of zhakals.

"Can we search some more?" Dick asked, fearing what Sally would say. The woman was tired, she probably wanted to go home. Oleg and Sergeyev meant nothing to her.

"Hold on a moment." She said. "Let's make contact with the base first."

She called the station and told Pavlysh she'd been to the settlement and was now at the *PolarStar*, but she hadn't found the two men. Then she asked how the children were. Dick almost laughed: how could anyone call Marianna a child? It was almost funny.

Pavlysh said everything was in order, then added,

"Come back here as fast as you can. I'll spell you."

"But I'm not tired."

"I have the life-sensor. Remember that? We'll never find them without it. They could be under the snow; you'd just miss them."

"You're right." Sally said.

"What does he have?" Dick asked, his hopes rising.

"This is an instrument to detect anything organic."

Sally assumed Dick had never heard the word 'organic' before and started to search for another, simpler, example, but Dick said,

"I understand. Vaitkus taught us chemistry."

The boat rose sharply out of the saddle between the peaks.

"Just one thing." Dick said. "Don't fly back direct, would you; make a wide circle over the mountains first."

"Pavlysh is right; it would be easier with the life-sensor."

"I know." Dick said.

"All right."

She agreed with Dick. Neither of them wanted to say it aloud, but both understood that if the men were lost in the snow every second could decide their fate. Had Claudia been in Sally's place, she would never have agreed to waste time circling over snow filled valleys; Claudia would have said it was in the lost men's best interest they return promptly to the station and then use the device designed to find missing mountain climbers. Sally was not so single minded. The two of them flew low, in enormous zigzags, combing a band kilometers wide.

They were right.

When they had already descended to the upper border of the clouds, and admitted to themselves they would have to cut off the search, Dick caught sight of a dark spot in the snow.

"That way!" He shouted.

The spot was unmoving. Sally saw it as well and sent the boat twisting at a sharp angle that nearly threw Dick out of his seat.

The spot grew quickly; then they could make out it was moving. It was an odd, shapeless mass; it grew and expanded. They were almost on top of it before they could see the mass was two men who were getting up and then falling down again, holding on to each other so tightly they could not be told apart.

When the boat landed in the snow some twenty meters in front of Sergeyev and Oleg the two could not see it; they were blinded by the snow's glare. As Dick and Sally got out of the boat and watched, the pair fell down again and, cursing dully, with difficulty, began to rise to their knees.

"Oleg!" Dick shouted, rushing forward to the slowly shifting pile of bodies. "Oleg, I'm here! Listen to me! Oleg! It's me! It's us! We have real wings now!"

ABOUT THE AUTHOR

Kir Bulychev is the pen name of Igor V. Mojeiko, who has been a special correspondent in Burma for Around The World [Vokrug Sveta] magazine in Moscow, where he oversaw the construction of a chemical factory in the 1950s. Later, he worked as a translator for the Pugwash peace conferences. Currently he is a specialist in South East Asia with the Russian Academy of Sciences' Oriental Institute. Since the mid-Sixties his SF stories of have been appearing in Russian popular SF magazines and newspapers, written under the pseudonym of Kir Bulychev to prevent career conflicts. Some concern Alice, a little girl of the 21st century whose adventures have taken her to the ends of time and space. Many deal with the fictional North Russian city of Great Gusliar. Others are space opera, for both teenagers and adults. More than two dozen have been made into popular movies, including *Guest From The Future, The Lilac Ball, The Secret of the Third Planet,* and *By Thorny Paths To The Stars.* His real name became common knowledge when he won the State Prize of the USSR for the scripts to the last two films. Among his translations into Russian are Robert Heinlein's *If This Goes On. . . .* , Ben Bova's **The Weather Makers,** and Ursula K. Leguin's *Nine Lives.*

Some ten million copies of Kir Bulychev's books have been published in Russia since the fall of Communism. His official website can be found at *http://www.rusf.ru.*

Kir Bulychev is married and lives in Moscow. He has a daughter named Alice.

Coming in 2000 AD from Fossicker Press:

Kir Bulychev's

Alice: The Girl From Earth

Contents:

The Little Girl Nothing Ever Happens To
The Rusty Field-Marshal
Alice's Birthday

Complete at last in English

DISCARD

EAST BATON ROUGE PARISH LIBRARY

3 1659 02245 4819

EAST BATON ROUGE PARISH LIBRARY
BATON ROUGE, LOUISIANA

ZACHARY

4/01

GRAY-JACKET 5.5 X 8

9 780738 81560